The Fragrant Concubine

MELISSA ADDEY

THE FRAGRANT CONCUBINE

Published by Letterpress Publishing
Cover and Formatting: Streetlight Graphics
Cover photo of woman by Heijo: www.heijo.photography

Epub: 978-0-9931817-8-8
Smashwords: 978-0-9931817-9-5
Kindle: 978-0-9931817-6-4
Paperback: 978-0-9931817-7-1

Your Free Book

MELISSA ADDEY

The Cup

The city of Kairouan in Tunisia, 1020. Hela has powers too strong for a child – both to feel the pain of those around her and to heal them. But when she is given a mysterious cup by a slave woman, its powers overtake her life, forcing her into a vow she cannot hope to keep. So begins a quartet of historical novels set in Morocco as the Almoravid Dynasty sweeps across Northern Africa and Spain, creating a Muslim Empire that endured for generations.

Download your free copy at
www.melissaaddey.com

For Ryan

Spelling and Pronunciation

I have used the international Pinyin system for the Chinese names of people and places. The following list indicates the elements of this spelling system that may cause English speakers problems of pronunciation. To the left, the letter used in the text, to the right, its equivalent English sound.

c	=	ts
q	=	ch
x	=	sh
z	=	dz
zh	=	j

Author's Note:
Legends of the Fragrant Concubine

THERE ARE MANY VERSIONS OF the legend of the Fragrant Concubine.

It is true that in 1760 the Chinese Emperor Qianlong conquered Turkestan. A Muslim woman from that region was sent to the Forbidden City as his concubine and named Rong Fei. It seems she was something of a favourite, being promoted twice and given many gifts.

Over time, other stories have grown up around her.

In China they say that her body emitted an irresistible natural fragrance and that the Emperor was besotted with her. She was homesick, but he gave her many gifts, including a bazaar, a mosque and a cook from her homeland named Nurmat. At last she fell in love with the Emperor and they lived happily ever after.

But in her homeland they say that the woman was named Iparhan and born to a family of rebels. Brought to court by force, she kept daggers hidden in her sleeves to protect her honour. Finally she took her own life rather than submit to the Emperor's desire for her.

I found myself wondering which woman was the real Fragrant Concubine. Which ending was true: the sad one or the happy one?

This novel is about what might have happened.

TERRITORIES OF THE
QIANLONG EMPEROR, 1760

before

HE TRAILS MY FOOTSTEPS LIKE *a whipped dog. When I turn to him his eyes flinch away from the cut, the ragged edges now held together with crude stitches, still seeping pus. He looks down, away, over my shoulder, fixes his gaze on the fastenings of my sheepskin jacket.*

But I have just seen something that took my breath away, that numbs both the stinging pain and the crushing defeat of all my plans. Something – someone – that makes my head lift up again.

"Did you see her?"

Nurmat's eyes flicker to my face and then hastily away. "Who?"

"That beggar girl."

He shakes his head, uninterested.

I turn away from him, look about. "She was begging outside the mosque after prayers. We have to find her again."

"Why?"

"So you can see her."

"Why would I want to see her?"

I ignore him, scan the crowd, twist my neck this way and that, oblivious to the passersby who stare at my face. But the girl has gone, slipped away somewhere. I turn back to Nurmat, catch him looking at the cut, his eyes filled with tears he cannot hold back. "We will stay here tonight."

"Why?"

"Find us an inn."

He obeys me without further questioning. He does whatever I ask of him now, since that one moment, the sharp blade's quickness against my skin. His shame is too great to rage against my plans as he used to. This morning, looking in the mirror, my fingers tracing the open wound before it was clumsily sewn back together, I had thought that all was lost, that I must resign myself to a different life. And there was a part of me that was glad. I thought of Nurmat's arms about me, of his mouth upon my lips, and I felt such desire for him, for my new life. But rising from my prayers I heard a plea for alms. When I turned to place a coin in the outstretched palm I looked into her eyes and my heart leapt in recognition. I must see her again, to know if I saw true.

When we rise the late summer morning is cool and the traders have not yet found their voices. We walk through the warren of the city streets until I am dizzy and sick with turning my head this way and that to find her. The market-day crowds began to grow all around us.

Nurmat lays his hand on my arm. "Iparhan," he begins. But I pull away, breaking into a run, pushing my way through the people. I stop so suddenly that Nurmat collides with me and sends me sprawling but I rise at once, ignoring the sting of my grazed palms.

"There!" I say. "There!" Her ragged skinny frame making its way through the crowds. Her face... I wait for her to turn my way and when she does I feel my body begin to shake. Her face is my face. From before the quick blade swept across my cheek. I pull at Nurmat's arm. "There!" I say.

Nurmat turns his head, blinks in confusion as he tries to follow my pointing finger. Then he sees her and grows very still. When he speaks his voice trembles. "No," he says. "No, Iparhan. You said it was over."

I lie to him then. I have never lied to him before. "She will take my place," I say. "I will use her as a spy. Nothing more. If I have information from the City then I – we – can bring about a rebellion. It is a new plan."

14

Nurmat grips my arm so hard it hurts. But not as much as the hope in his voice. "Swear," he says. "Swear you will not..."

I put my hand on his and I lie again. "I swear," I say. "A spy, nothing more. Bring her to me, Nurmat," I said. "Make sure she has no one: no family or friends to seek her out. Then bring her to me."

He nods and begins to follow her, moving away from me. In that moment I know that our happiness is lost. I could call him back to me, could change my mind and live a gentle loving life by his side.

But it is too late to turn back now.

Market Day

"REMEMBER, MY FRIENDS — ALL legends are true, even the ones that never happened. For in them we find ourselves."

The spit bubble I'm idly blowing bursts unexpectedly. I wipe the spittle off my chin with my sleeve and watch the crowd around the old storyteller disperse; a few small coins tossed his way by the more generous. He always begins and ends with this phrase when telling his far-fetched tales of wild adventure and passionate love, savage monsters and epic journeys. I don't know if he truly believes it or whether he just thinks it adds an air of mystery — after all, all storytellers need an air of mystery about them or they'd just be common beggars with a fanciful imagination. You need to stand out from the crowd here, have something special to make people seek you out. Market day is the day when such storytellers earn their living, and the market of Kashgar, sitting on the trading routes, draws more crowds than most. Being known as a good storyteller here is important.

Now he tucks the coins away and prepares himself for another performance, scratching his balls through his layers of ragged clothing and taking a long drink of water from a dirty old jug, chipped round the edges. He wanders off to find a quiet spot where he can relieve himself before beginning another tale of mystery and romance. His eyes are growing milky but he would know his way round these streets by memory alone. His space is stolen by a troupe of acrobats, flipping this way and that, walking on their hands as though it were the easiest thing imaginable. It isn't. I tried it once when I was a child. I had strong arms even then but I fell over almost immediately and struck my face on an old root. Got a nosebleed for my effort rather than applause.

I start my daily rounds at the mutton dumpling stall of old Mut, tucked down a little corner street on the edge of the market. "Anything for me?"

He shakes his head. He'd give me the split or burnt dumplings but he doesn't care for me enough to give me dumplings that he could sell. "You're too old to still be wandering the streets, girl," he admonishes me. "Find a husband and settle down."

He's been saying this for years. "I don't need a husband, Mut, I manage well enough on my own."

"No one can manage on their own," he says, keeping his eyes on the bobbing dumplings. "Everyone needs a family. People to look out for you."

I shrug and start to turn away when I feel a hand stroke my behind. I smack it away without even looking. "Get your hands off me, you fat good-for-nothing."

Mut's son leers at me through a half-chewed mouthful of meat and bread. "I'll marry you," he says thickly, not bothering to swallow before he speaks.

I make a face. "Spend my life as your slave? No, thank you. Why don't you help your father earn a living instead of sitting about pawing women and stuffing your face?"

Dejected, he goes back to his food as I head towards the main square. I'm almost out of earshot when he calls after me. "Someone was asking about you earlier!"

I ignore him. Maybe someone who caught me stealing food wants to find me and give me a hiding. I'm hardly going to seek them out.

I thread my way back through the crowds and settle down to watch the acrobats.

"Tell your fortune?"

I jump. The voice is right by my ear. I turn and there's an old woman behind me. Her clothes are nothing so much as layers of rags, and there's a thick sweet smell about her which I know is opium, though where she gets enough money for it I don't know; perhaps she uses the cheap stuff mixed with even cheaper tobacco.

I raise my eyebrows. "Slow day?"

She shrugs, her eyes darting about to either side of me, looking at the market-day crowds over my shoulders. "Once they see one person being told their fortune they all come running."

I laugh. "Only if it's a good one, eh?"

She grins, showing a surprisingly good set of teeth still in her head. "Of course."

I grin back. A slow day for her means a bowl of noodles for me. "You'll give me the usual?"

She looks about and lowers her voice. "I've something will make your day brighter?"

I shake my head. "No flowery dreams for me, thank you. Noodles are what I want."

She agrees, grudgingly making it clear it's to be a *small* bowl. If I refuse her offer she'll soon find someone else who will accept.

I settle down on a crumbling wall nearby and present my face for her inspection.

She picks up two wooden rattles and hits them together rhythmically, indicating a fortune-teller at work. The noise attracts people's attention, and two or three bystanders wander over to listen in on my fate.

She runs her hands over my face and looks at me intently. Her

18

voice is louder when she starts to speak, my fortune apparently being of more interest to the complete strangers hanging about than to me.

"A dainty face," she starts. "What a fine face for a poor ragged girl. Her face may bring her great good luck."

I've heard this fortune so many times I roll my eyes. She pinches my ear hard. I'm supposed to look rapt, not disbelieving. I try harder, fixing my eyes devotedly to her face and thinking of hot noodles. This seems to give my face the necessary attentiveness; she pats my cheek and carries on. "Good luck will come from this face," she practically shouts. "A great man will love such a face."

I try not to snort and she grabs my hands, lifting and turning them so the crowd can see. "Such coarse little hands here, so rough. Perhaps your face will bring softness to your hands one day. I see a great man, a man who will let your hands rest only on silk."

I can feel the onlookers getting closer; a few giggles tells me that the old woman's favourite kind of customers, silly young girls with more cash than sense, are edging forward, beginning to hope for their own turn.

"Silk, yes," she goes on. "Dress you in fine silks, he will, and give you jade pins for your hair. Your face will be your fate."

I know she's almost done with me. The real customers are lining up. She likes to keep my fortune short enough to draw them in, not long enough to let them wander away again. I can hear the chink of little coins being turned in impatient hands. My bowl of noodles is getting closer.

"Who amongst you can guess your own futures? What turns of fortune may come your way? Even now the Emperor of China, so far away in Beijing, sends his armies here and claims our lands for his own, from one day to another. Now we are his subjects, his to command. Our people have fallen, our leaders lie silent in their tombs, their heads taken as trophies."

There are some mutterings in the crowd. Quickly she brings their attention back to my shining future rather than their uncertain present. These people are tired of wars. There's been too much fighting in recent years. If the Emperor has taken our lands now, let him have them. Life goes on here on the streets as it always did. Our taxes go to a new master; different officials oversee the trade routes. What difference is there? Wars bring death; taxes bring the same old hardships that can be borne more easily. They want to forget the sorry past and dream of a richer future, so she presses on. "This young girl now, so raggedy and with rough hands, who but I could know she is destined for silks? Are there others who wish to know their fates?"

There are murmurs and little excited pushings amongst the nearest girls. She lets go of me so I stand up, ready to make way for fee-paying customers. She slips me enough for a small bowl of noodles as agreed and I nod, pretending that I am the one paying her. I move past her towards the nearest noodle stall when suddenly she turns and grabs my arm. Behind her sits an eager girl, clutching a coin and lifting up her face, hopeful of another rich generous man appearing in her own future. The fortune-teller ignores her. Her eyes are fixed on me but they seem glazed and her voice is slow. I suppose it's the opium taking effect.

"Where'd you get a perfume like that?" she asks.

I stare at her. "What?"

She leans into me and I pull back a bit for she certainly doesn't smell like perfume. She inhales deeply, her eyes closed. "That. That's…" She thinks for a moment and then shakes her head, almost losing her balance. She clings more tightly to my arm to keep herself upright and opens her eyes. "Don't know what it is, never smelt anything quite like that. Expensive, though. That's the kind merchants bring from a long way off and what rich ladies wear. Not the likes of you. Where's it from?"

I shake my head and pull away. "I'm not wearing perfume. I carry nightsoil, if you like the smell of piss. Where would I get perfume?"

"Some rich man?"

"I'm not that kind of girl."

Her eyes lose their glazed look and now she's focused on me rather than her restless customers. She's never looked at me so steadily or for so long.

I stare back at her. "What?"

She shakes her head, confused. "Don't know. I smelt a perfume on you."

"I told you, I don't wear perfume."

She's frowning. "I know. But I could smell it. It was very strong and then it faded away."

I wink. "Maybe the great man'll give it to me. You know, the one who's going to dress me in silks and have me sitting around doing nothing all day."

I think she'll laugh and let me go, or tell me to keep it down so her customers don't hear me being flippant about her fortunes. She doesn't, though. "Maybe," she says slowly, and turns away.

I puzzle over it for a moment, even sniff my own arm to see if I can smell an expensive perfume. I can't, of course. I smell of a faint stench left over from the dawn when I carried pails of nightsoil to be dumped away from the city walls. The tight-fisted foreman only gave me a thin vegetable broth for my troubles, though, instead of the coin he owed me. I made sure to be clumsy after that so that one of the buckets fell over, leaking a foul mixture of piss and shit all over the doorway of one of his best customers, a fancy house in the centre of town. The broth's all I've had today, so a bowl of noodles is more interesting right now than the opium-raddled ramblings of a so-called fortune-teller.

I order a small bowl and smile nicely at the vendor, hoping he might add a bit more. He doesn't. I take the bowl and squat nearby, scooping noodles into my mouth as quickly as I can. They're gone before I've had time to savour them.

I hand my bowl back to the stallholder and make my way through the crowds. It's slow work to move about on market day. The warren of narrow city streets, squeezed in by high sand-coloured buildings and lined with stalls, swarms with people. I'm surrounded by the bleating of sheep, bellowing of camels, the slow wooden wheels of carts and above all the chattering of people. Cages of live hens and partridges are everywhere, cackling and shrieking as they're lifted out by their feet. The women gossip their way from stall to stall making a simple purchase of dried fruit or nuts last hours. Meanwhile their menfolk are no doubt claiming to be equally busy buying stock – sheep or camels, perhaps even a horse. This, too, seems to take up a great deal of the day. There are acquaintances to nod at, relatives to embrace, wrestling to watch or even take part in, perhaps a spiced lamb pie to eat, bartering being hungry work even if you don't do much of it.

Here and there the Emperor's officials make their way about, consulting records that show them the names of merchants who owe them taxes. They have guards with them in case there's any reluctance to pay up. We're used to the sight of soldiers by now. Young men who fancied themselves rebels used to attack them in the narrow streets after dark – and paid with their lives. Most people kept their heads down and avoided trouble. But now the fighting is over. The Emperor has won and if all he wants is glory and taxes, then so be it. A little boy sticks out his tongue at the soldiers as they pass by but they don't notice him. They wouldn't care if they did. They don't expect us to love them.

I wriggle past two gossips and find myself close to a dried fruit stall where a rich lady is buying whole handfuls of dried raisins. My mouth waters for their sweetness. The lady is fussing over their quality, looking them over disdainfully as though she might command finer things. But raisins in Kashgar are the very best that money can buy and so she can sniff and look down her nose for only so long before she graciously permits the stallholder to sell them to her. Now she turns away, her servants bobbing alongside her carrying many baskets and bundles. She has been busy spending her money today. As they pass me I follow behind the most stupid-looking servant, the one who is carrying foods rather than being entrusted with the more delicate pottery or silks. One quick pull and a handful of raisins is mine. The motion makes the basket rock, though, and a twist of spices falls to the ground. I've already slipped away from them and found a low wall to crouch behind, the raisins hidden inside my too-big man's jacket, so I can watch the lady's fury as others might watch a play.

"Fool!' she shrieks.

Someone ought to tell her she sounds like a common peasant woman instead of the gracious lady she likes to imagine herself. The servant ducks, expecting the slaps coming his way. The first blow catches his shoulder instead of his head, which doesn't satisfy his mistress, so she goes for him again and this time, perhaps realising it is better to get it over with quickly, he doesn't move much and the blow of her hand knocks off his little cap. "Useless, good-for-nothing! The very next market I shall buy a new servant, for you're not worth the sorry few coins I paid for you!"

I grin and settle down in the dusty street behind the wall, cramming sweet raisins into my mouth till every last one is gone, even the ones that fell in the dust when they slipped through my fingers. A little scruffy white cat with a shrivelled leg rubs against me and I stroke it till it purrs and settles down to sleep on my legs, a small embrace from a living creature, a warmth I am unused to. For now my belly feels at least partly full and I sleep for a while in the afternoon sun, hidden from passersby.

It's early evening when I'm woken by drunken singing nearby. I hurry to the nearby mosque, anxious not to miss evening prayers. I pray at the back of the women's room and loiter about afterwards. Sometimes praying gets you a coin from a wealthy woman, it makes them feel pious to give alms to a poor street girl. I've never been taught to pray properly but I can join in with everyone else, go through the motions and murmur scraps of the right words. The bright tiles decorating the mosque are cold to kneel on without a prayer mat but I make do. When winter comes the mosque's a brief respite from the wind. But today no one feels generous and when prayers are over I move off through the crowds, which are now less focused on bargaining for household goods and are happily settling down to the real business of the day: entertainment. I can hear old tunes being sung, gasps at the acrobats who have moved on from their warm-up of walking on their hands and are showing off finer skills with juggling and injury-defying leaps and twirls in mid-air, using all manner of poles and ropes to thrill the crowd. In nearby inns there are drinking games being played, which start off with a literary bent involving reciting poems but become decidedly bawdy as the night wears on. Men sit in the street with their heads tilted back, being shaved or massaged, their tall felt hats on the ground beside them. They munch on almonds and figs, risking their throats being cut when they swallow too close to the strokes of the sharp blades.

I wander away, down other streets. There's one more place to visit before the day is over.

"So, can a pretty girl show me the many delights of Kashgar, eh?"

My grumbling belly has brought me to a small lane with a tall pole at one end, embedded in a yellow earthen wall. It's one of the women's lanes, a place where they wear more ribbons and silks than you'd think would fit on one body and where local men and merchants from further afield come to see what pleasures their money will buy. When I was a little girl I used to come and stare at them, till I found the customers began to stare at me too closely for my liking. These days I have to be careful round here, but sometimes it's a risk worth taking.

The man is fat and balding, and very drunk. He's barely standing straight. He has his cock in one hand, supposedly ready for action, though it looks a bit limp to me. If he were less drunk he'd see I'm not even dressed like a serving maid to one of the pleasure-women, let alone being one of them myself, but he's a merchant and this is what he is looking for. Merchants come here from all over and it is said that in Beijing they sing rude songs about the girls of Kashgar and their supposed charms. He's just right for me, though, too slow and drunk to grab hold of me. I push him away and he sways dangerously, grasps the pole to keep his balance and fumbles in his robes.

"Got cash," he burbles. "Got strings of it." Sure enough he pulls out a string of coins with his free hand. "How much, then?" he says, because even in his drunken state he can see I'm not running off, that all my attention is fixed on the many swaying coins threaded together on a red string.

I look at the dangling string of cash. Usually they hold up a single coin and I can sometimes grab it and run. I'm too quick for them to chase. But a whole string of coins... I could eat meat instead of noodles every day till next market day.

"Well?" says the man, and then he falls over and lies there at the foot of the yellow wall.

I'm scared he's died for a moment, but then he starts snoring. Much to my disappointment he's fallen on top of the string of cash, so I can't even grab it. I'm a strong girl but he's huge; I'd never roll him over in his state.

I look down the lane. A stout woman I've seen before, who runs one of the brothels, has come out of her doorway and is watching me. "Help you?"

I gesture to the man lying by my feet. "He's got cash and he wants a good time."

"You going to show him it then, are you?'

I shake my head.

She comes a bit closer. "Ah, you again. You keep coming back to look down the lane. Made up your mind to come and work for me?"

I shrug.

"Thinking about it?"

Of course I have been. What other choices do have? Winter will be here soon and how many more winters will I be able to survive alone on the streets? Last year I thought I would die in the cold. By spring I was nothing but bones, my skin stretched too tight across them. The lanes would mean warmth, food. But the price I'd pay for them… I stand silent before her while she waits for the answer I'll have to give one day. I can't bring myself to give it yet. I keep hoping I will think of some other way.

The woman laughs. "Well, some men like a quiet girl." She squints at me and makes her voice softer, coaxing. "I look after my girls. They wear silk, you know. Not all the girls do."

I look down. The fortune-teller's words about my hands resting only on silk come back to me and I wonder if this is what she sees for me each market day. If she really sees anything at all.

"I feed them well too," she says. "Doesn't do to have a scrawny girl about the place."

I look up and she smiles, seeing the first flicker of real interest. "Come and see."

I step back.

"Just a peek," she says.

"I won't stay," I say.

"Of course not," she says. "But a peek won't harm you."

I hesitate, then step forward. She smiles and takes my hand, but I snatch it away.

"All right," she says, laughing at me. "No touching."

We get closer to the house and she points me to a small door. I put my hand on the doorframe for a moment, then step inside.

There is a little courtyard with the house built around it. There's a terrace above us. In the yard are cushions, a table or two and a scrubby little oleaster tree, its fruit slowly turning to gold from grey-green. There are customers here already, half-naked girls sitting on their laps. I step back and bump into the woman who is right behind me.

"Don't worry about them," she says. "Come and see the other girls."

We step away from the courtyard into a room. It's painted in bright colours and there are a few women sitting about on cushions. One is having her hair combed; two are mending clothes. One is smoking a waterpipe, staring into the air.

"My girls," the woman says, waving a hand at them and smiling.

They turn round to look at me.

They're not girls. They look old and tired. The bright silks they wear are cheap and thin, with patches of faded colour where the poor quality dye has dripped away on laundry days. Here and there are stains that haven't washed away so easily. The smell of tobacco is thick in the air.

I turn to face the woman.

"Want to eat with us?" she says, smiling. "There's good food cooking."

I've already smelt the air for food and what I smell is old fat, used again and again. I shake my head and walk towards the door.

She grabs my arm a little too tightly. "Won't you stay?"

I shake my head.

She smiles. It's not the nice smile from before; it's wider and shows her missing teeth. "You'll come back one day," she says. "They all do. You can't last much longer on the streets, a girl your age. A child might receive alms; a young woman might get more than she bargains for. We'll be here when you come back. When the autumn sun's gone and winter gets cold."

I pull away from her and walk out, through the courtyard and back down the lane. I walk slowly, my back very straight because I'm afraid someone will chase me if I run, but my heart beats fast until I find myself in the safety of the market crowds again. The familiar sights – the knife stall with the decorated handles, the delicately balanced piles of eggs, the hat stalls adorned with every colour of velvet and felt shining with bright embroidered threads – surround me and I breathe deeply.

"Thief!"

The man grabs at me but I've already stuffed the hot *naan* into my mouth and made my way down a side street, the bread flapping down over my chin like a giant tongue. The market of Kashgar is no place for a grown man to try to chase a girl who can slip through the crowd at speed. I hear him shout again but it's already a distant sound. I'm safe.

I've found a dark corner between two buildings to crouch in while I eat. Not that there is much left to eat now for I can run and eat at the same time. Hands are better used to make my way in the crowd. My face contorted grotesquely as I made my way down the narrow back streets and now there is barely half a *naan* left. I finish what is left of it in seconds, barely chewing, struggling to swallow great chunks of it. It doesn't do to take your time with food when you might get caught.

I yawn. The earth walls here are hard but the area is growing quieter as the traders finally pack up, grumbling about a poor day's takings. The wind grows a little chill and I pull my hands into my sleeves. I could just stay here for the night I suppose; the earth is still warm from the day's sun and I can't easily be seen by anyone. I stretch out my legs in front of me and yawn again.

"You took some finding."

I leap into the air and come tumbling down, my knees hitting the ground so hard that I cry out. A strong hand slips over my mouth and another pulls me upright and steadies me, for my feet are somehow bound together, though I can't see by what. I try to turn to see my attacker but he doesn't let me move.

"Stand still," he says, his voice low in my ear. "I'll loosen your feet but you're to walk with me as though you were my servant, do you understand?"

I don't reply. There's a hiss before I feel a tiny patch of cold on the nape of my neck. It pricks and I know it's a knife. A sharp one. I nod, downwards only, keeping my head bowed so that my neck no longer touches the knifepoint.

"Good."

The man moves his hand from my mouth to my shoulder, stoops and cuts whatever was tying my feet together. I tense, ready to run.

"Don't," he says. He sounds calm, not angry, which somehow is more frightening. "I found you this time, I'll find you again."

I lift my chin. "Don't count on it."

He tightens his grip. "A man's holding you at knifepoint and you're talking back instead of trembling like a good girl should?"

"I'm not a good girl."

"No," he agrees. He sounds amused. He keeps a hand on my shoulder. I still haven't seen his face. His hand, though, I can see out of the corner of my eye. It's well formed and smooth, not calloused.

29

A young merchant's hand perhaps, not a peasant's. "Now," he says. "I'm not sure I trust you to walk behind me like a servant girl should. Maybe you ought to pose as my wife instead. That way I could keep a hand on your shoulder as we walk."

I don't reply.

"Awkward one, aren't you," he says. "Never mind, we'll soon cure that."

He keeps one hand on my shoulder and with the other puts away the blade and I feel him twist to grasp at something. He pulls away my ragged jacket in one hard movement.

I gasp. "Don't – don't!"

I struggle under his hand and at once he pins me tight again, his arm across my collarbone. I bend my neck and bite down into his arm as hard as I can. He's wearing good thick clothes but still he jerks away and curses. He cuffs the side of my head and I stumble to the ground. He hauls me to my feet again. "Stand still and be quiet," he says. "If you do that again you won't be standing up again in a hurry."

"Please don't touch me," I say. I try to keep the tears out of my voice but I can hear them trembling on my lips.

"Oh shush," he says. "As if anyone would want you for *that,* the way you look. And smell," he adds, with distaste.

Warmth steals over me. I look down to see he is draping a knee-length waistcoat over my shoulders. It's velvet, a finer thing than I've ever worn, embroidered with little flowers, split to panels over my hips. A rich woman would wear a pretty, full skirt under this and a gauzy-sleeved shirt. My stained trousers peep out from the bottom, spoiling the effect. Over the top of this he adds a thick sheepskin jacket, warming me further. It's growing dark now and there are few people left to see the young man with his well-clad wife as they leave the main market square and make their way slowly towards a pair of horses, tethered in the far corner, close to a narrow street. A lantern shines nearby but its flame is flickering, about to burn out.

Now the man turns me towards him. He's tall. I only reach his shoulder and have to tilt my head up to look at him. Broad-shouldered, with wide cheekbones, red-brown skin from a summer of sun and thick dark hair, he's a local. His mouth is wide while his nose is a little askew. His eyes are large and dark. He's looking at me as though I were a ghost.

Keeping his hands firmly on my shoulders so that I can't move he turns my face towards the lantern and peers into my eyes, then over every part of my face, as though looking for something. I stand rigid, waiting for him to throw me to the floor. What else would a man grab a girl for? I try not to shake but I am so afraid. I should have made my home with the brothel owner. At least I would have known what was coming and there might have been someone nearby to watch out for me if a man were too rough. Now I am alone with this stranger and no one will protect me from whatever he wants to do with me. My eyes begin to fill with tears.

He notices. His eyes come back to meet mine and he pulls away from my face a little, stopping his close scrutiny. He loosens his grip on my shoulder and his voice is soft when he speaks. "I am going to put you on this horse. I will take the other. Can you ride?"

I look down and slowly shake my head. Ride? Where is he taking me?

He nods. "Good. Then you won't be tempted to ride off without me, will you?"

He lifts me up onto the closest horse in one smooth movement, as though I weigh nothing. He fiddles with the saddle, shifting my legs to make me sit better. I sit rigid and wait. If I move quickly enough I can dismount and run into the alleyways while he is busy with his own horse. As soon as he turns away to mount I throw myself forward, yanking my legs upwards to get out of the saddle.

I find myself dangling headfirst, my face a hand's breadth from the ground. He bound my legs to the saddle's straps while he was adjusting my seat.

The man gets down from his horse and helps me back up. He doesn't speak until he's back in his own saddle. Then he looks over his shoulder at me. "Your horse will follow mine," he says, and urges his horse forward.

I almost lose my balance as we move.

"Keep your legs tighter together," he advises. "You don't want to fall from that height. And hold the reins, don't just let them drape over her neck like that. Stop holding her mane. Sit up straight."

I let out a little whimper as I let go of her mane and clutch at the reins and he nods with satisfaction.

"Doesn't take much to stop your cheekiness, does it? Now come on, do as I say, you'll have a better journey if you learn to ride a little at least." He narrows his eyes when he sees my hands, so tight on the reins that the horse's neck is pulled down, her chin against her breastbone. "Try not to yank on her mouth like that with the reins, she'll think you want her to stop. We've got a long way to go so you'd better learn fast."

I'm not sure how far we've ridden.

It's dark out here. It must be a few hours since we left the city walls behind us. I could smell the sweet ripe scent of the grapes and the mustiness of the overripe melons, rotting at the sides of the fields outside the city. We headed out east, towards the desert, I suppose, although no one heads straight for that, they go round it, so maybe I'm just confused. I'm tired and scared, although I still can't think what this man would want with me that he couldn't have had in Kashgar or immediately outside the city walls.

As we rode out of the walls I sat rigid on the horse, waiting for him to throw me to the ground and rape me, or kill me – though why he'd want to take my life I've no idea. I thought of calling out to him to ask him why he'd taken me but I was too afraid of the answer. Has he taken me for a slave girl? My shoulders slump at the thought. It seems the most likely reason. A life of drudgery and beatings awaits me, then, with perhaps the odd rough fumble when the mood takes him. My shoulders tense again as another thought occurs. Perhaps he is only a servant and his master has told him to bring a girl to him, one no one will miss, with whom he can – can do as he wishes? I try to stop thinking, my hands are shaking too hard and my lips are trembling with the approach of more tears. I try to think of anyone who will miss me in the market – but why would they? Who would miss a scruffy street girl – and if they did, if they briefly wondered where I was, they wouldn't come looking for me. No one cares what happens to me.

I am alone.

My horse suddenly stops, pushing her nose up against her companion's backside. The man has pulled up without warning and now he is dismounting. "We'll stop here," he announces.

I look around. It's thick darkness now. I can barely see his outline. I'd hoped we might go to a village or even a city, somewhere I could slip away from him. But this is nowhere. Why would we stop here? He approaches and I feel rather than see him untie my legs. Then he offers a hand to help me down. I don't take it. My hands are shaking but I don't want him to see how scared I am.

"Where's 'here'?" I ask, stalling for time.

"Part of the way there."

My fear makes me angry. "And where exactly is 'there'?" I ask.

33

"You will see when we arrive. Do you wish to eat or not?"

I climb down ungracefully, ignoring his guidance and nearly falling on the ground as a result.

"Make yourself useful," he says. "Pick up some kindling and wood."

I'm about to ask where from but stumble on a stick. I almost have to feel my way around the horses and nearby ground but I put together a few sticks and old brushwood, which he uses to start a fire.

He lifts down his saddlebags and squats beside them, reaches in and takes out some cold hard *naan* breads and a big yellow melon, a long oval in shape, heavy with seeds and thirst-quenching, tongue-tempting flesh. I love these fruits. They're from Hami, where the best melons grow. I've only had them occasionally, the odd bruised slice given as a kindness from a stallholder. He sets it on the ground and rummages about again, emerging with a wrapped up package, bloodied on the outside. Inside are thick chunks of fat lamb. I swallow as saliva rises in my mouth at the thought of it. I rarely eat meat. A doddery old *naan* vendor might not chase you far; a seller of richly spiced skewers of roasted meats most certainly would – and your ears would be ringing if he caught you.

He roasts chunks of lamb over the hot flames and warms the *naans* so that they soften up and taste fresh again. He slices the melon into crescent moons of pale golden sweetness. When the meat is spitting hot he tosses a *naan* to me and I hold it like a bowl, into which he lets fall chunks of the rich meat as it slides off the skewer on which it cooked.

I eat with both hands, taking unfeasibly large bites of the parcelled up bread and lamb, which I nevertheless manage to cram into my mouth. I finish one *naan* in moments and am given another and then still one more. The man raises his eyebrows but I ignore him, my eyes on the food. Whatever this man intends to do with me, he is at least feeding me and I know better than to turn down food. If I am to get away from him, I will be stronger and think better for having eaten well. When my belly aches with fullness I turn to the melon slices, heaped up so that only their skins touch the bare earth. The flesh is juicy-ripe and I eat more than my fair share, slurping at it till my chin is wet and sticky. The man watches me. He's eaten some of the bread and lamb, but not much.

"You'll have to learn better manners than that," he remarks, passing me the melon slices that should have been his share. I devour them and scrape the rinds with my teeth until not one bit of the sweet flesh is left.

The food has given me some courage. Perhaps he won't be a harsh master. I have never eaten a meal as good as this one. "Why do I need good manners? They just slow you down so you get less to eat."

"There will be enough to eat," he says, but his voice sounds odd when he says it.

"Where?"

He doesn't answer the question. He just looks at me. "How long have you been without a home?"

I frown at him while thinking quickly. I must make him think that people will be out looking for me. "What are you talking about? I live in Kashgar with my grandmother. My mother is a sickly sort, so she doesn't go out much. The two of them sit there all day cracking nuts and munching on raisins; the shells everywhere drive me mad. And the gossiping! So I spend most of my time outdoors. I'm to get married soon, though, so I suppose my husband won't fancy me going off here there and everywhere without so much as a by-your-leave. I expect I shall have to stay at home a bit more and mind some babies."

He shakes his head slowly.

"What?"

"Not what I heard."

My lies haven't fooled him. My voice was too light, too unconcerned. "What did you hear, then?"

He tilts his head, looks at the fire instead of me. He sounds like he's reciting a lesson. "You're fifteen. Your name is Hidligh. Old-fashioned name, from before we were Muslims here. Means fragrance. Your mother came from a poor peasant family near the city of Turpan. Your father was a young merchant from Kashgar. Met your mother on a market day in Turpan. Besotted with each other. Good match for your mother, of course, not quite so good for your father. His mother was a widow and she objected to the match. He was always travelling so your mother came to live in Kashgar, in the family home, much against your grandmother's wishes. Treated her poorly when your father wasn't there, fussed over her when he was. Local people felt sorry for her but no one did anything."

He stops and looks over at me. "Right so far?"

I think of this morning, of Mut's lazy son calling after me about the person who was trying to find me. I should have listened to him, should have been more careful. This man knows too much about me. "I wasn't there. Before my time."

He nods. "Your mother fell pregnant, your grandmother became more reconciled. Hoped for a grandson." He stirs the coals. "Cold winter. Your father got sick travelling in the cold and rain, the snow, the winds. Died. Your mother was devastated; his mother nearly went mad. Went to every fortune-teller in town and they all promised the same thing. A boy, yes, of course, a grandson to replace her son. They saw daggers, a palace, horses, power. A boy for sure."

I look up and meet his gaze. I have to brazen this out, make him doubt what he's heard. I cross my arms. "Do I look like a boy to you?"

He shakes his head with a small smile. "A boy with plaits?"

I make a face at him but he's not watching me, he's staring into the flames.

"So: the big day came, your mother had the baby – and it was a girl. Any care your grandmother was taking of her vanished. She dismissed the servants and turned your mother into a maid. She ranted at her day and night, how she'd brought nothing but shame and bad luck to the family, killed off its only living son and turned what should have been a boy to a girl in her womb out of spite." He stops, falls silent.

My earliest memories are of scrubbing floors. My hands were too small to hold a scrubbing brush properly in one hand so I had to use both. Sometimes the brush would run away from me and I'd lose my balance and fall forwards. A floor that needs scrubbing seems endless when you are very small. My mother died eventually, coughing and coughing while I scrubbed and scrubbed. Not long after that I stole a bunch of grapes at the market, too tiny to be noticed as my hand crept over the edge of the stall. When no one saw me and I knew I had been fed better that day than any other since I was at my mother's breast, I ran away and took up my life on the streets of Kashgar.

He stands, stamps out the few remaining coals so they won't start a fire while we sleep, then repeats his first question. "So, how long have you been without a home?"

He knows the answer anyway, no use in lying. "Always."

"What happened to your grandmother?"

I look up at the outline of his shape, faceless in the dark. "You must know that if you know everything else about me."

"She died a few years later. There were some things missing from the house on the day of the funeral."

When I heard the wrinkled old bag was dying I went back to the house and took everything that might be useful to me, mostly clothes which were too large but were warmer than my tight and shredded rags, plus a few coins I found and a small threadbare velvet pouch which I tied round my neck under my clothes to keep money in. Not that I ever

*had any for long. That was my whole inheritance. I heard her ranting in
her room and stood in the doorway. She saw me, thought I was a ghost.
Afraid, she told me she never meant to drive me away. When I came closer
to take her hand, feeling sorry for her all alone in that empty house, she
felt my cold little hands, saw I was flesh and blood. She spat then and
cursed me, told me I'd get nothing when she died. Her house had been
promised to some distant relatives who had* sons. *I dropped her hand and
left her there. Four days later I heard she was dead.*

I sit in silence, remembering the smell of dust and her ranting
echo in empty rooms.

He throws me a blanket that smells of horse. I wrap it round
myself and lie down. The blanket's thick but I grow cold as he walks
closer and stands over me. I suppose he'll take what he wants now. I
wait. My teeth and fists are clenched. I know it will hurt.

"Got a lot of riding to do," he says. "So get some sleep." He turns
and walks away, takes a blanket and settles himself a little way off.

I lie in the darkness. Slowly I unclench my fists but my hands
start trembling, so I ball them up again. When I'm sure he won't
touch me I finally risk asking what I really want to know. "Why did
you bother finding out all that about me? What do you want with
me?"

He doesn't answer.

I wait until I'm sure he is asleep. He knows a lot about me, but
there's one thing he doesn't seem to have realised. My poor posture,
whimpers and clutching at the horse's mane have fooled him.

I'm a good rider. I've worked with horses since I took to the
streets. Scraped their hooves clean and brushed them down, held
them for rich merchants and fed and watered them for everyone from
farmers to noblemen. Sometimes all the thanks I got was the muddy
impression of their fat master's boot in my hand from helping them

to mount. I got used to them, though, was unafraid even when I was so small they towered over me. When no one was looking I'd hoist myself onto their backs, even when it meant climbing up a wall to reach them. I'd sit there, feeling their warmth seep into my cold body, whispering to them. Later I'd have them walk a bit, when my legs were long enough for my commands to get their attention. A few times, out in the fields away from the main city, I'd find horses pasturing and learnt what it was to ride at a full gallop, terrified by the speed the first few times but always wanting more, till a farmer would inevitably notice his horse galloping around the field with a girl on its back. I got yelled at plenty of times and got a beating twice, but it didn't put me off. So here I am, a poor girl, who should never have been on a fine horse in her life, and I can ride.

My horse is fast but it's not long before I hear hoofbeats behind me, and although I urge her on I know she can feel my defeat because she's not really trying. If he caught up with us that quickly when I had a good head start then there's not much hope. I slow her down and finally stop, then sit there waiting in the darkness for him to reach me.

I wait for him to pull me down from the horse and beat me but he just pulls up alongside. He leans towards me without dismounting and takes the horse's bridle. His voice is flat. "You're going to be hard work," he says, and turns both horses back the way we came. Now he knows I can ride we go faster.

I try not to wonder why he needs us to hurry. The possibilities frighten me.

We ride the next day and night too. I've never been on a horse this long and I'm tired of the jolting and the ache in my thighs. We stop a couple of times. Walking when you've been on horseback for hours is agony: I stagger when I dismount and then hobble like a wounded duck to relieve myself behind bushes. The food runs out and now all I am given is a handful of raisins. Here, in a scrubland far away from any landmark except the odd blackened stump of a dead poplar, with no idea of a destination, there's something gritty and wan about them, as though they need the noise and hustle of a market to give them their true flavour.

It's dawn and I'm drooping over the neck of my horse, half-awake, when at last we stop again. We're in the most barren place I've ever seen. Rocks, sand, rocks, sand, some more rocks and more sand. A huge old dead poplar tree, its bark shredding away. Its branches are decorated with tiny scraps of cloths, tied as symbols of past wishes made. Probably wishes to escape death in the desert. Nothing else. There are sand dunes in the distance but my eyes must be not working properly through lack of sleep, because they're taller than houses, many many houses stacked on top of each other.

I think this madman has actually brought us into the Taklamakan Desert. Any thoughts I might have had of trying to escape from him again fade away. No one can survive out here alone.

We're going to die for sure.

"Here we are," the man says. He dismounts and approaches my horse, then stands for a moment, looking up at me, his eyes tired and somehow sad.

I'm wary. "Where are we?"

"Home."

"Live under a rock, do you?" I ask. I try to sound sharp but my voice comes out shaky.

He doesn't laugh. "Get down," he says. "That's home." He points.

I was mistaken. Rocks, sand, rocks, sand – and a house. It's only one storey high, built low and broad, quite big. Sand has piled up on one side almost as far as the flat roof, and it's made of earth so your eye passes over it thinking it's just a strange shape for a dune. I can only see two windows and they're quite small. It must be dark in there.

I look back at the man and he's watching me. "Is it what you expected?"

I don't know. I don't know what I was expecting. I think I'd stopped expecting anything. "You live here?"

"Yes."

I stare at him, eyelids aching, hands trembling, for once unable to come up with a quick-witted response. "Why?"

It's the only thing that comes to mind. Why would someone with the money for clothes and food and horses live here? No one lives here. They struggle through here only if they get lost, mostly they take their goods along the well-worn trading routes no matter how long the detour, doing their very best to avoid this place.

He takes hold of my reins, turns the horse and then lifts up his hands to me. "Get down."

I almost fall off the horse into his outstretched arms.

Arrival

I SEE HER FROM THE WINDOW. *Drooping in the saddle, skinny as a twisted stick. Her face pale with tiredness, looking at the house and seeing nothing until Nurmat speaks. I cannot hear his words but she looks again at the house – and sees it. She blinks, startled by its sudden appearance but still too exhausted to be as wary as she wants to be. Nurmat speaks again and she looks down at him, tries to refuse to enter. He holds up his arms to her then, a coaxing gesture like a man with an untrained colt, promising kindness and good food in return for obedience. Grudgingly she relaxes her legs, slips down from the horse's hot flanks. She almost falls into his arms and I see them tighten about her for a moment, to stop her collapsing onto the sand as her legs give way beneath her. For one brief moment Nurmat holds another woman in his arms and I cannot help myself: I draw back a little, shocked by even the illusion of betrayal.*

She stands, shivering, her arms close by her side, seeking to contain what little strength and warmth she has left. She does not look about her. When Nurmat gestures her forwards she stumbles towards the door and I draw back from the window, tilt my head to hear Mei's bustling steps going to welcome them in.

I saw the traitors' army come too, our own family, their banners held high, their soldiers fresh and fierce, heading towards the walls of our fortress, coming to join the Emperor, to pass on our family secrets. Our men were weary from fighting, our women and children wept with fear *at this treason, this new onslaught from the Emperor, emboldened by his new allies.*

I stood, halfway between child and woman, longing to be a man, to carry weapons and join the fight. I watched the fighting from high up until my mother, a gentle woman, drew me away.

I hear footsteps as the girl passes by my room, blindly following Mei.

For one moment I think of Nurmat's arms about her, her weakness held up by his strength, and something cold comes over me. Perhaps I should turn her out into the desert. To starve or die of cold, whichever comes first. Something in me is afraid of her somehow, as though she is stronger than me.

Then I hear Mei's steps pass my door and behind her the shuffling steps of the girl, being led to a room where she will be put to sleep. Every step is an effort to her and I chastise myself for my foolish fears.

She is mine, for what other choice does she have?

The Taklamakan Desert

I WAS WRONG ABOUT THE HOUSE being dark inside. The windows are small and outside the desert is still a pale grey, but this room shines.

There are candles and lanterns everywhere, burning brightly. There are ornate and colourful wooden carvings all the way round the walls. Large silk and velvet cushions, heavily embroidered, are scattered so extravagantly I could sit down anywhere and find one ready for my horse-sweaty backside. There's a long low table, which a very small old woman is busily filling with little bowls of raisins, almonds and honey. There's a larger bowl filled with yoghurt and I can smell hot bread cooking.

The little woman has a back that is bent forward so far that it's an effort for her to look up at us as we enter. Her deeply wrinkled face is like a tortoise craning up from under its shell. I stare at her. Beneath the layers of wrinkles her features are different to ours. She's Chinese, her old skin paler, more yellow-tinged than reddish-brown, her eyes slanted more deeply than ours.

She nods to my captor and then looks at me. Her eyes widen and she takes a little step backwards. Then she takes in my ragged clothes topped off with the velvet and sheepskin the man provided. She looks down at my dirty nails, up at my frightened, exhausted face and her own face grows sad. "Welcome," she says. She speaks our language well, but with a strong accent, which I've heard before in the market.

Merchants who hail from Beijing speak like her. She indicates that I should sit down. "At peace?"

It's the local greeting. The simple, ritual reply that I ought to be giving is: *At peace – and you?*

I've never felt less at peace in my life and even a standard response I've given a thousand times in my life eludes me. I stand, swaying, in the doorway. This room is too much for me, too many colours and patterns, too much warmth and comfort, the smell of fresh hot food too great an assault. It seems I've arrived but I don't know where I am, nor why I've been brought here.

The man pushes me forward. "She is tired," he says. "A good enough horsewoman, but unused to such distances and I have not been able to feed her as well as I would have done had we not been heading this way. Feed her up, then she can sleep."

The tortoise woman nods and heads through a doorway, emerging in moments with a platter of hot *naan* breads in one hand. "Sit," she says.

I take two hobbling steps forward, then sink down onto a pile of cushions. The man steps quickly to the table, takes a hot *naan*, smears it with honey, throws a fistful of almonds into it and accepts a bowl of tea from the tortoise.

"I'm going to bed," he announces, and leaves the room through another doorway.

If I were less tired I'd follow him, even to his bed. He's the only person I know here and he's treated me well so far, whatever his future intentions. But I don't have the strength to stand.

I sip burning hot tea and slowly eat a soft *naan* with honey but even I can't manage much. When she sees my eyelids drooping and my chewing slow down the old tortoise gently takes the bowl of tea away and offers me her hand. She pulls me up, then shuffles off ahead of me into an equally colourful and comfortable room, but with fewer candles, making it glow softly rather than gleam like the first room. There's a *kang* made up with blankets. I sit down and shudder at the unaccustomed warmth coming from the heated bricks. The tortoise mistakes my reaction. "Not warm enough?" she asks. "I can put more wood on the stove."

I shake my head, dazed by the heat and food.

She crouches down in front of me, pulling off my worn boots. "What's your name?"

I try to speak but hardly any sound comes out and I have to try again. "Hidligh," I manage in a croaked whisper.

"My name is Mei," she says. "Let me take your clothes. I will give you new ones. These will be full of lice."

I clutch at my clothes but I'm so tired that her little calloused hands pull back my fingers one by one from the cloth and in the end I sit, slumped, as she strips every bit of clothing off me.

"Sleep," she says, and pushes my shoulder so that I lie down. She seizes my legs and swings them up. Then she heaps blankets over me. She stops for a moment, looks down on me, frowning. Then she shakes her head and leaves the room. I can hear her little puffs of breath as she blows out each candle she passes, the room growing dark as she leaves me.

I try to focus, to think about where I am and how to get away again, but the heat of the *kang* seeps into me and I close my eyes.

In the warm darkness two things wake me: the rustling of clothes and a fragrance. Someone is moving about in the room. I lie very still. The rustling comes closer and my nostrils fill with perfume, muddling my thoughts. I feel a person sit on the bed, close to me.

I swallow. "Who's there?" I manage to whisper, hoping it is the little bent woman, Mei.

A flame flickers and a lantern is lifted. At first the light blinds me but when it gets closer to my face I blink and shrink back. In the darkness, a hand's breadth from my nose, is a young woman's face.

She's beautiful. I see that, but only after I've drawn away from the huge scar that runs across her face. It traverses her whole cheek and comes too close for comfort to her left eye. Her skin elsewhere is smooth. She looks like an overripe peach split open by too much rain in the height of summer, perfection ruined.

She still smells perfect, though. Like a wondrous fruit warm in the summer sun and yet somehow like its own delicate springtime blossom as well: an impossibility.

Her dark eyes are fixed on me. Slowly she reaches out a hand and touches my cheek, lightly stroking my whole skin where hers is damaged. She looks over every part of my face in silence. Behind her another lantern is lit and I see my captor standing, watching us.

Their silent scrutiny is unnerving. "What do you want with me?" I blurt out.

The woman sits back a little. Her voice is soft. "What did you think Nurmat wanted you for when he took you?"

I shake my head. "A slave. A…" I stumble over the word wife; no one would steal a raggedy street girl to be a wife. "A concubine?"

She nods and speaks over her shoulder to the man, Nurmat. "She's not stupid. I can train her."

Her voice has a cold eagerness that makes me wriggle backwards, edging up against the wall so that I'm sitting upright. I pull the blankets around my naked body as though they might protect me. "Train me for what?"

The woman ignores my question and gets up. I'm relieved she's no longer so close to me and hope she'll move further away, but she stands still, looking me over. She has long thick hair, arranged as several fine plaits that fall down her back from under a little embroidered cap. She wears a full skirt and a velvet waistcoat. Her scar is worse than I first thought, a throbbing red on her pale skin, still fresh, made only days ago. Rough stitches and scabs are still in place, crusting brown bridging the pale silk skin. Her perfume is extraordinary, though. I can't help my nose stretching out towards her a little.

Nurmat, behind her, speaks. "We don't have to go ahead. We could be free of all this."

He can't see the woman's face from where he stands, but I can. Her eyes glisten with tears for a moment and then her face hardens. There's a rage in her eyes that scares me so badly I feel a trickling on my thighs and know that I've pissed myself in fear. I press my spine up against the hard wall trying to lean away from her.

The woman composes her face, then turns away from me and walks past Nurmat. "I have made my choice," she says, and leaves me alone with him.

Nurmat looks at me and then down at the dagger on his belt. I wait. I wonder how quickly I could move if he came for me but he's standing between the door and me. I can't feel my legs.

After a long moment his shoulders slump. He nods at me with an unhappy smile. "Looks like I have no choice," he says, "So we'd better learn to work together so we can get this over with quickly. My name is Nurmat. Are you hungry?"

The sudden reversal leaves me trembling. My lips are cold. "A little," I manage, although my stomach rumbles loudly, giving away my lie.

He nods. "I'll send Mei to you so you can be washed and dressed."

I've barely time to unwrap myself from the soaked blanket when Mei the tortoise drags in a heavy tub, steaming water, cloths, combs and rose scented soaps. She strips and remakes the bed without comment, then turns her attention to me. I'm scrubbed down in a very short space of time, kneel to have my hair washed and by the time the soap's been rinsed away she's laying out fresh clothes for me to wear. I reach out to touch them. A soft white cotton shirt with long billowed sleeves, a floor-length intricately patterned skirt woven in bright blues and reds, a thigh-length waistcoat in red velvet which fits me better than the one Nurmat covered me with in the market of Kashgar and a pair of good quality leather shoes with little heels which make me walk like the acrobats on their ropes.

Mei nods when I've finished putting it all on. "A good fit," she says. "Tiny bit loose but you'll fill out when you've eaten a few good meals. Now let me do your hair. Then you can go to eat with Nurmat and Iparhan."

"Who's Iparhan?" I ask.

Mei's voice goes flat. "The woman with the scar."

"Why does she want me here?"

Mei's wrinkled tortoise face is guarded. She opens her mouth as though to speak, then thinks better of it and closes it again. She picks up a comb. "Time enough to talk of why you are here later," she says and starts work on my hair. She drags a comb through it with a few choice words on my part. Days on horseback against a desert wind have made it even more tangled than usual. Once it's smooth she braids it tightly into many tiny plaits.

I protest. "I usually just have two."

"Nonsense. Only married women have two plaits – too busy to be braiding so many every morning. A young girl like you should have lots."

Once the plaits are done she finishes each end with a tightly wrapped blue ribbon and then puts a little velvet cap on my head. It's blue and has red flowers embroidered around the band. I reach up and feel its stiff newness. I had a black cap before, a man's one because it was bigger and kept my head warmer than this one, but it was worn

49

and frayed. I don't ever recall having new clothes. My skin feels tight with cleanness.

Mei gazes at me without speaking. She looks a little afraid.

I try to break the silence. "Do I look nice, then?"

She nods, a slow reluctant movement.

I frown. "Can I see? Do you have a mirror?"

She hesitates too long. "No," she says. "Come and eat now."

I think she's lying but I make my way to the door. There's a quick flash of silver light behind me. I'd swear Mei has just hidden away a mirror.

The main room is laid out for a meal again, this time with thick *lagman* noodles, roast lamb and vegetables. I stand in the doorway, awkward in my new clothes and clean skin. I'm not sure who else might be around, but the room is empty apart from Mei, who starts bustling in and out with more plates of food. Above the smell of the cooking I breathe in that scent again, the one I now associate with the woman Iparhan. I look about the room but can't see her.

Nurmat appears from the doorway opposite me, the one that leads outside. He sees me and his eyes widen.

"What?" I ask.

He pauses, then shakes his head. "Nothing," he says, although his eyes stay fixed on me.

I don't like being stared at. "What's that perfume?" I ask, hoping to distract him. It fills the room. Not even rich women smell like this.

Nurmat looks pleased. "The perfume is Iparhan's. She always wears it."

"Is that why you call her Iparhan? What's her real name?" Iparhan just means Fragrant Girl. It's not a real name; it sounds like a nickname, like being called Little Melon if you're a bit plump.

He shakes his head. "She's been called Iparhan for years. No one uses her real name any more."

I step further into the room, thinking she must be there somewhere for her perfume to be so strong. But it's just Nurmat and me in the room. "She's not in here."

He grins suddenly, looking younger and more cheerful. "She is, you know. You just can't see her."

I look at him to see if it's a joke but he's looking round the room carefully, at the hangings and the long curtains hanging either side of the small window. He even looks at the larger cushions as though she might be inside one or underneath it.

I make a face. "What is she, a magician?"

There's a cold hard sharpness on the back of my neck.

"Too slow."

I move fast to the other side of the room and look back. Standing where I was standing is Iparhan. She's the same height as me, and she's holding a dagger where my neck was.

By my side Nurmat is laughing. "You always beat me at this. Were you behind the door? I thought I checked."

She doesn't answer, just reaches up to a rafter and pulls her whole body upwards so that it lies flat against the ceiling above where I was standing, just her arms holding her in place. I can see them trembling with the effort but she stays in place for several breaths before she swings back down again.

Nurmat looks impressed. "That's a new one."

She ignores his praise and sits down.

Nurmat nudges me and I sit, as far away from both of them as I'm able. I don't like their sudden changes of mood, from the soft voice and then eyes full of rage I saw on Iparhan's face to Nurmat staring at his dagger and then his tired joviality towards me. I don't know what might come next. I find myself holding my breath and flinching

51

when they move. I try to sit still and force myself to breathe. All I'm thinking is: how do I get out of here when the desert surrounds me?

They wash their hands and start to eat. I hesitate, but food is food. Mei joins us, passing little bowls of food to each of us, making sure our plates are full. The food is good, I'm clean and warm and well dressed. I ought to feel comfortable, but I'm too anxious and on edge.

Iparhan turns to Nurmat and indicates me as though I'm not even in the room. "It's going to take longer than I'd like. She speaks like a peasant." She gestures at my sticky fingers and chin. "She eats like one too."

Nurmat looks me over and smiles. "Perhaps you should explain why she is here," he suggests. "Then she might know why she needs to behave differently."

I cross my arms and sit back against the cushions, chin up. My heart's pounding. My mouth is dry with curiosity and fear. "Yes," I say, trying not to let my voice tremble. Instead I sound too loud and almost cheerful, as though we were talking about someone else. "What *am* I doing here?"

Silence. I look at Iparhan but she seems to be ignoring all of us, gazing into her bowl of tea as though mesmerised. It takes a moment before she begins, her voice too quiet after my loudness. "What do you know about the besieging of Yarkand?"

I blink. This is not the beginning I was expecting. "What?"

She looks up, suddenly impatient. Her voice is sharp. "The siege. Of Yarkand."

"Not much." I try to think fast, afraid of arousing her anger. Yarkand? The end of the war, when the Emperor of China finally claimed our land as his own? What does that have to do with me? "I know that the Sultan cut off the heads of Burhan ad-Din and Khoja Jihan and showed their bodies to the commander of the Emperor's army." I begin tentatively. Iparhan's face contorts in a painful grimace and I hurry on, unsure whether I'm saying the right thing. "I know that pretty much ended any rebellions, and now Altishahr is the 'New Dominion' – *Xinjiang*." I shrug and try to end my piecemeal history. I don't think I'm saying what she wants me to say. "We all belong to the Emperor of China now," I finish lamely. I wait for her response.

She's staring at me, appalled. "Is that the whole of your understanding of the conquest of our homeland?"

What more does she expect of me? I spread my hands. "What else would I need to know to live on the streets of Kashgar?" I say, which is the truth, but she glares again, so I try to do better: "We were one of the great cities of Altishahr. Now we're one of the cities of Xinjiang and part of the Empire. So what? I see Emperor's Bannerman officials hanging around all the time, collecting taxes and swaggering about looking pleased with themselves. But trading goes on as it always did. Life goes on as it always did. Not much changes. Not for real people."

She's frowning. Suddenly I'm almost angry with her. She may be strange but clearly she wants for nothing, not even out here in the desert, sitting on her fat cushions and being fed mountains of food. "Real people need to eat." I tell her. "Only rich people worry about who is ruling them. Rich people who want the power for themselves."

She shakes her head, as though she can't even think where to begin in correcting me.

"You still haven't answered my question," I tell her. "What has any of that to do with me? I've never had anything to do with the war. I've been too busy trying to feed myself and stay out of trouble. Why would you bring me here?"

"I need you to do something."

I don't like the sound of this. What could I do for her? She has money, she could ask anyone to do anything for her if she offered them enough money. What does she need doing that cannot be bought with silver? Why does she need me and not anyone else she could have chosen?

"I don't understand," I say, although I'm not sure I want to hear her explanation.

She takes a sip of the cooling tea and looks down into the bowl as she speaks. "Two hundred years ago—"

I stop her at once. "Two hundred *years* ago?! I don't want a history lesson! I want to know why you brought me here! Who *are* you?"

She looks at me for a moment. "My family is of the White Mountain brotherhood. My grandfather was Khoja Afaq."

I blink. I may have lived on the streets but everyone knows her family. They are – or were – effectively our rulers. Her family lived in Kashgar on a great estate, guiding both religious and secular affairs. All their lands were seized by the Emperor's officials, turned into grain storage or offices for his administrators. "But I thought your family was…" I stop. I was going to say 'dead'. They were wiped out. I thought they'd all been killed and yet here is one of them. I'm gaping at her. "How did you escape?"

She ignores me. "To rule we had to have the support of the Zunghars, but they grew too demanding and we rebelled against their control. When we did, the Zunghars captured my grandfather Khoja Afaq, my uncle Khoja Jihan and my father Burhan ad-Din, and imprisoned them in Yili."

"That was four years ago," I say. "There was plenty of coming and going in Kashgar when that happened. But trading goes on. Doesn't matter who rules the cities, they always want them to keep trading. That's how they get their money, by taxing merchants. Can't be frightening off the merchants, even if you are the Emperor of China."

She looks as if she might strike me. I draw back. Perhaps I should keep my mouth shut. This is a woman who's lost every member of her powerful family and who no doubt has a price on her own head. Not a person to be trifled with.

She's speaking again. "The Emperor of China had been trying to take Altishahr for many years. Now he believed he had a chance to do so. He offered us our freedom and the rule of both Yarkand and Kashgar if we would be his tributaries. But my family refused. We had heard that the Zunghar had rebelled in the North and so we too rebelled."

I make a face. "Why be allies again with the Zunghar when you'd rebelled against them in the first place?"

Her voice goes cold. "We are the people of Altishahr. We would rather join forces with the Zunghar than allow the Emperor of China to reach out his greedy hands and take away our freedom. His empire cannot take over the entire world. He had to be stopped."

I hold up my hands. I'm not about to argue with her. I think I might not even live to regret it if I do. "Whatever you say."

"The rebellion angered the Emperor. He sent a huge army to take Altishahr by force. He would not accept failure this time. In this he was aided by a traitor."

I don't understand any of this. It's turning into a history lesson after all and I keep searching for my place in it. But these are emperors and rulers and noble families she's talking about, the people who make history. Where does a street girl fit into it? I try to hang on to the last thing she said. "A... traitor?"

"My father's cousins, greedy for influence and resenting my father's command, refused to support our rebellions. Instead, hoping for privileges from the Emperor, they sent their forces to support the Emperor's army. My uncle Khoja Jihan was killed. The Emperor threatened the local Shah, demanding my dead uncle's head and that my father Burhan ad-Din should also be handed over, to do with as the Emperor pleased. The Shah was a coward and he handed over

Melissa Addey

both the head of my uncle and the body of my father, whom he had executed himself." She stops, her breathing a little too fast.

I sit up straight, my attention finally caught by something she's just said. "The Shah handed over your uncle's *head* and your father's *body*?"

"Yes."

"Why not two heads? Or two whole bodies, come to that, with the heads still on?"

Nurmat cuts in. "The Shah said that the head of Burhan ad-Din had been mislaid."

"Mislaid?"

Nurmat nods.

How you can mislay a head is the least of my concerns. "So your father and uncle were both killed and you came here to hide?"

Iparhan nods.

"And Nurmat?"

She hesitates, flushes. For one moment the red scar disappears into the rose of her cheeks and her face is perfection.

Mei stands and begins to clear the table. "They are promised to one another. Their families were friends. Nurmat and Iparhan are to wed one day."

I raise my eyebrows. "What's stopping you getting married now?"

Iparhan's face is hard, but her voice is quiet. "I will not marry until I have exacted revenge."

She sounds like she's said this more than once. I look to Nurmat. "You don't mind waiting?"

Nurmat smiles. It's a sad smile. "I'd wait for ever for her, of course," he says.

I think he's said this more than once too but it sounds as if it's beginning to grate on him. "So you're hiding here," I repeat, then ask

56

the question that's still burning in my mind: "But why do you need me?"

Iparhan leans forward. I lean back. She's suddenly too eager, too focused on me. I wish I hadn't kept asking my questions, perhaps I could have delayed the reply. "Now that the Emperor has taken Altishahr our traitorous cousins are preparing to travel to Beijing. There they will be given imperial honours for their part in the Emperor's victory." Her voice is shaking with rage. She pauses for a moment, then takes a deep breath. "There is a daughter. She is going to be given to the Emperor as a concubine. It is supposed to be a great honour and if she pleases the Emperor her family will receive many more gifts and privileges."

It's still not an answer. I don't see why she's even bothering to tell me about this girl. "He must have lots of women," I say, hoping to calm Iparhan. "I expect he'll barely notice her."

Suddenly her face is close to mine. I start back. "He *will* notice her," she breathes and her dark eyes are too dark, too fervent. "'She' will be you—and it will be your task to be noticed."

I don't even think. What she's suggesting is so impossible it's not even worth thinking about. "No."

She sits back, a half-smile on her lips. "Yes," she says simply. "We need an insider. We need a woman who is close to the Emperor, who can ask questions, who will hear of plans being made. You will take the place of my cousin. You will endear yourself to the Emperor. Then you will talk of your homeland. What could be more natural? He believes your family to be his loyal allies, so he will let slip information which will aid us."

"Aid you to do *what*?"

She answers without meeting my gaze. "Start a rebellion."

I'm sure my mouth falls open in shock. "How would you do that? Do you have an army you haven't told me about?"

"The people will rise up if they have a strong leader. We have a network of those who wish to reclaim our land."

I have my doubts about anyone raising an army that can withstand the Emperor's troops. Now he's made his conquest, after years of fighting, he surely won't let it go that easily. But I don't really care about her ridiculous plans of fighting the Emperor of China. I'm shaking at the very idea of what she's suggesting. "It can't be done. Everyone would know I'm not from a noble family."

Iparhan nods. "You will have a few months here first. You will learn how to behave like an imperial concubine. By the time our cousins set out for Beijing you will be able to pass yourself off as the girl. We will intercept them and you will take her place."

I clutch at this. "What happens to this girl, then? She's hardly going to step out of the bridal palanquin and say, 'Oh, by all means take my place,' is she?"

Nurmat looks at Iparhan. She says nothing, just looks back at him.

I shut my eyes for a moment. I can feel tears of fear welling up. I'm sorry I asked the question. "I don't want to know. Then what?"

Iparhan presses on. "Once you are at the palace you will be given a title, your own rooms and servants, clothes, money. You will be kept in splendour – this place will be a hovel compared to it."

I shake my head. I'm beginning to feel sick. "You're crazy. It's just not possible."

She's coaxing me now, her voice pitched low and soft. It doesn't sound natural coming from her. "All you need to do is live your life. There will be gardens to walk in, other ladies to keep you company, wonderful food to eat. You may keep a pet. There will be games, visits to the summer palace and the hunting lodge, boating on the lakes. Your life will be –"

I stop her. "Oh, yes. My life will be one long round of pleasure and happiness, I'm sure. Until my 'brother' comes to visit and he sees a complete stranger masquerading as his sister. Then what?"

She shakes her head. "We will arrange the timing of the changeover so that you are almost at the palace when it happens. The court will send out a palanquin for you to ride in. You will be wearing a wedding veil. Once you're in the palace your 'brother' may visit you only if you are ill or if there is a very special occasion. Even if he does, he will not see your face. He is a man; you will be an imperial concubine. He will wait outside your rooms and send in his compliments. Once you enter the Forbidden City he will never see your face again. You will live there for the rest of your days and be our spy."

The tears I was trying to hold back spill over. I stand up too fast. My heart's pounding and I think I might throw up. I need to get away from Iparhan's dark eyes and the madness coming out of her mouth. My legs feel weak beneath me and I have to lock my knees in place to stand upright. "I'm going to bed," I say and my words are an ugly distorted gulp.

Iparhan stands as I do. "We need an answer tomorrow morning."

I pause in the doorway and look back at her. I think of the endless grey desert outside, the way Iparhan talks of the hapless concubine-to-be who is her own cousin. No one knows or cares that I'm here. No one would know or care if a dagger stopped my heart. "Do I have a choice?"

Her silence follows me to bed.

I don't sleep. Instead I lie awake fully dressed and think. This could be my way out of life on the streets. Concubine to the Emperor of China! I would live in comfort for the rest of my life, would never again feel the pain of hunger cramping my belly. I'm quick and smart, I could learn what must be learnt to pass myself off as a lowly concubine, couldn't I? It's not as if I am trying to impersonate an Empress. I could find out whatever Iparhan wants to know and then she can raise her rebellion and succeed or fail – it will make no difference to me. My life will go on, secure within the gilded cocoon that is the Emperor's Forbidden City. What harm can come to me there?

But… but… their plan is a folly. For all their talk of the luxurious life I would lead, how can they possibly expect it to work? The women chosen to be concubines for the Emperor will have come from the best families. They will have spent their whole lives being prepared for their role in his court, in his bedchamber. And I? I have spent my life scraping – not even a living – only enough food to keep me from starving, enough warmth to keep me from freezing. Besides, they want me to be a spy, to ask questions that may raise suspicions. I will have to draw attention to myself, which will only risk my position further, exposing the deception. It can't be done. And I know enough to know that if it can't be done; someone will suffer for it when the deception is revealed – and that someone will be me.

By dawn I am decided. In the early light I slip out of the room and make my way to the outer door. I touch the thick sheepskin of Nurmat's jacket and slip it on. It engulfs me but it's warm. I think I might need it. I open the door and step out.

It's freezing. The desert is the unpleasant colour of dirty, peeling, dead skin, a grey undulating endlessness.

I look more closely at the old dead poplar tree. What few branches it has left poke into the sky, black stumps against almost-white. From the stumps flutter tiny shreds of cloth: red and green, yellow and blue. Each tiny scrap a prayer or a wish from some unknown person. Under the tree is a large dome of pale mud, hard baked by the sun. The scraps of cloth should be faded, unravelling from years of past-forgotten dreams. The mud-domed tomb should be better shaped and dusty with age. But the scraps are brightly coloured and the dome is misshapen and cracked as though it was made by unskilled hands and then dried out too fast. I move closer to it and look down at it, then rest my left hand on the poplar, looking out across the dunes. The bark crumbles and gives way under my touch.

I see a small shed tucked into the edge of a dune and hear a snort, telling me that the horses are stabled there. In the distance are the mountains I think would lead me back to Kashgar. I take a deep breath and prepare to move towards the shed when I hear a thud and find I cannot move my left arm.

I look down and see a dagger pinning the sheepskin jacket I am wearing to the tree. I look up and see Iparhan, standing in the doorway of the house, a second dagger in her hand. I turn slowly to face her, my left hand still pinned to the tree.

The wind changes direction and I get a mouthful of thin dry sand. I cough. I try to keep my eyes on her though. I'm afraid of where her second dagger might land if she lets it fly but I can't let her see my fear. "Whose tomb is this?"

She keeps the dagger lifted in her hand, ready to throw. "My father's."

"But you said—" I stop. "So when the Shah said he'd 'mislaid' the head of your father, he hadn't."

"No."

"Who did the body belong to, then?"

She shrugs.

"So he came with you? You, your father, Nurmat and Mei?"

"Yes."

"And what was the plan?"

She sounds proud. "He would have roused the people behind him and Altishahr would have rebelled against the Emperor."

"And your role in all of this?"

She is silent for a moment. "I was to be the Emperor's concubine."

"The spy, you mean."

"Yes."

"What went wrong?"

"My father died of a wound that rotted his flesh. We buried him here."

"And decided to do it all yourselves?"

"Yes."

"But something went wrong?"

She's silent. I look at her for a moment. In the cold her skin is bone white, the scar purple.

"You couldn't be the concubine because of the scar. You needed someone else to take that part."

She dips her head.

I sigh. "Why me?"

She doesn't answer.

"Because you thought no one would miss me?"

She moves away from the house and comes towards me. I'd like to step back but her dagger is keeping me firmly attached to the poplar. She hesitates, looking me over. That same searching look.

She pauses, then speaks quickly: "I look like my cousin, the one who is to be the concubine. And you look – enough – like me." She sees my puzzled face. "Your height, your build," she adds. "Don't you think you look like me?"

I shake my head, confused. I can't say I see myself in mirrors that often. The hat stall in the market has a mirror, but I've only glimpsed myself in passing. Certainly I don't think I look like Iparhan, who despite her scar is beautiful. I frown. "But the Emperor will never have seen this girl before anyway – oh, what does it matter? At least the silk in the palace will be better quality for my hands to rest on, I suppose."

Iparhan frowns. "The silk?"

"Nothing. Talking to myself."

We stand in silence. I'm thinking fast. I have two choices: defy her and die, or agree to her plan. I try to push back the conclusion I came to in the night's darkness: that the plan is impossible. Instead I look up and meet her gaze directly. "I'll do this for a warm bed and a full belly," I say, trying to sound unafraid. "And a quiet life in a forgotten part of the Forbidden City once your crazy plan is done with. Do you understand? I don't want to be your comrade in arms or a part of whatever glories you have in your mind. I want to be left alone when this is over. And you must keep me safe. You must teach me every trick I will need to stay alive. I have to know how to dress, how to move, how to do whatever it takes to stay alive."

"You agree to my plan?"

I spread my hands open, the left one pinned to the tree, the other shaking with cold and the realisation of what I am agreeing to. "If I ran away now, in front of you, what would you do?"

She looks down and then hardly moves. I hear a *thud* and my right arm jerks back. Now both my hands are pinned to the tree behind me, my arms pulled open in a gesture of submission, the second dagger's handle still trembling.

I nod and start to laugh. "I thought so."

She watches me as I laugh and laugh. I can't seem to stop. I struggle to breathe and my lungs hurt but the laughter carries on without air.

Eventually my laughter fades and there's only the hissing of the sand dunes.

She pulls out the daggers in swift movements, her eyes never leaving my face. I look away from her as soon as she's finished. Her eyes burn too brightly for my liking. Back in the house Nurmat and Mei are standing waiting for us.

"I'm alive," I say. "So that must mean I've agreed to her plan, don't you think?"

Nurmat leaves the room, Iparhan following behind him. Mei looks concerned.

"Well," I say to Mei with blustering confidence, "I must be able to survive in a palace if I can survive on the streets. At least they'll feed me and keep me warm. It can't be much harder than my life up until now, can it?"

Mei looks at me without answering.

"Don't bother to reassure me," I say.

"I will do all I can to help you," she says, although she doesn't sound confident. "But we don't have that much time, perhaps only a couple of months. First things first, you have to learn good table manners."

"If you had just one meal a day and only if you stole it or begged for it or worked hard for it, you'd eat in whatever way got the food into your belly fastest."

She nods. "But you'll be a court lady now. And court ladies have more food than they know what to do with. They've no idea what it is to be hungry. So they just pick at their food."

"What do you know about court ladies?"

She smiles, revealing her secret. "I was a maid in the Forbidden City."

I stare at her. "What are you doing here, then?"

"I had served my time. I was released to be married. I married a man from Yili and when he died I carried on living there."

I narrow my eyes and lower my voice. "Until they kidnapped you, too?"

She hesitates, looks behind her, then nods.

"To teach them about the Forbidden City?"

She nods again.

"Don't you mind?"

Mei answers cautiously, her voice low. "I had no children. My husband had died. Besides," and there is some pride in her voice, "I was always a good servant to my mistress."

I feel sorry for the little bit of pride left which leads her to make the best of her imprisonment. "And who was your mistress in the Forbidden City?"

"I was maid to the Lady Wan. One of the Emperor's concubines."

"Did you live there a long time?"

"They were such *happy* years. My mistress was so *kind*."

We both jump. Iparhan is standing in the doorway and she has just mimicked Mei's voice. We stare at her, for she does it perfectly. It sounds like Mei speaking.

She uses her own voice again and it's cold. "This is not the time for reliving your past. Get on with teaching Hidligh some manners."

Mei obediently starts hurrying in and out of the room, setting down all manner of little dishes on the table, each filled with local delicacies. Roasted lamb with herbs, kebabs spiced with ground cumin and chilli, various vegetables and noodles, as well as *polo* – a dish of rice with mutton and vegetables. It's usually served at banquets and the only time I've eaten it was when I managed to get my hands on the scraps from a wedding.

I gaze at the food and shake my head in disbelief. "So," I manage. "How *does* a court lady eat?"

"Don't reach for anything, just nod towards it," Mei says. "I will pass it to you."

I nod in an exaggerated way towards the *polo*. Mei passes it to me. It's glistening with fat and the smell makes my mouth water. It's a dish eaten with the fingers, and I try to eat in a way that suggests I am only picking at it, but greed overtakes me and I take a heaping scoop, which allows grains to fall from my mouth and fingers.

"Peasant." Iparhan is watching me and mutters it quietly, but it annoys me. I let my mouth hang open as I chew as noisily as possible, slurp the hot tea placed by me, then exaggeratedly suck each of my fingers clean even though there's not that much food on them. Mei shakes her head but I wipe my mouth with the back of my clean shirtsleeve, then belch loudly when I'm finished. I look over my shoulder at Iparhan, eyebrows raised, daring her to make another comment.

She's looking away, out of the door towards the desert. From where I'm sitting all I can see is the scar on the curve of her cheekbone.

The Lie

W HAT ELSE COULD SHE SAY *but yes? What other choice does she have? Nurmat watched her standing in the women's lane, shifting from one foot to the other, nervous, desperate, one step away from selling her body for a filling meal. She scraped her food up from the dirt by the traders' stalls or caught it mid-air as it was thrown to her, like a mangy dog.*

"She has spirit, though," says Nurmat. "She can ride," he adds.

"Spirit is nothing without food in your belly," I tell him.

"She tried to escape," he says. "Several times."

"She failed," I remind him. "Several times."

He doesn't answer.

"She has accepted my proposal," I say. 'She had no other choices and besides, what street girl wouldn't do anything for a life of ease and luxury like the one I am offering her?"

My own life of ease and luxury, the noble daughter of a noble house, was swept away when the Emperor's men beat on the great doors and demanded the heads of my father and uncle. As the heavy doors swung open and the hideous bloodstained bundles were passed from the defeated to the victorious, there was a great wail from the high walls.

Each of us turned our faces to the sound, only to see the silent fall of my mother through the air, her multi-hued skirts rippling against the grey sky. Hidden away for her own safety she had not been told of our subterfuge, only seen what she believed was her husband's dead and mutilated body being given to our enemies. Her despair so great she chose to leave me, her only daughter, to an unknown fate. I was left with a mortally wounded father and no guidance from my mother. I stood alone.

Except for Nurmat.

"It is dangerous," Nurmat says. "She may forget how to behave. She may be found out."

I shrug. "If she is found out she will be executed and no harm will come to us," I say, although my heart beats faster.

Nurmat turns to me so that our faces come very close together. His voice is low. "Iparhan. You still swear it?"

I keep my eyes on his while my heart beats faster still. I can see before me so plainly what really intend to do that I cannot believe he does not see it himself, that the bloodied image does not rise up before him. "I swear," I say. "She is to be a spy. She will gather information and I will use it – we will use it – to further our plans for rebellion."

"Nothing more?"

I lift my free hand and cup his cheek, stroke his warm skin. His eyes close at my rare touch. His breath is on my lips. "Nothing more," I say.

The House in the Dunes

"**I**'M NOT BATHING WITH HIM in the room!"

Iparhan's face is white. Her scar stands out, a red streak of fury. "Take off your clothes and get in the bath, you stupid girl."

I turn away from her. "No!"

Iparhan's voice drops to a hissing whisper as she comes close to me. Her teeth are so tightly clenched I think one of them might crack. "Your bath will be filled by men. You will be soaped and rinsed by men. They will wash your hair. They will touch every part of you. They will pat your legs dry while they kneel before you." She's so close to me now I can feel her breath on my lips. "Which part of your body do you think their faces will be next to when they do that?"

I step back, trying to avoid her fury. "They'll be *eunuchs*!"

Mei is busily filling the tub, taking no notice of either of us, nudging past with each new pail of water.

Iparhan picks up a handful of dried rose petals and scatters them into the bath. Their scent warms the room more than the clouds of steam. Her hands are shaking. "Take. Your. Clothes. Off. Get. In. The. Bath."

I turn to Nurmat. "Shut your eyes."

He holds out his hand, which has a scented soap in it. His face is serious. "I am supposed to bathe you. I have to be able to see."

"You're a man, not a eunuch! This is ridiculous. Can't I just act ignorant when I get there and insist on bathing alone?"

Iparhan leans over the bath and tests the water. "Get in."

I'm so angry I rip my skirt as I try to undo it. Mei comes to my rescue and I pull off everything as fast as I can so I can get into the tub and have something, even if it's just water, covering my naked body. Mei leaves the three of us alone then, taking my clothes with her to mend. Iparhan stands by the small window as Nurmat kneels by the side of the tub and rubs the scented soap between his hands onto a small soft cloth.

The autumn moon has long since died away and a bitter cold surrounds us. Because of her past, Mei is designated my tutor for most things, and I'm glad of it, for I can't bring myself to willingly spend much time in a room with Iparhan. Mei serves me with care and kindness, as though I were her beloved mistress, not a fellow prisoner.

My only interest in Iparhan's scheme lies in learning enough to protect myself. Mei rebukes me for looking at her when she talks to me, for paying her any attention at all. "You must not laugh at what I do. You must not even notice me. I am a servant. I am invisible to you."

I make a great show of ignoring her as I eat but this is not enough. "You are not supposed to *act* ignoring me," she chastises me. "You have to be oblivious to me. Forget about me. I am a maid. I am nobody."

I sigh and keep eating, trying to manage chopsticks with grace. Mealtimes come sooner for me than for Nurmat and Iparhan. They eat at normal times but I'm fed several more times a day. They were right. You can't eat as I've been accustomed to when you're not really hungry. So I begin to pick at my food, with Mei having to coax me. I'm aware that my starved angles are filling out into the slender curves of a rich woman and I'm glad of it. A bit of extra fat on me may be my saviour if this plan goes awry. I attempt to get some noodles into my mouth in an elegant manner but several fall out of my mouth. I catch them but my white cuffs get sauce on them. Behind me I hear an impatient sigh. I don't bother turning round. Iparhan's perfume follows her everywhere. If I can smell it, then she is in the room.

"What do you want?" I ask. I'm afraid of her daggers and her eyes that are too dark, too certain. I compensate for my fear of her by speaking rudely to her, by showing a bravado I don't feel.

"You need to learn poetry."

I roll my eyes. "Poetry? Why would I want to do that?"

"All cultured women at court can recite poetry."

I give up on the noodles. I look pointedly towards some vegetables and Mei passes them. At least eating them is a bit easier. "Well," I say through a mouthful. "You'd better teach me some poems then, hadn't you?"

Iparhan looks away from my half-filled, fast-chewing mouth and addresses the cushions.

"Blossoms fall
Mist rises
She arrives in darkness
And fades in the light
How long will this spring dream stay?"

She looks back at me.

I grimace. It sounds like the merchants from Beijing but I never understood them, even when they shouted. This just sounds like a whining child, all ups and downs. "I don't speak that language."

Her lips tighten. "It is Mandarin and it is what the court speaks. You had better learn or you will understand nothing of what goes on."

I shake my head and help myself to more vegetables. "I can't learn a whole new language in a few months. Besides, he knows I'm from Kashgar, doesn't he? He surely doesn't expect me to speak his language?"

"You need to know what is being said around you – or possibly about you."

She's right. I can't get by anywhere if I don't know what is being said. I shake my head in despair at what I have to learn. A whole new language. This is madness. I sit for a moment in silence, my confidence sapped.

She looks at me and waits.

I lean back against the cushions and repeat the sounds back to her. My version sounds like a child talking garbled nonsense, whining to its mother for sweetmeats. Mei stifles a laugh.

When Iparhan leaves the room, glowering at my incompetence, I turn to Mei. "I need to know," I say. "What happened to Iparhan's face?"

Mei sits back and sighs. This makes her cough, something she does regularly. She takes a drink of water. "Iparhan's father and uncle ordered Iparhan to leave their side although she was unwilling. She wanted to stay and fight but they insisted that she escape from the siege and come here. It's a safe place and the family had many taels of silver to hide away for as long as necessary. Nurmat is a distant cousin, they have been promised to each other since they were children. He too had intended to stay and fight but was ordered to make his way here and protect Iparhan. Her family was afraid that if they lost the battle against the Emperor and were killed there would be no one left of their family line, so they wanted to save the two of them. Nurmat has never cared for war. He wanted to marry her many years ago, take her away from all of the fighting and rebellions and family feuds. He said they could live quietly somewhere out of the way and be happy together. But Iparhan got it into her head that she must stand by her family until they had defeated the Emperor. When her uncle died her father made his way here. But his wounds began to rot and when he died she vowed she would not marry until she had avenged them.

You've seen how she can hide herself, how well she can use weapons. She trains every day."

I know this. Iparhan spends most days outside. She trains in the dunes of the desert. The cold, the heat, the wind and blowing sand never seem to affect her. Her daggers fly straight and embed themselves in the blackened poplar trees, which are scarred and shredded all over with her rage.

"And the scar?"

Mei looks down into her lap. "Nurmat hated the idea of her marrying the Emperor, even for show. He did not want her to be a concubine to the Emperor before Nurmat had taken her as his wife, if indeed at all. They argued. He begged her to marry him first, to live together as husband and wife and that then she could go and be a concubine. She refused. She had to be a virgin for her first night with the Emperor. Nurmat was enraged at the idea. He attempted to take her maidenhood before it was taken by the Emperor."

I frown. I can't imagine this of Nurmat, who worships Iparhan. "He forced her?"

Mei slowly shakes her head. "He didn't try very hard. He was drunk that night and was a little rough perhaps in trying to persuade her. And she refused, she said she would not come to his bed until she had raised a rebellion against the Emperor. She threatened him with her dagger, said if he took her virginity she would kill herself out of shame at not being able to carry out her revenge on the Emperor. Nurmat took the dagger out of her hand." She stops.

"And?"

Mei speaks fast. "And he cut her face. He said if she was disfigured the Emperor would never take her into his court, but he, Nurmat, would still love her."

I gape at her. "It wasn't an accident?"

She shakes her head. "No."

"And she still refused to lie with him?"

"Yes. Nurmat thought that would be an end to her plans but she saw you in the marketplace and chose you as her replacement. You will allow Iparhan to take her revenge."

"And then they will marry? Not before?"

"She is a warrior at heart, not a maiden. She took a solemn vow not to marry before she has her revenge. She is stubborn. She will not change her mind now. She wants to see the Emperor dead – probably at her own hand – and these lands returned to their people."

I sigh. "She's hardly going to come face to face with the Emperor in battle. I believe he has generals and foot soldiers to do the fighting. So long as she leaves me alone once she's finished. I'm doing this for a warm bed and good food. I don't want her causing trouble for me for years and years to come."

Mei is silent. She opens her mouth, then closes it again. Then she starts again but ends up having a coughing fit. I fetch her some water. When she's breathing properly again I get up. "We'd better carry on, then. Wasn't I supposed to be learning how to eat noodles without them falling down my waistcoat?"

Clothes are worse than table manners. Although my new clothes are warm and clean, I'm clumsy in them. A long wide skirt, after being used to trousers, is difficult to manage. I regularly trip over it or catch it on everything from protruding hooks to, memorably, Mei's head, sitting on cushions near a door I come through. Nurmat laughs so hard he cries.

"It's that sort of accident that will give me away at court," I spit at him, and he shakes his head at my sudden temper.

I pull on yet another long skirt, this time in a vivid pattern of green and blues, then stand while Mei fastens my green waistcoat's little buttons, which I always fumble over. "Shouldn't I be wearing court clothes?"

Iparhan, watching me, shakes her head. "We know that our cousins have decided the girl must wear clothes that show where she is from. They wish to flaunt their allegiance to the Emperor. She is to be a daily reminder of his conquest of our lands." She looks enraged.

I shrug. I've got enough to cope with without wearing entirely unfamiliar clothes. At least I know how these ones should look – if I wore court clothes I might put the wrong things on or wear some item in the wrong way and give myself away. Besides, I've seen drawings of the headdresses the court ladies wear and I don't know how they balance them all on their heads, what with flowers and dangling hairpins. My plaits are easier. But the billowing sleeves of my shirts are a problem.

"Get them out of your soup," admonishes Mei.

I curse and Iparhan frowns at me.

Nurmat laughs out loud. When he's not arguing with Iparhan he can be funny, with a lop-sided smile and a laugh that makes me laugh too. "I want to be there when you do that in front of the Emperor," he says. He mimics my trailing sleeve, dripping with soup at the elbow while uttering a string of such coarse words that I get a helpless fit of giggles. For the rest of the meal the two of us hold up our sleeves at intervals and mouth obscenities at each other. Mei shakes her head and laughs at us, although even she is tiring of our game by the end of the meal. Iparhan ignores us.

The shoes are worse. They have a small elegantly raised heel and I am used to walking in men's boots. I stumble and fall regularly. Nurmat gets used to catching me in time after the first bad sprain.

Iparhan is displeased with my clumsiness. "You still have the same feet—you're not foot-bound," she admonishes. "What's the matter with you?"

Exasperated, I kick them off. They strike against the door, making a clatter that brings Mei to see what the noise is about.

"I have the same feet but wobbling about on stilts!" I yell at her.

Nurmat fetches the shoes, grinning at my temper, then kneels in front of me holding them. They're made of finely tooled leather, with little flowers etched into them. I put a hand on his shoulder and feel the warmth of his cheek against my thighs as he slips them back on. I blush and step backwards from him and in doing so very nearly fall over again.

Nurmat laughs. "The day will come when it will all seem natural."

I sit down, slumping forwards, my face resting in my hands, my feet, encased in the foolish shoes, tucked under me. I'm too tired and worried to reply with any spirit. "I'm not sure it ever will, you know."

Perched high on a stack of cushions, Nurmat focuses his attention on Iparhan. By his side Mei, also on a stack of cushions, looks down benevolently. A fit of coughing mars her regal performance as the Empress Dowager but she recovers and nods graciously to Iparhan to continue her demonstration of the perfect kowtow.

Iparhan advances very slowly, head high, hands by her sides. As she nears Nurmat and Mei, her knees bend without seeming to affect her upper body at all, for it remains upright until she is fully kneeling before them. Then she folds herself in two, her forehead touching the ground. Lifting her head she calls out in a clear voice: "I wish your Majesties ten thousand years!"

She touches her forehead to the ground twice more and then rises in one smooth movement, as though lifted by invisible arms.

"Ten thousand years?" I say from behind her in my place in the corner of the room. "Who wants to live that long? Wouldn't a hundred do?"

Iparhan ignores me. She is kneeling down again.

"Yes, yes," I say. "I got it the first time. Walk forward. Kneel down, touch your forehead to the ground three times, ten thousand years, get up again."

Mei lays a finger on her lips. "You must do it three times," she says.

"The whole thing? Three times?"

"Yes."

I sigh and sit down on a cushion with a bump. "This is going to take all day. Doesn't the Emperor get bored of it?"

Iparhan has finished her set of nine reverences. "Your turn."

I stand and step forward to take my turn.

Iparhan sighs behind me. "I wonder how long it will be before you fall over."

I turn and make a face at her. "Watch me."

She does, and I fall over as I try to stand up. Nurmat tries to help me but we end up in a tangled mess on the floor.

"Much use you are," I scold him.

"Much good *you* are," he retorts, straightening my skirts as we stand. "I've never seen such a clumsy girl."

I swipe at him but he ducks too fast for me and I nearly slap Iparhan, who's standing behind him, her face cold.

Iparhan and Nurmat are praying. I sit and watch them, then suddenly interrupt.

"Praying!"

Iparhan pauses, then turns to face me. "What?"

I speak fast, excited. "You have to teach me to pray!"

She is disbelieving. "You don't know how to pray?"

I shrug. "Who do you think was going to teach me that? No, I can't pray. But I need to. It will help me fool them – it's a very good distraction."

Iparhan's face freezes. "A what?"

I sigh. "Don't get all upset. I just mean, when I am in the Forbidden City, they'll know I am a Muslim, won't they?"

Iparhan is unforgiving. "I'm not sure you are, if you don't even pray."

I ignore her. "They will be expecting a Muslim woman. So of course I must be – I must pray, and only eat certain foods, and make a big fuss about it all, so that they'll be so busy trying to accommodate my requests they won't spend time wondering whether I really am who I'm supposed to be. You see?"

Iparhan barely speaks to me for the rest of the day, but Nurmat agrees that I must be educated in the fundamental aspects of our religion, in which I am sadly lacking.

And so I have to listen to long passages from the Qu'ran, then practice my prayers so that I don't stumble over the words or actions.

"You will have to fast as well," points out Iparhan.

I laugh at her. "You want me, who used to be near to starving, to fast?"

"You must," she says simply.

I walk out of the room, but we both know she's won the next day, when I pay more attention to the rules governing the food I may or may not eat, although privately I think that when I reach the court I may play the part of a good Muslim girl but I will not mention any need to fast.

"Enough!" I shriek. "Enough!"

Mei tuts. "What a fuss. What a baby," she scolds.

"It hurts!"

She shakes her head, focusing on my second earlobe. "You must have pierced ears. Even a peasant girl has pierced ears," she says.

I moan as the second lobe is pierced and pull away as she finishes. "I thought it would never end," I say.

"It hasn't," she says sternly.

"There's one in each ear! What am I, a pin cushion?"

Mei wipes a drop of blood from the first earlobe. "The Emperor's ladies dress in the Manchu fashion. That means three earrings in each earlobe. You'll have pearl earrings, little strands of them, one strand hanging from each hole. You must look like a court lady," she adds, her voice lowering to a warning. "You cannot raise their suspicions. If they find out - "

I back away. "No."

"You have to."

I hold out my hands to stop her advancing on me and stand my ground. "No. I'm doing enough. I'm learning a ridiculous amount of new things every day. I'm being made to learn a religion backwards. I am *not* having triple piercings. I'm a Kashgarlik girl, not a Manchu. If the Emperor doesn't like it, that's just too bad. He should have picked another Manchu girl to add to the rest of them."

Mei lets her hands drop and shrugs. "Suit yourself," she says. "At least you've got enough piercings for these parts."

My shoulders slump with relief. "I've got a headache," I say. "I can't remember all the things I'm supposed to be learning."

"It will come," says Mei soothingly.

"I doubt it." I sit down on the cushions in a huff. "I want some noodles."

"I'm busy," says Mei.

I sit up straight and give her a withering stare. "I am an imperial concubine," I say with as much grandeur as I can muster. "Bring me my noodles the moment I ask for them or I'll tell the Emperor and he'll have you beaten for being a disobedient wretch."

Mei chuckles and goes to the kitchen.

Now it seems I must learn how to flirt.

"You can place your hand on a man's arm," suggests Mei. "Or pull gently at his sleeve, to draw his attention to something you wish him to see, to share with him."

"Such as?"

Mei sighs at my lack of imagination. "A beautiful landscape. A flower. Yourself."

I can't imagine such a moment between myself and a man.

Nurmat holds out his arm and I tug at his sleeve. He pretends to be pulled to the ground by my strength. I make a face at him and he laughs.

"Stop your foolishness," Mei chastises us. "You must learn to draw the Emperor's attention, his interest."

I roll my eyes but I learn to pull gently at a sleeve, to smile coyly, to glance up from under shy lashes. I feel like an idiot and my smiles feel like grimaces. I cannot imagine how they would attract anyone.

The moon grows and wanes again and again. Slowly, so slowly, the days begin to come.

"I wish your Majesties ten thousand years," I say, and rise to my feet.

Nurmat laughs out loud. "You didn't fall over! For once, you didn't stumble!"

He jumps off the pile of cushions and picks me up, swings me round till I shriek with dizziness. Mei comes to see what all the fuss is about.

"She did it!" yells Nurmat. "She did the whole kowtow and she didn't stumble. She got up in one move and kept her back straight, like Iparhan does."

Mei smiles, but Iparhan, silent on the cushions where she had played at being Empress next to Nurmat's Emperor, continues to read the Qu'ran and ignores our laughter.

The dice are thrown and it's my turn to recite a poem. I don't pause. The words flow from me with something approaching rhythm. Iparhan's eyebrows go up.

"The poet's name?"

I'm smug. "Li Shangyin, Tang dynasty."

She nods. It's the first time she hasn't had to correct me. I struggle to hold a coherent conversation in this strange new tongue, but I can recite an awful lot of poems. I hope the Emperor's happy to talk in riddles.

I reach out for a bowl of tea that's not there and Mei places it in my hand. I don't thank her. I don't even acknowledge her.

She claps her hands in delight. "You are a lady!" she says.

We grin at each other before I remember my training and gesture to her to leave me. She goes and I sit alone for a few minutes. I've been here for several months now. The Emperor has already sent for Iparhan's traitorous cousins and they will be planning their journey. Soon they will leave, and when they do, we will be in their shadows until they reach Beijing. Somewhere outside the Forbidden City, as an unknown girl steps from her own carrying litter into the imperial palanquin… I think of her for a moment, this faceless girl. Each of us chosen for a destiny not of our own making. The path I have been forced on to will collide with hers and at that moment the girl…

I stop thinking about her. I am about to be cast alone into a new world and my own fear is growing so great I cannot summon up any more fear for another girl's destiny. She must remain faceless to me. My eyes fill unexpectedly with tears and I dash them away. I've always been alone, I tell myself angrily. At least this time I will be well fed and dressed with a warm bed at night, for the rest of my life, even if I do have to share the Emperor's bed from time to time. *How bad can it be?* I think to myself. I say it over and over again in my head, *how bad can it be, how bad can it be* and I do not let myself listen to the reply. I have tried to escape and I have been caught every time. Now I can only step forward blindly and hope I never have to find out how badly it might end for me.

I spend the rest of the day sat in silence, turning my new skills over and over in my mind. Are they enough? Yes, I can dress well and walk well. I can perform a kowtow smoothly. I can recite meaningless poems and converse – poorly and only for a few moments – in Mandarin. I can flirt very badly and I can eat without noodles falling down my clothes. I am not sure any of this is enough. I may have prided myself on being quick-witted but will that be enough when there are quick blades waiting if I am found out?

The next day I wait but it seems no one is going to teach me anything new nor test me on what I have learnt so far. Iparhan is in a foul mood. She snaps at Mei, she turns away from Nurmat. She acts as though she cannot bear to be in the same room as me. We eat in silence, everyone's eyes lowered, our attention supposedly on the food although none of us seems to be eating much.

At last Mei stands. "It is time to begin," she says.

"We'll begin tomorrow," says Iparhan, without looking up.

"There is much to be done," says Mei.

"Tomorrow," says Iparhan.

Her tone makes my fingers clench and twist with fear. I daren't ask what we will be beginning tomorrow, but I don't sleep well.

I eat my breakfast in silence, in an empty room, my tired eyes aching. Only when I have finished and Mei has cleared away the food do

Iparhan and Nurmat enter. Iparhan is holding something, which she drops into my lap as though it burns her fingers. "You will acquaint yourself with this," she says and heads immediately for the door, Nurmat following her.

When the door closes behind them I pick up the object. It is an album of paintings on silk. The first shows a maid, peeping through a crack in a door leading to a bedchamber. Inside the bedchamber, only their feet visible, are a man and a woman engaged in lovemaking. I hastily turn the leaf over to the next painting although as soon as I do so I begin to blush. In this painting two lovers embrace outdoors, surrounded by blossoms. Their robes are pulled up so that the woman may grasp the man and guide him inside her.

Painting follows painting. They grow more and more explicit, the couples entwined in every possible way, their most intimate parts clearly shown. There are kisses, embraces, all manner of positions. There is a man who is coupling with two women, one older and one younger. There is a man with four women in a garden, all in various states of undress. There are couples on beds, in boats, in gardens, in baths. In one a man kneels before a woman, his lips on her, while her head is thrown back in pleasure. When Mei brings me some tea I nearly drop the album, flustered.

"It came from the Forbidden City," says Mei. "The Emperor will have many such albums for his pleasure. She takes the album and shows me a picture of a couple that is engaged in looking at just such an album of drawings together. "It is possible you will be shown such paintings. You will also be expected to know how to assume some of the positions. A woman destined for the palace would have been taught such things."

I can feel myself grow hotter. "How will I know what to do?" I ask.

"You will practice."

Iparhan's voice is so close I nearly scream. I manage to gasp instead. She is standing in the doorway, with Nurmat behind her. Her voice is too loud.

Nurmat looks uncomfortable. "She could just look at the pictures," he suggests. "She is not a fool, she can imagine for herself…"

"We will not discuss this," says Iparhan. "It will be done and that is all. She cannot appear uneducated in this. She must please the Emperor. Otherwise all this is for nothing. We will begin now."

Nurmat comes closer to me and reaches out his hand for the album. I hand it to him at arm's length. He opens it and discards the first painting, the one where only the couple's feet show. Instead he turns to the next picture, where the couple sit entwined at the moment of penetration. He examines it for a moment and then sits himself on a chair, his feet flat on the floor. He gestures to me to come to him. I look at him in silence, uncertain of what he means to do. He surely does not intend to enact these scenes? I can already feel Iparhan's anger, her unhappiness. It is filling the room. Nurmat gestures again.

"Come, Hidligh," he says. "You must sit on my knee as the woman does in this painting."

I don't move.

I can see that Nurmat is almost more uncomfortable than I am. His voice is curt, unlike his usual manner. "Come," he says.

I get up very slowly and move a little closer to him.

"You need to try each of these positions," says Nurmat. "You must know how to assume them should the Emperor wish you to do so. Some are more difficult to attain than others, so you must have practiced."

I move within his arm's reach and he stretches out and takes my arm, pulling me towards him. "So," he says, his voice tense. "You will sit with one leg between mine. The other is raised up and you will rest your foot on my knee. Then you turn your upper body so that you can embrace me."

I stumble my way into the position, my face hot and red, my movements awkward. I am too close to Nurmat. His breath is on my cheek. His arms are wrapped around me. My right leg is trapped between his thighs, my left foot is resting too close to his most intimate parts. At other moments when we have touched we have been in motion – when I have fallen and he has caught me, for example – a brief touch and then we have come apart again, not sat like this, in an embrace which is watched over by Iparhan. Her face is perfectly still, her hands, which are by her side, are shaking.

"And the next one," says Nurmat.

I want to cry. There are dozens of paintings. The idea of enacting each one, under Iparhan's barely controlled gaze, is horrible. The silence in the room, broken only by Nurmat's terse orders and the rustling sounds of our clothing and bodies fumbling to execute them, is excruciating.

But I have no choice. Day after day we enact the positions from the album, over and over again. Some are difficult or even painful to maintain. All, with Iparhan watching over us in silence, are uncomfortable.

One morning Iparhan does not appear. It seems she has a fever, so while Mei takes her foods and medicines, Nurmat and I sit together and eat breakfast, before taking up the album. Many of the positions we can now perform from memory, so we begin without discussion or referring to the paintings. At least our daily repetition means that some of the positions have become physically easier. My muscles no longer ache. I sit on a chair, padded with cushions, and lift my legs so that my ankles rest on Nurmat's shoulders, my knees pressed back against my breasts as he kneels between my thighs. There is a pause.

"I don't remember the next position," I admit. It feels easier to speak without Iparhan in the room.

Nurmat nods. "I think you sit more forward and wrap your legs around me," he says.

I adjust my position. Our faces are closer and our bodies more tightly pressed together. "It's difficult to hold," I say.

"Cross your ankles behind me," he says.

I try, although he has a broad chest and my legs only just reach far enough. The relief of not having Iparhan here, watching over us, makes me giggle a little, and Nurmat also lets out his breath in a little laugh, the tension easing despite the intimacy of the position.

"On to the next position, then," says Nurmat. He consults the album, then lies down on the floor, holding out his hands to me to help me as I lower myself over him, sitting astride him on my knees. Once I am settled he places his hands on my waist and helps me to raise myself up and lower down again, over and over again. I struggle to do it gracefully, but Nurmat does not smile at my efforts. His grip on my waist tightens a little and he speaks to me softly. "Slowly," he says. "Slowly. Hold my arms so that you keep your balance." His face has grown flushed. I lean forward so that I am holding his upper arms, his muscles bunched beneath my hesitant grasp. I slow my movements, trying to follow his guidance. Below me, he closes his eyes. As I lower myself onto him I feel him grow hard beneath me and see his lips part, his breathing grow faster.

I rise up, pull away from him as quickly as I can.

His eyes fly open. "I am sorry," he says, his voice hoarse. "I did not – I was not…"

I manage to step over his legs, although I almost stumble. I head towards my room, but find my way blocked by Iparhan. Her eyes are bright with fever, her face is flushed. Beads of sweat are on her forehead. She leans against the doorframe, unable to hold herself upright without its support.

"What are you doing?" she asks.

I don't answer, only push past her, the only time I have ever deliberately touched her since I came here. I go to my room and lie on the bed, my eyes closed as Nurmat's were when he grew aroused. My thoughts spin. Does Nurmat desire me? It's not possible. He has Iparhan. Except... except he does not, of course. She refuses to consummate their betrothal. She will not marry him. She will not share her body with him. And so... and so now he has become aroused whilst enacting these scenes with me. I twist on the bed, turning one way and another as I try to think my way out of the situation. What if he forces himself on me? I turn away from the thought. It is not in Nurmat's nature, I believe. The greater danger for me is Iparhan, who would surely kill me from jealousy if she even suspected such an interest in me from Nurmat. Does he care for me? Does he love me? I do not know what to think. I lie awake for hours while the day slowly passes and still my thoughts whirl and I cannot see the way ahead.

I awake in darkness to perfume all around me and Iparhan's dagger against my throat. I lie very still. My voice is hoarse with sleep and fear.

"What do you want, Iparhan?"

Below the scent of her perfume is the smell of hot fever: sour, dried-up sickness. "You are trying to seduce him, to draw him away from me"

"He wants you," I whisper. "His eyes were closed. He was thinking of you." I only hope it is true. I sit up in bed and feel the dagger move away. I breathe more deeply. She's a dark shape in the night. My eyes ache with tiredness. I can think of nothing that would placate her.

"Marry him, Iparhan," I say, weariness bringing truth to my lips. "You can't keep a man waiting for ever."

"I cannot marry—" she begins.

"He's yours, Iparhan," I say, into the darkness that holds all her sorrow. "Forget your obsession with raising an army against the Emperor and marry Nurmat while he's still yours. Before he grows weary of waiting. Before he begins to look elsewhere. But he is still yours."

"I am his," she says. "I do not know if he is mine."

She gets up and stands over me. I know she could kill me, that one quick movement could end my life, remove me as any threat to the love between Nurmat and herself. If she does so, though, she will lose her chance to know the thoughts of the Emperor and use them to feed her plans for rebellion. If she cannot exact her revenge then she cannot marry, according to her own vow. My breath stops and I listen in the darkness for the movement of her arm that will end my life.

She hesitates and then leaves the room.

I touch my breast and feel my heart trembling. I lie awake for a long time in the dark, my skin cold under the blankets and my eyes full of tears, which slowly trickle down my cheeks. My life is hers to take at any moment. My only protection is her desire for revenge and the part I can play in achieving it. If I fail to carry out her dreams then I am worthless to her and to be worthless to Iparhan is to be dead.

"This afternoon, you will take a bath," says Iparhan.

I glance at her to see if she's thinking of last night. I wonder briefly if she means to drown me rather than stab me, but she's already speaking to Mei.

"She has to learn to be bathed by other people," she says. "She will be bathed by eunuchs there. She cannot be shy about it."

I shrug. "I don't care if the two of you bathe me," I say.

Iparhan turns to me and her eyes are very dark. "Nurmat will bathe you," she says, and her voice trembles. She stops, as though she does not want to continue. She looks towards Mei who nods, although she looks a little wary at this turn of events.

Iparhan goes on. "In the bath water will be my perfume."

I look up. "Why?"

"When you smell that perfume what do you think of?" she asks.

"You," I say. "No one smells like that but you."

She nods. "You must have something that is special," she says. "Something the Emperor remembers. You must stand out. He must think of you first when he thinks of his ladies. He must spend time with you alone, not with all the others. You need to spend time with him if you are to know his mind."

I nod eagerly. This is a clever trick. I will need all the help I can get to stand out for the right reasons rather than for any errors I may make. The perfume will be a valuable tool in what I'm coming to think of as my armoury.

Iparhan isn't smiling. I think about the little vial that carries her scent, a tiny golden-yellow thing, held with silver clasps.

"Who gave you the perfume?" I ask, but I know the answer already even as I ask the question.

She gets up and leaves the room. I look to Mei.

"Nurmat," says Mei. "An engagement gift."

Iparhan pauses in the doorway. Outside I can hear the horses' bridles jingle. Recently Nurmat brought a third horse back to the stable. Later today I will be bathed by him. I'm anxious. Iparhan's face is dark. I think the poplar trees had better brace themselves for her daggers. Today she will show no mercy. Her scar is turning an ugly purple as it heals, with little puckers where the scabs have dried and flaked away.

Since yesterday I have kept my distance from Nurmat and he has not looked me in the eye. I don't know what will happen now. How much longer will we be here? How much longer can this situation be held in stillness? Nurmat and I cannot be together in the same room, yet now he must bathe me. Iparhan hates me, yet she cannot kill me.

Iparhan leaves and I slump down onto a cushion with relief. The house seems lighter when she is not here. I look up at Mei.

"Come and tell me more of your outlandish stories about the Forbidden City."

Mei chuckles. She likes to tell me of daily life in the palaces and for my part I ask her endless questions. The more I know about the Forbidden City the better prepared I will be.

She offers me a tea and settles herself next to me. "There is a great moat around the Forbidden City," she begins, her voice as dramatic as any storyteller. "It is three times deeper than a man's full height and wider than fifty paces across. The walls surrounding the City are red and so smooth no-one could climb them without falling. There are four gates: the great gate of the South, called the Meridian Gate, the North gate, called the Gate of Divine Might, and the smaller gates called the East Glorious Gate and the West Glorious Gate. There are four watchtowers, one at each corner."

I'm not that interested in the walls and gates. "Tell me about daily life. What do I eat for breakfast?"

"You will be served up to one hundred dishes at every meal."

"One hundred dishes? At one meal? For one person? Don't be silly."

"Truly."

"Even I can't manage a hundred dishes."

She laughs so much her cough gets worse and I have to pass her tea to sooth her.

"You don't eat them all. You eat whatever you have a fancy for. Then your servants will eat the leftovers."

"So they'll all be watching me thinking 'Oh, don't eat that dish, that's my favourite.'"

"Probably."

"Tell me about the rooms."

"You must look up. In the throne rooms especially. The ceilings are a wonder of carving, painted in gold and red, with dragons writhing round them."

"And the private rooms?"

"Beautiful as well."

"All of them?"

"All of them."

"Was your room beautiful?"

Mei laughs at me. "I was a maid, not a concubine. Our rooms are hidden away at the back of the palaces. They were no better than soldiers' barracks – half of them were falling down. They leaked and the wind blew in during the winter months."

"Why don't they mend them?"

"We were servants. They thought they were good enough for us."

I think about the strange world I am to be sent to. Magnificent palaces with crumbling barracks hidden behind them. "What else?"

Mei thinks. "There are no men allowed in the Forbidden City at night except the Emperor and the Court Physician who is on duty."

"Apart from the eunuchs."

"They don't count."

"How many are there?"

"Perhaps three thousand."

"Three *thousand*? All eunuchs?"

Mei nods.

"Iparhan says it's a disgusting practice," I say.

Mei nods. "It is a great sacrifice. But many of the boys and men who choose that path do so because they can then feed their families. They are poor people, with few choices in life. Iparhan is a nobleman's daughter, she has never known such hardships."

"And I'm to be bathed by eunuchs? Or is Iparhan just teasing?"

Mei raises her eyebrows.

"All right," I concede, "Iparhan doesn't know how to tease. So that's true?"

Mei nods. "You won't be left alone for an instant. You'll have a eunuch sleeping on the floor beside you, for protection. You'll have them all around you, whatever you do."

"How annoying," I say, though in truth, secretly, it sounds comforting. There were nights in Kashgar when I would have been grateful to have someone sleeping nearby for my protection or even just to know I was not alone.

"What will I see when I first go there?" I ask.

"The Outer Court," she says promptly. "The City is made up of two parts. First the Outer Court, with great temples and throne rooms. Behind those is the Inner Court, which is made up of gardens and all the palaces of the Emperor and his family. That's where you will live."

"And is there a marriage ceremony?" I ask.

Mei shakes her head. "Iparhan says that the rank chosen for her cousin as concubine will be below the four highest-ranked concubines, so there will not be a full ceremony for you. There will be a ceremony before you enter the palace and then you will be presented to the Emperor. Once that has been done, you will be a concubine of the court."

"So I'm not really married to him?"

"You will be married as such," says Mei. "The Qing dynasty allows all children of the Emperor to be equal. Your own child could be chosen as the next Emperor above the Empress' children. So in that regard you are as much a wife as she is. But of course at court your rank is very important. And because you are from a newly conquered land they may celebrate your arrival more lavishly than a concubine of your rank would normally receive. The Emperor has chosen a concubine from Iparhan's cousins' family to reward their services to him and to emphasise the conquest of Xinjiang."

"What's he like?" I ask.

"The Emperor?"

"Yes."

Mei pauses. She looks down. "You will probably not see a great deal of him. He is a busy man."

"I'm supposed to spend as much time with him as I can," I point out. "If I'm to spy for Iparhan."

"He likes poetry."

I sigh. "I do *try* to learn the poems," I say. "There's just so many of them."

"He writes them too."

"Heavens. Does that mean I'll have to learn his as well?"

"Probably."

"Wonderful."

Mei smiles. "He has other interests. The Emperor loves to ride."

"Really?"

"Of course. He's a Manchu. They've very proud of their heritage. They're supposed to be able to fire an arrow whilst riding at full gallop."

"And can they?"

"They practise a lot, so they probably can."

"What are they firing arrows at?"

"Animals when there isn't a war. He has a hunting lodge set in huge grounds and forests. He goes there as often as he can. You'll go with him."

"Hunting?"

"Probably just watching. But the whole court goes."

I snort with laughter at the vision of dainty concubines tiptoeing about in a forest, ruining their nice clothes, tripping over fallen trees.

"Will I be the only lady without bound feet?"

Mei shakes her head. "None of the Emperor's ladies has bound feet. He is a Manchu, remember. Their women do not have bound feet and the practice has been banned. It still goes on of course. Every time new concubines arrive to be chosen there will be some sent home in disgrace because their feet are bound. You will not see a lady with bound feet amongst the women of the court."

"Why am I learning Mandarin if he's a Manchu?"

"They speak Mandarin at court. Manchu is only used for a few words. It is an old tongue now, no one uses it for everyday speech."

"Is the Emperor a nice man?"

Mei shrugs.

"Come, Mei. Iparhan never speaks kindly of him. She spits his name. She says he is a greedy man, that all he wants is endless new conquests."

Mei nods but doesn't speak.

"But she's never met him. And you have, Mei. So what's he like?"

Mei looks sad. "He loved the Lady Fuca."

"The first Empress?"

"Yes. She made him a little carrying purse once, a plain thing such as the Manchu warriors used to have before they became emperors. He was so proud of it, he wore it on his belt."

"So?"

Mei tries to make me understand. "He wears robes covered in

gold embroidery," she explains. "His belt is covered in jewels. He shines. And then on this magnificent belt, hanging by other purses woven in gold and bright colours he hung this little purse, like something a peasant would wear. Because he loved her and because she had remembered and honoured his ancestors and their way of life, which he reveres."

"He can't be all bad, then, is that what you're saying?"

Mei pats my hands, which are growing softer by the day, mostly thanks to her creams that she insists I use almost hourly. "You do not need to love him," she says. "To love him can bring jealousy from other women, even poisons to your table. Do what you must do, but make your own life at court. Make friends. Enjoy a soft life. Do not seek out the Emperor too closely."

"I'm supposed to seek him out," I protest. "If I don't then I can't get information for Iparhan and if I don't do that…" I trail off.

Mei leans towards me and lowers her voice. 'When you get to the court," she all but whispers, "You must seek out Lady Wan."

"Your old mistress?"

"Yes. She is a kind woman and if you tell her that I sent you to her, that I think of her still, she will help you however she can. Perhaps she is not a great favourite but she has lived happily at the court for many years now in peace and contentment."

I like the sound of this. "And how can she help me?"

Mei is serious. "You need to be warned about the factions."

"The what?"

"The factions amongst the Emperor's women. There are many women in the Emperor's court and they fall into different factions. They change often. One woman might form an alliance with another and then turn against her, for jealousy. You must know which women are in favour and which are embittered by their lowly status in the

Emperor's eyes. You must know who is trustworthy and who might work against you."

"Work against me? What would they do to me?"

Mei becomes aware she is frightening me. She pats my hands again. "Do not fret about it now. We cannot know which women you must be wary of until you are at court. Got to Lady Wan and beg for her help. Tell her I served you as I once served her. I am certain that she will be kind to you."

"But…" I begin.

Mei shakes her head at my questions. "You will be taken good care of no matter what happens, whether you are a favourite or not. Your hands will rest only on silk."

I feel cold and pull my hands away from her.

The room is filling with steam. Through the clouds of it I watch Mei pour in the last bucket of water. She takes the tiny vial from Iparhan and opens it, allows a few drops to fall into the bathtub. Iparhan's perfume fills my nostrils as though she were standing with her skin touching mine. Mei nods and leaves.

Now the three of us are alone and although the water is warm I am shivering. Nurmat's hand, large, warm and brown, touches me and I flinch. He draws back for a moment but then seems to make up his mind. One hand lifts my hair and holds it up, the other, holding the cloth which is wet and scented with rose soap, slips over my shoulders and the nape of my neck in a smooth movement, rubbing my skin with soap and water.

By the window Iparhan shudders, then swiftly steps to my side and grabs my hair from Nurmat's grasp. With two bone pins she savagely twists and fastens my hair so that it will stay up on its own. I wince as the sharp ends scrape against my scalp. "You need both hands or you'll be there all day," she snaps at Nurmat.

She returns to her place but then as his hands slip beneath the surface of the water and the scent of the roses and her own perfume grows stronger she gasps something under her breath and leaves the room. Nurmat and I are alone. The heat of the water is bringing a pink flush to my skin exceeded only by the heat in my face turning my cheeks a darker rose. I try to imagine myself to be in the Forbidden City, a concubine to the Emperor, bathed by eunuchs as a matter of course. I close my eyes, the better to believe that Nurmat is a eunuch, not a man.

With my eyes closed I can hear his breathing, which is faster than it is even when he's been riding. I feel its warmth on my cheek and then on my shoulder, on my arms and knees, which are not covered by the water. His hands have lost their hesitation and now he lifts my limbs to better reach behind my knees, between my toes, under my armpits. The little cloth is dipped again and again in the water, rubbed with the soap, then stroked over my back, my thighs, my belly. It follows the curve of my breast and to my shame I can feel my nipples harden under his hand. The heat in my cheeks is unbearable and I open my eyes, thinking somehow to make him stop, to form words which might bring an end to this moment. But he takes my face in his hands, turning me towards him. I look at him, bracing myself for his gaze, but I see he's taken my instructions to heart. His eyes are closed. He is washing me by touch alone, his nostrils filled with the scent from the tiny vial. In this moment I know that he is washing Iparhan, not me, and I begin to tremble as he lifts the little cloth to my face and wipes each part of it, across my forehead, down my nose and then a little circle over my lips, which part under the pressure. He lets his hand slip down and in the warmth and wetness of the scented water he uses only his fingers to clean between my thighs. I close my eyes for a moment and then I can take no more.

I spring from the tub, splashing water everywhere, leaving Nurmat soaked. I grab at a cloth to dry myself and wrap it round me but Nurmat has risen to his feet. He takes my hand and leads me to a seat by the window, pushing me gently so that I sit down while he kneels by my side. From his pocket he takes the vial and opens it, releasing Iparhan's heady scent once more. I shake my head but he ignores me and with one finger dips into the little pot. He dabs the perfume onto my skin, down the nape of my neck, then across each collarbone and then, reaching down, he slips a hand under the cloth I am wrapped in and puts a little on each of my thighs. The room is filled with her perfume again, that smell of delicate spring blossom and rich summer fruit. Nurmat, kneeling by my side, has closed his eyes and now he inhales deeply.

I reach out and put one hand on his shoulder, where his shirt is open, and my fingers can brush his bare skin. He opens his eyes and my hand shakes at the love in his eyes. I push him away from me, hard, and he loses his balance and topples backwards to the floor.

"I'm not her," I hiss, and rise to leave the room. I don't get very far.

Iparhan is in the doorway. She's as upright as ever, poised as ever, but tears are running down her face. Nurmat is unaware of her; he sits with his eyes still closed, breathing deeply, perhaps imagining a compliant Iparhan bathed in his love. I stand facing her, she in her long skirts with her little plaits under a red cap, me wrapped in a damp cloth.

"He looks at me and sees you, Iparhan," I say, afraid of what she might do, but I see the rage build up in her eyes and her lips tighten.

"You still believe he is mine?" she says, her fists clenched by her side.

I want to reassure her but I hesitate. I know that Nurmat sees Iparhan instead of me, but the longer he looks, the more likely it is that he will eventually see me.

I open my mouth to say something to calm her, whether it's true or not, but Iparhan shakes her head.

"It doesn't matter," she says, her voice too loud. She addresses Nurmat. "It's time to leave."

"Leave for where?" I ask stupidly.

"Beijing."

I gape at her but she ignores me and continues to speak to Nurmat. "I have received word. Turdan's sister has begun her journey to the Emperor and we must intercept her before she reaches the Forbidden City. We leave in the morning."

I look over my shoulder at Nurmat. Slowly, he gets to his feet. He and Iparhan gaze at each other for a moment and I know that in their minds her plans, so long discussed, are being made a reality. They know everything that is about to come and I know nothing. I feel a deep terror. All this play-acting, this transformation, this pretence is about to come true. I've almost treated the past few months as a game, with food and a warm bed as my prizes. I've grown used to Mei's pampering and her wrinkled smiles, believed that the tricks I was learning would help me to win against the odds. But the truth that I have always known is now here in front of me: if I lose this game I will forfeit my life.

I think of the moment when I chose, laughing without air in my lungs, of Iparhan's daggers trembling in the tree trunk, pinning my arms open, rendering me helpless. I had no real choice then and now it is too late to turn back.

Nurmat clears his throat but his voice is still husky when he speaks. "I'll prepare the horses," he says and walks towards the door and Iparhan.

As he passes he inhales the scent I wear.

Mei

MEI IS STANDING BY THE *doorway, a dripping pail in one hand. I make sure to shove her as I pass, my shoulder hitting her squarely so that she has to drop the pail and grab at the doorframe to avoid falling. I have so much anger inside me, so much pain that I must let it out and she can say nothing to me, cannot stop nor reprimand me.*

But she does.

"Iparhan," she says, and I pause, my back still turned to her, facing out into the cold blackness. She does not often address me, preferring to keep her distance, wary of my temper.

I wait but she does not continue. "What do you want?" I ask over my shoulder. My teeth are ground tight together, it costs me an effort to unclench my jaw enough to speak.

"Beware of the path you tread," says Mei, and her soft voice has an edge to it I have not heard before.

Nurmat's plan is simple.

"We will go away from here," he says to me, his warm hand holding my cold one. "We will be married. We will have children. We will put all of this behind us. The Emperor has what he wants. Let him have it. You have suffered too much loss. I will not let you suffer again. I will love you always and keep you safe."

I stand before my father's grave, the desert wind whipping at my mother's skirts, the only clothes I brought with me. Slowly I draw my hand out of Nurmat's and place it on my father's misshapen tomb. "I will not rest until Altisharh is returned to our people," I say, and see Nurmat's face grow pale. "I will carry out my father's plan. When the Emperor sends for his concubine I will make my way to the Forbidden City."

Nurmat grabs for my hand, pulling it away from the hard clay but I speak before my hand has left its rough surface. "This I swear."

He faces me and there are tears in his eyes. "You will break my heart," he says.

I do not answer, only reach for my horse's reins and pull myself into the saddle, my muscles stiff with shivering.

Mei's wrinkled face peers up from her hunched shoulders. She is afraid of me, I can tell it by her shaking hands. But she stands her ground. "You have a plan," she says. "I see it because it is there to be seen. Nurmat does not see it because he does not want to see it. The girl does not see it because she has no notion of herself. She has only ever thought about survival. But your plan will destroy you all."

"My plans are none of your business, old woman," I say. "You do not understand. I must reclaim my country."

Mei shakes her head. "Your plans are shaped by grief and pain," she says. "You claim to seek restitution."

"Yes," I say. "Of my country. For my people."

"No," she says. "You seek revenge. And it will destroy you and Nurmat, the only other person you care about in this world."

I step closer to her, look down into her narrow eyes. "You are a nobody," I say. "You will keep your mouth shut."

"Or else?" she asks. "Do you plan to look after me in my old age, Iparhan? Do you plan to take me with you when you leave this place?" My eyes blink before I can stop them and she nods. "And when the food and fuel for the fire is gone, will you send more? I do not think so."

"Finish making the bread," I say, turning away from her. The cold air strikes my face and I have to force myself to step out of the house's warmth into the darkness.

Journey to Beijing

I T'S DARK.

I stand, shivering, in the doorway. I can't see much beyond a few steps. I can hear the horses nearby, stamping and huffing in the cold air. Iparhan's with them, she left the house before I did. My teeth chatter together so hard that even when I clench my jaw they don't stop, only start to grind back and forth instead.

Nurmat appears out of the darkness. "Are you cold?"

I shake my head.

Nurmat tuts at my shaking and pulls my sheepskin coat tighter round me. When our skins brush against one another his hand lingers.

I grab his arm hard, pulling him close to me. "Stop it," I hiss, my fear sinking my nails into the skin of his wrist so that he winces. "Stop thinking I am Iparhan. I need you to be my friend now, not some half-wit whose head is turned by a perfume and his imagination."

He turns his face away to where Iparhan's appeared, standing in the doorway. The two of us stand silent as though we had been caught kissing.

She doesn't move any closer. "Ready?"

I stay silent and Nurmat nods.

"Then mount."

I turn back to the doorway where Mei has joined Iparhan. She looks small in the flickering light from the house, her face hidden in shadows. I ignore Nurmat and make my way back to the door. I embrace Mei, feeling the bent bones of her back. "Thank you," I say.

She returns my embrace and murmurs something I don't catch in my ear.

"What?" I ask but Iparhan has taken my arm and is leading me to the horse. Nurmat throws me into the saddle and busies himself with the straps but all my attention is on Mei. "I didn't hear you," I call out to her but she stands silent. The horse shifts beneath me while Nurmat and Iparhan mount their own horses.

I can't see Iparhan's face well enough to read her expression but her voice is cold. "Ride," she commands.

"Mei," I call again. "I didn't hear you."

Her old voice reaches me through a sudden wind that whirls sand around us. "A mirror," she calls out. "Look in a mirror."

I hear a whistling sound and a dull thud. By my side Iparhan is holding a whip. She leans over now and brings it down – crack – on my mare's rump. Startled, she leaps forward. I grab at where the reins should be to try and stop her but then realise that Iparhan has secured my horse to hers and left my horse without reins. I have no control over my own mount. I clutch at the horse's mane and twist in the saddle to look back as we build up speed. To my horror I see Mei slowly crumple to the ground, her small outline framed in the light of the doorway.

"Mei!" I scream. The sand whirls up from the horses' hooves and into my open mouth, making me choke. I cough and spit, the hard grit in my throat immoveable. I almost fall, unable to keep to the horse's rhythm for all the coughing.

"Cover your mouth," yells Nurmat, riding just behind me.

I pull my jacket collar up with one hand while clinging on to my galloping horse. If I throw myself from the saddle I will end up under the hooves of Nurmat's horse.

We gallop for a long time. The horses are fresh, the early morning is cold. But at last we have to slow down. At once, I throw myself to one side, landing hard in the grey sand. I stagger to my feet and look up at Iparhan, who has stopped her horse and wheeled it round so that she can look down at me.

"Mount your horse, Hidligh," she says. Her voice is calm.

My voice comes out in a hoarse wail. "You killed her!" I scream up at her.

Her face stays expressionless. "Mount," she repeats.

I back away from her. "I will not," I say. I find tears rolling down my face and sob, the tears trickling into my mouth when I open it. "Why did you kill her?"

"She was no longer useful," says Iparhan, unmoved.

My legs are trembling too hard to stand. I fall forwards, on my knees with my hands sinking into the cold sand. "You could have sent her home to her family," I say.

"She had no family," says Iparhan from above me.

"I have no family," I say.

"Get her up," says Iparhan to Nurmat. I hear him leap down from his horse and then his arms are about me, lifting me into the saddle. I sit slumped, hands loose by my side.

Iparhan moves her horse a little closer to me. "Look about you, Hidligh," she says quietly.

I keep my head down.

"Look about you," she repeats.

Slowly, I raise my head. I avoid her eyes and look about. Sand. Tall dunes. The odd scrap of a bush, struggling to survive.

"I can leave you here," says Iparhan. "Or you can hold on to your horse's mane and ride."

I look down at the dead grey sand beneath my horse's feet. Slowly I move my arms and take my horse's mane into my clenched hands.

We sleep, ride, sleep, ride. The first night we dismount I sit in silence. When Nurmat gets the fire going he brings me hot flat bread filled with chunks of lamb, like the first meal he ever gave me. I chew the lamb without tasting it, then sit and hold the empty bread until it grows cold, knowing that Mei's crooked old hands kneaded and baked it yesterday. Then I lie down and sleep, the shrivelled bread clutched by my side.

As we ride the next day and for many days after, tears trickle down my face while I think of Mei's wrinkled tortoise face and her hunched back. I hear that shrill whistling and see her bent back crumple to the ground. I turn over her last words to me. A mirror. Look in a mirror. Why?

Each night I dismount and walk a few paces in agony before I fall asleep. My body, grown used to bathing and scented soaps, reeks of sweat and horses. My thighs are red with drips of piss and the rubbing of the saddle. I smell unwashed. I don't care. I don't speak. I only obey orders I am given. I am numb.

I have no idea where we are but many many days go by before I care enough to ask. "Where are we?"

Iparhan seems surprised at hearing my voice after so long. She twists in her saddle to look me over. "We are very close."

"To Beijing?"

She snorts in disbelief at my ignorance. "To Turpan. Now we will join the trading caravans on their way to Beijing. There is safety in numbers and we can follow behind my cousins."

The caravans are immense. Camels, horses, mules and donkeys, all are weighed down with burdens. Some carry medicinal rhubarb, fine teas and brick teas, hazelnuts and other foods. There are silks and velvets. Others carry pearls, jade, tourmaline or amber as well as fierce looking guards. Occasionally the trade routes are interrupted by yaks bearing huge quantities of jade from the local rivers. Guards stand on the riverbanks and wait for jade to be lifted from the waters, while clerks note down weights and colours - white, green, red, yellow, brown and black. The Emperor's court has an insatiable appetite for jade, and Altishahr has it in bountiful quantities.

Iparhan's expression grows bitter whenever she sees jade being taken in this way. "So it begins," she mutters. "All that we have is his. Our jade. Our women. Our taxes. Our crops. Our labour."

Up ahead of us, a party of armed riders surround a covered palanquin in which sits the Emperor's future bride. Its slow rocking must make for either an uncomfortable or a soporific journey. I wonder whether its occupant is excited or afraid. I wish I didn't know that she should be afraid of the dark-robed figure that rides by my side. I wish I did not have to watch the palanquin's slow rocking, day by day, as the paths of our fates converge. As we move onwards I wonder sometimes about whether I could attempt another escape or whether my path is now set, whether it has been carved into a jagged lump of jade, at the bottom of some river where no human hands can touch it nor erase the choice that has been made for my life. I wonder whether that choice has been made by divine hands in heaven or whether some darker hand has inscribed it.

Days pass and then one morning Iparhan begins to smile. I find even her smile frightening. I've hardly ever seen it and anything that makes her smile worries me.

"What?" I ask, wary of this change in her.

"They say," she says, her voice louder than usual, "that the lady in the palanquin ahead has an extraordinary fragrance. It is not a scent that can be bought. It comes from her very skin. The Emperor was so bewitched that he commanded she should be his bride."

I look at her, waiting to understand what she is doing.

Behind us a merchant leans forward on his horse. "Is that so?" he says. "I thought as much. I smelt a very fine perfume when we passed their party at the inn the other night. I said at the time it was not a perfume I had ever smelt before."

I gape at him but Iparhan turns on her horse and smiles radiantly. "You were right, then!" she says with admiration. "You must know your perfumes. Of course, a man so well-travelled..." She stops, shrugging charmingly, as though to imply that such a man would be an expert on any manner of topics.

The man beams and straightens his shoulders. By the next night the whole of the caravan knows for sure that the unseen lady in the palanquin is destined for the Emperor himself and that her body emits a natural fragrance so heavenly that she cannot be seen in public for fear that men might not control their carnal desires. I turn to Nurmat when I hear this and he looks away.

Every night Iparhan slips away from us. One night I follow her and watch her approach the tent that holds her cousin. I want to call out a warning as she slips a hand into the folds of her skirt, but hold my tongue. I see her hand emerge holding the tiny vial with which Nurmat anointed me. One quick motion and it is applied, her hand slipping over the threshold of the tent's folds. I turn away as she comes back towards my hiding place.

"Goodnight, Hidligh," she says without pausing as she passes me.

The rumours surrounding the girl grow in magnitude. Now we hear that her family anoints her daily with camel's butter, anxious to enhance and maintain her newly developed natural fragrance. Iparhan rolls her eyes when she hears this. "Idiots," she says. "It'll go rancid and she'll stink of the stuff."

We travel for so long I begin to think we will never arrive anywhere, just keep riding and riding forever. But at last there's a change in our surroundings. Up ahead are the walls of a great city and around us are ever-growing crowds heaving towards them. The faraway traders of fine goods in great quantities are now surrounded by locals, peasants carrying loads of firewood, vegetables, camellia flowers, fruits and other fresh goods on their backs, in little hand-carts or occasionally on the backs of reluctant mules. I look at Nurmat.

He nods. "Beijing."

My throat grows tight as I look at the walls again. Somewhere within them lies another, hidden, city. And my future, whatever it may be. My hands tighten and I keep my head down.

Up ahead, the family's caravan of horses and camels breaks off and heads in a new direction.

I tug at Nurmat's sleeve. "Where are they going?"

"There's a senior official at the palace. He has invited them to his house for the night, so that the bride can be prepared in comfort before she enters the Forbidden City. The house sits within the walls of Beijing but outside of the Forbidden City. They are making their way there."

"Are we following them?"

By way of an answer he jerks his chin forwards at Iparhan, already riding ahead, her horse following the family at a discreet distance. Nurmat and I turn our horses towards her.

It's dawn and barely light. A sharp wind blows our skin to chilly paleness, marred by goosebumps. We're in the gardens of a fine house, hung all about with red lanterns and long strips of red silk tied to trees and columns, embroidered with gold characters, which I can't read.

"Happiness," whispers Nurmat, when I point to them.

I shake my head. Happiness is not what I am anticipating. How can we possibly enter such a house without being seen? We've already had to dodge servants bustling about everywhere. The house is in an uproar, even though it's so early.

"What are they all *doing*?" I ask Nurmat. Iparhan has left our side and slipped round the corner of the house. I can't help wishing that they'd find her, that one footfall in the wrong place will alert someone to her presence.

"Getting ready for the imperial ladies," Nurmat replies.

"What imperial ladies?"

"They come from the Forbidden City to bathe and dress the bride ready to be taken to the palace. They're important women in the court, wives of senior officials and military men."

"Does that mean I have to dress the same way as her so we can swap later on?"

He looks at me as though I have said something stupid and doesn't reply.

We wait. My legs are cramped from the half-squat we've been in for hours, the cold dew is making my clothes damp and I'm afraid. I try to focus on the cramp and the dampness, as well as on my urgent need for a piss. The discomfort stops me from thinking about what lies ahead.

When it comes, it happens so fast I hardly understand. I catch a glimpse of Iparhan's figure in the garden and am about to turn to Nurmat when his hand is clasped firmly round my mouth. With his other arm he lifts me. My legs, freed from their long-held position, shriek in pain as they unfold. I kick but his grip is too strong. In a moment he has moved from our hiding place in the bushes to the wall at the back of the house where Iparhan is waiting. As we reach her she turns her back on us and begins to climb an ancient wisteria, its barely budding branches giving her easy places to place her hands and feet. She's above our heads and then disappears into a window. I struggle against Nurmat.

"Keep still," he says, and there's no gentleness in his voice.

From above I see Iparhan's hand throw out a rope, which falls down the wall to our head height.

Now I think Nurmat might release me and urge me to climb. He doesn't. He takes a cloth from his pocket and binds it about my mouth, so that I can't speak but he now has two free hands. With one he hoists me over his shoulder, with the other he grabs hold of the rope. I struggle.

"Don't," he says. "I mean it."

I hang over his shoulder like a sack of rice while he climbs. I had never realised how strong he is, not even when we used to mock-wrestle. Then, he would let me win. Now, I know there's nothing I can do to escape.

I'm tipped over the windowsill, Iparhan grabbing at my clothes to help pull me into the room. I land mostly on my right thigh with a bruising thump. Nurmat climbs in behind me and I hear them fasten the window. Still winded, I sit up and look about me, trying to understand where I am.

The room is large and well appointed. A *kang* marks it as a bedroom. There are artfully arranged flowers in a little niche, various silk hangings with unfamiliar characters on the walls. Several large chests are open, fine clothes spilling out of them. The room is rich with the scent of Iparhan's perfume.

There's been a struggle. One of the wall hangings is askew. The covers on the *kang* are dishevelled and most have fallen to the floor. There's a broken lamp. I'm afraid to look further. I know now that when Iparhan left us in the garden she came here, and the girl whose room it is does not seem to be here. Where is she?

Iparhan catches me looking about and jerks her head.

My eyes follow the direction she's indicating before I quickly turn my face away. I caught a glimpse of a coverlet, wrapped about a shape that is partly hidden behind a clothes chest.

Iparhan turns to Nurmat. "Help me," she says.

I stare at the floor and feel the shape pass by me as they lift it to the window. My skin shrinks from the silken brush of the coverlet as it passes me and I feel a trickle of piss down my legs. I sit in the spreading puddle, not moving. They're not gone long. I wait as they rearrange the room, restoring order. When Iparhan comes over to me and begins to undress me I don't stop her, sitting limp and unresisting as she strips me. She sops up the wetness around me and wipes me down. The last thing she removes is the gag around my mouth. She looks into my face to see if I'll suddenly scream but I know we've gone too far now. To be found in this house now, as we are, would mean certain death. I've thought of escape before but even I know that it is too late for escapes. I gaze back at her and when she takes my hand and pulls me to my feet I walk naked across the room with her to the *kang*. Nurmat gazes out of the window as we pass.

Iparhan tucks me up into the *kang* and then sits on the edge of it. She speaks fast. "The ladies from the palace will arrive shortly and they will wash and dress you. They do not expect you to speak much Mandarin. The clothes laid out for you will be unusual to them. They are red, as befits a wedding to the Emperor, but they are made in our style. You may need to show them how they should be worn. Your brothers and father," and she does not even pause over this falsehood, "will not see you until you descend to the palanquin which will be brought for you. By then you will be veiled for your wedding day, so they will not see your face. Follow the ladies to the palanquin. Climb inside. Sit still. When you arrive at the palace within the Forbidden

City you will be taken to meet the Emperor and his court. From then on, I cannot guide you. You must make your own way."

I shake my head and my voice is small and hoarse. "I can't do it, Iparhan," I say. "I can't."

"You have trained for this," she says.

"I can't do it," I say, my voice beginning to rise above a whisper. "It'll go wrong. They'll know I'm an imposter as soon as they look at me."

Iparhan unsheathes her dagger and very slowly, with care, lays its tip against the hollow of my throat. "Remember who you are supposed to be," she says. "Endear yourself to the Emperor so that you will be of use to me later."

I look up at her in silence.

Nurmat turns from the window. "The Imperial Guard is arriving, along with the eunuchs and ladies," he says. "I just saw them turning the corner of the road outside. They will be here shortly."

Iparhan rises, sheaths her dagger and pulls out the little vial. She tips it onto her finger, then dabs the contents on my neck. Her perfume fills the air. She turns to go and I grab at her hand. It is cool to my touch. She looks down at me, almost in surprise.

My voice deserts me. "Please," I mouth.

She pulls her hand out of my grasp. "Remember who you are supposed to be," she says and turns away. A quick movement and both she and Nurmat disappear through the window.

I am alone.

I lie still. I try to think, try to imagine what is about to happen, but I can't marshall my thoughts. They're made up of blurred, unformed pictures in my mind, which don't come together to provide me with answers. I have to think, I have to remember how to behave. One thought only is clear in my mind. I am not brave enough for this. I did not understand the risks. Yes, yes, I told Iparhan and the others I would be risking my life but it was a figure of speech to me. I thought I could trick and turn my way out of any danger if it happened. I was arrogant from years of fighting for survival on the streets. Now I have seen two innocent women die – Mei and the unnamed girl, the wrapped body that passed me. And the danger has not even truly begun. How many more lives will be lost to maintain this illusion I am engaged in? And when will my own life fall forfeit to this dangerous game?

There's a whisper at the door. I lie still. I don't know how to answer or even whether I should answer. My mind whirrs.

My silence is taken for assent. The door opens. Slowly I turn my head towards the sound.

The doorway is filled with colour and pattern. I blink, trying to understand the many-headed creature standing before me.

A gaggle of women peer in at me. In front, filling most of the doorframe, stands a larger, older woman. Behind her and to both sides are more faces.

The woman falls to the floor and kowtows. She does it with ostentation and the others, taking up most of the landing behind her, quickly follow suit, taking direction from their leader. When they've finished they stand and crowd into the room. There are eight of them. Behind them, still on the landing, stands a group of men, who look very young. Beardless and with soft plump faces, chattering in high voices, I take them for the young sons of the ladies, until I realise I'm seeing eunuchs for the first time.

I'm still lying in the bed, face turned towards them, motionless except for my eyes.

The older lady steps towards me with a commanding smile. "Your ladyship," she says. "This is a wonderful day. And an honour for us all to prepare you for your union with the Son of Heaven."

I gaze at her. I understand most of what she's saying but I don't know what to say in reply.

Her smile falters for a moment. She must think there is something wrong for me to just lie like this, expressionless, motionless. But she's not a senior lady for nothing. "Your ladyship must be overwhelmed with the joy of the occasion," she presses on.

One of the ladies behind her whispers. "Does she speak any Mandarin at all?"

The older lady beams at this reminder. Of course. I am not a simpleton. I am foreign. What a relief. She raises her voice and speaks very clearly. "Your ladyship is *very happy* today," she affirms.

I blink at her. I feel as though my body will not obey me. I make a small movement as though to sit up, though I'm not sure I can go through with the whole motion without simply tumbling off the *kang*.

The ladies dart forwards and the most senior pulls me upright, completing the motion I've started. They smile. I'm showing signs of life. This is better. Now that they are close to me I hear them whispering to one another.

"She really does smell of perfume."

"Probably something they wear in those parts."

"No, I heard it said she smells of it *naturally*. That it comes from her own *skin*."

I see each of them discretely sniffing the air.

"Your ladyship will have a *bath*, now. Then we will *dress* you," enunciates one loudly. They have obviously decided that they must only use loud simple words and gestures with me. It's just as well. I speak very little Mandarin and there's not much I can manage to take in at this moment. I have to give them something and so I manage to nod. This sets off a wave of smiles and nods. They are on firm ground now. They begin giving directions and orders at high speed. I see eunuchs hurrying away and servants bustling about. A large wooden lacquered tub is wrestled into the room and an endless procession of maids begins to traipse back and forth with pails of hot water. The room fills with steam. The ladies begin to sweat. Their robes are made of heavy silks and seem to consist of multiple layers – long skirts that peep out under calf-length heavy robes with wide sleeves. On top are long waistcoat-like strips of fabric with a great deal of decoration. Looped over these clothes are many long strands of colourful beads, which swing back and forth as they rush about the room, threatening to entangle the ladies with each other's corals, ambers and jades. Their carefully made-up faces shine with perspiration under heavy headdresses.

The tub is full. The ladies advance on me. I'm almost lifted into the tub by their many eager hands. I slip into the hot water and sit there, my vision still blurred by steam and the many colours surrounding me.

The ladies vie with each other to be part of the bathing process. Soap is passed from one to another. Impatient hands reach out for little scoops with which to pour water over me. I am being washed by a sixteen-armed spider. There is soap everywhere, water everywhere. Rubbing, stroking, pulling, scrubbing. I go limp and close my eyes, allow them to do whatever they want with me. The heat stops my limbs from shaking. I think, *breathe. Smile. Be helpful.* People are reassured by small gestures, by meaningless pleasantries.

More water is used for rinsing and I'm pulled from the tub a vivid scarlet colour. Again the hands descend to smooth me with many creams and unguents. As my skin fades to bright pink they mull over my hair. They have been given instructions to dress me according to our traditions, not theirs, and this is confusing them. I make vague motions of plaiting and when they try to make one large plait I shake

115

my head and indicate many with my fingers. They are mystified but tentatively begin many smaller plaits. When I nod and encourage them with a smile, they proceed at speed, murmuring in confusion at the unusual style, which seems too plain to them. They consider decorative options and finally bind gold and scarlet ribbons at the end of each plait and weave in tiny red flowers and strands of gold. My own dark hair has all but disappeared beneath a river of red and gold by the time they are satisfied.

The clothes provided to dress me are once again a surprise to them. They're a surprise to me too. Although the clothes are the same as I've worn before in structure, these are made in a rich red silk and then covered in intricate gold embroidery. Formalised waves, flowers and birds adorn them so thickly that their weight makes my knees weak and knocks me off balance. The long skirt is stiff with gold, the shirt, which would normally be white, is also red and the scarlet waistcoat is lavishly adorned with more embroidery and studded with pearls. On top of all this I'm helped into a heavy jacket of red silk with wide sleeves. A cap of red and gold is perched on my head. Long looped strands of pearls are layered round my neck and dangle from my – strangely only single pierced – ears. They apply makeup, which feels heavy on my skin.

As one, the ladies step back to look me over. I can see that the lavish use of red silk and gold embroidery is pleasing to them, as are the pearls. The style of the clothes they're still finding it difficult to reconcile themselves to. They try to adjust the way the clothes sit, perhaps thinking that by a tweak here or there they will magically become like their own. Their heads tip to one side as they consider the overall effect. Reluctantly they agree amongst themselves that certainly, if not traditional, I look *exotic*. This will have to do. I am, after all, foreign, and so looking odd is to be expected. Time is slipping by and the Emperor can't be kept waiting for his bride. They lift a red gauze veil over my head and the senior lady takes my hand to guide me. I'm not certain that my face is fully hidden but we're already out of the door. At the last minute I think of Mei's words but there has been too much going on and I forgot to look for a mirror in the room.

I stumble down the stairs. Ladies, maids, eunuchs and guards are everywhere, trying to keep out of the way and managing to do the opposite. I feel slow and heavy, weighed down with gold and pearls, with layer upon layer of thick silk. My hair pulls my neck backwards; my skirt pulls me forwards. The heels I'm wearing are higher than I'm used to. Were it not for the firm grip of the many ladies I would surely fall.

An older eunuch, wearing an elaborate hat with a peacock feather stuck in it, meets us at the foot of the stairs. He motions us into a large room in which are laid out tables bearing various large documents covered with writing I can't read, stone tablets, and other items. I look about me and freeze.

There are a number of men and women here dressed in the Altishahr style. The family of the bride. I wait for one of them to cry out, to say that I am not their daughter or sister, that I'm an imposter. I feel one of the ladies push me slightly and the trembling in my legs makes me fall to my knees. As I do so the whole room follows suit and I realise we are all kowtowing to the tables – or rather, to the items on them, which I assume are in some way important, probably sacred. Perhaps this is my marriage ceremony.

The bowing loosens my veil and I clutch at it, the only thing keeping me from being found out, but other hands have already taken hold of it and are adjusting it as I rise. My face remains covered. Slowly I'm turned around and led outside, the family following behind me.

Outside the house the courtyard has been transformed. The

silence of the pre-dawn has been replaced with chaos. There are guards everywhere, hundreds of them. There are eunuchs. There are the members of the household, their own servants as well as what appear to be many animals whose coats and feathers are dyed bright red. I want to lift the veil to see if it's just the fabric making them appear red, but the ladies are holding my hands too tightly. Ahead of me is a huge palanquin, like a carved version of my own clothes, shining gold and red. The roof is topped with gold birds and bearers await my arrival.

I step out of the house and jerk back from a crashing and wailing sound. Trumpets, gongs and drums greet me. Firecrackers are let off all around me. Bright streamers are thrown under my feet. I hesitate but the ladies are unperturbed and half push, half pull me onwards. I'm helped into the palanquin, which rocks alarmingly.

Once in, the ladies hold open the curtains and one after another the members of my 'family' kneel in the dust of the courtyard and kowtow to me. I sit silent and rigidly motionless, waiting for their eyes to see what's really in front of them, but they're too swept up in the festivities. This wedding is their reward for loyalty to the Emperor, payment for the treachery to their own family, and they know more favours and riches will come their way if I please my future husband. Their faces beam with pleasure at the sight of the rich clothes, my many jewels, at the noise and pomp surrounding me. My actual face, hidden beneath the crimson gauze, is of little interest at this moment.

The last bows are made and the ladies drop the curtains. I'm left alone inside my new tiny world.

I feel something uncomfortable under me and shift position, thinking of the layers of thick gold making up flowers on my skirt. But the discomfort remains. I reach under myself with my left hand and find a familiar vial. I unstopper it and once again Iparhan's perfume fills the space. I apply the perfume, then hide the vial in a small pocket of my skirt.

Sitting in the palanquin, I'm bathed in a strange dim red light as the sun shines through the scarlet walls and roof. I can hear chattering and people milling about. I sit and wait, my eyes strained by the strange light and the blurring effect of my veil. I look down at the clothes I'm wearing, the gold embroidery stiff on the silken skirt. I fiddle with the sleeves of my jacket and feel something wet. I look down at my hand and see blood. It takes me a moment to understand that my right sleeve, silken red, is soaked in red blood, that the colours match one another so well it can't be seen, only felt. I squeeze my arm, trying to feel pain, seeking a wound that isn't there and then become very still. This blood is not mine but has come from the girl I've replaced. Carefully I wipe off the blood onto the red seat of the palanquin and then hold the sleeve away from me with cold fingers, hoping that it will dry quickly, that I will never again have to feel that wetness on my skin. I try to breathe.

There are loud shouts outside and running feet. I feel my body tremble, from my tapping feet up to my chattering jaw. At any moment I expect to be discovered. They must have found the dead girl's body, or seen a smear of blood from where my sleeve brushed through a doorframe and understood that something terrible has happened. I clench my hands and wait for the curtains to be ripped aside, for a hand to reach in and grab me, pull me out. I get ready to run, but curse myself for my stupidity. I can barely move, I don't know where I am and dressed like this it would be impossible to hide. I will have to rely on new skills here – my old street tricks will not save me now.

The palanquin tips and I gasp as it's lifted and begins to move forward. I lift one shaking hand and pull aside the curtain just a little. The bright clear daylight blinds me after the dim redness inside but I see hazy rows of people kowtowing as the palanquin passes them and then the gates of the house as we leave them behind and enter a street. I let go of the curtain and as I do so I catch one brief glimpse of two dark-robed riders traveling away from us. Iparhan and Nurmat are gone.

I feel sick. The palanquin tilts and sways as I'm carried along, there are shouts as we pass through the streets, one phrase repeated over and over again, the only words I can make out in all the noise.

"Make way! Make way! Make way for the Imperial Phoenix! Make *way*!" The call is sometimes interrupted by a thud and a shriek as some too curious or too slow passer-by impedes the progress of our procession and receives a blow with a staff for their impudence.

I try to breathe slowly and deeply but the rich scent of the perfume and the iron tang of the still-wet sleeve, the sway of the palanquin and the shouts of the street make my head spin and my stomach dip. I feel the sharp rise of vomit in my throat and swallow again and again to force it back.

The swaying goes on for an eternity. I lose count of how many times I swallow.

From inside my scarlet cocoon I can hear the streets grow ever busier. I hear beggars asking for alms, street vendors calling out their wares, enticing housewives by enumerating the many fine quality of their goods or cooking up meats so that a thick smell of roasting seeps through my red and golden walls. It makes me gag. I can hear children and singers and once I even hear a snatch of a storyteller beginning his tales, as fanciful as any back in Kashgar. I shut my eyes and imagine I am back in my home town, that in a moment I'll leap out from this carrier as its rightful occupant, some fine lady, boxes my ears for the cheekiness of having sat my ragged arse where her silk-clad backside should be. I'm comforted for a moment until a shift makes me tip a little and I feel the heavy silk slide against my own skin and know that I'm no longer clothed in rags and that the rightful occupant of this chair is lying dead somewhere, her corpse denied mourning while my own body takes her place and her destiny.

The palanquin stops suddenly. I wait for it to move again, to hear curses and more shrieks as the staff is wielded against whatever obstruction is in our path. But we stay still, and then I hear a loud creak. I tilt my head to line up my eye with a tiny gap at the side of the curtain and see the hinges of a huge red gate slowly open.

The Red Wall

WE RIDE TO THE HOUSE that our silver has bought. I leave Nurmat with the horses and make my way to the bedchamber I have chosen for myself. I stand at the window and look out. The view from here is as I was promised – this house abuts the outer wall of the moat. Across the dark water rise the red walls of the Forbidden City. This area is to be the newly appointed Muslim quarter, in honour of the Emperor's new bride. Here I will be close to my own people, those who may support our cause, as well as close to those who come and go from the red walls – the servants, messengers, supplicants and emissaries. I rest my hands on the windowsill and look at the wall. It rises more than four times the height of a tall man and is pierced four times: the gates of the South, North, East and West. Behind that wall lies the Forbidden City. The palaces, the great halls, the Emperor and his women. Today Hidligh will take her place amongst them.

My hands grip the sill more tightly. Tonight as dusk comes Hidligh will no doubt be called on. She will be taken from her own palace and ushered into the bedchamber of the Emperor. She will be undressed and given to him to do with as he wills. By the morning she will no longer be a virgin.

I let go of the windowsill, bring my stiff hands up to the fastenings of my travelling clothes. Slowly, I unfasten each one, letting my clothes fall to the ground until I am stripped bare.

Nurmat's fingertips caress me. "Iparhan," he whispers. "I cannot lose you to another man. I cannot bear it. Lie with me. Lie with me now."

I pull back from him. "I cannot," I say, my voice made harsh with my desire for him. "I must be a virgin for the Emperor's bed, or I will be discovered. I am sworn to this path, Nurmat."

He moves so fast I do not feel the pain, only see the glint of his knife come close to my eye and pull back for fear it will touch me. Only when I see his face grow pale and feel a wet heat trickle down my cheek do I realise the knife has already touched me. I begin to raise my hand but stop before I touch my own skin, afraid of what I will find there.

Nurmat is shaking but he reaches out for me. "Forgive me," he says. "Forgive what I have taken from you. You can no longer go to the Emperor but you will stay in my arms forever and you will be as beautiful to me as you were the day I first saw you."

"What have you done?" I ask, my voice a whisper. "What have you done, Nurmat?"

There are footsteps on the stairs and Nurmat enters the room shoulder first, carrying the weight of our bags. As he puts them down and straightens up he sees me. Naked, framed by the dark windowsill and the sun's pale winter rays. He stands still, a hunter confronted by his prey, afraid to believe what he sees before him.

I try to keep my voice steady. "We cannot marry yet," I say. "I have not taken my revenge."

Nurmat nods, uncertain of what is happening.

"But we are so close to our goals now," I say. "So close that I thought perhaps…" I allow my voice to grow soft. "I thought perhaps we, too, might be close. For one night," I add, mindful that I cannot risk my offer being misinterpreted by a too-eager Nurmat.

He does not speak, only steps forwards and takes me in his arms. There is nothing gentle about his embrace. He crushes me to him, his breath fast, his face buried in my neck. "I have dreamed of this moment, Iparhan," he says.

I am about to reply but he all but throws me onto the bed, half his clothes already removed. His lips are on mine, hot and hard, his arms about me, every part of my body caressed, kissed and grasped. His hands are everywhere upon me. I cannot help being aroused, even though I had promised myself I would not give way to passion, that I would stay cool and calm inside myself, no matter what he did to me. I find myself reaching for him, pulling him to me, my lips on his lips, my teeth on his skin.

But when he kneels between my thighs he checks himself. "I will be gentle," he promises me, his voice shaken with desire, and I can see the effort it costs him to hold back, to enter me with care.

It hurts, of course, but it is that gentleness, the moment's pause he takes, which allows me to cool the heat rising within me. So at the moment when ecstasy overwhelms him and he cries out my name I push away the desire that threatens to pull me towards him. Instead I turn my face away and look out of the window at the red wall. I close my eyes and see blood, trickling.

The Forbidden City

ALL I CAN HEAR IS the sound of running feet. The bearers move more freely now we have left the overcrowded streets behind us. The guards, running alongside, add their own noise – their shoes heavier, their armour and weapons rattling.

I reach out a tentative finger and touch my sleeve. It's dry, hard with the invisible blood shed by its former wearer. I let it go, then pull aside the curtain a crack, barely enough to see out.

We're crossing a paved courtyard, although I've never seen a courtyard this size. I blink and pull back the curtain a little more. It stretches into the distance. At the edges of my vision are high red walls. Here and there we pass huge buildings with swooping rooftops, topped with golden-glazed tiles and beyond them the tops of trees. A guard, trotting alongside, catches a glimpse of movement from my curtain and turns his head. I let the silken folds fall back into place.

My breathing grows faster remembering Iparhan's last words of advice – *remember who you are supposed to be.* Her warning. *Endear yourself to the Emperor.*

She didn't need to say, *or else.* That, I can say to myself.

We come to an abrupt halt. Hands pull aside the curtains and are then offered to me. Tentatively I reach out and take them, am helped out into bright daylight, where I stand, in the shadow of a huge building. There are many steps falling away behind us, explaining the additional jolting I felt before we stopped. In front of us is a massive doorway.

I stand uncertain, wondering whether I should step through it. I look back at the guards and bearers but they all stand immobile, their faces empty of any expression. I look back at the doorway. Only now do I notice a small doubled-up figure prostrate before me, completing a series of bows. I step back a little as the person unfolds. A soft face and meek expression. A eunuch. He's only a little taller than me, although older, perhaps thirty years old or more. His well-made robes are a deep blue, decorated with delicate embroidery.

"Your ladyship," he murmurs. He speaks my language, but in a voice so soft I have to lean forward to catch his words. I smile. The relief of hearing my own tongue is so great that I forget what's about to happen until he reminds me.

"I am your humble interpreter, madam," he says.

I nod.

"My name is Jiang and I will accompany you as you meet the Emperor," he says. His eyes pass over my clothes and the veil, which hides my face from him.

I try to nod again but my neck feels stiff.

Shadows move in the doorway and what appears to be a very senior eunuch comes forward. His robes are magnificent and he looks stern. Jiang virtually fades away into a very low bow. His murmur to me is almost silent. "The Chief Eunuch."

I wonder whether I should kowtow and start to bend my knees. I'm wrong. The Chief Eunuch is already on his knees, kowtowing to me while I hastily straighten my legs. He begins to speak and my interpreter's lips move at the same time, without pause, without hesitation. I wonder how many times he's repeated the same greeting, perhaps to every woman brought here to be the Emperor's new bride. "Your ladyship," he says. "On this most auspicious day, it is my honour to welcome you to the Forbidden City. I beg of you to accompany me into the presence of the Son of Heaven, his Imperial Majesty, the Emperor."

I nod uncertainly and start forward towards the doorway. The Chief Eunuch looks startled and holds up a hand to stop me.

"Shouldn't I enter?" I ask.

The Chief Eunuch blinks at me. "There is a correct moment," he explains. I look at him, confused, and he elaborates as though to a child, "An *auspicious* moment."

We stand like idiots for a few moments and then the Chief Eunuch, based on a signal I fail to see, waves me forwards.

We enter the darkness. I can barely make out my surroundings, only that I'm in a cavernous room and that it's full of people.

The Chief Eunuch turns to me. "Allow me to assist your ladyship," he says, and with one quick gesture he pulls away the veil covering my face. I blink and tighten my hands into fists to stop from grabbing at it. Without it I feel naked. Slowly I raise my eyes to see my future.

The room is enormous. With the haze of the veil torn from my eyes, even its darker recesses can be seen. The floor is simple enough, but I remember Mei talking of the decorated ceilings and my eyes follow the lines of the great gold columns up to their tops. The ceiling is extraordinary. There's not a single part of it that isn't shining with gold and painted carvings. I try not to gape like some country bumpkin and instead look about me. All around the room are people in dazzling robes. Every hue of thick, quality silk is on show, every kind of motif that can be embroidered or picked out in jewels is here.

Standing apart is a group of women. One, who is slightly turned away from us, is wearing a bright yellow robe as well as a complex headdress, which makes her head look too big for her body. The headdress is blue and has a bird rising from the centre. All around it dangle pearls and other jewels.

"The Empress Ula Nara," whispers Jiang.

I nod.

"And some of His Majesty's other ladies."

Clustered around the Empress are more women, wearing similar robes, although they're in every possible colour – purples, blues, apricot orange, golden browns. Their huge hair is absurd. It's drawn up onto what looks like a small plank of black lacquered wood laid horizontally above their head, decorated all over with combs, flowers and hairpins. It's huge and looks like a balancing act just to keep it upright. I can't help wondering which one will tumble off first. These then, are the Emperor's other concubines, the women that I am about to join. I think of Mei's warning about their rivalries, the factions they may be part of, alliances made and lost through jealousies and success or failure.

The women stare at me. One, a wrinkled old thing, offers a timid smile. One looks me up and down, as though considering a beast at the market or a length of cloth. She purses her lips, and nods to herself, as though she has decided on a price for me. I'm not sure I've been valued very highly. Two watch me with their heads tilted to the same side, as though they were twin dolls, their faces curious, a little wary. I'd find it hard to tell them apart if I saw either again. One glowers at me under arched eyebrows, then turns her head and mutters something to the lady closest to her. They both smirk. I feel my palms grow damp. What if they can see at a glance, these women from illustrious families, that I am nothing but a street rat, whose fine clothes and gold-entwined hair do nothing to cover up my lack of breeding? My brief period of training is nothing compared to the years of preparation these women will have gone through to be chosen as brides to the Emperor.

The other women in the group glance briefly at me, then turn their faces away as though I am of no consequence, although the rigidity of their necks as they turn away tells me they want to look at me for longer, that they want to know more about me, to find out how my presence here will disturb their precarious equilibrium. Perhaps they are fearful of me – the newest and youngest recruit for the Emperor's bedchamber. *If they only knew how much more afraid I am of them*, I think. And which woman should I be most afraid of? Who has the greatest power here?

Slowly, the Empress' head turns towards me.

She hates me, I think. I look away and try to gather myself. *How can she hate me? She's never seen me before.* I glance back at her, thinking that my nerves are causing me to see what is not there, but her eyes, unwaveringly fixed upon me, leave me in no doubt. *She hates me.* My mouth feels numb. I can feel my hands tremble. I wish I could hide them.

All eyes are on me. Then all eyes turn to the other end of the room. I follow their gaze

The Emperor is seated on a large throne made of carved wood, lacquered in red. His head is bowed over some papers he is examining. To one side of him is a plump old woman with a square-faced jaw, seated on a similar throne. They are both wearing the same bright yellow robes as the Empress with intricate embroidery featuring dragons and other symbols. Their robes make those of the courtiers look insignificant. For a moment I see Nurmat and Mei, sitting on the heaps of cushions in the little house in the dunes, waiting for me to practice my kowtow.

The Emperor seems to finish whatever he was doing. He folds the papers neatly, passes them to a servant and looks up. I know he's almost fifty years old but he looks younger, not even forty. He sits very erect. His face is a long smooth oval with a very straight nose and full lips. The Chief Eunuch whispers something and the Emperor beckons me forward.

I look to Jiang who gives me a small but frantic nudge. "His Majesty should not be kept waiting."

I hiss back at him. "I can't speak Mandarin well enough. You need to come with me."

He shakes his head. "*Go.*"

The room falls silent as I make my way towards the throne. I'm afraid I'll trip at any moment. I'm also afraid of what will happen next. No doubt he'll speak to me and I won't understand. This is the moment when I will give myself away in some foolish way, by some tiny slip. I look back at Jiang but he stays put and waves me on.

I reach the throne without falling. As I approach him the Emperor stands. He's taller than I expected and bends his head slightly to look down at me. I come to an uncertain stop. Should I kneel and wish him the ten thousand years of life I spent so many hours training for?

"Welcome to court," he says, and smiles.

I can't help it. I gape at him. He speaks my language!

He laughs at my expression. "I speak all the languages of my empire," he says. "I have been learning yours in preparation for meeting you."

I stand in front of him, not sure what to do next or how to reply. I feel like a dolt.

He looks me over thoughtfully. "Your clothes are not court dress," he remarks.

He sounds curious, not angry, but there's a sudden silence and I can feel the tension rise in the room. No doubt it's inappropriate to be incorrectly dressed in the presence of the Emperor. Will someone be in trouble for this? Is it a bad omen?

I curse Iparhan's traitorous cousins for their stubborn insistence on this clothing but I have to face it out. "They're – they are the traditional clothes of… " I stumble as I was about to say Altishahr and remember who I'm speaking to. "Xinjiang, Your Majesty. I thought it would please you to see them."

He smiles at once, a broad, happy smile and I feel the court relax around us. "Of course. Turn around."

I turn awkwardly on the spot.

"Charming," says the Emperor, looking at my hair. "All those little plaits."

I put a hand up to them. "There'll just be two tomorrow, Your Majesty," I say without thinking and immediately feel heat rising from my neck to my face.

He frowns. "Why?"

My cheeks are scarlet. "I will be m-married," I say, stumbling over the word, hoping that he will not think me presumptuous, as a concubine, to declare myself his wife. "Married women wear only two plaits."

He chuckles. "Then I will look forward to seeing you with only two plaits."

The court laughs.

I risk a sideways look and see the Chief Eunuch gesturing to me. I step back a little but the Emperor holds up his hand. "One more thing."

I stop.

"I have been told that you have a special attribute."

I look at him.

"I have heard that your body emits a natural fragrance."

I look down. Here comes the first of the illusions that have been created for this game – a move I can play to keep my pieces safe. Word of the perfume has already spread and now I can prove that yes indeed, I am perfumed.

"Is it true?"

I am afraid. What if this trick does not work? "I've been told so,

131

Your Majesty." It comes out as little more than a whisper and he has to lean forward to catch it.

He smiles. "Come closer."

I step forward tentatively.

"Closer than that," he says. "I am not a hunting dog, to scent you from so far away!"

Everyone titters politely.

I step closer. He leans forward, so that our faces are only a hand's length apart. His eyes are bright and mischievous. I try not to shake. He inhales loudly, putting on an amusing show for the courtiers, but as he does so his eyes close. They reopen changed, his gaze on me softer and more wondering.

"It is your own scent? Not a perfume?"

I think of the tiny vial hidden in the folds of my skirt. *Endear yourself to the Emperor.* I take a deep breath. The perfume trick has worked. "Yes, Your Majesty."

He steps back and appraises me. "Remarkable. It reminds me of lotus flowers."

He sits down and gestures to the Chief Eunuch who hurries to him, and whispers in his ear. There's a pause and some consultation of documents and then the Chief Eunuch steps forward for my official presentation to the court. His voice is loud but what he says is too fast and complicated. It only sounds like a gargled song to me but there's a murmur of approval from the court as well as some laughter.

I turn to my translator, Jiang, who has crept up behind me and who now whispers to me. "You are to be known as *He Guiren* – Lady He."

The Emperor and Empress Dowager watch me from their thrones, waiting for my face to change in response to the announcement.

I shake my head. "What does that mean?"

"*Guiren* is your rank. You are sixth-ranked, which is an Honoured Lady, and *He* will be your new name."

I'm taken aback. "I have a new *name*?"

"Yes. It means Perfect Purity. So you are the Honoured Lady of Perfect Purity. A very auspicious name, especially as the Qing dynasty's name also means Purity."

"Why did they laugh, then?"

"The name He can also mean lotus flower, because it rises perfectly pure out of the mud. The Emperor has asked for your name to reflect your scent."

I look back at the Emperor, who smiles as he sees understanding dawn on my face. I give a tentative smile in return. The Chief Eunuch is gesturing at me, so I step forward and perform a kowtow. I stumble slightly as I stand but at least I don't fall over. The Emperor holds out an object like a sceptre to me and the Chief Eunuch indicates I should take it. It's as long as my arm and in parts almost as thick, made of a dark carved wood and inset with three panels in white jade. There are characters and flowers carved over every part of it. I've no idea what it is.

Seeing my puzzled face the Emperor leans forward from the throne to explain. "It is called a *ruyi*," he says. "It is a blessing, a symbol of good luck for our union."

I nod and try to look suitably impressed, although I can't read the writing on the jade panels.

The Emperor reaches out and traces the carved characters with his finger. "It says that all the world is now at peace," he says, smiling. He raises his voice a little so that everyone can hear. "Now that Xinjiang is part of our empire's family and Lady He has joined the ladies of the court, the world is at peace."

The court applauds.

I wonder what Iparhan would say but bite my tongue. I smile at him and he smiles back. I step away, holding the *ruyi*.

The Chief Eunuch calls out more announcements and I tilt my head towards Jiang for an explanation.

"Your father and brothers are to be given a fine house and many gifts," he murmurs. "They will live close by, in the newly created Muslim quarter of Beijing, just outside the walls of the Forbidden City."

I think of the men and women I saw for a few brief moments in the house on the outskirts of the city, who kowtowed to me believing me to be their sister, their daughter, their prize for the choice they made in turning away from their own family and lands, the allegiances of centuries. Their smiles, their pride. I think of the touch of the coverlet as it passed me, its wrapped burden made to disappear forever through an open window while hot piss ran down my thighs in fear.

I shudder.

The Chief Eunuch is by my side in an instant.

"We have not cared for your ladyship well enough," he says. "My humble apologies. You are tired and chilled from your journey here. You will be conducted to your rooms at once." He makes a tiny gesture and other eunuchs appear by his side. He instructs them at speed and bows very low to me as I'm guided from the room. I look over my shoulder and see him return to the Emperor, who is now examining a new document, oblivious to my departure. I look for the Empress, but she has disappeared.

My palanquin is waiting and I climb back in. I keep the window curtain open to cool my hot cheeks. I look down at the carved *ruyi* resting in my lap and revise the hurdles I have passed so far. My supposed family members are outside the walls of the Forbidden City, never to see my imposter's face again. I've not done anything terrible in the presence of the Emperor, have not yet given away my fraudulent identity. These thoughts should soothe me, but all they lead to is what may be coming next.

I'm whisked along stone-clad expanses, through endless gates and courtyards, past magnificent temples and palaces, their rooftops surmounted by strange little figurines. We pass golden-glazed roof tiles, red walls, monstrous golden guardian lions on pedestals, red columns, carved white stone, the colours and shapes repeated infinitely. It makes me dizzy.

We pass through a large red and gold gate and everything changes. Now we must be in the Inner Court that Mei told me about. There are more gardens with tall pines, smaller trees and bushes. A few are showing their first buds, creating, from a distance, the illusion of a gentle green haze. Here and there, nestling in the warmer nooks are early-blooming flowers. The cobbled pathways grow narrower and we pass close by many small palaces and shrines, their gates guarded by stone lanterns as high as my head. Carved wooden screens in red or dark wood shape the outlines of windows. Looking through the palace gates we pass I see little courtyards here and there with glimpses of flowers and trees within them. Once I hear a child laughing, but I don't see anybody, only a few other palanquins bobbing along in the distance.

The palanquin pauses briefly in front of a gate, which we pass through. We stop and I climb out. By my side, slightly out of breath, is interpreter Jiang, who must have trotted alongside us for the past few minutes.

We're in the courtyard of a small palace like the ones we passed coming here. The courtyard has three tall pine trees and many pots holding pink and white camellia bushes. The roof, its edges curved like a temple, reaches out over shining red columns. Blue and gold decorated outer walls are carved everywhere with wooden panels, forming balustrades, window and door frames in brilliantly bright colours as well as shaped ceilings over the walkways connecting the doors of the building. The carvings around the door are of many rich fruits and delicate flowers, piled high like the best market stalls of Kashgar.

Before me are gathered a group of men and women. One eunuch, who appears to be their leader, is about forty and very well dressed in brilliantly colourful robes. He's tall and thin, with a weathered face and a stately demeanour. Around him are other eunuchs, mostly dressed in simpler robes of sober blues and greys. The women all wear long pale green or blue robes with their hair in one long plait tied with a small red ribbon. They look to the senior eunuch as though for a signal. Sure enough, he drops to his knees, as does Jiang at my side, all of them performing a kowtow.

I wait for it to be completed and then the tall eunuch approaches me, his manner poised like an actor stepping onto a stage. His voice is high pitched, but louder and more certain than Jiang's soft murmuring. "My name is Huan, Lady He, and I am your first attendant. All that gives you pleasure is my desire. All that displeases you is my sorrow and disgrace."

I look to Jiang, who has spoken at the same time, repeating the words in my own tongue to be sure I will understand. "Thank you. Is this where I will live?"

"Yes, my lady. And we are your humble servants." He reels off a string of names, indicating various faces. I very quickly stop trying to take them all in. I will focus on just the two of them for now. Huan, because he is the most important servant, Jiang because he is my mouthpiece. I must stay alert, must stay focused on the people who will matter most in my new life.

"Who else lives here?"

"The other ladies."

"Do I have my own room?"

Huan looks shocked for a moment but hastily recomposes his face. "This is all your own palace. The other ladies have their own palaces, the ones you passed as you came here."

I've made an error but I'm truly taken aback. All this is mine? It's huge. Quickly, I recompose myself. "The Emperor is very generous," I say. "I had not expected to be given my own palace at once. I know I am not as highly ranked as other ladies here." I hope this sounds suitably humble and grateful. Sure enough, Huan's face clears. I heave a small sigh of relief.

He steps back. "Let me show you through the rooms of your palace, your ladyship."

Huan and I walk up a few steps onto a walkway and enter the palace. By my side, a constant shadow, is Jiang. When Huan speaks loudly to my left, his meaning comes to me from my right, in the soft murmur of Jiang's voice. Both have the same way of walking, toes turned out, bodies pushed forward, their legs close together. It gives them an odd, mincing pace. With one on each side I find myself falling into the same strange walk before I hastily correct myself and walk normally.

Inside we step into a sitting room. It is decorated in pale blue, with lavish use of gold and carvings. I hear birds singing and look about before I catch sight of two birdcages. The occupants flit about the cage and make a pleasant chirping sound. I approach them and then freeze.

Standing before me, in a shadowy corner of the room, is Iparhan.

I feel the room sway, hold out my hand, open my mouth to speak her name and then darkness falls.

I come to with a face very close to mine. The terrified eyes of Jiang are fixed on me. As I open my eyes he almost screams for Huan, who is by his side in an instant. I am half-lying on a couch, my shoes have been removed and a more junior eunuch is anxiously rubbing them. I feel very hot and then realise I've been heaped over with silk covers of every size and colour.

I try to speak and make a soft moaning noise, causing Jiang to whimper. Huan is firmer.

"You must drink this," he orders, and I sip some foul-tasting brew, which makes me gag. I wave it away but he persists.

"Iparhan," I say, when I can speak again.

"What is ipar-han?" asks Huan. Jiang shakes his head, mystified. I push them aside and sit up, looking into the corner of the room again where Iparhan stood. She is still there, although seated now. I rise, shaking. So does she.

A mirror. I am standing before a mirror. I make my way as close to it as I can and reach out, the very tips of my fingers brushing my cold hard reflection. Only now do I realise that I have never seen myself dressed as a lady. I never saw a mirror in the house in the dunes. I forgot Mei's instruction to look for a mirror in the room where I was dressed this morning. I think of the first time I ever saw Iparhan, when she stared at my face, searching over every part of it, touching my unblemished cheek, of Mei hastily hiding a mirror from me the first time she dressed me. How Nurmat checked my face when he first held me in the dark side street of Kashgar, how he stood frozen when he first saw me washed and dressed. His arousal when we enacted the images from the pillow books. How he saw me naked in the bath, his hands reaching out of their own accord. Now I understand. I look like Iparhan. With my rags taken away and clothed in rich colours, my hair swept back and powders enhancing my face, I am like her sister. Not twins, not so close, but if someone did not know us...

I stand in silence, my fingers still resting on the cold glass. Mei's last words echo in my mind. "Look in a mirror," she said. What did she need me to understand? Why does Iparhan need me to look so much like her? By the old poplar she had brushed over us having a 'similar' height and build. But this is much more than that.

As I gaze in the mirror, my mind full of questions, I suddenly realise that the two eunuchs are standing behind me. Their fearful faces reflect back at me through the mirror and I try to steady myself. I am behaving very strangely. I have to think of an explanation – and fast.

I turn to them. "I resemble a – a sister who died many years ago," I stumble, inventing as quickly as I can. "The heat – the journey – I thought of her. She would have been so proud of me today… of my great good fortune in being chosen by the Emperor himself."

They look hugely relieved but still think it important to check. "You thought of her. You did not – *see* her?" says Huan.

I shake my head, walking away from the mirror as though it is unimportant, although in truth I just want to stand in front of it and stare again at the reflection – at my face, which is no longer mine. "No, no, I was just… tired."

I can see they immediately thought of ghosts, that I have diverted them sufficiently. Now they can resume their fussing. I am made to rest, to drink more of their vile drinks, asked whether I wish to wear more comfortable clothes.

"May I see the rest of the palace?" I ask at last, hoping to escape the mirror in the corner.

Room after room unfolds. There's a bedroom with a huge *kang* piled high with silken covers and draped with long curtains, far larger than the one I thought so luxurious in the desert house.

A matching bedroom makes me turn to Huan. "I thought you said I wasn't to share with another lady?"

"If the Emperor should choose to visit you and wish to stay the night," says Huan, "then he will stay in a separate room."

"Why?"

Huan looks perplexed at this questioning of timeless protocol. I curse myself. I must stop asking questions that reveal my ignorance. "The Emperor never stays a full night in the same bed as one of his ladies. Once congress has taken place he will retire to another room."

I nod as though this makes sense. It doesn't. But I make a note of the word 'congress' as a reminder to myself. I might have forgotten and called it something coarser. I will have to watch my mouth.

We move on. Every room is luxurious and filled with beautiful things. There are flowers, paintings, scrolls with delicate calligraphy, decorative screens, carved furniture, mirrors, and cabinets. Everywhere there is a sweet smell of sandalwood, coming from the many items of furniture. Everywhere are gems, paint applied in brilliant hues, mosaics. On most surfaces pretty little items await my use or amusement – stone incense burners, implements for writing, fans, as well as little game boards, all their pieces tiny, exquisite carvings. It all begins to blur together – the scent, the brilliant colours, the endless new ornaments. I feel dizzy but I try to keep a suitable look on my face – somewhere between impressed at my good fortune and the natural acceptance of a noble lady surveying suitably adorned rooms, perhaps only one level more elaborate than those with which she would have been raised. It's a difficult expression to maintain.

There's a huge receiving hall, a miniature of the magnificent one in which I met the Emperor, which contains an altar and a throne.

"For His Majesty's visits," says Huan.

We pass again through the sitting room, where I avert my eyes from the mirror, then make our way to a dining room with enough space for a banquet should I choose to hold one and a bathroom with a gigantic lacquered wooden tub for bathing, so heavy it stays in its place always, unlike the one in the house where I was prepared to come here. Later I find that hidden away from my eyes are many more rooms, far plainer, which smell of food, sleep and bodies rather than incense, sandalwood and precious perfume. These are storage rooms, kitchens and my personal servants' sleeping and eating quarters. Such necessities are considered none of my concern, they exist to service my needs rather than to delight my senses and therefore must not be seen, heard or smelled.

We go back to the sitting room where I sit with my back to the mirror and Huan nods imperceptibly to a maid. In moments I'm brought tea. It's a tea beyond the imaginations of the common trading route tea merchants selling their so-called 'fine' teas. This is delicately perfumed and as I sip, a beautiful flower unfurls its scarlet petals within the depths of the bowl. I sip it gratefully while discreetly trying to shift my feet into a more comfortable position. My new high shoes hurt me but I daren't mention them, no doubt I ought to be used to them. Huan observes the slight grimace on my face and rises from his place opposite me, kneels, then gently removes the shoes and sets them aside, slipping a cushion under my feet.

I look down at him, surprised. "How did you know?" I blurt out.

He smiles. "It is my duty to know everything about you, my lady," he says, rising and going back to his place.

I hope he knows nothing at all about me. I wonder if he can tell that I'm not a noblewoman born and bred and shift uneasily in my seat. His eyes and Jiang's are on me at all times. Any error I make will be seen at once. I pray that they put down any slips to my being a foreigner. But now Huan seems to have other things on his mind. He clears his throat. "Because your ladyship is from the newest part of His Majesty's glorious empire, you must instruct us how to care for you. His Majesty has given orders that all must be done to ensure your happiness."

I wait for clarification.

"Your clothes, for example..." He pauses and both he and Jiang examine me with concerned expressions.

This is what I dreaded. Something is wrong. I curse Iparhan for having made some error, for not having noticed something that will give me away. "What about my clothes?"

The two eunuchs look awkward. Huan clears his throat again. "They are not in the Manchu style and yet we understand you are to continue wearing them. Your chests of clothes were sent to us ahead of your arrival so that we might prepare them to be worn and examine how they are made. As they are not..." He clears his throat for a third time.

I'm worried. "I desire only to please His Majesty," I say hesitantly. Their faces smooth out. I'm on the right track. "You must speak freely so that I may know how I may please him best," I finish, hoping it's the right thing to say.

Huan lowers his voice and Jiang does likewise. A mistake, because this means he is almost silent.

I lean forward, and Jiang hesitantly repeats Huan's words. "The clothes are not, er, *elegant* enough for your ladyship's new status," he breathes, blushing as he does so. "What you are wearing now is of course suitable for your wedding day but the rest of the items..."

"I know the style is different," I say, struggling to understand what he's saying.

"It is not the style," they hasten to reassure me. "We can of course replicate your ladyship's traditional costume. It is the fabrics, the embroidery..."

I think back to the Emperor's clothes and those of the court women, how they outshone the courtiers. "You think they should be more elaborate?" I ask tentatively, hoping I've guessed their delicate hints.

They beam at me. "*Yes*, your ladyship."

I could cry with relief. Is this all that's bothering them? "You must have them made however you think best," I say quickly.

They spring into action before I've even finished speaking. Maids are dispatched and return bearing huge chests of clothes, which are pulled out and spread on the floor to be examined. Huan and Jiang kneel on the floor and hover over them, trying to understand the strange new garments, glancing up at what I'm wearing for confirmation.

"So there is a skirt," they mutter. "With a shirt? And then the waistcoat?"

I stare at them. I've never met people like this. They're like two old women with their bustling and concern over minor details, or little girls with favoured dolls. I feel lost. I had thought that at least I knew how to talk my way round most people, but these men are unlike anything I've ever encountered. Is this how I'll be spending my days? Fussing and fretting over clothes? *Until Iparhan comes wanting information,* I think, *Iparhan and her face that matches mine...* and quickly push the thought away with a small shudder.

Huan catches the motion and looks up at me. "And an outer jacket?"

I nod. "If it's cold enough."

Huan sits back on his heels and looks up at me with concern. "Beijing winters are cold beyond your imagination, your ladyship. There is snow and ice everywhere. The streams that run through the Forbidden City freeze over. And the *wind...* "He shudders theatrically.

I think of the freezing desert wind and the snow-capped mountains of home and try to look suitably impressed. The Emperor may have learnt my language but clearly his people have no notion whatsoever

143

of my homeland. I might as well have arrived from a made-up world, a fairytale.

Jiang joins in the inspection. "And then there is a little cap?"

I indicate the heaps strewn before us. "Yes. As you can see, there are plenty to choose from."

From their pursed lips I can see that none of the caps meet their standards. Huan is holding up a waistcoat and comparing it to what I am wearing. "They seem very…"

"Very?"

"… small?"

I frown. I don't understand what he means. I'm beginning to panic. Is this how I will fail? Not because of some big mistake but because I don't know some tiny sartorial detail? "They fit me," I say, feeling my hands begin to tremble again. Have they ever seen the girl whose place I have taken? Do I not fit her clothes well enough?

"Yes. Very – very *fitted.*"

"Is that wrong?"

The two of them look at one another. I wait. Huan tries to explain. "Did you see the other ladies? In the throne room?"

I nod. Where is this leading?

"Their robes are more… loose-fitting."

I did notice. Their exquisitely decorated robes hung shapelessly over their bodies. Fat or thin, shapely curves or flat-bottomed and mean-chested, you could hardly tell when they were all standing together. I think of the girls of Kashgar, who try to make their waistcoats just that little tighter at the waist, just that little more curved at the chest, to give them a waist and bust more shapely than those with which they might have been blessed by nature. The wide skirts which float outwards when a girl dances.

I try to explain. "They make a woman more shapely. More… womanly." I draw a shape in the air with my hands, trying to show them what I mean. The two of them ponder the imaginary shape in silence. "So that men will find them... attractive?"

They consider this in doubtful silence before Jiang ventures to Huan, "Perhaps His Majesty will appreciate something a little different? Like Lady Ling?"

Huan's eyebrows go up but then he nods, first slowly and then a little faster.

"Who is Lady Ling?" I ask.

"A favourite of the Emperor," says Huan thoughtfully. "Han Chinese, not Manchu. Different." He smiles. "Like you, my lady."

The rest of the day passes in chaos. A selection of my clothes are picked out to be ripped apart for patterns and taken away to an army of unseen dressmakers who are told to replicate them many times over, but in fabrics and with decorations befitting my new status.

Once the clothes have been dealt with Huan approaches me and slowly undoes a few of my plaits. I sit still and await his verdict. I'd rather he focused on my hair and clothes than investigating anything else. So far their attention to my clothes has stopped them asking any other questions about me.

"Your hair is very unusual, my lady."

Jiang, watching him, interjects. "She said it must change from many plaits to only two from now on, as she is married."

Huan frowns, rubbing the loose hair between his fingers to feel its texture. "Two plaits? Down your back?"

I nod.

He shakes his head. "Your ladyship will look like a maid." He gestures and a maid rushes forward. Huan indicates that she should turn her back so we can see her hair. One thick plait hangs down her back, tied with a small red cord. Huan points to it. "Two plaits, one plait – what difference will there be?"

I pull one of my tiny plaits over my shoulder. The red flowers and gold ribbons in it shine. "Can't you do things like this?"

He considers them. "Perhaps…"

I wait.

"Gemstones," he says at last. "Your plaits must shine like a treasure house."

Jiang smiles. "Huan is an excellent hairdresser," he says. "Our previous lady, who is now gone from us, would have no one but him do her hair."

"How did you come to both be given to me then?"

"We begged to serve together," says Huan.

Jiang adds shyly, "I was taught by Huan when I arrived here and he saved me from many beatings, being older than I."

"Beatings for what?"

Both of them blush and look away. Jiang's murmur drops so low I can barely make out his explanation.

"When a eunuch is very young, my lady, he… struggles to control… his… his urination. Due to the operation – to make him a eunuch."

I can't help it, I wince.

Huan nods gravely. "Often eunuchs are derided for this, madam, for the… smell."

Jiang continues alone. "So new eunuchs are severely beaten for such crimes. But Huan, being older than I, knew what fate might befall me and would wash my robes and hang them to dry in secret, so that I might not be punished for my odour."

I'm about to reply but a loud cry makes me jump. It's repeated over and over again, first far away and then drawing closer, before fading again like echoes. "Draw the bolts, lock up, careful with the lanterns. Draw the bolts, lock up, careful with the lanterns." I hear a voice reply from my own courtyard and turn to Huan. Jiang answers.

"All those who had business in the Forbidden City today have left. The gates are to be locked up now; only the Emperor and his family and servants will remain."

I speak without thinking. "And the court physician on duty tonight."

Their eyebrows go up simultaneously. "How do you know about the physician?"

I think of a wrinkled tortoise face and bent back. "I knew a woman who was once a maid here." They wait for more but I stay silent. I don't trust my voice not to waver if I speak again.

Huan claps his hands. "It is time for your ladyship to eat. A meal has been prepared."

They lead me back to the dining room and the gigantic table. I sit down at one end. Perhaps ten servants are already in the room, gazing at me. Huan and Jiang hover behind me as dishes are brought in. Mei was right, I think. Soon almost the whole table is covered in tiny dishes, which are uncovered before me. Each has a tiny strip of metal stuck in them. I prod one cautiously.

"For your safety, my lady," says Jiang.

I twist round to look at him. "Safety?"

"They are strips of silver. If there is poison in your food, the silver will go black."

I've never heard of such a thing. "Are you sure?" *Poison?* I think to myself. No one mentioned the possibility of poison before I came here. How many more hidden dangers are there?

They nod, earnest.

I shrug and pick up the chopsticks laid out for me. Huan hurries to intercept me. "One moment, my lady." He gestures and a eunuch steps forward and begins tasting the dishes, a little bite of each.

My eyebrows go up. "What's he *doing*?"

Huan looks surprised again. I've asked another stupid question.

I must keep quiet. "Your taster, my lady. An additional precaution against poisoning."

It takes some time but at last I'm allowed to start. I want to try everything but almost immediately run into difficulties. Huan offers me a dish.

"Pork dumplings, my lady."

My chopsticks are halfway to the plate. I stop. "I can't eat that."

Huan looks bemused. "Dumplings?"

I shake my head. "Pork."

He looks down at the offending items. "You don't like pork?"

I adopt a devout tone. "I'm a Muslim. I cannot eat it. It is forbidden."

He blinks and I see the servants' eyes move slowly the length of the table.

I sit back in my chair, relishing having put them on the back foot. I was right. Being a Muslim is going to be helpful to me. "How many of the dishes here are pork?" Huan begins to indicate them. I hold up a hand to stop him. "Take the pork dishes off the table."

The servants start readjusting the dishes. Many are taken away. I pick up my chopsticks again and then pause. "These ones remaining – do any contain pork fat?"

Several more are removed.

I can see Huan getting concerned. The bountiful table looks diminished. They can hardly doubt my religion, at least, the amount of fuss I'm making. "These other meats – have they been blessed?"

"Blessed?"

I make it as simple as possible. "As they are being killed – they must have prayers said over them, otherwise…"

I stop. Incomprehension on every face. I point with my chopsticks. "Pass me all the dishes that are vegetables only. No meat."

There are frantic changes. I now have ten dishes before me rather than close to a hundred. The endless table looks bare. Still, I have rice, noodles, vegetables, sweetmeats. I begin to eat. A thump to the floor and a blur of movement makes me stop. Huan and Jiang, along with the other servants, have fallen to the floor, on their knees, their faces hidden. I look down and then touch Huan. "What are you doing?"

His face, when he looks up, is streaked with real tears. I drop the chopsticks in alarm. Something has gone badly wrong. My heart is suddenly thudding. "What is it?"

"We have failed your ladyship. You go hungry because of our ignorance."

I snort with laughter and have to turn it into a cough. I want to tell him that hunger, real hunger, is not ten dishes of good hot food. That hunger isn't even one missed meal but many, one after another until the gnawing in your stomach almost disappears into a numb acceptance. I open my mouth and then shake my head. I can't tell him this. I'm supposed to be a noblewoman, a suitable consort for an Emperor. What would she have said? I frame the words carefully and try to keep a straight face. "You've a great deal to learn about how to serve in my household. Tomorrow a servant must go to the new Muslim quarter in Beijing and find a – a priest of my people who will direct them in how to buy meats for my table. For tonight..." I pause at the enormity of the lie. "...I will have to go hungry."

They all hide their faces again. I want to tell them not to be so ridiculous. Instead I ignore them and eat the bountiful food before me, enjoying such delicacies as sweet potatoes, chestnuts and peanuts. Then I stand, forcing them all to rise with me and begin clearing the table, their faces downcast.

Huan and Jiang, meek now, follow me back to the sitting room. I decide I can't live with the daily reminder of my similarity to Iparhan. Whatever it means, whatever is to come of it. "I am not fond of

149

mirrors," I say. "Can that one be removed? It is…" I think about what might constitute a valid excuse. "It is a temptation to pride, which as a Muslim woman is sinful."

They look taken aback but within moments the mirror has been removed. I feel my shoulders slump with relief.

An edginess is creeping over me at what is about to happen next. I look about me and take a deep breath. It has to happen sometime, I can't put it off any longer. I knew what playing this part would entail and I will have to go through with it. "What time will he come?" I ask.

"Who, my lady?"

"The Emperor, of course."

Their heads both tilt to one side. "He may not come here."

Have I made another error? "Do I go to him, then?"

There is a pause. "His Majesty," says Jiang, choosing each word with care, "might not see you at all today."

I take this in. "Tomorrow, then?"

There's a pause.

"When *will* I see him, then?"

Jiang makes a gesture of helplessness. "His Majesty's desires are not ours to know."

I'm confused. "But he will want to see me?"

Huan hurries to reassure me. "Of course. Of course."

"When?"

"That, we cannot know."

I must be missing something. "Does the Emperor see one of his ladies every night?"

They consider this. "Usually."

I think of the small group of women I saw standing in the throne room. It can't take him that long to work his way through us. "How many ladies are there?"

"Several dozen."

"*What?*"

They hurry to explain. "Of course, not all are as exalted as yourself and the Emperor's most important ladies. You are part of a small, elite group. There is the Empress Ula Nara. Then there are the Imperial Noble Consorts, the Noble Consorts, the Consorts, the Imperial Concubines, the Honoured Ladies such as yourself. But after those there are many more ladies of far lesser rank and in far greater numbers. All are housed within the Forbidden City."

I might not see him for a long time. Iparhan wants information from me. What will Iparhan do if I don't give her what she wants? And the information she wants can come only from time spent with the Emperor.

Huan sees my face cloud over and he speaks gently. He must think I cherish some foolish notion of being one of the Emperor's favourites. "Be patient, my lady."

I try to smile but Iparhan's face – now too similar to mine – rises up before me and I turn away from him.

Night comes. I peep into the courtyard and see glowing lanterns everywhere. Inside the *kang* is warmed and the pink and gold hangings around my bed are loosened to prepare for the moment when I'll be cocooned inside them.

The maids help to undress me. I've already found a moment to hide my perfume vial in a little sandalwood box down the side of my bed. Now that I see the maids up close they are practically children; the oldest looks barely thirteen. I'm given a soft loose robe in which to sleep. I'm shown how to use crude salt on a finger to clean my teeth. Perhaps ladies don't care about spitting in front of their servants because they're used to having people watch them wash and dress. I don't care because I've spat in the street a thousand times, so I pass this trial easily. Even using a chamber pot in full view of the servants doesn't bother me; I've pissed in alleyways enough times. Huan keeps up a running commentary on the next day's plans. I barely hear him; I'm in such a daze of tiredness.

"The second lunar month brings us the festival of the Azure Dragon – we call this the Dragon Raising Its Head. All homes must be expressly cleaned to honour the occasion and special dishes of pancakes and noodles will be eaten. Should you wish to visit a temple, a sedan chair will come for you in the morning."

I try to show some interest. "The same one I had today?"

"No, my lady. That was a bridal chair, used for the day when a new lady enters the court. From now on your chair will be orange, like those of the other concubines. The Emperor, his mother and the Empress ride in yellow chairs. Everyone else rides in red chairs."

I try to shake away the ache in my head. I must concentrate. "Is everything colour-coded like this?"

He smiles. "Yes, my lady. It will all seem natural soon."

They finish preparing me for the night. I'm halfway into the bed when I suddenly remember. I turn to Huan. "Which way is North?"

He looks startled but points. I think about the right way to face and then kneel on the floor and ostentatiously begin my prayers, bowing and murmuring. A hush descends. I'm grateful my face is mostly hidden from view and that none of them will know if I make a mistake. As I finish I keep my head bowed. How long will my tricks and illusions keep me safe here? A real, unbidden prayer comes to my mind. *Let me be safe here.* I stand and see twenty pairs of eyes fixed on me in amazement.

"It is how I pray," I say, trying to keep a straight face. "And you must find me a little mat on which I may kneel."

They continue to gape. I climb into the bed and pull the curtains closed. "Goodnight," I call through the thick folds.

I hear the thump as they all hit the floor to bow to me. "Goodnight, your ladyship."

I look up at the painted and gilded ceiling and listen to them leaving the room. When they've all gone I lie awake and think. I am shaking with exhaustion after less than a day here. The constant tiny errors I am making, the endless ritual and routine that all these people know backwards... I will need an escape plan. If this all goes wrong – and how can it not – I need to have food and simple clothes hidden away. I need to find a way to leave the Forbidden City. Tomorrow I will begin to put together my plan, for I can't believe this illusion won't shatter into a thousand pieces the first time true pressure is applied. My head aches from trying to keep my wits about me. I will have to remember to say the right things, to behave correctly, day after day after day. Perhaps for the rest of my life. And if I forget, for just one moment, it could lead to my life being a great deal shorter.

I look down at my hands, lying on the blossom-embroidered pink silk coverlet and think of the words of the old opium-riddled fortune-teller.

I see a great man, a man who will let your hands rest only on silk.

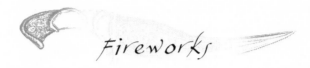

Fireworks

N IGHT COMES AND FIREWORKS RIP the sky apart across the city, celebrating the marriage of the Emperor to his new bride. Nurmat is happier than I have ever seen him. He is all gentleness to me, all smiles to strangers we pass in the streets. We eat at a food stall and then walk about the Muslim quarter, learning the streets, greeting those from our homeland.

Later in darkness I sit by the window looking out over the moat while Nurmat lies on my bed, his fingers lightly stroking my back.

"Of what are you thinking, Iparhan?" he asks softly. Perhaps he is hoping that I will reply that I am thinking of him, or of his caresses in this bed.

"Hidligh," I say. "I need someone to watch her, to report on whether she is playing her part well. I need to know how close she is to the Emperor so that I can judge what questions she should ask of him. I may have to bribe a maid."

Nurmat yawns. "You need a eunuch, not a maid," he says. "The maids are nobodies. The eunuchs are far closer to their mistresses."

As a child, the last offspring and much-desired daughter of an aging mother, I ran wild. I longed to play with the boys but my mother disapproved. "Weapons are not suitable playthings for a girl," she chided me gently. She made sure my horses were soft creatures, docile and trusting, not the warhorses I longed for.

The servants became my playmates. I rode on the menservants' backs, *urging them on like racing steeds, laughing when they reared and snorted, attempting to throw me. I coaxed them to let me play with daggers and then swords, begged to mock-fight them when they had other tasks to perform. And so I grew: my aim more accurate, my seat in the saddle better than even my older brothers'. My ability to disappear from sight when my mother came looking for me was aided by willing servants, my sworn allies.*

"A eunuch?" I repeat.

There is no reply. Nurmat's eyes are closed, his face half buried in the covers, his soft young skin flushed with sleep.

The Inner Court

THE INNER COURT IS A strange place.

A whole day can be taken up with being bathed and dressed in ludicrous finery. Each day my plaits are variously interwoven with pearls, corals, jade, strands of multi-coloured silk, fresh flowers (which Huan changed three times that day just to keep them fresh and scented) and even, on one memorably dull day, with *zhe zhi*, tiny shapes intricately folded from paper to resemble animals and birds, then hung on red silk strands from my dark hair. They took hours to fasten and I had to sit still while it was done, stifling my yawns.

I'm fed dish after dish, sitting all alone at the great table for my meals, then I sit in the garden or one of my rooms. I might play a game with the eunuchs, learning new moves on the board while picking at sweet cakes or little snacks. I might look at paintings or talk to the caged birds, some of who talk back in creaking voices. I sip fine teas, their leaves and floral additions changed with the hours of the day or my mood. I go to bed. This is a day.

At first I'm expectant. I wait to be summoned by the Emperor. I'm jumpy, nervous. But there is no summons. No word. Not even a suggestion that I might be called on as his companion. The work that goes into my clothes, my hair, my grooming – what is it for, if not for this expected summons which is so long in coming? I want to ask questions but I daren't reveal my ignorance. Perhaps this is normal. Perhaps the Emperor never calls for his new ladies until... until what?

What do I have to do to be noticed? I'm nervous of being called for, but if I'm not called for then how can I get the information Iparhan wants? What will she do to me if I fail her in this? When I think of this I finger the hollow of my throat, where Iparhan laid her dagger against my skin. It becomes a nervous habit with me, a quick flutter of my fingertips against the hollow of my throat.

I set about protecting myself. I've not lived on the streets for nothing. I need to know the Forbidden City and its people as I knew the streets of Kashgar, but first I need an escape plan. You should always have somewhere to hide if things go wrong.

I ask for some cakes. When no one is looking I hide a few in the pockets of my skirts, then squirrel them away under my bed, along with a sleeping robe that could serve as clothing should I need to run away. The robe may look plain compared to my other clothes but it is at least Manchu in style and I would stand out less wearing it than I would in my foreign-looking, elaborately embroidered clothes. This little parcel will serve as my security in case I should have to escape. Each day I hide new food away and throw the old food into the pond in my garden where the fish eagerly rise for the crumbs I throw them.

Then I ask Jiang to show me Beijing from one of the watchtowers. "I've never seen it," I say to him. He calls for my palanquin and takes me to the very back of the Forbidden City, to the North-West corner and the watchtower there.

I stand in the uppermost storey, only too aware of the armed guards standing close by. Jiang chatters away to me while I try not to let my true feelings show.

"You can see most of the Forbidden City from here," says Jiang. "The Inner Court, beginning at the far North of the City and stretching South. That is Empress's palace there, and that is the Emperor's. That one close by is the Palace of Motherly Tranquillity, it is where the Empress Dowager lives. The surrounding palaces are those of the other court ladies and yourself. Then further away you can see the Outer Court. His Majesty's officials and courtiers come there of course, on official business and for ceremonies. Then if you turn this way you can see the city of Beijing itself…"

I try to drown out the sound of his voice and focus on what I need to know. I keep an interested look on my face, I nod and turn my face where he points as though listening to him but inside I have a horrible sinking feeling.

From where we stand I can see, not Beijing, which I had little interest in seeing anyway, but instead the outer walls and defences of the Forbidden City. The moat that Mei told me about is huge. Where its dark waters meet the Forbidden City rise the red walls of my new home. They are too smooth to climb, too high to jump from even if I could scale them. I would risk a broken limb at best, at worse a cracked head. There are only four gates in and out of the huge palace complex, and each is heavily guarded. Escape will have to be a last resort.

I need to protect myself from any dangers of which I am as yet unaware. I think of the Empress' face when she first saw me and remember Mei's warnings of the 'factions' amongst the women of the palace. "I wish to visit Lady Wan," I announce to Huan.

He pauses in his work, wrapping thin strands of purple silk in my hair, from which dangle tiny white jade creatures. "Lady Wan?"

"Is she still here?" I ask, wondering if perhaps she has died since Mei left court.

"Oh yes," says Huan. "But why would you wish to meet her, my lady? She is quite old and lives a very quiet life. She is not much in favour."

"Does the Emperor dislike her?" I ask.

"No, no," says Huan. "He is quite fond of her, but he no longer calls on her as a companion."

"I had a maid who served her," I say. "And she spoke well of her. I would like to meet her. What does she look like?"

"She is fully four and forty years old," says Huan, as though suggesting that she is practically on her deathbed. "She was known for the beauty of her hair and the fineness of its arrangements, but now it is no longer black and much of it is – ahem – missing."

"Missing?"

He lowers his voice theatrically. I've already learned that Huan will seize any opportunity for dramatic pronouncements. "She is *bald*, my lady."

"How does she have her hair done, then?"

"She has one of the best hairdressers in the palace. He spends hours creating wigs for her. If you see the Lady Wan you will be astonished by her hair. It is perfection. Even the Empress appears not to have such fine hair nor so beautifully dressed. But they are all wigs."

Lady Wan's palace is not far from mine and with all due ceremony, involving a train of servants and much fussing beforehand over my hair and clothes, we make our way to her.

She greets me with fluttering kindness, her heavily painted face almost cracking as she speaks. Her hair is spectacular. It towers above her, stretched across a thin black board. From it are suspended crimson peonies made of silk and tinkling golden strands. Her hair is three times the size of her head.

"My dear," she says, her voice breathy, girlishly pitched. "What excitement!"

Having experienced just a few of these empty days I have to agree. Meeting a new face will be the highlight of my day for sure. If she's

159

been here for many years I might even be the highlight of her year. She may remember this as The Year I Met Lady He.

We are settled in with tea, little cakes and fruits piled high in elegant platters. I gesture towards them thinking to start with something polite. "How pretty," I offer.

Lady Wan almost blushes. "The Son of Heaven is all kindness," she says. "The fruits were a gift from him."

I nod and smile.

"Do you miss your family?" she asks.

"I'm sure my family is very happy in the accommodation the Emperor has provided," I say, afraid she's about to suggest a visit to me from them, something I'm very keen to avoid.

"Of course," she says. "His Majesty is most generous." She pats my hand. "Visits are not allowed in the general way of course, but should you ever be gravely ill remember that he may grant permission for them to attend you should it serve to help your recovery. He is a kind and generous man." She smiles at the thought of him.

I make a mental note never to fall ill enough to warrant a visit. "Do you attend the court very much?" I ask, hoping to steer the conversation away from myself.

"Oh no," she says. "I lead a very quiet life. I was always a shy girl," she adds with an awkward little laugh. "I have lived here for many years now, very happily, with only the company of my maids and eunuchs."

This is my way in. "I had a maid back in Kashgar," I say. "She served you many years ago."

"Really?" says Lady Wan. "What was her name?"

"Mei."

She looks disappointed. "A common name," she says. "What did she look like?"

I speak without thinking. "A tortoise," I say. I feel stupid at once, for Lady Wan will not know what I am talking about.

But her eyes light up. "Mei!" she says. "She had a bent back."

I had thought Mei's bent back was due to her age. "Yes," I say.

Lady Wan is all smiles. "She was my favourite maid when I was very new here," she says. "I did not wish her to leave me but her time was up and she was free to marry. How did she end up in Xinjiang?"

"Her husband was from my homeland," I say.

"And is she happy?" asks Lady Wan. "Is she well? Does she have children?"

I can't bring myself to tell her the truth, to hurt her with the image I carry of Mei, her crumpled body lying in the half-lit doorway of a house soon to be swallowed up by the dunes of a fearsome desert. "She was a good wife and mother," I say. "Everyone who knew her loved her. She served me for a little while before I came here, so that I might be ready to join the Emperor's court. She was very good to me." I can feel my eyes glisten and try to look away.

Lady Wan reaches out and pats my hand. "We never forget those who are kind to us," she says. "Mei was my faithful servant. I am so happy to know she is well and surrounded by those who love her. And she must have told you so much about the Forbidden City!"

"She did," I say. "But she also told me that much would have changed and she told me that you... that you might help me by telling me... about the other ladies at court?"

Lady Wan sits back a little in her chair. "The ladies are all very kind, of course," she says. "We are honoured to be part of His Majesty's court."

I will have to tread softly. "It is an honour, of course," I say. "But Mei told me that I should be aware of the different... characters of the ladies? So as not to offend anyone? I am very young and she said that I should know something of their... history? Will you tell me about them?"

Lady Wan nods slowly. "There are various ladies of lesser rank," she starts. "You do not need to concern yourself with them." She thinks for a moment. "Except perhaps Lady Wang," she adds. "Lady Wang is of a lesser rank but she is very ambitious for a higher position. And..." she pauses.

"Please go on," I say.

Lady Wan's soft voice grows quieter. "She is known to have a temper," she says. "She slapped a maid – which is forbidden."

"Why?" I ask.

"A woman's face is her fortune, even if she is a maid," says Lady Wan. "You cannot damage a maid's face. The Emperor was very angry with Lady Wang and she had to pay many taels of silver to the maid's family."

I think of the way in which my own face has become my fortune and nod. I'll try to steer clear of this woman. She sounds unpleasant. "Are there any ladies whom you count as friends?" I ask.

She brightens. "Consorts Qing and Ying are my very dear friends," she says. "They too lead a quiet life here. Their palaces are adjacent and Consort Qing has the guardianship of Lady Ling's eldest son. They are almost a little family. You should seek them out," she adds. "They would be good friends to you."

I'm glad to hear there are some women here who may be friendly. "Doesn't Lady Ling look after her own children?"

"Oh no," says Lady Wan, looking shocked at the suggestion. "It would not be correct. Besides, she is with child at present and must be treated with all due care. This will be her fourth child and she has been assured that it will be another son."

"She must be in favour with the Emperor then?" I suggest.

"She is," says Lady Wan. "She has given the Emperor a son and two daughters. She is ranked as an Imperial Noble Consort, only one rank beneath the Empress. She is often called to the Emperor's rooms."

"She is his favourite, then?" I ask.

She nods.

"Why does the Emperor like her?"

"She is dedicated to his needs," she says. "She is pleasant in her demeanour to him and she has proven herself fertile. Her children are strong and healthy. She was a beauty in her day and even now is considered a woman of charm."

"Is she pleasant to anyone other than the Emperor?" I ask.

Lady Wan hesitates. "She is very ambitious for her children," she says. "No Emperor has ever been born to the ruling Empress. Every son chosen for the throne has been the offspring of a concubine. So if a concubine bears a son who pleases his father she could one day become mother to an Emperor. Lady Ling hopes to achieve this. She is kind to those who do not stand in her way but to those whom she sees as rivals..." she trails off.

"What do you mean, rivals?" I ask.

"Those who have borne sons for the Emperor," says Lady Wan. "Those women who have borne no children, or only daughters, count her as a friend – and they seek her protection, which she will give freely. But those who have borne sons are afraid of her, for she is a formidable woman at court and has the Emperor's ear."

I think this over. Certainly it's not my intention to bear sons for the Emperor but Lady Ling is likely to look at me and see a young woman new to court, who may well bear children in due course. I'll have to watch my step with her. I don't need enemies at court. I believe I've already made one but I don't know why.

"Can you tell me about the Empress?" I ask.

Lady Wan looks sad. "I have known the Empress Ula Nara

since she was a young girl. We both entered the Forbidden City as concubines when the Emperor was still a prince," she says. "She was full of romantic notions and hoped for the Prince's favour. But the Prince was in love with his Primary Consort, the Lady Fuca. They were very well matched." She gives a small smile. "We concubines were hardly ever called for – he was so happy with Lady Fuca. When he became Emperor, he made her his Empress, as we all expected. But Ula Nara was beside herself with jealous grief. The years went by and still she hoped for the Emperor's favour. Having failed to attract the Emperor's attention, she tried to endear herself to his mother, the Empress Dowager, by being the very model of a dutiful daughter and becoming an expert in court etiquette. There is no-one as well versed in the rituals of the Forbidden City as she is. But despite her efforts, the Emperor was still uninterested in her."

"What happened when the Empress Fuca died?" I ask.

Lady Wan's voice drops to a whisper. "She took a fever and died so quickly that none of us were prepared. In his anguish at her death the Emperor went almost mad. He ordered mourning throughout the Empire and even had people executed for not showing proper grief for his Empress. We all of us feared for his health. He said he would not appoint another Empress, that he could not bear for another woman to take her place. But his mother, the Empress Dowager, insisted. She said it was not fitting for the court to be without an Empress, and she recommended Ula Nara as a worthy successor. Reluctantly, the Emperor agreed, although he waited until the full mourning period was complete before he allowed Ula Nara to be made Empress."

"Was she happy?" I ask.

Lady Wan slowly shakes her head. "The Empress was at first overjoyed. But soon it became clear that the Emperor did not really favour her. Of course she was the Empress and he accorded her all proper respect, but she was called frequently to his rooms for only a few years – during which she bore him three children – and then he began to call for her less and less. It is known that he no longer calls for her."

"Doesn't he like her?"

"She is a very jealous woman. She has often made her displeasure known to the Emperor when he has shown an interest in the other women of his court. She is known to hate Lady Ling because she has been shown much favour. The Emperor finds such jealousy tiresome but the less favour he shows to Ula Nara, the more she craves it."

I swallow. I was right. The Empress must find any new concubine arriving at court a galling sight and now I am that new concubine. "How do I stay out of trouble?" I blurt out.

Lady Wan pats my hand. "Oh my dear," she says. "I have scared you! I did not mean to. The court is not an easy place for a young woman. Those of us who have been here many years have found our own ways to be happy. For myself, I have always lived a quiet life. I am not ambitious and so perhaps I have not risen very high – but then I have lived a happy and comfortable enough life here, with my servants and my own pastimes. Consorts Qing and Ying – well, they have found their own happiness in their friendship together. If you are not ambitious, then those that are will not consider you worth troubling themselves with."

I nod, as though grateful for her advice. I'd take it, too, if I were on my own here. A full belly, a warm bed, servants and whatever pastimes a lady here is allowed – boring, perhaps, but how bad could such a life be? But I'm not free to take a quiet path. Iparhan wants information and that means that I must choose a path that will take me straight to the Emperor – and incur the wrath of the ambitious women who surround him.

I let the talk pass on to other things and when we leave Lady Wan clasps my hands. "Visit me again!" she begs. I agree that I will. She's frightened me but what she's told me has put me on my guard and for that I'm grateful. Besides, I'm sorry for her, she seems lonely.

In my palanquin, being carried the short distance back to my own palace, I think over what I've been told. I feel as though I've been set down in a nest of snakes and told to tell them apart, the venomous from the harmless. It seems that I can count Lady Wan as a friendly face, and perhaps her friends Consorts Qing and Ying will prove friends to me too. But Lady Wang seems one to watch and I am certain Lady Ling is watching me. As for the Empress... I bury my face in my hands for a moment. How am I to survive with Iparhan outside the walls and the Empress within them? I seem to be trapped between two women, each of them half-crazed with their own obsessions.

"Poor Lady Wan," says Huan once we are home. "She is more than twice your age but she will never be promoted now. She was young when the Emperor was young. He has his pick of younger women now and she is old and wrinkled. But kind," he adds. "She has never been a schemer."

"It sounds like everyone else is," I say. "It's scheme or be forgotten. As it appears I have been," I can't help adding.

"The Emperor will not have forgotten you," Huan promises. "No other lady dresses or smells like you."

Huan and Jiang are intrigued by my perfume. At first they are curious. They beg to know my secret.

I plead innocence. "I was born this way," I say, lying for all I'm worth. "In my cradle, I smelt like this."

They gape at me. Then I notice that they've begun to take an immense pride in this 'wonder' that is my supposed natural fragrance.

They tell all the servants of every other palace that, yes, indeed, their mistress is naturally perfumed.

"The perfume-maker has been called to every lady's palace," says Jiang, eyes sparkling. "He has been ordered, cajoled, bribed with many taels of silver and threatened with whippings. He must make new perfumes for every lady. Every perfume must be better than those requested by the other ladies. All of them must be better than yours."

This rivalry worries me. I don't want to draw unnecessary attention to myself, especially from the more ambitious or jealous women. But Huan and Jiang are happy. "Every lady must be known for something, madam," they assure me. "And your perfume is without equal, for it is not made by the hands of a man."

I think of the tiny vial hidden in my bed and nod gravely.

Wary of losing this unique gift they anxiously ask me what they must do to ensure the perfume does not depart from my body.

"Who knows?" I say. In truth, the perfume itself is causing me some concern. I am known for it – so what happens if it runs out? I use it sparingly, but use it I must, or its absence will be remarked on. What if Iparhan refuses to give me more until I have provided her with information? I try to plan for the day when I am without it. "No one has ever found a way to make it stronger nor weaker," I tell them. "It could leave my body at any time."

Worried, they put their heads together and ponder. It's imperative that I should keep my unique scent. They make lists of possible substances that will support and enhance my odour. Their latest agreement is that it must be something I eat. As the Emperor says I smell like a lotus flower, then it must surely be the lotus. With this in mind I'm served lotus seed cake (even though I prefer sweet sesame buns) and stir-fried lotus roots. The roots are also served pickled, in soups, stews and deep fried. I find them a bit stringy, but I eat them by the plateful while the two of them stand behind me, beaming.

They fill my rooms with vases of lotus flowers and have planted so many in the garden pond it's a wonder the fish can still move. The petals and leaves are used to adorn dishes on my table. The dried seed cups are used for decoration and even added to the carvings around my doorways. They only make me worry even more – with all these reminders of my 'natural' perfume, what will happen if I no longer have access to it?

"I'd like *something* other than lotus flowers embroidered on my clothes," I say, when the first batch of them arrives back from the dressmakers. Lavish silks in every possible colour are spread out before me, made into skirts. Waistcoats in velvets and more silks are paired with them. All of them are covered in embroideries and gems picking out the shape of the lotus flower. Every shade from purest white through to deepest pink illustrates the petals. Green stems and wide-open pad-like leaves twine about them, growing up from rippled blue waters. Dragonflies and songbirds twirl about their petals, skimming the water below. Silver threads trace the delicate shape of the seed-pods. They are extraordinary.

The palest, most see-through gauze imaginable makes up my new shirts. Most of them are indecent without a waistcoat on top.

"I can't breathe!" I complain as the buttons are done up.

Huan stands his ground, adhering doggedly to the new principles of dress to which he's now sworn. "Your ladyship said they should be *fitted*," he remonstrates. "To enhance your ladyship's exquisite figure."

"I still have to be able to breathe and eat!"

Along with my new clothes arrives a gift. Gifts have been arriving since I got here, from various courtiers, anxious to ingratiate themselves, from new officials posted to my homeland, from lesser ladies of the court. Most of them are small, delicate gifts of precious stones, or perhaps platters of towering fruits and flowers.

The new gift is a large parcel, which, unwrapped, reveals a length of exquisite green silk. It is decorated with fine embroidery but Huan tuts as soon as he sees it.

"What's wrong with it?" I ask.

"The Emperor hates the colour green," says Huan. "The lady sending you this is hoping that you will not know this, that you will perhaps wear it in His Majesty's presence and so displease him. Fortunately you are surrounded by good servants to protect you from such trickery," he adds, snatching the offending fabric away.

"Who sent it?" I ask.

Huan inspects the accompanying seal. His lips set firm. "Lady Wang," he says. "We will know not to trust her from now on," he adds.

"You could have it made into a skirt that I only wear when I don't see him," I suggest. "It's not as though I've seen him since I got here," I add.

Huan mutters something uncomplimentary under his breath about Lady Wang and has the fabric made into a skirt, which he rarely allows me to wear.

Huan and Jiang are excited.

"There is to be a great celebration," they tell me.

"Celebrating what?"

"The conquest of Xinjiang."

I'm puzzled. "Hasn't that been done already? The Emperor claimed it months and months ago."

"Such celebrations must be planned," they explain. "It requires much time. However, the celebrations will begin in a few days. There will be a procession of soldiers, who will display their prisoners of war. The Emperor and the court will watch them from the Meridian

Gate, celebrating the peace which will now come to his empire, both through his army's victory and his marriage to you."

I don't like the thought of the attention this will draw to me but at least it's a chance to remind the Emperor of my existence. Meanwhile Huan and Jiang flutter away to consider my clothes and hair.

The orange silk allowed by my rank shimmers in the pale spring sunlight, making it high summer. Blue silk waves are embroidered at the hem. Across my skirts and waistcoat fly phoenixes. My cap is blue and gold, my plaits woven in the same colours with silken cream lotus flowers placed here and there. I'm shown what I look like in a mirror but I inspect myself only briefly. The face looking back at me reminds me too much of Iparhan.

We leave the Inner Court behind, heading for the huge public spaces, and finally arrive at the Meridian Gate, the tallest building, where I'm guided to a seat looking out across the vast complex. I bow towards the Emperor, who seems to barely acknowledge me, to his mother, who looks me over and then turns away and to the Empress.

Her eyes slide over my clothes, my hair, my face. Her own face does not change. It is like a mask, her eyes still, her neck turning where she wishes to look. Her expression is blank, as though I am not there, although she is looking straight into my eyes. I lower my gaze. She is frightening me. First hate, then nothing. What is she thinking?

I feel lost in a sea of dazzling robes and unknown faces, most of them turned towards me. My clothes mark me out here, I am the only person dressed in this style. Courtiers bow to me and I try to acknowledge them, though I'm unsure of which rank requires what sort of response. In the end I fix my eyes firmly ahead of me on the spectacle below us, hoping to avoid any further errors of etiquette. I can hear whispers amongst the crowd and make some of them out.

"Did you note the casket by the Emperor? It contains the left ears of the two rebellious Khodjas, a trophy."

It contains one of their ears, I think. *I don't know who the other one belongs to. The second left ear that should be there lies beneath a scarred poplar tree in the desert to the far west of here, under a dome shaped inexpertly by Iparhan's grieving hands.*

Below us a parade begins, with countless troops declaring their spoils and victories, while the Emperor looks on, smiling benevolently. Still I can hear the whispers from the courtiers.

"Oh, the prisoners of war. Are those the troops or some of the nobles? Is that their general who…"

"Who knows. They all look the same to me."

"Even the new concubine?"

"They're all the same. Dog-Muslims, my husband calls them."

I was wrong. There are people here dressed like me, in the style of Altisharh. They are the prisoners of war, dragged here to be displayed and gloated over. My eyes suddenly fill with tears of fear. If anything should go wrong with this plan, if anyone should find out who I really am, I too would be displayed below – and executed afterwards. My little escape bundle seems ludicrous. I wipe the tears away discreetly, hoping no one notices, and bite my lip as hard as I can to distract myself.

The Emperor has composed a poem commemorating the celebration and now it is read aloud:

"The casketed Khodja's heads are brought from desert caves;
The devoted Sultan knocks at the palace gates…
By Western lakes, the might of Qing Eternal is decided,
At the Meridian Gate our triumph is thrice proclaimed.
From this day forth, we no longer stay this military course.
My people, sharing joyful plenitude, now shall take their rest."

I think of Iparhan, somewhere in Beijing, hearing this poem immortalising her father and uncle's deaths as nothing but the crushed

171

and fallen enemies of the victorious Emperor. Her rage brings my fingers fluttering to my neck over and over again and by the time the procession is over the hollow of my throat is red with rubbing.

At last we can leave. Huan strides ahead, clearing the way for me to get back to the safety of my palanquin and palace. I'm almost shaking with relief. It's clear many courtiers think little of my people and I've no desire to be anywhere near the Empress.

But Jiang catches at my sleeve. "The Empress Dowager," he hisses. "She has summoned you to her."

I bite my lip again and taste blood. Slowly, I turn and make my way back to the three thrones. The Emperor is speaking with one of his generals, oblivious to me. The Empress Dowager is waiting for me to kneel to her. Barely an arm's length from me is Empress Ula Nara, who watches me as I approach.

I stumble as I rise from my kowtow and feel my face grow hot and red under their gaze.

The Empress Dowager is a tall woman, made larger by the grandeur of her robes and the squareness of her jaw. She dispenses with the niceties of greetings. "You cried," she says. "When the prisoners of war were displayed."

Her eyes must be as sharp as a hawk's. "Yes, Your Majesty."

"Why?"

The truth would be impossible. "I – I am a little homesick, Your Majesty," I stutter. It's a poor excuse but it's all I have.

She nods. "All the ladies are at first," she says. "You will grow accustomed to your new life and the world within these walls. Each lady finds her own way to be happy." She considers me for a moment. "Or not."

"Yes, Your Majesty," I say, keeping my voice soft so she won't hear it trembling.

She doesn't speak again, only looks closely at me, her eyes travelling over my clothes and hair. Then she makes a dismissive gesture, a quick jerk of the chin. I step backwards with care, afraid of stumbling again. As I move away I risk a glance over my shoulder. The two women, Empress and Empress Dowager, are watching me leave. I trip as I get into my chair and only Huan's steady hand saves me from falling.

I'm not sure what to do. Staying away from court will not allow me to fulfil Iparhan's wishes. Being in the gaze of the court is terrifying. I find myself seeking out distractions, ways to forget why I am here and avoid having to make a move.

Yapping brings me to the window. Two tiny dogs are frisking about under Jiang's delighted gaze.

"Whose are they?" I ask.

He jumps up, flustered. "My lady! They are my pets. They are bothering you. Naughty. *Naughty!*" he shrieks at them.

I laugh and sit down on the steps, holding out my hands to be sniffed. "Can I play with them?"

I hold them down while he brushes their silken coats. "Are cats allowed here?" I ask.

"Would you like a cat?"

"A kitten?"

The next day Jiang comes to me with a half-wild black kitten, enraged at his capture, who hisses and backs away when I hold out my hand. When I seize him by the scruff of the neck and lift him up to look at me he flattens his ears and spits. It takes only a few hours and a small dish of egg yolk to tame him. I call him Fury and he lives up to the name, attacking lizards in the garden. When he swiftly graduates to snakes I stand and look on in horror while the eunuchs shriek and poke ineffectually with brooms. Fury wrestles the snakes

173

to their death, risking their gaping mouths and slashing fangs while his still-tiny body whirls through the air. He always wins and his smugness in victory is palpable.

Slowly my palace becomes a menagerie. There are caged birds everywhere, hanging above the walkways, in the garden, even in my sitting room. Some are set free every day, to whirr about in the evening sky before returning to their familiar roosts. Others are taken for a 'walk' in the courtyards and gardens each day, sitting inside cages that swing back and forth from the end of long poles.

I have fish brought to the pond in my garden. A greedy heron lives there and can eat a pail of the wriggling, glinting, bodies a week.

The beloved little dogs of the various eunuchs are allowed free rein. The courtyard and palace fill up with chattering and barking, mewls and squawks, as well as the shrieks of maids and eunuchs either playing with the creatures or running about keeping the place tidy, following small trails of destruction. It's a vast improvement on the endlessly refined silence of days passing. I like to sit in my garden, stroking the ears of a panting dog and watching Fury stalk shadows. It lets me forget why I am really here. Perhaps, I think, I could just live here quietly, like Lady Wan. But the little rough patch on the hollow of my throat tells me otherwise.

Huan is in the doorway with news although he seems reluctant to divulge it.

"Well?"

"The Empress has summoned you."

I can feel my heart speed up. "Summoned me for what?"

"She wishes you to visit her in her palace."

"Why?"

Huan looks uncomfortable. "She has been known to request visits from His Majesty's other ladies," he admits.

"For what purpose?"

Huan twists a little under my worried gaze. "She rarely calls for one of the ladies. When she has done so in the past... it has been to ascertain..."

"Ascertain *what*?" I ask.

"She calls for those ladies of whom she is jealous," says Huan in a rush, trying to get it over with quickly. "She will try to frighten you away from His Majesty, to dissuade you from any ambitions you may have in his regard."

"I've not even spoken to him since my first day here!"

"Even so. The Empress disliked the attention given to the celebrations for the conquest of Xinjiang. She sees you as part of that."

"I attended because I was told to and I left as soon as I could," I protest.

Huan is already busy planning. I could have done with him in Kashgar, he's born for survival in difficult situations. "You will dress humbly," he says. "Perhaps in the green silk Lady Wang sent so that the Empress will not think you are dressing to please the Emperor. You will show her every respect and you will agree with whatever she says. Spend as little time there as possible."

He's making me nervous. "What do I say to her?" I ask.

"Nothing, if you can help it," says Huan. "She will twist your words against you."

I'm shaking by the time Huan is finished with me. My hair would shame him under any other circumstances. I have two plain braids, adorned only with green ribbons. I wear the ill-wished green silk skirt with a plain white shirt and a hastily-made green waistcoat. I'm dressed as humbly as is possible without borrowing a robe from a maid. Huan bites his lip at the sight of me but calls for my chair and watches me from the palace courtyard as I am carried away.

We travel down the narrow lanes linking one palace to another. The day is overcast and the little paths are gloomy. Spent lanterns hang everywhere awaiting nightfall. I wish they were lit now, to bring some warmth and light to this unwelcome journey.

At last we turn through a gateway into a large courtyard. The Empress' palace is far larger than mine. The courtyard is full of fragrant white flowers and should be a delightful sight, but the eunuch waiting to greet me is unnervingly silent. He bows and gesture to me to follow him into the palace. I do so, feeling more and more nervous as I enter.

I'm show into what must be the sitting room. If I thought my rooms were lavish, I was wrong. This room is more elaborate than anything I could have dreamed of. There is a huge screen at one end of the room, decorated in gold and black silk with a pattern of flying cranes over a mountaintop. It stands taller than a man and gives a heavy air to the room. Indeed, the whole room feels heavy and silent, too full of precious objects, as though they are clustered here to bring comfort or show status rather than for beauty or because their owner liked them. I stand uncomfortably in the room until the eunuch indicates a chair by the window. I sit and a maid brings a little bowl of steaming tea and a small dish of sweets. The two servants withdraw and I am left alone, with no indication of where the Empress is or when she might arrive.

I glance at the refreshment I've been left with but I don't touch it. There is no second bowl of tea – am I going to wait here alone for a long time? Or does the Empress not want to eat and drink with me? A small voice inside me tells me I don't even trust the food and drink in this palace.

I look out of the window. Her courtyard garden is silent and still. My own garden is full of animals and bright flowers, but here all is quiet, there are not even any birds. Her flowers are all white, set against artfully piled-up dark rocks in strange formations. It's a cold, hard space.

I shift in my seat. How long will I be kept waiting? Is this some sort of obscure punishment by the Empress, to summon her rivals into her palace and then have them sit in silence, alone and nervous? If so, it's a very effective way to display her authority over a woman of lesser rank.

I stand. Sitting is making me uncomfortable. If I'm to be kept waiting here for a long time without being free to leave – and I don't believe that I am free to leave – then I may as well look about me.

A niche in the wall provides a frame for what is probably a poem, although I can't read it. On a golden table are displayed four *ruyi*, the first a simple though beautifully carved rosewood, the second made of almost-black sandalwood inlaid with rubies. The third is an ornate green jade. The fourth is magnificent, with intricate gold filigree studded with precious gems and characters. These four pieces must be those given to Ula Nara as she was promoted through the ranks of the Emperor's women, the fourth one being when she was made Empress. They are her talismans of success in the Forbidden City and displayed here as though on a shrine. What promises did she make to her gods to be rewarded with the dizzying climb from concubine to a golden throne at the Emperor's side?

I sit down again and sigh. I've been waiting a long time now. The tea has stopped steaming. I dip a finger in it. It's grown cold. I sniff my finger to see if I can smell anything untoward but I can only smell tea. I tap my feet on the ground for a while and then without thinking I do something I haven't done for a long time. I blow a spit bubble. I look cross-eyed down my nose at it as it shimmers and grows. It bursts and I wipe my chin and try again.

"Is this how they raise the daughters of Xinjiang's noble families? Or just you?"

I jump to my feet as the spit dribbles down my chin. The room is empty but the Empress' voice was clear enough. I wipe my chin with a shaking hand and look about me. There's no one here. Her voice came from the far end of the room and there is a door there. I wonder if perhaps she's in an adjacent room. Cautiously, my breath fast and shallow in my chest, I make my way towards the door. But it's firmly closed.

"Behind you."

I whirl round. There's no one. My breath is loud now, it fills the room with my fear. The tall dark screen looms over me, black and gold. Flying cranes and snow-topped mountains.

Eyes.

The Empress is watching me through the gap in the panels of the screen.

I step back, a little scream in my throat and suddenly she is here in front of me, stepping from her hiding place, her robes dark purple, her face a hand's breadth from mine.

"Answer me."

I want to step backwards but there's nowhere I can move to but the closed door behind me. "W-what?"

"Are all the daughters of the noble houses of Xinjiang allowed to blow bubbles from spittle or just you? Or are there no nobles in your cur-ridden land? Have we been sent nothing but a street rat, a flea-infested stray from the back alleys, a prisoner of war masquerading as a woman fit for an Emperor's court?"

I'm trembling and my lips move without noise. I'm struggling to hold her gaze. Does she know everything about me or is she just spitting out every insult she can think of?

"Your – Your Majesty – I – I didn't know you were…"

"Clearly not," she says. Without moving her head she allows her eyes to slide to one side, taking in my untouched tea and sweets. "You have not partaken of the refreshments I offered you."

"N–no," I manage.

"Why not?" She moves slightly to one side of me, giving me an opportunity to back away from her, towards the tray bearing the cold bowl of tea. I nearly back straight into it and stop myself just in time. She has followed me across the room, matching me step for step. She looks down at the offending refreshments. "Drink. Eat."

"I – I would rather..." My voice trails off. Refusing is not an option. I move my fingers down by my side without taking my eyes off her face and feel about until I touch the small bowl. I lift it with trembling fingers and feel a little tea slosh over the side, wetting my hand. I don't dare react to it. I bring the bowl to my mouth and take a sip. It tastes only of tea. Cold, slightly bitter, tea. I drain the bowl as fast as I can, my throat clenching with every swallow, then set the bowl back down, my hand still wet.

"Eat," she commands. Her voice is steady, her face is blank. Her eyes stay fixed on mine.

The sticky sweets feel as though they are gluing my teeth together. There are too many to be eaten at one sitting but I eat them all, my jaw aching, my throat too dry. I choke a little under her fixed gaze and put my hand over my mouth, afraid of spraying her purple silk with half-chewed food. Finally it is over. I wait. I daren't speak.

Her face moves forward. She is so close her breath is on my lips and her eyes are blurring into one all-seeing eye, the eye of some monster from a storyteller's dark mind. "Welcome to the Forbidden City, concubine," she says.

I don't reply. I stand still and wait for more – for her nails on my cheek, for her fingers round my throat.

She doesn't move. "Return to your rooms," she says at last.

I back away, expecting her to follow me but she doesn't. She stands where I left her, staring at the wall behind where my head was as though seeing something else there.

I run. I forget any pretence at dignity, at graciousness, at elegance. I run through her rooms, afraid I will lose my way and somehow find myself faced with the Empress again. I see the door leading to her garden and run at it, slamming both hands into it so that it opens too fast and I almost fall down the steps. My bearers look up, startled.

"Run!" I cry at them and almost throw myself into the chair. It lurches upwards, one of my legs still dangling out of it. They run, the chair shuddering at the pace, my body jolted.

I feel sick. I'm afraid of why. Am I scared? Or poisoned? At last we come through the gate to my own garden and I am out of the chair before it's even fully stopped and running to one of the great metal urns that is filled with plants and a small tree. My fingers press against the back of my tongue and I heave again and again, a horrible flow of tea and sweets pouring over my hand and into the earth.

Jiang is at my side and screaming for Huan. Huan takes one look at me and calls for water, which he makes me drink, then thrusts his own fingers into my throat so that I retch again and bring up dirty water. Huan half-drags me back into the palace and to my bedroom. He dismisses everyone but Jiang.

"Were you poisoned?" he asks, all but ripping my green silk clothes from me and lifting me into the bed.

"I don't know," I say. My voice is hoarse from crying and gagging. "She made me eat and drink even though I didn't want to. Then I felt sick. I didn't know if it was poison but I was afraid."

Huan finishes covering me. "The water will have cleaned your stomach," he says. "It may not have been poison."

"She made me eat," I repeat, starting to cry. I can't think how to describe to Huan the fear I felt. Saying that the Empress kept me waiting and then made me drink tea and eat sweets... how does that describe what I felt, the fear that surrounded me?

Huan waves away my explanation. "The Empress has frightened many women," he says. "You will stay away from her."

"If she calls for me again..." I begin, shaking at the thought.

"She will not," says Huan. "She tries to frighten the new women, she tries to make sure they will not be rivals to her. She will have finished with you now."

I begin to sleep badly. Night after night I dream of the imperial women. I see the Empress' dark eyes watching me through a screen of green silk, ripped as though by unseen claws. I see Lady Wan's wig tumble, leaving her bald. I see Lady Ling with an endless parade of children who surround me and yank at my clothes, pulling me down to the ground with their little hands while their mother watches, smiling. I wake sweating and ask myself what I was thinking of, to agree to Iparhan's plan. When I sleep again I feel once more the thud as her dagger pinned my sleeve to the blackened poplar tree and I have my answer: I had no choice.

The weather turns warm and one morning when I wake the maids are rushing about. Piles of clothes, blankets and coverlets, kitchen utensils and more make their way from the palace in armfuls, chestfuls, cartfuls.

I watch from my sitting room. "Where are they going?"

Jiang answers from under a heap of silk clothes. "The imperial gardens – the summer palace, my lady. We leave tomorrow."

"We?"

"The whole court, your ladyship. To escape the heat."

"Heat? It's not even mid-spring. It's just started getting warmer!"

He's serious. "The summer brings many illnesses – miasmas,

plagues. The hot winds are very injurious to health. The Emperor always leaves as the warm weather arrives."

"Where is the summer palace?"

He draws me a map. I study it and frown. "It's barely any distance. We could walk there. The weather can't be that different."

He shakes his head. "The summer palace is built on the lakes. They draw the cool breezes."

"And where do we live there?"

"You will have another palace. Just as lovely as this one, but far more suited to the summer heat."

The procession my household joins is endless. Palanquins. Guards everywhere. Maids and eunuchs in a blur of blues and greens.

Inside my chair I'm nervous. I keep my curtains closed at first, peeking through them only occasionally. I'm afraid that somehow one of my 'family' might seek to see their 'daughter' ride by. But I peek out at the moat as we cross over it. The waters are a dark murky green. As we cross the bridge from the Forbidden City's gate into Beijing itself I see that the streets are lined with bamboo screens standing higher than a man's head. We're making our way through this strange bamboo-coloured tunnel, behind which I can hear the noises of everyday street life. I pull the curtain fully aside and call for Huan. He hurries to me.

"Why are there all these bamboo screens?"

"The Emperor must not be seen by commoners, madam."

I shake my head and let him go back to his place in the procession. I feel safer now, and I leave the curtains open for the cool air they bring and watch my guards and servants as they march alongside me. Then I doze for a little while.

A familiar voice brings me wide-awake and sweating in an instant.

"Find out how a eunuch is made. Every detail."

I look out, startled, straight into the eyes of Iparhan. She's wearing a guard's uniform, her hair pulled back tight simulating a queue beneath her helmet. Her scar suits her soldiers' garb.

I gape at her.

"Find out," she says. "I will come for the answer."

She is gone. I clutch at the window, look both ways. My maids and eunuchs, my guards, look back at me. One eunuch hurries to my side.

"Do you desire something, my lady?"

"I – I am unwell," I choke. My chest feels tight and I struggle to bring air into my lungs.

My palanquin stops. Huan is sent for. He gives me ginger sweets and exchanges the fan I was holding for another, as though it might better provide me with fresh air. "We will be leaving the city soon," he promises. "Your ladyship can see now, the kind of foul airs that beset the city at this time of year."

I nod, as though a warm spring wind could have made my skin pale and clammy, my throat retch.

Reassured, he fans me for a little while and then gives the signal for us to continue.

As we lurch on our way I think over what I saw and heard. Was it a dream? I was dozing. Perhaps I dreamed of Iparhan, who is never far from my thoughts. Maybe I thought up a demand from her for information I couldn't possibly have. *Find out how a eunuch is made.* Why? What need could she have for such information? I wipe the sweat that has risen under my eyes and on my upper lip. I try to fan myself. I hear the streets grow quieter and pull back the curtain, half-afraid I will see her again. Only my own familiar household figures are nearby. Beyond them, now, are open fields and a cool breeze lifts towards me. I gulp it in and try to assure myself I was only dreaming.

But I know I wasn't. Iparhan has made herself known to me at last. And she wants information. Why she wants it I can't begin to imagine. But if she needs it, then I need it. Thankfully it doesn't involve the Emperor. Yet.

I should be amazed by the summer palace. It is a place of exquisite, unending gardens, encompassing hills and valleys, lakes and buildings. Some of the buildings are Chinese in style and seem familiar to me now. But my own chair is carried to a newer part of the gardens, where very different buildings await me. They are huge and made of carved stone, unlike anything I have seen before.

Huan is proud of their strangeness. "European, my lady," he tells me. "Built by the Jesuits at His Majesty's express command. The other ladies will be staying in the Chinese buildings but you have been given this palace for yourself. It is called the Immense Ocean Observatory."

The servants are already rushing inside, carrying all my belongings, preparing to make everything inside perfect for me. I try to look about me. The stone rises above us, shining white in the bright sunlight. Nearby are huge, fantastical fountains, each spout of water emerging from the mouth of a bronze creature – the twelve animals of the Chinese zodiac. Some of the spray, carried on a soft breeze, reaches my face and I startle.

"Your ocean," says Huan, smiling.

I try to force a smile on my face although I cannot take any of it in.

I ignore offers of food and bathing, rest and entertainment. I ask for Huan and Jiang to bring me tea and to sit with me, alone.

They comply, still concerned for my wellbeing. I wave away sweets and herbal teas, offers of a physician.

"I want to know how you came here," I begin, addressing the

floor, unable to meet their eyes. I feel nauseous at what I have to do and it makes me abrupt. "How you were – made."

They look shocked. Huan frowns. "Why, my lady?"

I haven't thought of a reason. There is no good reason to ask them to tell me about the pain and shame of their early lives. "I – I want to know more about your lives. You – you have been so kind to me and looked after me so well…" I stumble to a halt but their faces have softened a little, soothed by my praise.

Huan takes the lead. "I suppose such things are strange to your ladyship," he says. "Do you not have eunuchs in your land?"

I shake my head.

He nods, serious, then begins. He sounds as though he is telling a story of a far-off place, not his own painful experiences. Perhaps this is how he bears it, by telling his own life as though it were a legend. "Just outside the gates of the Forbidden City in a tumbled-down building dwell the 'knifers'. They have done their work for generations. Boys are sold into service as eunuchs, but any man who wishes can go to them and for six taels of silver they will be castrated, their manhoods lost forever."

I can't help leaning forward. "What happens to them?"

"The man lies on a low bed, and the knifer will ask him if he is certain he will not regret his choice. When he answers that he will not he is given a tea to drink that stuns his nerves. Then tight bandages are wound about his legs and stomach, before three men enter to hold him down. His private parts are bathed in hot pepper water to numb them."

I brace myself for what is to come. Huan takes a deep breath and goes on. "The knifer has a small curved knife. Using quick cuts he removes the – the-"

He comes to an uncertain halt, fearful of damaging my ladylike ears.

I try to imagine what he is trying to say. "Both – parts?" I ask tentatively. "The – and also the...?"

Huan nods.

I wince but gesture to him to continue.

"He takes a metal plug to fit into the man's – hole, that he may not lose the ability to urinate. They cover the wound with water-soaked paper and the man must walk about the room for three hours, supported by the knifers. Then he must lie in that same room for three days. He may not drink nor urinate. Some men become delirious. At the end of those days they pull out the metal plug so that he can urinate. If he fails to do so because the passageway has sealed itself, then he will die in agony.

The three of us sit in silence for a moment, thinking of those men who sacrificed everything in the hope of a better life and in doing so lost the poor life they had. Huan seems drained, his face a little pale.

Jiang picks up from Huan. "After two or three months the eunuch is fully recovered and he may join the household of a prince, where he will be trained for perhaps a year. Every prince of the dynasty owes the palace eight eunuchs every year, who must be trained, inspected and confirmed free from disease and uncleanliness."

I nod. "And the – the parts?" I ask. "Are they – disposed of?'

The two of them look appalled. "Oh, no, your ladyship," says Jiang. "We keep them for ever – if we are buried without them we will not be whole in the afterlife."

Huan has recovered a little. "And they are necessary for our promotions," he adds.

Jiang leaps to his feet and rushes away. I sit in silence for a few moments with Huan, both of us staring into bowls of tea, now grown cold. When Jiang returns he is carrying a small jar, wrapped in a delicate piece of pale blue silk. He hands it to me and I hold it as though the little container might break.

Jiang looks at me holding it and his eyes glisten briefly with tears. I gently pass it back to him and he holds it for a moment and then leaves the room again, this time more slowly. I watch him go and when I look back at Huan he is watching me.

"I am sorry," I say, and I mean it. "I did not wish to cause you both pain."

He looks at me a moment longer, then nods. "I know," he says, his voice gentle. "But you are very young, my ladyship. You are only a child. And a child does not always know that there are some questions that should not be asked."

I turn my face away a little so he won't see the tears rise up at being chastised. His gentleness is a greater punishment than his words. But he touches my shoulder as he stands and later on, as our household goes about its day both of them are kind to me, as they have always been.

Now I have what Iparhan needs. When will she come for the information? Will she wait until we return to Beijing, for that single moment when we are travelling, when she can impersonate a guard, a maid? Or can she find me even here, even within the palace grounds? I wonder whether I could escape before she comes for me. Here, with none of the high red walls or the moat of the Forbidden City, might I be able to slip away more easily?

I sit, with no appetite, in front of the dishes laid out before me. The sweets and vegetables are good. The cooks have been trying, with very little success, to cook traditional foods from my homeland. Today, the *polo* rice dish is a disaster. It drips with grease. I tried to explain how to make it but having never made it myself before had to describe the end result rather than the recipe. I told them it should be generously fatty but this coats my throat and I have to ask for a sharp plum juice to cut through the layer of oiliness.

Huan's eyes fill with tears of despair. "Beat me, my lady. I have failed you."

"Oh, stop that!" I snap at him. "It's just too oily. Tell the cooks to try again another day."

There's the now-familiar thump as everyone hits the floor in a miserable bow. I feel like bursting into tears myself. It would be easier just to eat the food they make here; it's probably delicious. Their attempts at my food are laughable. I feel like a fool for insisting on it – I'd have eaten anything when I was on the streets, while these poor wretches think I'm a high-minded noblewoman who can't soil her dainty Muslim mouth with the food of infidels. I get up from the table and walk away, the dishes half-tasted, the knock of heads on the floor echoing behind me as I walk into my bedroom and climb onto the bed, pulling the curtains about me, wrapping myself in the tumble of silk coverlets, tears welling up.

Underneath me is something hard. I reach down and find a tiny flat tablet of wood. On it are painted the first rays of a rising sun over a lake. Nothing else. I turn it over in my hands but I understand it well enough. And I also understand that I cannot hope to escape this place. Iparhan will find me anywhere.

Dawn comes. I slip from my bed, placing my bare feet with infinite care as I tiptoe past the sleeping eunuch whose turn it is to watch over me at night. My bed curtains close behind me, masking my absence from view. The eunuch stirs but doesn't wake and I push the doors open. Thankfully they're kept oiled so no creaks give me away. I wish I'd brought a thicker robe with me, but that would have made more noise. It may be early summer but it still feels cold at this time of day.

I make my way past the fountains and then follow a small path down to the lakeshore. My back is cold on the white stone balustrade.

I shiver and look about me but I'm alone. I peer into the water and the fish rise to the surface, hoping for crumbs that I have not brought.

"At least you understand pictures even if you can't read."

I don't turn to greet Iparhan, just wait in silence. She sits by my side. I look at her feet, spread out in front of her. She's dressed like a maid today, the pale blue robe skimming her ankles. Her feet are bare, perhaps to walk more quietly. They're wet with dew. I never heard her coming.

She grows impatient, snaps her fingers in front of my face. "I can't stay all day," she says curtly. "Stop staring like an idiot. Tell me what I need to know."

I turn. Her face is so close I can see how the scar, now fading to a pale pinked-violet, almost enters her eye. It makes my own blink in sympathy. I try not to stare at it, to keep my gaze fixed on hers, but it's unnerving.

"Do you want to know anything about the palace?" I ask tentatively. "About my life here?" I want to blurt out what happened with the Empress, my fears of the scheming women surrounding me but I am afraid she will be angry that I have unwittingly turned people against me.

"I don't care how you fill your pampered days," she says. "I asked you for information. Do you have it?"

I nod.

"Well?"

"How much do you need to know?"

"I told you. Everything. Every detail."

I take a breath and begin Huan and Jiang's story, the tale repeated over and over again throughout the palace walls and centuries. I keep my face turned away from her and I tell her only what is true of any eunuch. I hold back what I know of Jiang, the beatings received for wetting himself and how Huan helped him, hiding the evidence of his disgrace and washing his robes so the smell wouldn't give him away. Their closeness now. I refuse to let her steal the pain of my kindly servants and use it somehow for her own plans. I'm aware that I almost gabble the details, that I rush them so that I will not have to think of the suffering of the thousands of eunuchs all around us, of the many more thousands that were here before and will come later. Finally I finish. I look at Iparhan but she is unaffected.

"What happens to their private parts?"

"They keep them forever in a jar," I say, omitting the description of Jiang's soft trembling hands on mine as he passed me his little silk-wrapped treasure. "They can never be promoted without them. They need to be buried with them so that the gods of the underworld will believe them to be whole men."

Iparhan snorts. "Infidels."

I want to slap her. Want to make her see Huan and Jiang's eyes, downcast before me. My hand itches.

She presses on. "Do they really stink? I've heard the saying 'he stinks like a eunuch'."

I shake my head. "They have difficulty containing their urination at first and are beaten for it. But once they've been trained they master the flow and smell no different to you or me."

"You had better smell finer than a eunuch," she says. "Do you still have the perfume?"

"Can't you smell it?"

"Yes. Do you need more of it?"

I nod and she passes me a new vial. I take it and drop it in my pocket without looking at it. I don't want her to see the relief in my eyes, I don't want her to know that I was afraid of running out of it.

"How do you discipline the eunuchs?"

I sit back. "Why do you need to know so much about their lives, Iparhan? Didn't Mei tell you about them?"

"I did not need the information then."

"Why do you need it now?"

"That is not your concern."

I wait but I can see she'll say nothing else. The rules governing the eunuch's lives are known to all here. Huan instructed me in them shortly after I arrived, so that I could govern my household. "If they run away they're caught and imprisoned for two months, beaten and sent back. If they do it again they're put in a *cangue* for two months. It's a wooden frame. It stops them lying down or feeding themselves. Some of them die in it. If it happens a third time they're banished to Manchuria for two and a half years, or if they stole something precious they're executed away from the walls of Beijing."

"And for minor matters?"

"For laziness they're whipped one hundred times and then have the wounds dressed. Three days later the dressings are removed and the same place is beaten again to 'raise the scabs'."

Her interrogation doesn't stop. I have to get up to demonstrate the way they walk, imitate their high-pitched voices. Describe their daily duties, from the highest to the most menial. Their careful protection of any hedgehogs found in the gardens, believing them to bring great good luck. Their gambling and the silly little dogs over which they fawn as young mothers with their first child. Their sorrow at not being able to ascend the altars of the main deity in the temples – being deformed they are considered not clean enough to do so. Their sensitivity to taunts about being a 'spoutless teapot' or a 'tailless dog'. The petty squabbles between them. Their tender care towards the women and children who are their only reason for being.

"I've told you everything," I say finally. "There is no more."

"Good," she says. "Now, the Emperor."

I stiffen.

"Have you been called to his bed?"

191

"No."

Something flickers across her face and is hidden. "Why not?"

"I don't know."

Her voice is cold. "I need you in his bed. You're no good to me if you do not lie with him."

I'm angry. "I'm not a whore."

"Yes you are," she says. "You agreed to become a concubine so you would be fed and housed. What else is that but a whore?"

The anger leaves me in a rush. My dreams of living here peacefully were the dreams of a fool. Of course Iparhan has found me. I must play my part or she will follow me for the rest of my days, wherever I might hide. I lean forward, resting my hot forehead on the cool stone of the wall and listen to the sound of the fountains splashing. I let my eyes close. "Don't do this to me again, Iparhan," I say softly. "It was cruel to ask them so many questions. And for what? Why would you care? How could it possibly aid your plans for rebellion? Don't make me hurt the only people I know here."

She doesn't answer. I keep my eyes closed a moment longer, waiting for her to speak, then raise my head.

She's gone.

I'm afraid of the information I've given to Iparhan. I think back to my days in the little house set among the Taklakaman dunes, how I seized on any scrap of information about the Forbidden City, ready to use it to my own advantage once I got here, to be used as a trick, an illusion, a distraction. How will Iparhan use what I have told her? All I know is that she is planning something and that my only protection is to play the part she has given me and give her what she wants. I need to get closer to the Emperor. I try not to think of the Empress.

Most days I walk by the lake. The weather has turned hot and my heavily embroidered silk skirts do nothing to keep me cool. Besides,

I have a secret task that I need to perform alone – throwing the stale cakes, breads or fruits from my secret hoard to the fishes. Back at the palace I replenish my supply daily.

Across the lake rises the Emperor's own palace. I look across the waters and wonder whether I will ever be called to his rooms. I think of ways I might draw his attention but they seem foolish and unlikely to work. I find myself kicking loose pebbles into the water, frustrated by my lack of ideas.

One morning I find someone already at the water's edge, in a scholar's dark robe. His back is to me and I see he's a painter, for he's putting the final touches to a silk painting of a pink lotus flower. Two butterflies dart across the silk, one large and dark, one small and pale.

"Pretty," I venture.

He turns to face me and I step back. Although he's dressed as a courtier, he's not Chinese, nor even from my homeland. He's a foreigner, a European. Old, nearing seventy, with a full white beard and a stooped back.

"Lady He."

"How do you know who I am?"

He chuckles. "I have been here many years," he says. "A new member of the court is worth learning about."

I hope he doesn't learn too much about me, but he seems friendly. "I don't know your name."

"My name is Lang Shining."

"You don't look as though that's your name."

He chuckles. "My original name, then, for you who have such sharp eyes, is Giuseppe Castiglione. I came here many years ago from Italy."

I try to pronounce his name and he has to correct me. "You're a court painter?"

"I am whatever His Majesty requires me to be." He smiles, rueful. "Except, perhaps, that which I would most like to be – a spiritual advisor."

"Are you a priest?"

He nods. "A Jesuit. I followed Our Lord's work to this country many, many years ago but I think perhaps He has in mind for me other lessons. Patience, perhaps."

"I might need to learn that too," I say and he nods. His wry smile tells me he already knows that I've not yet been called for.

"I gather your new name was meant to reflect the lotus," he says. "May I be so bold as to offer you this painting?"

I'm pleased. The palaces I have been given are luxurious beyond words but nothing in them really feels like it belongs to me except the animals. I take the painting and have it hung in my bedroom.

I wake with a start. Loud bangs echo across the lakes. I clutch at my nightclothes. Has Iparhan come? Has she somehow stormed the palace at the head of an army? I pull aside the bed curtains and almost walk into Jiang, who is standing in the darkness just outside, his back to me.

"What's happening?" I whisper.

Jiang turns, lifting up a small lantern. He forces a smile onto his face. "Imperial Noble Consort Ling has been safely delivered of a son, your ladyship. Tonight there are celebrations throughout the Summer Palace."

My thudding heart slows. I make my way to the window. Firecrackers leap into the air, turning the sky many colours. I can hear music from the palaces and chanting inside the temples. The sounds all carry well here, floating across the waters.

I sit in a chair by the window, looking out onto the fireworks reflecting in the lake. The fireworks and celebrations seem far away, in another part of the world, from which I'm separated by the lake before me. The court is celebrating Lady Ling's success while my failure keeps me here alone. I get up and Jiang springs to his feet. "Bring me something to tap my ears," I say. "I want to sleep."

I see the distant figure of Giuseppe and hurry down to the lake to speak with him. I think he might be a useful ally to me. A man who's been at court so many years and is friendly may be able to help me.

"Painting again?"

He opens his arms to demonstrate the lack of painting tools. "Today I only think about painting. Another day I will paint. I am not as busy as the Emperor is in his daily life."

I try to make my voice sound careless. "Do you know how he passes his days?"

He nods.

I was right to seek him out. Giuseppe can help me to understand more about this place and how I can get closer to the Emperor. "Tell me."

"On an ordinary day there are a great many demands on his time. He wakes very early, with the sun. He washes and dresses, then eats breakfast. He enjoys reading history but cannot do so for long, for his ministers and officials await his presence to discuss matters of state."

"Such as?" I wonder whether this is a time when he hears reports from Xinjiang.

"Reports of weather conditions and harvests, passing judgement in serious legal cases, progress on special projects such as the building of temples. And of course there are many, many petitions from his subjects."

I think of the papers he was reading before and after our first meeting. "Doesn't he get bored?"

"He is very conscientious. But after the work of the day is complete he eats his main meal in the mid afternoon."

"Does he have ridiculous amounts of food too?"

He chuckles. "I am sure that however many dishes are brought to your table, far more are brought to his."

I shake my head. "Can't he just order his favourites?"

"He likes bird's nest soup and duck, but mostly he favours game, for he is a keen hunter. But you have seen for yourself how meals are prepared here. Abundance is all."

"And afterwards?"

"He is at liberty to read or write poetry, to paint, attend the theatre or view his art collections. Or to practise his calligraphy, which is very fine."

We walk a little further in silence. Finally I work up the courage to ask what I really want to know. "And his – his evenings?"

"He eats only a light meal at sunset."

"What's a light meal in these parts?"

He chuckles to acknowledge the truth of my question. "Then he prays. He is a Buddhist, sadly for me."

"Neither of us is successful with him, then."

He chuckles. "You still have many years ahead of you, Lady He. I am sure you will be more successful than I."

I shrug. "So – his evenings?"

He smiles, understanding what I'm really asking. "Part of his evening is spent with a companion, who I believe is usually chosen in the morning. A tray is proffered with the names of the palace ladies written on little tablets. He chooses one and she is then informed. This gives her the opportunity to prepare herself – I understand it may take some time," he adds, with a hint of mischief.

"I was told he would not stay the night," I say, wondering if this was just nonsense, stories put about by the servants to make more of a mystery of the event.

"He does not, if he is visiting you. He will stay in the other bedroom."

"And if I visit him?"

"Then you will be escorted back to your own palace."

"Why?"

"The Emperor must get a good night's sleep so that he can be rested for his duties in the morning."

"So he thinks we ladies might snore, or kick him in the night?"

He laughs out loud, startling a heron by the water's edge. "I think it is a protection against assassination. Or perhaps against infatuation." He grows a little more serious. "Either of which are grave dangers to a ruler."

"Well, he needn't fear either from me. I've only been near him twice and I'm not sure he even remembers me."

Giuseppe stops and looks at me. "I am sure he does," he says with kindness. "It is only a matter of time."

"Everyone says that," I say, kicking a large pebble into the lake.

"Then they are right," he says. "And may I offer some humble advice, Lady He?"

"Go on," I say.

"I can tell that you wish to know more about the court. But be careful what questions you ask, and of whom."

"Why?"

"There are many secrets at court, Lady He."

"Are there?" I ask.

He stops walking and turns to face me. "We all have secrets, Lady He," he says. "I am sure you have your own, do you not?"

I can feel my mouth turn dry. I force a smile and quickly swallow, trying to bring back my voice. "I suppose everyone does, " I say. "I'll be sure not to ask the wrong questions."

Giuseppe regards me for too long a moment, as my smile struggles to stay on my lips. "A wise choice," he says at last and although his voice is kind, his eyes are searching and I find it hard to hold his gaze.

The hem of my skirt, the green silk from Lady Wang, is soaked in dripping mud. The dogs followed me on a walk and now they rush in and out of the water, full of excitement, wetting me and ruining the silk. I suppose Huan will not mind, I think. He never liked this skirt anyway and I'm not that fond of it myself after my encounter with the Empress. Above the yapping I hear another high-pitched sound and turning, find Huan and Jiang running through the gardens towards me, shrieking.

"What is it?" I ask as they reach me.

They're panting from their headlong rush and rosy-cheeked. "My lady, he is here!"

I've waited so long I don't even know what they mean. "Who?"

"The Emperor. We received no prior warning! He is making his way to your palace. You must be ready to receive him!"

I gape at them. This moment, so long awaited, has come too soon.

Huan is almost wailing at the sight of me. "Green! Why did you have to be wearing the green?" he moans, indicating my skirt. "And mud everywhere. How did that *happen*?" He doesn't wait for an answer, just stretches out his hands beseechingly towards me.

I take a step in the direction of the palace. Heedless of protocol they each grab one of my arms and begin to run back towards the palace, forcing me to run between them, my wet skirts clinging to my legs. Within a few strides I'm out of breath. It's a long time since I've done any running.

Inside is chaos. Maids and eunuchs run in all directions, some ensuring the palace itself is prepared, others with animals in their arms, hiding them away. The muddy dogs cause even more horror than my clothes. When we arrive a wave of servants come towards me, sweeping me towards the bathroom. Hands engulf me, tearing off my clothes as we go, so that I reach the room entirely naked. Behind us, maids on their knees clean the floor of the mud I have dripped through the rooms. Water splashes everywhere, I narrowly avoid soap in my eyes and already I'm out and dried, being hurried back to my room, where clothes are thrown this way and that. Huan is combing my hair, his usually gentle hands ripping through it so hard that I cry out.

"Hush," he begs me, almost weeping. "You must be ready for His Majesty. This is your moment!"

I bite my tongue hard to stop myself swearing at the pain.

Normally I dress myself, with maids helping here and there with fastenings and passing items to me. The dressing and hairdressing is a leisurely pastime, designed as much to kill time as to prepare me for an empty day. Now I'm being dressed like a child, my limbs not my own. In a few brief moments I'm resplendent in shimmering silk, velvet and gauze. Pink and white lotus flowers rise up from the pristine waves of my blue silk skirt, reaching towards the magnificent golden waistcoat as though it were the sun. My sleeves bear the outlines of wheeling birds. My still-damp plaits are interwoven with gold threads and interspersed with tiny pink lotus flowers carved from tourmaline, glinting against the gold.

Jiang is almost hopping in the doorway. "I can hear his approach," he whimpers.

Huan pulls me to my feet. I nearly fall flat on my face. The heels on my shoes are higher than I've ever worn before. I'm almost his height.

"You are ready," he pants. I'm about to reply when he turns on the other servants. "Get out, get *out*," he cries. "Get ready or I'll have you all whipped!"

There is a rush for the doors, as each servant tidies their own appearance and hurries to their stations.

Huan turns back to me. "You should be in the receiving hall," he hisses. "Come."

But I stand still. "I need to be alone." I say. "Just for a moment."

Huan and Jiang's looks of horror would make me laugh if I wasn't so scared. "Alone? *Now*?"

I nod vigorously. "You must leave me. Now!"

I've never raised my voice to them and they both take a step back, then reluctantly leave the room. I almost throw myself at the bed, slipping my hand down the side of it to find the tiny gap where the vial of perfume is hidden. The hot water splashed all over me will have washed off the scent. Hastily I dab more of it on, then hide the vial again before running to the door of the bedroom and making my way through to the receiving hall. I arrive panting and turn immediately towards the windows, looking for the Emperor's palanquin. Sure enough there is the imperial yellow chair in my courtyard. I put a hand to my throat and then take a deep breath, waiting for him to step out of it. This, then, is the moment I become a whore and a spy.

"You were expecting me, Lady He?" A deep voice, amused, behind me.

I turn to face the Emperor, already seated on the throne, surrounded by his own servants and mine.

Dream

BELIEVING HIMSELF USEFUL NURMAT HAS *been making enquiries in the Muslim quarter and beyond for the past month and more. Now he has gathered together allies to our cause. Those of our own country, who, like my own family, have been crushed beneath the Emperor's armies and seen their leaders fall. Who have lost wealth and power. And those from further afield, the countries bordering our own, fearful for the future should the Emperor look beyond his New Dominion and see further conquests to be had. They too, come to us and swear loyalty to our cause. They talk late into the night, making and remaking plans.*

We rode fast, away from the fortress. The darkness of the night concealed our escape and by morning we were far away from the Emperor's banners.

My tears fell as we rode. My mother gone, my uncle gone. Our position lost. My father wounded. He said, through gritted teeth, that he would recover and we would carry out our plan for rebellion, but I knew already that he would not survive. The pain on his face as we rode told me he had not long to live. Nurmat rode with his mouth in a grim line and behind him, her old face frightened, rode Mei. She knew that our power was waning, that we were clutching at the last vestiges of our status, and she feared for her life.

The little house in the dunes waited for us, our hideaway, prepared many years before and now newly stocked with food and goods. Nurmat helped my father inside while Mei, her old body stiff, hobbled along behind, ready to cook and clean for us.

I sat on my horse, the incessant desert wind blowing my plaits. Hot tears turned cold on my cheeks. Slowly I slipped down from the saddle, lifted my head, wiped my eyes and went to my father, my face showing none of my growing fear.

The men talk on and I listen with only one ear. Perhaps I should be planning uprisings, but in my mind is only one image, an image I see every night when I go to sleep. A battle rages around me. The Emperor's face, close to mine, blood tricking from his mouth, as I plunge a dagger deep into his chest and twist the blade. To others it might be a violent image, to me it is soothing. I fall asleep when I have this image in my mind, the relief of his life draining away so great that my muscles can at last relax and allow me peace in the darkness.

The Hunt

I FALL TO MY KNEES AND perform the elaborate kowtow I've
practised so often. Where I once cursed the never-ending bows and
the discomfort of the position, now I'm grateful. I have a chance to
slow my breathing although as I stand for the final time I'm well
aware that my face is flushed.

The Emperor is smiling. "Lady He."

"Your Majesty. I'm – I am very honoured to receive you. May –
may I offer you some refreshment?" My eyes slide towards Huan, who
makes a quick gesture that has maids hurrying off in all directions,
soon to return with teas and sweets.

He waves me over. "Come and sit with me," he invites, indicating
a chair which is not yet there but is hastily provided by the ever-
attentive Jiang. "I am sorry I have not visited you before. I have been
very busy."

I sit down, my skin still damp from the bath, awkward under his
gaze. He looks at me, curious. "Do you still have the lotus scent?" he
asks.

I imagine the tiny vial and for a moment I think he knows about
it. I feel my cheeks grow even redder but try to control myself. Of
course he doesn't know, how could he? I think quickly and hold out
my arm to him, newly anointed. "I believe so, Your Majesty."

He takes my hand in his and lifts it to his nose, smells and then
smiles, letting go of my hand as he does so. His skin is very soft. "It
is still there," he says, with some satisfaction. "Truly, like a lotus."

I wait for more questions, but he seems to take it for granted that one of his ladies should be naturally perfumed. Perhaps, I think, he's surrounded by such wondrous things all the time – works of art painted on silk, carved sandalwood furniture, the striking chiming clocks of which I've heard he's fond – that a woman whose very skin releases a scent beyond the skill of the court perfumer is not such a strange thought to him. Instead his mind has turned elsewhere. He looks about the room.

"I used to visit this palace as a child," he says. "It belonged to one of the ladies of my Honoured Grandfather. She was very fond of songbirds. Are you fond of birds?"

"Yes, Your Majesty." I indicate a couple of the hanging cages. "I have many birds myself." As I finish speaking I hear a sharp yap, immediately muffled.

But he has keen ears. "And a dog?" he asks.

I nod, ignoring Jiang's mortified face. "Yes. Several. I have quite a few animals here."

He frowns, looking about. "Where are they, then?"

I'm a little cautious. The court is so formal. He might object to the noisy chaos that is usual in my palace. "They have been taken to other rooms so as not to bother Your Majesty," I say.

He shrugs. "Have them all brought here."

It takes a while. The newly washed and still damp dogs, Fury, my birds, even the latest pail of fish for the garden are brought for his inspection. The room grows noisier with each addition. But he seems pleased rather than put out. When the last dog has joined us he looks about and then chuckles.

"I see you are fond of animals, as you say."

I nod. "They keep me company, Your Majesty."

He tilts his head. "As I do not visit you often enough, is that it?"

I shake my head hurriedly, thinking he's offended but he only laughs. "My mother says you are homesick. Perhaps I should come and see you more often, or next time I visit you will have elephants here."

I smile more broadly. At least he has a sense of humour. Perhaps spending time with him won't be as bad as I feared. If my being 'homesick' has drawn him here then I'll have to pretend to be homesick more often. I'm about to ask him what animals he favours but he's risen to his feet and I follow his lead.

"I must go now," he says.

I nod, although I'm disappointed. Given his past record, I probably won't see him for another few months. Before he reaches the door he turns back.

"Lang Shining told me he enjoys his walks with you. He said he gave you a painting. May I see it?"

A eunuch hurries to my sitting room and returns with the painting of the lotus and butterflies. He examines it, nods and then makes his way to his chair. I bid him farewell, standing on the steps surrounded by my servants and animals, then return indoors.

"I didn't know what to call him," I confess to Huan. *Of all the things not to know,* I curse Iparhan for not telling me this basic information.

"'Your Majesty', of course."

"Doesn't he have a name I can call him – like…" I stop, about to say "like Hidligh", and correct myself. "Like my childhood name?"

Huan shakes his head. "That is no longer your name. You are Lady He now."

"Does no one here have the name they were born with? Not even the Emperor?"

"Especially not the Emperor."

"What was he called as a child, then?"

Huan lowers his voice and looks about as though we might be overheard before answering. "Hongli."

I find myself whispering too. "Why are we whispering?"

"His childhood name is now taboo. As he became older he was given the name Prince Bao. That name is also taboo. Now he is the Qianlong Emperor of the Qing dynasty."

"Can I call him Qianlong?"

Huan shakes his head as though I've said something very stupid. "Qianlong is the name of his reign, not his own name."

I give up. "So I'll just call him *The Emperor*, shall I?"

Huan ignores my tone. "Yes."

I sit back in my chair. The visit has tired all of us; the strain of getting ready and then being in the Emperor's presence – we are too used to days of nothingness. And I can't help feeling disappointed. I was ready to play my part, to ask questions. I thought I would have to lie with him and although the thought frightens me it also somehow draws me. "He didn't stay the night."

Huan shakes his head. "If he had planned to do so we would have been warned this morning." He sighs. "I wish he had, then I could have arranged your hair more elaborately." He tuts, looking it over.

I wave him away, suddenly weary of his fussing. "Hair isn't everything in life, Huan. You sound like Lady Wan's hairdresser. *Why* didn't he want to stay the night?" I was dreading being called to his bed, but now I feel as though I've failed. Did I do something to displease him?

Huan, insulted by my disparagement of his favourite task, only shakes his head and repeats his mantra. "In due course, my lady. In due course."

I send an invitation to Giuseppe to come to my palace. He has helped me and I need to keep him as an ally. He joins me at dusk, as the birds set out on their 'walks' or are set free for their evening flights.

I offer him tea and little mooncakes. "Thank you."

"For what?" he asks, sipping tea.

"You mentioned me to the Emperor and he came to visit me."

"I am sure he was intending to visit you anyway," he says.

I shake my head. "I could have been here for years without seeing him."

He chuckles. "I am sure now you will see him more often. He was most taken with you."

I find myself leaning forward. "Really? What did he say?"

"That your palace was very noisy."

I make a face. "It is. Did it annoy him?"

"Not at all. I believe he found it refreshingly different."

"Did he say when he was coming again?"

"His Majesty does not share his plans with me," says Giuseppe. "But I am sure you will see him again soon."

I sit back in my chair. "Perhaps," I say doubtfully.

But the spell has been broken. The next time the Emperor visits he catches us unawares yet again. Barely a week has passed and the weather is growing ever hotter. Fortunately I'm better dressed this time but I'm sitting on the steps of the building with the dogs while Jiang tries to groom them, as ever with limited success. The birds, hearing the yapping of the over-excited dogs, respond with their own shrieks and cries. Meanwhile Fury begs for food, yowling more and more loudly as we ignore his greed to focus on the dogs.

"I can hear your palace from the other side of the lake," comes a voice.

We leap to our feet and then fall to our knees. The Emperor is standing by the fountains below us, having dismounted from his chair. Behind him stand his many servants, most looking appalled at the spectacle of us.

"Take them away," I hiss at Jiang, who begins to scramble about with a few other servants to try and collect up and hide the various animals.

"Oh, leave them," says the Emperor. "Bring chairs outside. It is a nice day. We will sit by the fountains and you shall continue whatever you were doing."

His commands supersede mine and the carved throne kept for him is brought outside, as are teas and sweetmeats. He ignores the sweets but drinks the tea, encouraging Jiang to continue the grooming. Jiang, aware of his own weaknesses in this respect, calls for other servants, who hold each dog still for him so that for once the grooming is undertaken with some decorum. Meanwhile Fury is given his favourite egg yolk and some of the birds are set free to hop about us. Fury watches them, tail twitching, egg yolk dripping from his eager whiskers.

"You really do like animals," observes the Emperor. "Did you have many as a child?"

Of all the questions I dread, it is questions about my childhood that worry me the most. My 'family' were the Emperor's allies – how much does he know about them? Would he know what kind of childhood I am supposed to have had? I improvise. "Only a small cat, Your Majesty," I say, thinking of the autumn sun in the marketplace of Kashgar and the filched raisins I enjoyed in the company of the small crooked kitten.

He nods. "You were not allowed any other pets?"

I shake my head and make a sorrowful grimace, somehow implying a strict family upbringing. I don't even know if this is right. What if he knows that 'I' had a spoilt childhood, denied nothing? He may seem friendly towards me, kindly in his manner, but I can only imagine what would happen if he were to find out that he has been duped, that sitting by his side is not a noblewoman from a family of his allies but a street rat, a girl who picked up food from the ground if it was tossed to her.

He smiles, benevolent. "You may have as many as you wish here," he says.

I indicate the chaos around us. "I believe I already have, Your Majesty."

But having seen how many animals I have he begins to send me all manner of creatures, even a hedgehog, which the eunuchs revere and which disappears into my garden, to be found only when it wants to be fed fragments of honey glazed buns.

"I like your palace," the Emperor tells me. "It is unlike the others here."

"It's as noisy as the market of Kashgar," I say in an unguarded moment.

"Tell me about Kashgar," he says at once, turning to face me.

I describe the market stalls and he listens, sometimes with his eyes closed to better take in my descriptions. I try to remember mentioning being carried in a palanquin, to describe my 'servants' buying raisins for me.

He continues to visit me often and soon only a few days pass between his visits.

Iparhan was right. He loves to talk of Altishahr – although I have to remember to call it Xinjiang. His new toy, his new conquest. He likes to hear how different it is; it makes him feel that he has taken a far-off land, a whole new country, not merely an adjoining region.

"You must miss it greatly," he says, and I see that he likes this thought, that he's beginning to think of me as a rare bird, longing for its home. I don't try to relieve him of this idea. If it pleases him, if it makes him visit me more often, then that's all to the good.

"I do miss it," I say.

He nods gravely, then reaches out and covers my hand with his. "I will try to make you happy here," he promises.

I smile and wait for him to let go, but he keeps his hand over mine for a little while and when he rises to leave my hand feels cold without his touch.

"Tell me what here is strange to you," he says one day.

"Your Majesty?"

He waves a hand. "In your daily life. What is different from your life before you came here?"

I think of carrying heavy pails of piss and shit alongside the stinking nightsoil men, of old Mut and his hot dumplings tossed to me if they broke up in the pan and were therefore unfit for his paying customers. Nights sleeping out by the tombs. Stealing food, having fake fortunes told to bring in the crowds. The women's lanes edging closer as my only option. I'm silent, but he's expecting an answer and I have to think quickly. The sound of the fountains brings an acceptable answer to mind.

"We have bathhouses. We call them *hammam*s," I say.

"*Hammams*," he says, turning the unfamiliar word over in his mouth. "How are they different to being bathed here?"

"They are very dark," I say. "With domed ceilings. Full of steam. And little old women scrub you clean when your skin has been steamed like a hot dumpling. Then they throw buckets of cold water at you, to refresh the body and make you glow."

He listens intently. "Do you miss them?"

I keep a straight face. "The little old ladies? No, Your Majesty. They are very strong and they show no mercy."

He laughs.

Then a few weeks pass without his visits. I find myself looking out for him, going quickly to the window if I hear footsteps in the courtyard, even though I know that if he were arriving there would be more than a few footsteps outside. But in the end it's Jiang who comes to me, his face holding an exciting secret. Behind him hovers Huan, his usual upright bearing entirely spoilt by almost hopping from one foot to the other.

"What is it?" I ask.

"Your chair is waiting for you, my lady."

"I didn't order it," I say, wary of perhaps another unwanted summons from the Empress.

"His Majesty ordered it. He wishes you to meet him."

I'm already on my feet. "Where?"

"Close to the Hall of Martial Valour. In the Outer Court of the Forbidden City."

"Why are we going there?"

Jiang shakes his head, eyes shining. "I do not know, my lady."

I make my way towards the palanquin and pinch his arm as I pass. "You're lying, Jiang. You're a terrible liar."

His giggle tells me I'm right as the pair of them hurry out after me.

The ride is shorter than our journey here, since we are not caught up in a huge procession – just my own palanquin, with a plainer chair following me for Huan and Jiang and an escort of guards surrounding us. Our footsteps echo as we cross back over the moat's bridge and enter the Forbidden City's gate. The Outer Court feels very quiet, for everyone is in the Summer Palace. When we stop I find myself outside a small building, capped with a domed roof. The Emperor is already waiting. I step out of my chair and begin my bows.

"Never mind that," he says. "Look!"

I look, then turn back to him, unsure of what I'm supposed to be seeing.

"A bathhouse!" he says, grinning like a boy. "It was built in the

Yuan days and no one uses it now but when you said the bathhouses in Xinjiang had domed roofs I remembered it. There is a well just there for water," he says, pointing, "and I have had it cleaned and prepared for you so that you may use it as a *hammam*." He pronounces the foreign word with care and pride.

I stand, speechless.

"Do you like it?" he asks. "Come and see it inside. Tell me if it is done well."

I step inside the dim room. The walls and floor are tiled and the ceiling reaches up in a perfect dome. It's already been filled with steam and my heavy silk clothes are rapidly becoming damp. By my side the Emperor stands rapt, gazing upwards through the steam. The heat makes our breathing faster and the tiles echo back our words in the darkness.

"Do you like it?" he asks again. His voice is a little anxious.

I reach out and touch him for the first time, placing a tentative finger on his arm. I'm glad the steam and dim light in here hides my face. "It is perfect, Your Majesty," I assure him. "I believe I am standing in a *hammam* in Xinjiang."

"Except for the little old ladies," he reminds me, chuckling. Without warning he puts an arm about my shoulders and pulls me towards him, resting his chin on my now-damp hair. "You will have your own eunuchs and maids to bathe you here. They are at your mercy, not you at theirs."

I stand very still, feeling his body pressed against mine, smelling his scent. I've never been so close to any man except Nurmat. This is not like being close to Nurmat. I feel stiff and awkward but as he continues to hold me to him I relax a little into his embrace. I cannot remember a time when someone embraced me for this long; I have no memory of being held like this.

"I must go now," he says, satisfied. "You may stay here and bathe, if you wish." He pats my shoulder, releases me and makes his way out.

I stand alone in the dark steam, unsettled by the feeling of loss I feel at no longer being held. Jiang and Huan, having seen off the Emperor, come to find me and hover uncertainly when they see me motionless in the darkness.

"Is something wrong, my lady?"

I shake my head and struggle to bring my words together. "I only mentioned the bathhouses in passing," I say. "To – to make conversation. But he..." My voice trembles and I stop.

Huan beams with pride. "The Emperor is a kind man," he says. "And he cares for you. He wants you to be happy here. I told you this day would come."

I nod and stumble my way towards the chair. I hadn't thought to be so moved by a gift, after all the Emperor has only to wave a hand and buildings can be built up or torn down again. But his good-hearted notion of soothing my supposed homesickness makes my eyes sting with tears. Since my mother died, no one has cared about how I might be feeling. I wonder whether Iparhan ever considers my happiness. I know she does not and for the first time I ask myself where my loyalties would lie, if I had to choose.

Now when the Emperor visits I laugh with him more readily, and I'm sorry to see him go, not only because I am failing to meet Iparhan's instructions in joining him in his bedchamber, but because I would like to spend longer in his company.

Soon it will be autumn and Huan begins to plan my winter clothes. He has little fur caps and waistcoats made, as well as heavy outer coats.

"I feel like a beast to be hunted," I tell him, as I try on a skirt and jacket, both thickly trimmed in fur.

He nods, pleased. "Hunting season is almost upon us. It will not be long now until we head for the hunting lodge."

"Is everyone going? The whole court?"

"Oh yes. There will be many thousands."

"Thousands?"

Huan shrugs. "All the court. All the servants – cooks, dressmakers, cleaners, maids, eunuchs. All the courtiers, the officials, their families. Then of course there are the beaters, the groundsmen, the woodsmen – they will all meet us there."

"How far is it?"

"Seven days' travel."

"That's very far!"

"Well," he concedes, "It can be done in three days. But there are staging posts along the way, where the court may rest for the night. The Emperor loves to hunt but he is mindful of his duty to his mother. The journey is in part to provide her with interest and entertainment, with fresh air in the hot months."

I make a disbelieving face. "The hot months are coming to an end."

Huan raises his eyebrows.

I make a gesture of surrender. "Very well," I agree. "We are going to the hunting grounds to please the Emperor's mother and protect her from the terrible heat of the autumn, when all the rest of us will be wearing furs against the cold. How filial of him. And in order to pass the time on this journey of his mother's the Emperor will hunt. When do we leave?"

"In the next few days. There will be a rite before we leave, when all of the Emperor's family will gather together and pray to the ancestors for their blessing, promising to honour their memories in a glorious hunt and prove themselves worthy of their Manchu heritage. You will enjoy it."

The night before our departure I make up my own little bundle of goods. I put in my simpler clothes and then pause. But then I add some fresh food. I cannot rest easy.

Our first glimpse of Chengde comes on the seventh day. Built into a hilltop, gleaming palaces and temples rise from the trees.

"Is that where we stay?" I ask Jiang. "Will I have my own palace?"

He grins. "You will have your own tent."

"*Tent*?"

"The Emperor prefers to stay closer to the hunting grounds. Everyone stays in tents. They are very grand of course, but tents nonetheless. The Emperor's grandfather was very fond of staying in a tent. He said he felt at one with nature, as though he was a Manchu warrior of old."

I shake my head. "You're teasing me. We're going to live in tents? All of us?"

But he's right. The tents are laid out like the Forbidden City, the same configuration of private palaces and great halls, with added rows of tents for the many people who would normally reside in Beijing but now live in the same city of tents as their emperor. The tents are luxurious, with hangings, screens, silk coverlets for our beds and scented chests for our clothes, but they're still tents, and it's not long before I hear that other ladies in the encampment are unhappy.

"The ladies are grumbling," reports back Jiang.

"Why?"

"They are not fond of the hunt. They find the tents draughty, not refreshingly cool, and they miss their gardens. It is fun for the men, of course; they go hunting. For the ladies there is little to do."

"There's not much to do back at the palace either," I retort. "Is the Empress complaining too?"

"The Empress never complains," says Jiang.

Melissa Addey

"Except about the Emperor's other ladies," I say.

On the first day that the hunting parties set off I stare after them in amazement. There are more than a thousand men taking part in today's hunt. It takes hours before they all disappear, and the duck whistles, hunting horns and dogs, the shouts of the men, can be heard all day.

"There can't be an animal from here to Beijing that won't hear them coming," I tell Huan. "How will they ever catch anything?"

"The animals are surrounded," he explains. "Beaters drive them towards the hunting party. There are little clearings here and there amongst the woods and when the animals reach them the hunters may shoot them easily."

"Easily sounds like the right word," I agree. "There can be no skill in it at all."

He shakes his head at me and places a finger to his lips, indicating that I shouldn't make such comments. I smile and say no more.

I find Giuseppe again, standing amongst the red-leaved trees.

"My Lady He," he greets me.

"Don't you hunt?" I ask. "The horn has already been sounded."

He shakes his head, smiling. "I'm a little too old for such pastimes now," he says.

He's painting and I stand behind him to watch. It's a huge piece, depicting the Emperor and his men hunting stags. The colours are rich and the size of it allows for some idea of how many men are engaged in the hunt, although the true number wouldn't fit in a painting ten times the size.

"How do you know how it all looks if you do not follow the hunt?" I ask.

"Oh, I have been on many hunts over my years at court," he

says. "I remember them all too well. But painting and riding do not go hand in hand. Now that I no longer hunt, I am free to paint my memories."

"I thought the Emperor could draw his bow and let fly arrows whilst riding," I tease him. "Can you not paint whilst riding?"

He chuckles. "It would be a poor sort of painting." Suddenly his expression alters. "Your Majesty," he says and bows.

I turn to see the Empress standing behind us. I feel like hiding behind Giuseppe but I only bow to her and wait. I'm trying to think how I can avoid going anywhere with her, if she were to invite me to go with her to her own tent, for example.

She looks me over. "Are you enjoying the hunt, Lady He?"

"It's very interesting," I stammer. It's a stupid answer and I can feel myself flushing. I have to be more on my guard, I think. I should have noticed her approach and made my escape before she could even reach me.

"It's very dangerous," she corrects me, a little smile playing on her lips. "There are wild animals all around us and hunters have been known to let fly an arrow in the wrong direction."

I don't answer. If she wants to frighten me, she's doing it well enough alone, I don't need to help her.

She waits for an answer, then when she sees I have none to give she turns and walks away without saying goodbye. I let out a breath of relief and look at Giuseppe.

"It seems the Emperor's attentions to you have not gone unnoticed," he says. He looks serious.

I shake my head. "He's not even called me to him," I say. "What will she do to me if he does?"

It's late afternoon and the encampment is drowsy. Many ladies sleep in the afternoons so as to be fresh for the banquets often held in the evenings. Their servants take advantage of the peace to rest from their labours or carry out less demanding tasks. Most of the men are out hunting. Only the elderly or the infirm, the women and the servants are about.

I'm restless. The encampment makes me more visible than I'd like. I'm not hidden away in a quiet part of the Forbidden City or protected from close scrutiny by the waters of the lake palace. Instead I'm watched wherever I go, for my clothes mark me out. The Empress' talk of arrows worries me. Is she planning for me to have an accident? I retire to my tent where I feel safer. But there's a strange noise just outside and at last I investigate, too curious about the soft huffs coming from directly outside the tent flaps.

It's a horse. Saddled but riderless. It's nosing at the walls of my tent, munching at some tasty grass that is growing at its edges. I stand and stare at it for a moment before I notice that it's trailing a broken cord, which must have been keeping it tied up, maybe to a tree during a pause in the hunting. It has perhaps snapped it by pulling and then, unnoticed in the tumult of the hunt, has wandered back to the camp. I wonder if there is some poor riderless courtier cursing it out in the woods. I stroke the horse, which snuffles into my hand, hoping for tidbits. I look about but there's no-one nearby to ask for food. The only food I have is in hidden in my little escape bundle thrust under my bed.

My breath stops. My bundle. The woods. A horse.

I could escape now. I could take my little bundle, slip it into the saddlebags. I could lead the horse to the edge of the woods and then mount it, ride away and change my clothes at the first opportunity. The gemstones in my hair alone would keep me fed for many years. No-one would notice I was gone until enough time had passed for me to ride a long way off. If I am questioned while I lead the horse away, I can pretend helplessness and say I was searching for its owner.

The bundle fits into the saddlebags. My hand shakes as I take the horse's cord and urge it softly forwards. I think it will not obey me, but it is placid enough. I try not to look about me, afraid if drawing attention, but for once no one is looking my way and I walk slowly, so slowly I think my heart will stop, towards the woods. There is a steep drop with a little path that leads into the woods and I find myself holding my breath as I make my way down it, gradually dropping out of sight of the main encampment. The only thing I allow in my mind are the words in Mandarin to explain (with wide eyes and a hesitant, girlish demeanour) that I thought I heard a man calling for help just down this path and since I saw this riderless horse...

The woods are empty. I can hear the hunting horns further away but I can't see anybody. I allow myself to turn and look behind me. There is no one there. I daren't change my clothes until I am further away from the encampment, so I bunch up my skirts and hoist myself into the saddle. The horse, now calmer, accepts me as its new owner, standing still as I mutter a few choice words that haven't passed my lips for months. My pink silk skirts are heavy with silver embroidery and do not sit well on a horse. My purple velvet waistcoat, as I told Huan, is too tight. It's suited to sitting about in a palace, not riding. I loosen a few of the buttons, although I can't undo them all. The fine gauze used to make the shirt underneath it is all but see-through. I undo as many as is still decent and take up the reins.

I'm uncertain of what direction to take, but I pick a path which I believe will take me back to the main road by which we came here from Beijing – but leading me through the woods first, so that I will have time to get my bearings and dress in simpler clothes. I can hear the beaters coming closer and I turn the horse away from them. Judging by the sun the hunt will be over soon and the men will return to camp with their spoils. We've seen all manner of game brought back in the past weeks. Deer, hare, ducks, boar. Even a tiger on one day. The Emperor rode past beaming with its body draped over a horse behind him. There was a celebratory banquet.

We come to the edge of a large sun-dappled clearing. The horse shies and will not enter it. I urge him onwards, first gently and then with a firm kick of my heels.

It's a mistake. As we enter the clearing there's a crashing from the undergrowth opposite and suddenly I'm facing five large, dark boars emerging from the golden leaves. They're frightened and their tusks are huge. The horse rears at the sudden apparition and it's all I can do to hold on. I wheel him about, thinking to turn back from where we've come but now there are shouts and the horse pulls away from my command and turns back to face the boars. They stand, irresolute, then charge towards us. As they do, one after another falls, arrows quivering in their flanks. They scream and my horse rears again. I shout and grip on to him with my knees, feeling myself beginning to slide off. Just in time his feet touch the ground again and I can scramble back into a better position on the saddle. I look about me and from all the sides of the clearing ride out the hunters.

At their head, the Emperor.

We stare at each other for a moment while several men run forward and finish off the thrashing boars, their squeals abruptly cut short with large knives. Blood spurts and the hunting dogs accompanying the party bark frantically, held back by their handlers.

My horse, now among other familiar horses, becomes calm. I let the reins go a little, my hands still hurting from the effort of keeping him under control.

I don't know what to say. I'm surrounded by men in their hunting coats and faced with the Emperor. I'm a concubine on horseback, my skirts rucked up, my waistcoat unbuttoned. My hair would no doubt make Huan weep. I am everything I should not be. In my saddlebags, should anyone think to look in them, are plain clothes and a parcel of food, all but announcing my plan to escape.

I bite my lip and then, glancing at the boars, I see that the lead one is stuck by an arrow that belongs to the Emperor – I recognise his feather colours, used by him alone. I think of the storyteller of Kashgar and at once it comes to me, what will make this a triumph and not a disaster. I have to speak fast, I have to explain myself before questions are asked to which I have no answer.

"Thank you," I say, looking directly at the Emperor. "You saved my life."

He frowns but I press on. "I was walking and this horse came riderless from the trees. Then I heard the boars and I was afraid, so I tried to ride the horse away from danger. But I rode the wrong way and –" I gesture towards the lead boar "– had it not been for your skill with the bow he would surely have gored my horse and brought me to the ground."

I know it's the right thing to have said as soon as I finish saying it. The men's shoulders relax. I've shaped a story that offers glory to the Emperor and his men and casts me as a lady in need of rescue rather than a wild girl on horseback appearing where she has no right to be. I see a few of the men chuckle and slap each other on the back, see one of the men closest to the Emperor turn to him and say something jovial which I can't make out. The Emperor rides towards me. I wait for him, wishing I could rebutton my waistcoat, but that would be too obvious.

He brings up his horse close to mine, facing me. He's still frowning a little, but not angrily. "You can *ride*," he says, and I hear his surprise.

I think of the Manchu heritage to which he clings and decide to align myself to it. "The women of Xinjiang are fine riders," I say, thinking of the Mongols who are our neighbours and are known for their women warriors and hoping he will too. "I have ridden since I was a child," I add, with enthusiasm. I might as well tell at least a part-truth. "It is a wonderful pastime."

He sits back on the horse, still regarding me for a moment while I wait for his true feelings to emerge, then a broad smile grows on his face. "Are you a good rider?" he asks. "I mean, can you gallop?" he adds. "Or must you be led?"

He seems to have forgotten I reached this clearing by myself but I answer truthfully. "I love to gallop, Your Majesty."

He purses his lips and his eyes shine. Next thing I know he's slashed a whip across the back of my horse, which leaps forwards. I'm surprised but I keep my seat and urge the horse on, across the clearing, past the startled hunters and into the woods. I glance behind me and, sure enough, there is the Emperor, his horse also at a gallop, leaning forward in his determination to catch me up, laughing. Behind him is a chaotic muddle of hunters, beaters, dogs and hangers-on, all taken by surprise, all trying to turn themselves round to keep pace with us and failing miserably.

To ride fast through woods is hard work. I've never done it before and I have to duck my head repeatedly although one branch does catch my hair. I have to look ahead and guide the horse whilst keeping my body and head low on its back. It's not long before the Emperor has caught up with me – after all he's an accomplished rider and no doubt has the finest horse available – and for a little while we ride neck and neck, before I slow my pace and he matches me, until we gradually come to a halt. Close behind us comes the noise of the hunting crowd but for a moment we're alone.

He grins. "You told the truth. You are an excellent rider." His glance takes in my disheveled hair, which has been shaken loose of its plaits. My pink ribbons and purple gemstones must be scattered across the woodland floor. He suddenly laughs out loud and reaches out to stroke my cheek. "An excellent rider," he repeats with satisfaction, before gently pulling the last ribbon from my hair. He looks down at it and smiles, then tucks it into a little pouch at his waist.

By now the others have reached us and I sit up straight and try to tidy my hair, at least away from my hot face, and tug at my waistcoat, which I know must be revealing rather more than it should. The Emperor calls to two of the men and tells them to take me back to the camp. I nod and turn my horse to follow them but as I leave he calls out to me.

"Lady He!"

I look over my shoulder. The warm sun shines down on my face and suddenly I feel free, as though my escape plan had worked and I am far away from the court and all the fears it has held for me since I arrived. "Your Majesty?"

"You will ride with me again."

I grin, a huge, happy grin. "Yes, Your Majesty."

"Tomorrow!" he calls.

I nod eagerly and he laughs at my enthusiasm, then turns his horse away and leads the hunting party back into the woods, while my escorts guide me back towards the camp, where I insist on the saddlebags being taken directly to my tent.

Huan's face is a mask of horror. "My lady!" His shriek brings the other servants running. His eyes are wide and panic-stricken. "Have you been *attacked*?"

I look down at my loose hair, unbuttoned waistcoat and crumpled skirts and grin again. "I have been out riding with the Emperor." I say. "On horseback," I add, in case he's imagining this to be a euphemism for something else.

He hustles me inside, out of sight of any passers-by. "On horseback? On a *horse*?"

I giggle. "Yes."

I explain what happened while he has me undressed and washed, then redressed and my hair rearranged. The servants keep their mouths shut as they follow his orders but their eyes and ears are kept wide open. By the evening the whole camp knows that I can ride a horse, that the Emperor saved me from what is now described as a whole herd of wild boars and very possibly a tiger as well, and that we rode together for many, many hours. Meanwhile, now that he knows that the Emperor wishes me to ride out with him again, Huan has a dressmaker stay up all night to modify my clothes for riding, making some of my widest skirts into a kind of wide-legged trouser which allows me to sit better on a horse but still maintain some elegance, as well as hastily loosening some of my waistcoats. My hair still has to be dressed with due care, but he binds it more tightly and doesn't risk adorning it with precious gems, settling for more of his paper creations in the form of tiny woodland creatures, appropriate to our surroundings.

There are a lot of 'casual' passers-by about in the morning when the hunt sets out. Not the other ladies, who are conspicuous by their absence, but courtiers, both men and women, gather to watch us depart, while servants seem to dawdle at those tasks which keep them close by. The Emperor has ordered a horse for me today and we ride out together.

He seems at ease out here in the woods. He talks of past hunts, explains how hunting is seen as a way to develop one's skills for battles. He can let fly arrows whilst riding with ease, and indeed this is a skill that he insists all his soldiers should exhibit, ordering that they should practice it often and calling for demonstrations by archers on a frequent basis.

"Who taught you to hunt?" I ask.

"I was educated from a young age in such skills," he explains. "My days were very long, for I had to learn all the skills of war as well as the skills of peace. My grandfather, the Kangxi Emperor, took me hunting at this very place once when I was only eleven," he adds. "He wounded a great bear, and invited me to take its life. But as I drew near it reared up and charged towards me. He managed to shoot it in time so that it crumpled at my feet."

"Were you scared?" I ask, picturing a small boy in front of a wounded, raging bear.

He's proud to be asked the question. "I stood firm before it," he says. "I did not move. My grandfather said I was destined to live a charmed life."

I shake my head. "You were a brave child," I say.

"I am a Manchu," he says, as though this behaviour might be expected of any Manchu child.

When I next see Giuseppe he laughs at me. "I hear you outrode the Emperor himself," he teases.

I shake my head, smiling. "Hardly. But it was fun."

He continues to paint while he talks to me. "He has talked of you often. He was most impressed. I believe he thinks you are almost a Manchu yourself."

I make a dismissive gesture but my cheeks grow warm. "Only because none of the other ladies ride."

Giuseppe turns to me. "Indeed," he says, eyes twinkling. "That is what makes you memorable to him. I think you are fast becoming a favourite."

My cheeks are too hot and I shrug, then mutter some excuse and leave him. Back in my tent I take the food I had squirreled away and throw it out, then give the plain robe to one of the maids as a gift. Whatever comes now, I will not run away. The life here may be worth keeping my wits about me for after all.

The Emperor takes me riding with him several times after that. Not every day, but on days where the quarry is small or harmless, where the hunt rides close to the camp. He is solicitous of my wellbeing, arranges for servants to carry cooled teas and snacks for me and sends me back to camp once I have ridden with him for a few hours. For my part, I relish the outings. I love to ride and to have a horse that is not stolen and no particular destination in mind makes the excursions relaxed and pleasant. I enjoy the fresh air, the leaves, the animals we spot. And the Emperor's company becomes a deeper pleasure to me. Here he's talkative and light-hearted, freed from his duties. Messengers still arrive daily with official documents and work for him, but he brushes much of it aside and concentrates only on those actions that must be taken. For the rest, he revels in his freedom, the company of the hunting parties and his strongly held belief that in coming here, in carrying out these hunts, he is maintaining his duty to his Manchu heritage.

I watch him shoot a deer herded towards us, his horse still moving while he pulls the bow back easily and lets fly the arrow which kills it immediately.

"May I try?" I ask.

He turns to me at once. "Of course," he says, passing me his own bow. He watches, grinning, as I try to pull it back to let fly an arrow. It's impossible; I can't even pull it back by a hand's width. "I must be stronger than you think," he says and waves a servant forward with an easier bow, but I don't have his aim and my arrows fall pitifully wide of any target.

The nights begin to grow cold and the complaints of the ladies grow louder. I hope our time here will last a little longer but Huan tells me the farewell banquet for the hunt is being planned and before I know it I'm being seated with many hundreds of people. It is the first time I've attended a court event after that first one to celebrate the conquest of my homeland. Although I get a few stares there are other foreign dignitaries and with the diminished attention I am more at my ease. I know there are officials and courtiers here from Altishahr, but to my relief they are not seated near me. I was dreading awkward questions about my family but I'm spared.

"May I offer you some of this? It is delicious."

I look up and meet the eyes of Lady Wang. I've not been sat so close to her before and it's my first chance to observe her. She's young, perhaps my own age. Her eyes are very long and narrow, her eyebrows plucked to accentuate them, arched high on her forehead. She's pretty, but her calculating expression makes her seem older than she is. She's holding out a little dish that clearly holds five-spiced pork, a favourite dish here.

I glance at the dish and back up at her. "I don't eat pork, Lady Wang." I don't feel the need to be polite to her. She is a lesser rank than I am and this is the second time she has offered me something inappropriate, her outer semblance of friendship masking a deviousness I don't care for.

She keeps a steady smile on her face. "Ah yes," she says, loud enough for anyone nearby to hear. "Your religion forbids it. Does it also forbid sleeping with your husband?"

There's a titter from some of the younger, lower-ranking women who despite their lesser status have already been called to the Emperor's bed. I feel myself flush but am distracted by a eunuch who is bowing low by my side. I turn and see he is holding out a platter containing sliced melons. Hami melons.

"From His Majesty, direct from Xinjiang, for your ladyship," he announces, and I see Lady Wang's face stiffen.

I lift the nearest slice, dripping with juice, and take a bite. The

227

memories it stirs are so strong that I put the slice down and stop chewing for a moment, before slowly beginning again and swallowing. I remember raiding the melon fields close to Kashgar or being thrown the odd slice by traders as the day's trading drew to a close. But the strongest memory is the last time I tasted these melons, the night Nurmat stole me away from Kashgar and wooed my shriveled belly with a whole melon to myself. I pass the melon on to other ladies and knowing the gift to come from the Emperor they are forced to comment on how fine the taste is and ask about other crops from Xinjiang. I answer them without thinking, my voice a monotone while I think of Iparhan fattening me up in the little house in the dunes, preparing me for this uncertain future.

Further up the table I see the melons being presented to the Empress and see her look at the platter, then down the table to where I am sitting. Her gaze meets mine for a moment but when I bow my head to her she does not respond, only waves away the slices of melon without tasting them.

Morning, and we begin our journey homeward. I send a message to the Emperor thanking him for the gift of the melon. The answer I receive puzzles me.

"The Emperor is pleased that you enjoyed his gift and believes that soon you will no longer miss the dishes of your homeland."

I feel a moment's panic. "Is he sending me home?" I ask Huan.

He shakes his head, confident. "Hardly, when he has been paying so much attention to you of late."

"What does he mean, then?"

He shrugs and turns away to cuff a maid for dawdling over the packing. "All will be revealed, I am sure," he says.

The seven days of travel are slow and tedious. I miss the riding and the fresh air, jolting about in my hot, dim palanquin. At last we reach Beijing and then the lakes of the Summer Palace. It feels like coming home.

We enter the complex as part of the procession of other ladies' chairs, but my chair comes to an unexpected halt and when I look out I see that the Emperor's chair is waiting for us. We join him while the other chairs set off along the lakesides towards their own palaces.

The Emperor leans out to speak to me. "I have a surprise for you," he says, beaming.

I can't help smiling back. "What is it?" I ask. Probably another pet, I think. Maybe even a horse.

"Follow me," he orders and his chair sets off, my own bobbing along behind.

We make our way through the gardens and bridges leading across the lakes to my own palace and I wonder what he has in mind. Has he had a new garden planted? Or given me some new furnishings? We reach the fountains and stop. I step out, blinking in the bright daylight after the dim interior of my chair. My servants are gathered on the steps. They fall to their knees, their faces pressed to the ground.

The Emperor steps out and waves me over. I join him and he points to one of the kneeling servants, dressed in a plain robe like the others.

"Your new cook," he announces.

"A cook?" I repeat stupidly.

He nods. He's proud of something. "I know you miss the foods from your homeland," he explains. "So I have had sent here a new eunuch, from your own lands, who can cook any traditional dish of Xinjiang that you desire."

I smile broadly. This is a welcome gift. At last Huan will no longer have to weep and berate himself or the other servants when they produce terrible renditions of foods I've described to them.

"Then you will have to dine with me," I say, a little surprised at my own boldness. "So that you can taste the dishes from the West."

He's delighted at the notion. "Yes!" he says. "Rise," he adds, as an afterthought to the kneeling man. "Present yourself to your new mistress."

The man rises and I take a step backwards, fighting to keep from crying out.

The man is Nurmat.

Dressed as a eunuch, now bowing low to me and quietly speaking his name before meekly returning to a kneeling position before us. Nurmat.

The Emperor turns to me, so pleased with himself that he doesn't notice the stunned expression on my face. "He is from Kashgar," he says. "And he can cook all of the dishes of your homeland. He says he makes very fine noodles. I look forward to eating them." He gestures to his servants that he's about to leave.

I manage to wet my lips and speak to him, although my tongue feels big and clumsy in my mouth. "Th – thank you," I stutter. "You are too kind to me." I fall to my knees to kowtow, as much to hide my face as for correctness.

He nods and smiles, then climbs back into his chair and within a moment is gone, his chair making its way away from us along the lakeside.

I get up very slowly and stand looking after the Emperor's cortege as it leaves the grounds of my palace, my back turned to the servants, who are still kneeling. When someone touches my arm I jump and startle Huan, who has come to my side.

He's pleased – and proud. My status within the court is rising with each new mark of favour. "His Majesty must care greatly for you," he says with confidence. "He has thought of what new thing might please you and has ordered that it might be done. He is not so thoughtful to all his ladies."

I don't turn round. "Dismiss the servants," I say.

He blinks, but immediately does so. When I hear the last footstep falling away I turn to him. "Where did that man come from?"

"The cook? He is a eunuch. From your own homeland. Made a eunuch once he was already a man. Lucky for us. It was difficult to find a eunuch from your region, and only a eunuch could serve you, of course."

I nod slowly. "Of course," I repeat.

He smiles. "Tonight you will have a meal that will remind you of home," he promises. "Will you come inside now?"

"In a moment," I say.

"Is anything wrong?" he asks.

"No, no," I say quickly. "Nothing."

He bows, then makes his way indoors.

I stand alone by the fountains, hardly daring to enter the palace that I had begun, tentatively, to think of as home. Now it is filled with fear for me.

Fear

I AM AFRAID. NURMAT HAS ENTERED the red walls and I am left alone.

He was displeased at the role I gave him to play. No man wants to be a eunuch, nor even portray the illusion of one. But I coaxed him; I promised he would advance our cause.

"Guide her," I said. "She is a foolish girl who cannot even bed the Emperor. Do all you can to advance her at court. Impress the Emperor with good foods at her table. Make her seem special in his eyes, remind him of his conquest. No doubt it will make him lustful," I add with disgust. "Doubtless a man like that needs to feel powerful before he desires a woman."

Nurmat caresses my face, his fingers covering up the white outline of my scar. "I will miss you, Iparhan," he says gently. "I long for us to be together." "We will be," I promise. "Soon. You need only guide her towards the Emperor and in what she must ask. We will find out his secrets and then we will strike. A rebellion will be raised. We will reclaim Altishahr and then…"

He smiled then and kissed me, left our home to go beyond the red walls.

Once within those walls he will spend much time by her side. I have disparaged her to him many times but in truth I know that she is doing well. The Emperor may not have come to her bed but he is wooing her as he has wooed no other woman. Her servants are fond of her. She has even managed to endear herself to another woman of the palace, a task beyond most concubines. She has not been found out. She carries herself with *grace. And I know that when Nurmat sees her again he will be reminded that here is a woman who has not only my own appearance but the nature he wishes I had been born with – spirited but kind, longing for nothing more than affection and happiness, for a gentle life.*

I am afraid.

The house in the dunes reeked with the smell of the rotten wound festering in my father's leg. I tried to clean it, my lips tightened against gagging, my hands steady although my legs trembled. When he began to see things that were not there and to babble nonsense I drew my own dagger and cut the flesh away although he screamed. But it was too late. The rotten smell had seeped into every part of his body and within a few days I was kneeling in the sands, shaping his tomb with my cold hands.

Nurmat believes he knows my plans but once the Emperor beds Hidligh he will find out their true nature. He will be trapped within the red walls and within the nightmare of my intentions. He will look back on every word I have said and know me for a liar. He will know the depth of my rage and the emptiness of our futures. I sit here staring up at those walls and ask myself unending questions.

Will he try to save Hidligh, if she has softened his heart?

Will he try to stop me when I take up my daggers?

Will he ever look upon me with love again?

I am afraid.

The Maze

I ENTER THE DINING ROOM IN silence and smell familiar foods. The meal spread out before me could be served in any fine house in Kashgar. All the dishes look as they should, although they're served in the same ludicrously high numbers, on the same little plates with strips of silver that my other meals are brought on. Tentatively, I seat myself. The servants beam, certain of success and praise but my face is very still. Slowly I help myself to a few dishes and put them in my mouth. The noodles, served with a fiery sauce, are good. The *polo* rice is perfect. There is a steamed multilayered bread which I know requires a great deal of skill to make, lamb soup, little pies and meatballs and much else. I have to acknowledge that Nurmat is a good cook. The food is delicious and all of it tastes exactly as it should. No more strange flavours and textures, no more odd Chinese additions to the traditional recipes of Altishahr. I should be delighted.

I'm very frightened.

Why is Nurmat here? He can't really have become a eunuch? If he's not, he's risking his life, for to be discovered as a whole man here would mean death, instant and unforgiving. I don't believe he's become a eunuch – his love for Iparhan's cause might be great but his desire for her body is greater and to have that dream taken away – no. So he's in great danger, as am I. Before today, I was always at risk of discovery, but as the days and months passed I'd begun to feel that I might be safe, that no one suspected my subterfuge. But now Nurmat's here my risk has grown much greater. There can be no scandal attached to me. There can be no question of my purity – when the Emperor has not even touched me! Nurmat's presence is endangering us both and for what – for noodles?

My mind and stomach churn together. I eat more and more slowly, nauseous with my thoughts. Is Iparhan tired of my slow progress? Has she sent Nurmat here to poison me? I can almost believe it. I feel so sick I think I might vomit at any moment. I look at the strips of silver but none have darkened and the eunuch designated my taster seems well enough, although his smile is fading with the rest of the servants' happy expressions as they see my face grow ever more solemn. And how would it benefit Iparhan's plans to make me sick? Or to kill me? Surely she needs me alive?

I sip my tea, which has grown cold, I've taken so long over the meal. The tea is served black and strong, as it would be at any tea stall in Kashgar's market, but the familiar taste seems strange in these surroundings.

I rise to my feet. The servants look at me in dismay. I've eaten very little. I think about what to say. My behaviour is too strange to go unremarked. I think of the Emperor's conviction that I'm homesick. I feel sick enough now.

"His Majesty's wonderful gift has brought back so many memories," I say, putting a hand to my head. "I am overwhelmed with sickness for my home."

At once their faces lighten. Of course. I am homesick. The food is so good it has made me homesick. They are all smiles and sympathy. Huan and Jiang hurry the others away and flutter round me. Their cooing voices, which I'd begun to find comforting, now make me want to strike them. At last I beg for rest and am put to bed early. Once the curtains close about me I can be alone.

I lie still, hearing the servants go about their chores, although they do so on tiptoe in order not to disturb me and their voices are low. I hear the last echoing calls from the courtyards and palaces as the Forbidden City's gates are closed for the night. I see the faint glow of lanterns slowly extinguished and at last there is silence.

I wait. I know he will come.

Every night I wait. Huan frets over the dark circles under my eyes, convinced that the late autumn and coming winter will finish me off if I am so sickly now. I yawn constantly. At last the night comes when Nurmat takes his place in my room to guard me while I sleep, a task that the eunuchs take it in turns to perform.

We wait in silence for hours, until there are no more sounds anywhere. Then I hear rustling as Nurmat gets up from his place by the door and makes his way towards my bed. I hear water being poured before the bed curtains are pulled back and he stands over me, a dim lantern from the door in one hand, a little drinking bowl in the other. He places the lantern nearby and sits on the edge of my bed, still holding the water.

"An excuse," he murmurs, holding it up. "You were thirsty and called for water."

I nod but stay silent.

Nurmat's voice is gentle, careful. "Are you well, Hidligh?"

No one has called me by my own name for the better part of a year. I can't speak.

He waits for an answer, then speaks again. "No harm will come to you," he reassures me. "I am here to help you. To watch and listen as you do. You cannot speak with servants as I can. Between us, we will discover much more than you could alone. You have not yet been called to the Emperor's rooms. I am here to help you in that. Iparhan needs you to be closer to him and many months have passed since you came here. We thought you needed help."

At last I find my voice, though when I speak my whisper comes out as a croak. "You're posing as a eunuch with the information I gave Iparhan."

He chuckles. "Yes. I would have tried to enter as a eunuch for any one of the palaces but then we heard the Emperor wanted a cook from Altishahr. It was too good an opportunity to miss; we knew it had to be for you. I spent two weeks cooking every dish you can imagine with an old woman from Kashgar. We cooked day and night so that I could learn all the recipes. She'd never received so much silver in her life."

My voice is cold. "Is she still alive?"

He's silent.

I lean forward so my face is closer to him. "You're risking your life," I hiss. "And mine, too. If you're found out…"

He shakes his head. "I am very careful," he assures me.

I want to scream at him but instead I grab his arm, digging my nails in as hard as I can. He flinches. My voice is a barely-controlled whisper. "Careful? You're posing as a eunuch! If you were found out it will mean death. For both of us."

He lays his hand on mine and I snatch it back. "Don't touch me."

"All will be well, Hidligh," he soothes me. "You are playing your part well. In Beijing they say that you are homesick and the Emperor dotes on you, that he has given you many gifts and shown you much favour. It is said that he is relishing wooing you, that he finds this new conquest romantic. Carry on as you are and I will help you however I can. Or leave me to make my own investigations and forget I am even here."

"I'll know you're here every time I eat!"

He starts to say something else but I'm too angry to let him explain himself. "Where's Iparhan?" I ask, for this is what really frightens me.

"In Beijing. In the Muslim quarter. She lives there, gathers information, corresponds with those whose plans are similar to hers both here and in Altishahr. I will be able to communicate with her more easily than you can. I can read and write. She has homing pigeons that can fly between us with notes. You'll hear the little whistles tied to their legs sometimes."

"You're risking my life!" I say.

"Live your life here as you did before," he says, still calm. "Forget about Iparhan and myself. We will call on you only when we need you to tell us something. Your task is to endear yourself to the Emperor and I hear you have been doing just that." He pauses. "But it is strange that he has not yet called you to his rooms. Why is that?"

I'm cold with anger and fear. "Get out," I say. "Get away from me before I scream and wake up everyone here."

He acquiesces, pulling aside the curtains and setting down the glass of water, before he turns back to me. "Are you beginning to care for him, Hidligh?" he asks.

I pull the curtains shut against him and after a moment I hear him lie down on his sleeping roll by the door. Soon enough he sleeps, but I do not.

The Emperor sends word that he wishes to dine with me. Although it's an honour – and certainly one that I can't refuse – I curse myself for my rash invitation. In the days that follow my heart frightens me. Sometimes it beats so quickly it feels like a fluttering in my chest and I stand, breathing fast, trying to still it with my fingers pressed against my waistcoat. Sometimes it beats so slowly that I feel heavy and my feet refuse to move.

I'm convinced Nurmat will try to poison him.

I call Nurmat to me, under the pretext of discussing the menu. I choose a moment when Jiang is busy elsewhere, so that no one can understand us when we speak together.

"The Emperor's visit," I begin, and then stop, unsure of how to phrase my fears. If I'm wrong and there's no harmful intention towards the Emperor, then perhaps my speaking of such a fear will put the idea in Nurmat's mind. If I'm right, he may lie to me and I'll be none the wiser.

He bows to me, mindful of the servants that surround us, even though we speak in a tongue they don't comprehend. They will be wondering what we have to speak of, an Honoured Lady of the Emperor's court and her cook. "All will be magnificent, my lady," he promises me, in a meek voice, as though he were truly just my cook.

I bite my lip but try to keep my face calm, as though this conversation were of no more interest to me than that of a good wife, anxious that her husband should eat well at her table. "Tell me about the dishes you will make," I say, to give me a chance to think.

He lists them. The list goes on and on, dozens of names and variations. Some I've eaten, some have never crossed my lips – dishes only served at feasts and on special occasions. I let the sounds wash over me and I see the servants lose interest in our discussion, for it's clear even without knowing our language that a tedious list is being related, with no room for mystery. At last Nurmat finishes.

"Very good," I say, my mind elsewhere. Then I sit back, although I would like to lean forward. "You know, of course," I say, as though the matter were of no importance, "that there are strips of silver in every dish, to identify poisons? And that there are tasters at every meal, who will taste each dish before His Majesty eats?"

He bows again but when he straightens his eyes gleam with a suppressed smile and I know he's heard the fear in my voice. "I will ensure there is a bountiful supply," he promises, as though the taster might be expected to eat whole mouthfuls of every dish, leaving none for myself or the Emperor.

I want to scream in his face to leave the palace. But I only nod and say, "Thank you, I am sure all will be satisfactory." I turn my face away and he bows and leaves the room. My hands are shaking. I tell the servants that there has been too much to do today and that I must rest.

By dawn all is in a fuss. The palace has been cleaned as though it were a miserable hovel. Huan stalks from room to room, dissatisfied with all he sees. The dining room is filled with hundreds of tiny coloured lanterns, to be lit at the start of the meal. All day servants dash back and forth with dishes, ingredients, knives. I am very nearly abandoned until the day draws on when it becomes my turn to be prepared. Today I'm in purple, with adornments in palest orange and early autumn flowers in my hair. I sit, shaking, while Huan readies me.

He frowns when he sees my trembling hands. "Are you well, my lady?"

I nod, my lips so pale that he tuts and applies a deeper colour to them. He takes a brief moment to reassure me. "The Emperor visits you often," he reminds me. "He has never found fault with you yet."

Until he's poisoned at my table, before my very eyes, I think. *I will die for this treachery.*

It's too late to plead sickness or lack of ingredients for a special dish. The imperial yellow chair arrives and the Emperor is in a fine humour. "Amaze me," he says, beaming. "I wish to taste all the flavours of Xinjiang."

I force a smile and lead him to the dining room, now glowing with lanterns and scented with incense. We sit down. Although only the two of us are dining, the room is filled with servants, his and mine. Among mine, Nurmat stands, silently watching. My legs tremble out of sight below the heavy tabletop.

The number of dishes I'm customarily sent seems paltry compared to the food on offer today, most of the items only ever seen at banquets. There are hand-pulled *lagman* noodles, thick in the mouth but light to the stomach, served at weddings as a sign of love – promising that the love being celebrated will last as long as the noodles are long; *polo* rice – glossy with flavoursome mutton fat and studded with chunks of lamb, raisins, carrots, apricots and onions; a whole lamb baked in the oven and kebabs of all kinds – from chunks of roasted lamb to minced lamb which is mixed with onions and cumin before being grilled, and then variations made with livers and kidneys. A dish with chicken pieces, potatoes, red and green sweet and hot peppers arouses the Emperor's interest. I explain that its name means Big Pot Chicken, although of course here it has been served as a dainty little portion. Small dishes of vinegars and heat-filled chili pastes sit ready for dipping into. There are soft breads, some plain and others filled. Hot-spiced broths send steam up from their bowls, filling the room with good smells. There are cold salads made of many vegetables, chopped and shaped into multi-coloured flowers.

The tiny strips of silver are all present. I check them as each dish is brought in, my eyes searching for any hint of darkness, of blackness overtaking their shining surfaces.

The Emperor, though, is happy. He waits for our tasters to try each dish, but while I watch them with fear, he ignores them, too used to their presence to give them any thought. "What are these?" he asks, lifting up a basket of little steamed dumplings, filled with pumpkin.

"They are called *manty*, 'the food of brave men'," I say.

He helps himself to them and pronounces them good, enjoying the new flavour. He presses his new favourite dishes on me, choosing the choicest morsels for my own plate. He asks questions about each dish.

"The *polo* rice is eaten with the fingers", I explain.

He follows my instructions and holds out a mouthful to me. I

241

have no choice but to open my mouth so that he can put the scoop of rice in my mouth. His fingertips brush my lips and tongue while Nurmat watches us.

The Emperor tries wine made of grapes, brought from Kashgar, which bring a flush to his cheeks and makes his laugh louder. I laugh too, although it costs me an effort to do so. My legs are shaking so hard that I expect him to hear the tapping of my shoes on the hard floor, but I manage to keep the heels from moving by bearing down on them with all my strength and he carries on, oblivious.

We finish with black tea and sweets, as well as dishes piled high with golden-hued dried melon strips and nuts. Fried *aiwowo* balls, made with glutinous rice, hold fillings of sugared seeds and have been topped with roasted sesame seeds.

When we have finished we sit a while and talk. I don't make very good conversation, for while we speak I'm watching his face – is he flushed? Sweating? Are his eyes steady? Does he breathe well?

"I heard you had a maid from the Forbidden City in your homeland," he says.

I blink, brought back to the conversation from my fears. "What?"

"Lady Wan told me," he says smiling at my confused face. "Here nothing is secret."

"Yes," I say carefully, conscious of Nurmat standing only a few paces away from me. "Her name was Mei."

"Does she still serve your family in Xinjiang?"

I shake my head. "She died," I say.

He pats my hand. "A shame," he says. " I would have had her brought to you if she was still living."

I blink back tears and offer him more tea, but once again I'm disappointed in his intentions towards me, for he rises, bids me farewell and returns to his own palace, leaving me alone. As soon as I can I undress, my clothes clammy with sweat. I call for a bath to be drawn of cool water and even though Huan shakes his head at the foolishness of a cool bath on a cold night, I insist and it is done.

The days are growing shorter and the nights colder. Soon we will return to the Forbidden City. Under Nurmat's tuition the other cooks and servants are learning to make the dishes of Altishahr, and so my table is loaded with good foods.

But I come to dread the nights when Nurmat is on guard. Even if I ignore him as silence falls across my palace I wake to his shadow leaning over me or to his soft voice speaking my name at the foot of my bed. In the darkness we talk, a little bowl of drinking water always held in his hand.

"Have you spoken with the Emperor recently?"

"Yes," I say reluctantly, knowing I can't lie. Every servant from my palace to the gates of the Forbidden City knows where the Emperor is every day. If he visits me I can't deny it to Nurmat.

"And?"

"And nothing."

"What did you talk about?"

"The weather. My animals."

"Did he ask for your company?" He is more interested in this than in any other information I might have about the Emperor. He wants to know when I receive gifts, if I'm shown favour.

I sigh. "Stop asking that. Don't you think everyone in the court would know by now if he had?"

"You should draw him to you," says Nurmat.

I blush. "I don't know how."

"Touch him," says Nurmat. "Reach out to him. Touch his hand. Pull at his sleeve to draw his attention to something. Smile at him more. Perhaps even touch his face."

I think of my time in training, how I was told to reach out to

Nurmat, how I caught at his sleeve and told him jokes to make him laugh, how I drew him towards me with gestures and requests for his attention. How I had to perform over and over again until the gestures became meaningless and empty. I think of the brief moments when the Emperor and I have touched. My fingertips on his sleeve in the bathhouse; his embrace of me and how his scent was still on my clothes afterwards; how I caught myself smelling them. How he drew the last ribbon from my loose hair in the forest and kept it in the pouch at his belt. I feel hot. The thought of deliberately reaching out to touch his warm skin makes me shake. "I will try," I mumble, beneath Nurmat's searching gaze. I try to turn his thoughts elsewhere. "How is Iparhan?" I ask, although I am not sure if I want to hear the answer.

"Impatient," he says.

I believe him. I imagine her raging outside the high red walls of the Forbidden City, awaiting news that will aid her plans. The eerie drone of whistles on homing pigeons flying over Beijing, which used to be a pleasant enough sound, now makes me want to hurry indoors to block out the sound, afraid of what messages Iparhan might be sending with her own flock, of what plans she might be making. I wish I could give her whatever she wants and have her leave my life for good, but the only way to do that is to draw the Emperor closer and I do not like to think of Iparhan when I think of the Emperor. The warmth I feel when I think of him, the fluttering in my breast, turns to something cold and dark when I think of her.

I make the most of the last days in the Summer Palace and walk by the lakes. In the distance, on a small rowing boat, I spot Consorts Qing and Ying, accompanying a little prince. I think back to Lady Wan's description of them. I could do with kind friends, I think, and when they come closer I ask them if they would like to take refreshments with me.

The two ladies glance at each other first, something I find out later they always do – checking that each is satisfied with what is being proposed, before turning back to me and nodding.

I arrange for chairs, tea and sweets to be brought out to them. Cautiously, they step from the boat and we make our introductions, then sit, while the servants light a little fire so that they can boil our water for tea.

"This is Prince Yongyan," says Consort Qing. The little prince just about manages to make an obeisance to me before rushing off to play with my dogs.

I ask how many years they've been at court.

Consort Qing counts and then smiles. "More than twenty years," she says.

I gape at her. "But you are very young!"

She smiles more broadly, flattered. "Not so very young," she says politely. "I am seven and thirty years of age."

She doesn't look it and I tell her so, at which she beams. "I was very young when I first came here. But of course His Majesty was also very young, and his first brides were of a similar age."

Consort Ying is younger. "One and thirty," she says, when I ask. She also arrived young, although after Consort Qing. The two of them have formed a close friendship over the years they have been here.

"Are many of the ladies good friends?" I ask.

They glance at each other and then shake their heads. "Most of the ladies keep to themselves," they explain. "There is much rivalry and each lady wishes for the attention of the Emperor, not for that of the other ladies."

"You are different, then," I say.

They nod in unison. "We are not…" says Consort Qing, while Consort Ying says "We have not…" There's a pause and then Consort Qing says carefully, "We have not been the most… favoured."

"We *have* been promoted," says Consort Ying.

"Oh yes," says Consort Qing nodding with vigour. "We have been promoted, certainly. But…" she glances at Consort Ying and then adds in a rush, "there are always new ladies and the Emperor's attention… can… wane."

"And there are those whom the Emperor has favoured," adds Consort Ying. "The Empress Ula Nara."

They glance at each other.

"Well," amends Consort Ying, "The Empress Dowager favoured her."

"And Imperial Noble Consort Ling is shown much honour, of course," says Consort Qing. "She has borne many children." She straightens her back a little. "I have the care of her son," she adds with pride, pointing to the little boy who is growing increasingly muddy along with the dogs, despite the pleadings of the eunuchs following him.

We talk a little longer. They're friendly but also wary. The Emperor's interest in me is well known, and yet they're puzzled.

"His Majesty dines with you often?"

"Yes," I say. "It is a great honour."

"And he has made you a gift of the bathhouse – the – the *hammam*."

I know that every lady in the palace has secretly made a journey across the wide courtyards of the Forbidden City to peer inside the little domed building. I nod and smile.

"But," says Consort Qing very carefully, "He has not yet…"

They both look at me and wait.

I look down, a little ashamed, knowing that they are wondering what is wrong with me. "He has not yet requested my… company," I say.

Their heads are tilted towards one another. "You have been here the better part of a year," says Consort Ying.

I nod and feel my cheeks getting hotter under their enquiring gaze.

Consort Qing pats my hand. "All in good time," she says. Her voice is kind but her eyes remain curious.

They leave me then, but begin to visit me every few days when their boat takes them in my direction. Perhaps they think I am also abandoned by the Emperor as they have been and expect that one day I will join their quiet little world. They are fond of boating and sometimes I join them, to dip our hands in the cool water, pick floating lotus flowers and allow little Prince Yongyan to admire his reflection in the ripples.

Close to my own palace there's another, smaller one. It's called the Belvedere, and the Emperor decrees that a room within it should be refurbished in the Islamic style and that I may use it for praying. It seems an absurdly large room just for me to pray in, but it's another mark of his favour and Giuseppe himself designs the decorations. He tells me that the name of the palace means 'Beautiful View' in his own tongue. My prayers have changed since coming here. I performed them as a trick at first, an affectation to ensure my religion could not be doubted. But I have grown used to the rhythm of them and here, in this peaceful room, I find myself praying without thinking of how I look or whether I appear pious enough. My prayers are one of the few times when I feel unafraid and so I undertake them willingly.

Sometimes the Emperor comes to the gardens of the Belvedere and waits for me. Today we've been sitting in the gardens for some time while Giuseppe paints us. When the Emperor gets up to go he doesn't look at the painting, knowing that it will be brought to him later, when it's complete. He nods to Giuseppe and departs. I'm not so patient.

"Let me see," I plead, like a child.

He waves me over and I join him. I look at the painting over his shoulder and frown. Sure enough, there is the Belvedere and gardens. The Emperor looks as he always does, although his head seems to be painted rather large – I know from the eunuchs that he prefers himself to look this way and by now all the painters know better than to paint him in any other way. Perhaps the volume of his robes make his real head look small and he does not like the effect. I smile at the large head and then turn my attention to my own figure. I frown. I am dressed as a European woman, in a dress tight at the waist and then frilling out into great skirts, with a giant hat, which Giuseppe has told me is called a *bonnet*. I step back.

"I look ridiculous," I say. "Why am I not in my own clothes?"

Giuseppe smiles. "I was thinking how different you look from your surroundings," he says, "and I wondered how you might look if your surroundings and your clothes were of one mind."

"But you have painted the Emperor in his own clothes."

"The Emperor likes to collect the exotic," he says. "These palaces and gardens, for instance, are European. They are not Chinese."

"And nor am I?"

"Nor are you," he agrees.

I look again at the picture and then turn away. I don't like how out of place I look.

There is a banquet that all the ladies attend. As the meal comes to an end platters piled high with honeyed walnuts are brought out.

"The Emperor wishes you a happy birthday," says the Chief

Eunuch, "And he wishes to honour your special day with your favourite sweets."

All eyes turn to me. I bow my head towards the Emperor and he nods back to me, smiling. He is the first to taste the sticky walnuts and everyone else follows suit. I had forgotten this was my official birthday and Nurmat must have prepared these nuts for today at the Emperor's request. It might as well be my birthday, for I don't know when my real one is.

Lady Wan, seated nearby, draws my attention to the Dowager Empress. "She's looking at you," she murmurs. "You should go to her and pay your respects."

I get up reluctantly and make my way to her. I perform a kowtow and she waits patiently for it to be completed.

"Are you less homesick now, Lady He?" she asks, direct as always.

I nod and bow again. "I am very happy here," I say meekly.

She tilts her head. "I hear you cry or seem sad when my son gives you gifts that remind you of your homeland," she says. "You cannot be entirely cured of your sickness."

I think of servants and how they love to gossip. How I wept after I saw the bathhouse and how I pleaded homesickness for my distress after Nurmat's arrival. All that I do is reported back to her, usually, it seems, with plenty of embroidery. "His gifts bring back memories," I say.

Her large dark eyes stay fixed on me. "Not pining for some past lover in Xinjiang?" she asks abruptly. "Your older sister, the Empress Ula Nara, has suggested that might be the case. She has… heard of such attachments."

I feel the blood drain from my face. This sort of idea, if embedded in her mind, could have me executed. "Of course not, Your Majesty. Only memories of my family and my childhood home, the customs there." I say quickly.

She gives me a slow smile. "I can see you still cling to your own customs," she says, indicating my clothes with a sweep of her long golden nail shields.

"Do they displease you?" I ask.

She tilts her head and takes her time, thinking. "No," she says at last. "They are a reminder of my son's conquest of Xinjiang. So they have their use at court; they remind visitors and courtiers of His Majesty's triumph. Your family was clever to think of it when they first sent you here. They must be good strategians." She pauses. "They chose where to place their allegiances, of course," she adds, evidently thinking of the treachery they showed their own family.

I bow my head and when I look up again she's dismissed me. I leave with my skin grown clammy. She's not a woman to cross. The Dowager Empress is Ula Nara's patron, having insisted that the Emperor should raise her to her high status, and since the Empress is clearly beginning to get angry about the amount of time the Emperor spends with me, even if he hasn't called me to his bed, perhaps I have unwittingly created another enemy here. If she knew of Nurmat's existence, of his being a man rather than a eunuch… I must get rid of him. I must make the Emperor call me to his bedchamber. Only then will I be enough in his confidence to find out whatever Iparhan wants. Once she has what she needs, perhaps both of them will leave me alone. I might still have the Empress' enmity but there could be a chance to be happy here if I didn't have Nurmat's shadowy nighttime visits to wake me, his constant requests for information, my fear of Iparhan's expectations. I need to be closer to the Emperor. I need to find a way.

Three days later Nurmat approaches me with news.

"It has been decreed that tomorrow will be the last day and night in the Summer Palace for this year. The day after, we will return to the

250

Forbidden City." I nod, but Nurmat goes on. "The Emperor has asked for his ladies to come to the maze tomorrow evening." He pauses. "With their lanterns."

I look up at him. His eyes are shining. "What does that mean?"

"The Emperor enjoys seeing the ladies of his court make their way through the maze," he says. "Each lady carries a lantern and each enters the maze alone. The Emperor sits in his pavilion at the centre and awaits their arrival. The lights making their way through the maze charm him. He finds it romantic," he adds, meaningfully.

I think about what he's said. "Is there a prize for the lady who reaches him first?" I ask, and see that I've guessed right.

"The Emperor often leaves the pavilion with the lady who reaches him first," says Nurmat. "If her company is pleasing to him. This could be your chance, Hidligh."

I nod, then call for Jiang. "Does anyone here know the secrets of the maze?"

He smiles. "I do, my lady."

I narrow my eyes. "How do you know its secrets if no one else does?"

"I used to play there as a child," he confesses. "When I first came to the palace. I used to run away and play there. I was beaten for neglecting my duties many times. But I learned its secrets."

I know this is my best opportunity. For once I have some knowledge that will help me get closer to the Emperor. He may be enjoying his slow wooing of me but I can't wait forever with Iparhan waiting in the shadows.

"Bring me Huan," I say and Jiang hurries away to do my bidding. Nurmat bows and leaves us, his face excited.

When Huan reaches me, I'm surrounded by maids who scurrying about with armfuls of silks. My clothes are scattered everywhere. He stands and stares.

"Tomorrow I will be joining the Emperor in the maze pavilion," I say. "You must make me lovelier than any other lady there."

Huan clears his throat, as though to soften the blow he is about to deliver. "The maze is hard to walk," he says gently. "Not every lady can hope to reach the Emperor's side. Most wander lost until they are rescued by their servants, long after His Majesty has made his way back to his palace."

"That is my concern, not yours," I say firmly. "Your task is to dress me appropriately."

He wants to test my resolve. "Appropriately for…"

"For a night with the Emperor," I say.

His gaze travels over the clothes laid out before us. He grabs a passing maid, pulls the bundle of exquisite clothes she's carrying out of her arms and drops them unceremoniously to the floor. "Fetch me the dressmaker," he commands.

I turn to Jiang who has been listening to all this. "Take me to the maze," I say. "You have to teach me its secrets so that I can reach the centre before any other lady. And we only have until tomorrow evening."

"It will grow dark soon," he protests.

"All the better," I tell him. "I will have to make my way through it in darkness tomorrow, so I should learn it in darkness."

The maze is made of carved grey stone and at its centre sits a pavilion, raised up so that whoever sits in it can see the shape of the maze and the lost steps of anyone in it. In the dusk, with no lanterns lit, it has a forbidding air.

"Show me quickly before it is fully dark," I say. "Then I can practice in the darkness."

Jiang shows me the main entrance and we begin. He walks

quickly, assuredly, a child sure of his playground. I follow behind him trying to remember each step I take.

"Did we turn left or right? Before this corner?" I ask him.

Jiang turns to face me, his face serious in the half-light. "You cannot hope to memorise each step," he says. "You must remember it as a whole, as you do your own rooms in the palace. You do not remember each step you take from your bedchamber to your receiving hall, do you?"

I shake my head. "I don't understand. My palace isn't a maze. Every room is different. This – " I gesture at the narrow path in which we stand, identical carvings on all sides, grey stone as far as we can see, " – this is all the same."

Jiang smiles. "No, my lady," he says. "It is not." He moves so that he is standing close behind me and then rests his fingertips lightly on my shoulders and head, turning me as he speaks. "This path, facing this way. When you look up you can see the far branches of the willow tree on the opposite lake. And when you walk this same path the other way the pavilion will be on your right, not your left." He leads me round a corner. "Here, when you look up, you will see the mountains in the distance."

"It will be dark!" I protest.

"Then the stars will be your guides," says Jiang. "On this path where we are standing, if you look up, the four small stars will be clustered like this," he gestures, "and facing the other way you will see the great bright star to your right. Do you understand now? You must look in a new way. Not down at your feet but all around you."

I fumble and turn as the darkness falls. I struggle to remember the stars, I cannot make out where the pavilion is. I make one wrong turn after another. The moon is bright, which helps me a little as it rises. As it travels across the sky I travel through the maze, my feet growing surer. At last Jiang leads me back to the beginning of the maze and I walk it alone as the moon vanishes and the sky turns from black to grey, my footsteps echoing in the emptiness.

We stumble back to my palace at dawn. For once all is quiet. Inside is intense focus. Outside the animals, banished in no uncertain terms, sulk by the giant flowerpots.

The dressmaker has worked through the evening and on into the night, his own helpers stitching, stitching whilst my servants kept them supplied with teas to stimulate, to keep their eyes from drooping. Huan's eyes are heavy with dark circles. I nod to him without speaking and make my way to my bed, where I collapse, waving away the maids who want to help me undress. I pull a cover half over me and sleep.

When I wake I'm hustled into a bath and emerge, my skin scarlet with scrubbing, my hair still damp. Silently the maids and eunuchs gather around me as we look at the newly finished clothes.

The skirt is deepest crimson, so thickly embroidered in gold that barely any of the silk shows through. Imperial dragons roar through rising waves. The scarlet waistcoat uses tiny gold fastenings in the shape of the omnipresent lotus flowers whilst delicate clouds outline my curves. The sheer gauze shirt allows the viewer to see the shape of my arms, the fabric making no real attempt to cover my skin. My shoes are shaped and adorned as fishes, swimming below the waves of my skirt. My customary cap is set aside in favour of a gold and pearl diadem, while blood red autumn chrysanthemums and ribbons of finest beaten gold await my plaits.

Huan's eyes are bloodshot and his wrinkles are showing but his smile is heartfelt. "You will be as a new bride," he says. "As you were the first time the Emperor ever saw you."

I nod and seat myself for his work to begin. He takes a bowl of tea to fortify himself and embarks on his masterpiece.

When my chair arrives by the side of the maze twilight is already turning to dusk and the lakes, from their daily blue, are turning black. A cool wind blows against me as I step out.

The maze is transformed. There are lanterns hanging everywhere outside of it, in all different colours, shapes and sizes. Two giant red lanterns frame the entrance and tiny yellow lanterns await each lady who will enter the maze. From here we can see the pavilion rising above the dark corridors of the maze, lit with hundreds of lanterns, surrounding a golden throne in which, from here, I can just make out the Emperor's motionless figure, awaiting our arrival on his golden throne.

All around me are crowds of servants. Bearers for every chair that arrives, eunuchs making last-minute adjustments to their ladies, maids hoping to watch the spectacle and not be sent back to their duties, hiding themselves amidst the chaos.

In the centre of this hubbub stand the women of the court.

Not all have yet arrived, but each is dressed beautifully. Their hair towers above their heads and there are so many flowers, both silk and real, entwined within our locks that together we seem like a moving garden.

I'm the only one who has chosen to wear the bridal colour of red. All around me are purple, blue, orange, pink as well as less showy golden-browns and silvery grays and even the risky, ill-favoured green, perhaps a sign that Lady Yehenara, still grieving for her child who died young, does not even wish to meet the Emperor tonight. My own clothes, picked out in gold, shine in the flickering lights of the many lanterns held by servants all around us.

The Empress stands apart. She has chosen to wear imperial yellow, with matching silk flowers in her hair. She is the only one of us allowed the colour and thus it adorns her as a reminder to all of us of her superior status. I try to stay with the other ladies but she signals to me to come closer. I reach her, then make my reverences.

She stands, still and silent, looking over my clothes. I am dressed as a bride, a young woman destined for a night with an eager husband. Slowly her eyes travel over me while I wait for her to comment.

"Red, Lady He?"

I bow. "Yes, Your Majesty." There's nothing else I can say.

"Do you know your way through the maze?" she asks.

I lower my eyes and shake my head. I'm afraid she will see that I am lying, or that she has somehow found out that I have spent a whole night here, learning the maze. That she will know that I have chosen a path that will bring me into direct conflict with her.

When I raise my eyes she is looking down at the dragons embroidered on my skirts, symbolising the Emperor. "Have a care which path you choose tonight, Lady He," she says at last, still not meeting my gaze. "The maze is a dark place in which to be lost."

She moves away and I let out my breath.

"We have not yet spoken."

I try not to jump. I've been joined by Imperial Noble Consort Ling. Hastily, I bow to her. She looks me over for a moment without speaking. She's a rounded woman, not fat but with an easy plumpness to her which speaks not so much of ample food, which we all have, but of her knowledge of being ranked second only to the Empress, of being an imperial favourite. She doesn't have about her the fluttering lonesome failure of poor Lady Wan, nor the diffidence of Consorts Qing and Ying, who stand on the edges of the crowd, speaking only with one another, nervously licking their painted lips. Her own clothes are embroidered with bats and persimmons, peaches and cranes, all signs of fertility, all subtle reminders of her four imperial children, her many nights with the Emperor.

I try to think of something to break the silence. "How is your son?" I manage. "I remember the fireworks to celebrate his birth."

She smiles. "My children are all well," she says, reminding me that she has already given the Emperor not just one son but two, and also two daughters.

"You have been blessed," I say, seeking for a platitude that might make her leave me alone.

"I have chosen the path I wish to take," she says. I remember Lady Wan telling me that no Emperor has ever been born to an Empress, that a concubine with favoured sons can hope to become the mother to an emperor and thus the highest ranked woman at court. Lady Ling's eyes travel over my crimson clothes. "Have you chosen a path, Lady He?"

I bite my lip. "I think I am still seeking it," I say, which is true, although perhaps tonight I'm starting out along a path, although I can barely make out where it might take me.

"Be careful where your path leads," she says. "I have never sought the love of the Emperor, but my children are my chosen path and those who bar my way will find it hard to walk onwards."

I try to think of a response but we are interrupted by an announcement from the Chief Eunuch and the ladies make their way forwards, each being handed one of the yellow-glowing lanterns. I take mine and wait to see what to do next.

The Chief Eunuch makes a gesture and suddenly we are plunged into darkness. Every lantern, except the tiny ones we hold, has been extinguished. The only light now comes from the moon, our tiny flickering lanterns and the great glowing Emperor's pavilion at the centre of the maze.

The ladies form into their ranks, ready to enter the maze according to status. First the Empress, upright and elegant, her pace

257

dignified. Then Imperial Noble Consort Ling, who strides off, her plump figure full of confidence. Consorts Qing and Ying take up their own lanterns. Holding hands they follow her into the darkness, before turning left, an immediate false step that will bar them from ever reaching the Emperor's pavilion. More ladies follow. I watch as Lady Daigiya and Lady Yehenara make their way in. Soon it is my turn and Lady Wan's, while behind us hover Lady Wang and Lady Chang as well as the lesser-ranked ladies, eager to outpace us if they could.

I wave Lady Wan forwards. "I will follow," I say, bowing. Lady Wan smiles back, pats her wig and straightens her shoulders, makes her way through the lengthening shadows towards the entrance and disappears into the maze.

I stand still for a moment and then begin my journey to the centre. I make my way through the towering gateway, turn right, then turn again and again before stopping. The stone walls rise above me and my first steps sound loud. Behind me I hear the tentative clatter of high-platformed shoes, as more ladies follow. I look behind me but I can't see them, they've already taken other turnings and are lost within the maze.

I stand still for a moment and then set down my lantern and walk into the darkness.

Behind the walls I hear little shrieks and the endless footsteps passing back and forth, seeking out paths that inevitably prove to be false friends. My own footsteps are few. I can see, shining above the intricate walls of the maze, the lanterns of the pavilion, where the Emperor sits, waiting. I take first one turn and then another, the darkness forcing me to check my pathway with my hands, running my fingers cautiously along the walls, mindful of my nail shields in lacquered scarlet, each painted with a tiny golden phoenix, the symbol of the palace's imperial women, the chosen ladies of the Emperor.

I look up at the stars to choose my way and hope that I have not forgotten their constellations.

I hear footsteps close by and without thinking I flatten myself against a wall. A dim light comes into view and I see the fast-bobbing lantern that illuminates the eager face of Lady Wang. I wait for her to see me but she is too focused on choosing her path and she misses me as she hurries past. I let out the breath I've been holding and turn away from her chosen direction.

The light of the pavilion fades and I know I'm drawing close. From a distance it shines, but here, at only a few paces from its steps, it barely sheds its light over the tops of the walls.

I turn and turn again and suddenly I'm standing in front of the pavilion, bathed in the light of more than a hundred lanterns. The gold of my clothes leaps into glittering relief and the crimson fabrics glow. High on a golden throne, observing my approach, is the Emperor. I make my way up the steps of the pavilion. He looks me over and smiles.

"No lantern, Lady He?"

I shake my head. "I found the way by my fingertips," I say.

I stand in front of him for a moment while he looks at me before he rises, taking up a lantern of his own. He steps towards me and I do the same without thinking. I lift my face to his and close my eyes. His kiss, when it comes, is gentle, his lips resting on mine for too short a moment before he takes my hand in his and leads me down the steps. I glance back at the now-vacated pavilion, filled only with shimmering lanterns, illuminating the empty throne which is all that awaits any other ladies who succeed in making their way through the hidden pathways of the maze.

We enter the twisting stone walls. I may know some of the secrets of the maze but he knows more. We never meet any of the other ladies, even though once or twice we hear them close by. Once I hear a sob on the other side of the wall and turn my head towards the sound, but the Emperor does not hesitate, only walks on. When we emerge it's not from the main entrance, but from a smaller side entrance. We walk, still silent, through the gardens and then down to the lake close to my palace. Under a willow tree a small boat awaits us, its oars manned by a young eunuch. The Emperor helps me into the boat. We sit, his lantern casting a dim glow over us, as we glide across the dark waters.

"The lotuses have died away for this year," the Emperor remarks in a low voice, as though to speak loudly were to break the shadows surrounding us.

I don't think, only hold out my hand to him.

He lifts it to his lips and turns it palm up. He inhales my scent, then speaks. I can hear his smile even though I can barely make out his face. "I was wrong," he says. "Tonight the lotus flowers bloom as though it were still summer."

The Gift

"**C**OME FORWARD, GIRL," SAYS THE old woman.

I step forward, my right leg dragging a little in a shuffling limp. My plain cotton robe is barely warm enough for the weather outside, but this room is well heated. The old hag must have cold bones. I bow deeply and as I rise up I see her wrinkled eyes narrow to inspect me.

"You limp," she says.

"Yes, my lady," I say, my voice heavy with the accent of an Altishahri peasant girl, a servile whine. "I was crippled as a child."

"And you are scarred," she observes, disapproving. "It's an ugly cut. I doubt any man would want you for a wife. But I suppose a woman would want you for her maid. At least you would not draw her husband's eye, eh?"

"I am a good worker, my lady," I say.

"I can barely understand you," she says. "Your accent is very bad. I suppose it is to be expected, coming from the New Dominion. Still," she says with some satisfaction, "I am sure your future mistress will not object. She's from that part of the empire herself, so presumably she will understand you."

This is the rumour I followed, that a maid was wanted for a great lady from my own lands. There can be only one woman who could be so described. "Are you not to be my mistress, then, my lady?" I ask, full of innocent ignorance.

"I wouldn't have a scarred cripple serve me," she says. "You might bring bad luck to my household. But I am related, you know, to the Emperor himself."

She pauses for effect, to impress me. I widen my eyes to look suitably awed. In truth she is a puffed-up liar; her blood-link to the Emperor so distant as to be laughable. But she wishes to ingratiate herself with him and I am her means to that end.

I tied scraps of cloth to the dead poplar above my father's tomb. Each strip one of my prayers, an unfulfilled wish. I wished for time to roll back, so that I would not have lost my family, my house, my future. But I knew it would not do so and so I made my vow. And in doing so I lost both my beauty and my chance for revenge to Nurmat. Until I saw the girl.

"I wish to present the Emperor's new concubine with a maid from her own lands," the old woman says, pleased with her idea. "It is said she is homesick or some such nonsense and that the Emperor is so besotted with her that he offers her every favour to woo her from her sorrow." She snorts. "A stupid girl if she cannot appreciate her good luck. But that is beside the point. If he wishes to indulge her foolishness then I will help him to do so. I daresay he will be grateful. It's a shame I could not find someone better formed," she adds, disappointed.

I wait, a paragon of patience and meekness. She shrugs at last and nods. "You will be obedient," she specifies. "There are severe beatings for a girl who is not an obedient maid within the red walls. It will reflect badly on me if you are not all you should be. You will be trained within my household and I will present you to the Son of Heaven when you are ready."

I have been ready for a long time.

The Bazaar

IT TAKES ONLY ONE NIGHT with the Emperor to change my status.
My servants beam. They hold their heads a little higher, and
speak with more assurance. When the Emperor calls me back to him
again and then again my newfound status is assured and I see them
grow confident in their future. I had not realised how many people's
fate depended on my own. Now that their mistress is truly favoured,
not with mere gifts but with access to the Emperor's bedchamber,
they can rejoice, knowing that their work has been rewarded, that
greater things might be in store for me – and them – one day. Their
efforts redouble. The dressmaker labours longer over the embroidery
on my clothes, knowing the work will be displayed before the
Emperor himself. Huan's folded paper creatures for my hair grow ever
more fantastical and are even painted or gilded, while more valuable
gemstones glitter between the woven strands. Elaborate gifts from the
more junior ladies are sent to me, each of them hoping for my favour
as I rise in the Emperor's estimation. No-one dares to send ill-omened
gifts, not even Lady Wang.

Only a few nights pass before Nurmat makes his way to me again. I
am expecting him.

"You have done well," he says, excited. "Now you will find out
more information and Iparhan's plans can take shape. We may finish
this business yet, Hidligh!"

I nod. This is what I had planned, that I would hurry along the

Emperor's wooing and that as a result I could find out more, find out whatever Iparhan needs to make her satisfied with me and leave me alone to live my life while she plans her rebellions and Nurmat pursues her for marriage.

Nurmat begins to list questions I might ask. I know I should be listening, should be remembering them all so that I can think how I might raise the topics with the Emperor, but instead I find myself thinking of our first night together, a night which fills my mind whenever we are apart.

The splash of water against the oars is all I can hear above the rushing in my ears and the hard beating of my heart. The Emperor still holds my hand in his, cradling it between his own two hands as though it were a kitten. His touch makes me tremble but his hands on mine stop them shaking. He does not look at me; his face is turned towards the lanterns on the shores, his demeanour peaceful and content. But I gaze at him, for once free to look at him without being observed by the court around me, without his eyes on mine. The lantern flickers with the rocking of the boat. His dark eyes are large and his skin very smooth, even on his hands, which I know are no strangers to weapons and reins. I raise my free hand and slowly stroke the back of his, tracing its contours in curiosity, as though he were a carving.

My touch makes him look down at my finger as it moves across his skin and he smiles, releasing my other hand. I look up at his face and tentatively raise both hands, slowly stroke his cheeks, cup his face in my palms. I forget that he is the Emperor and lean forward to kiss his lips.

"The borders are our hope," says Nurmat. "If he should threaten lands further than our own they will fight back and we can ally ourselves to them. Already they are discomforted by his endless quest for power. His empire has grown threefold in living memory and he is never satisfied. So ask about the borders, find out if he is greedy for more lands, his plans for the future."

His mouth opens under my lips and I almost draw back. But somehow I am drawn closer to him, so that I find myself held in his arms, my own arms about his neck, my hands stroking his long silken hair. I have never been held like this. I have never kissed like this, his tongue seeking mine, our mouths hot while our skin is chilled by the night air.

I can barely remember alighting from the boat, only that more lanterns, held by unseen figures, await our arrival and that the light around us grows and grows as we reach his rooms. His hands caress my shoulders and his fingers rest for a moment on the fastenings of my waistcoat. He half undoes it before he smiles and strokes my cheek instead, as though remembering something.

"My servants will help you undress," he says.

I want to cling to him. I want to say that I would rather he undressed me himself. When his fingers rested on my clothes I wanted him to go on, to undo each of the golden flowers holding my silken clothes together, to do it quickly so that I could feel his skin against mine. But my voice fails me and already he is making his way to another room.

Blinking, I find myself surrounded by unknown eunuchs and maids. I stand still, awkward again, my dark boldness lost in the light. At first I think they may be puzzled by my strange clothes but by the deftness of their ministrations I realise they have already prepared for this night, have already learned how to undo my fastenings, that they know all the elements of my traditional clothing, even though no other woman here wears such items. Perhaps they sent for my clothes, perhaps Huan taught them; who knows how long ago they all made ready for this night, so long in coming.

Stripped naked, I wait for a sleeping robe to be offered but none is forthcoming. Instead a senior eunuch gestures to me to follow him and

I walk behind him through the warm rooms, my bare skin raised into gooseflesh, not by the fear of what is to come but by my sudden, desperate, desire for it.

"I have found us many allies," says Nurmat. "Iparhan has the names of those who will rise up when given the word, those who can offer silver, horses, weapons. We must know if he has any inkling of their identities, if he suspects any of them so that we can assure their safety."

We reach the bedchamber where the eunuch bows and leaves me. The Emperor is nowhere to be seen and I stand alone, feeling small in the large room. I look about, wondering where I should put myself. There is a large carved bed, hung with silken drapes. A strange wooden chair, with arms twice as long as usual, as well as a padded silk seat and a cushioned headrest. Where one's feet would go, if sitting on it, is a large padded silken base. I stare at it for a few moments wondering at its form… and function. I decide against it and climb awkwardly onto the bed. It is heated, of course, and the silk covers feel like warm skin against my own. I lie there on the bed for a moment but my nakedness and the emptiness of the room makes me feel too exposed. The positions I was obliged to learn… will I have to perform them now? How will I know how to begin? I lift the top cover, intending to climb under it, seeking its protection.

"Stay where you are," says a voice.

I look up to see the Emperor closing a door behind him. When it swings shut it disappears, becomes part of the painted wall, showing a summer garden full of delicate flowers and birds.

The Emperor stands still, watching me as I turn a deep shade of pink. I have never been alone in a room with a naked man before. His long dark hair, usually plaited in a queue, is now hanging loose down his back. His chest is broad and his legs are long and well-made. I find myself glancing away from any other detail, too conscious of our nakedness. I shift uneasily on the bed and at once he smiles and comes forwards.

"I should not stare at you so, is that it?" he says, his voice gentle. I try to smile but my lips will not curve as they should. I have lost all my bravery and indeed all my desire. I am a little afraid, now.

The Emperor kneels by the side of the bed. I have never looked down on him before and I feel strange doing so.

"Lie back," he says.

I do so, feeling awkward. My hands are clenched. Now, I think. Now he will climb on top of me and...

He rises from his kneeling position, then sits himself on the bed and lifts each of my feet so that they are in his lap. Slowly, he begins to stroke each foot, from the toes to the ankle, over and over again. He does it for so long, without seeming to want more, that I feel my fingers slowly begin to unclench. My head sinks a little deeper into the bed. His hands are warm and his touch is firm but gentle.

Suddenly I need to know. "Why didn't you call for me before?" I ask, my words blurted rather than chosen.

His smile deepens and now his hands are on my calves. "I thought there was no hurry," he says, his voice low, the stroking motion not changing but slowly reaching upwards towards my thighs. "You were new to court and you seemed afraid. I wanted you to become mistress of your own palace and gardens, to feel at home here. I wanted you to be happy." His hands caress my thighs and I tense again, believing that I know where they will move to next, wanting but afraid. But his hands move smoothly past the dark hair between my legs and upwards, beginning to follow the shape of my belly. Again I wait for him to touch me more intimately, to fondle my breasts, and again he proves me wrong and instead sweeps up my arms. I feel a wave of disappointment, of unsatisfied desire. He rests his fingers on the hollow of my throat for a brief moment, feeling my fast pulse before easily moving to lie beside me, face to face, and his hands cup my cheeks and trail through my hair. He does not even need to pull me towards him, for the lake's darkness is upon me again and I press myself to him, to his kiss, his body, his embrace.

"If he grows suspicious," says Nurmat, "then withdraw a little, or ask some foolish question that will show that you are only a young girl, curious about many things. Then when he is lulled into believing there is no danger, you can ask more questions."

The Emperor half laughs at me. I am clinging to him so tightly, kissing every part of him, that he can hardly move. "I enjoyed wooing you," he murmurs. "I enjoyed surprising you with gifts. I enjoyed riding with you. It made me delay the moment when I would call for you as my companion." Suddenly he is kneeling between my thighs. "It will hurt a little, my love," he says in a whisper and the endearment makes me long for him. "I am sorry for it. But afterwards there will be pleasure again."

I cling to him and he takes me in his arms, then guides himself into me. I whimper at the stinging pain, but his arms hold me in a gentle embrace and his lips on mine wash away the sensation and slowly, slowly, he moves within me and I begin to feel the pleasure he promised. I find myself trying to match his pace and when I feel the pleasure begin to grow I wrap my legs about him and hear him groan. "My lotus flower," he says, his words a harsh whisper in my ear. "I should have called you to me long before this."

Afterwards I expect to be dismissed, to be sent back to my own rooms as protocol demands, but instead he holds me to him.

"Are you sore?" he asks as I nestle into his arms.

"No," I say. It is not true, of course. I am sore, but the pain is so wrapped up in the pleasure I felt that it makes me happy.

He smiles, as though he knows what I am thinking and holds me closer to him. Only when his embrace grows soft do I realise that he has fallen asleep.

In the red-yellow glow of the lanterns I observe him. His face is peaceful, untroubled. His arms grow soft about me. Briefly he even snores a little and I have to stop myself from giggling. I want to stroke him but I do not want to wake him. Instead I slowly move my fingers a hair's breadth above his skin, following the outline of his face, his arms, his chest. Gently I let my hand rest on his warm skin and he stirs a little but does not wake. I lie still and gaze at him, his closed eyes, his dark lashes and the tendrils of loose hair fallen over his shoulders. This intimacy is so far removed from what I was obliged to practiced in the dunes. Each position came naturally, I was not ordered to assume them. I was not embarrassed and uncomfortable. Most importantly, I was not watched over by Iparhan. She may be only on the other side of the red walls, but for now she feels far away. I feel his sleeping breath, slow and steady, on my temples until the easy warmth lulls me and I, too, sleep, a smile still on my face as I drift into darkness.

"There are even those who think like us here in Beijing, in the Muslim quarter," says Nurmat, "and they will have questions of their own, of course."

I wake to the sounds of bathing and dressing. His many servants, clustered about him, pay no attention to me but he turns and smiles.

"I must go," he says. "You will be taken back to your own palace."

I feel suddenly bereft but I nod. I wonder if he will want to see me again but I daren't ask. Standing before me, in his imperial robes, he is the Emperor once more, not the man who held me in his arms last night.

One of the eunuchs offers him a tray. His smile deepens and I recognise from Giuseppe's description the little tablets marked with the names of the palace ladies. I lower my eyes, not wishing to seem presumptuous but my hands grip the silk coverlet. He flicks through the tablets before holding one up. "Will this one do, do you think?" he asks.

I can't read all the characters they use but these ones are familiar and I know it is my own name. I blush and nod and he laughs, then drops it back on the tray, face down to indicate his choice. "Tonight, then," he says, and he's gone. I hold the warm bedding to my nose and inhale his scent, then realise his scent is on every part of me, as mine is on him. I stroke my own hair, my own skin, as though it was his, my eyes closed for a few moments until I remember where I am and open my eyes to see the servants waiting to dress me.

When I return to my palace, my servants are gathered by the steps. They should be packing to take us back to the Forbidden City but instead they are kneeling, faces to the ground, like the day I first came here. My hair is unbound and my clothes are disheveled but Huan's smile, as he lifts his face to greet me, matches mine in happiness.

"Your ladyship," he says, and cannot speak further, his voice choked.

I rest a hand on his shoulder and look about me as though all were new to me. Another servant's head rises to look at me but I turn away from Nurmat's gaze and make my way into the palace.

"… and above all we need to know which nobles from our homeland are still his strong allies or if any seem to waver in their support," finishes Nurmat.

I nod slowly, still feeling the Emperor's warm skin against mine, against my breasts, my belly, my thighs.

"Do you understand?" presses Nurmat.

"Yes," I say, to make him go away.

"Then as a reward for your nights with the Emperor I have a gift for you," he says, smiling. From his pocket he pulls out a new vial of perfume. He holds it out and I take it, but along with it he drops a little wooden tablet into my palm. On it are carved some characters. I look at them but they mean nothing to me.

"What does it say?"

He grins. "The name of the perfumer who made that perfume. Have it sent to him and he will know you are its new owner and provide you with it for the rest of your life. He is sworn to secrecy. Once this is all over you will still be here and you will still need your supplies of it."

I frown. "Won't Iparhan want to keep wearing it?"

He shakes his head. "I will find her a new perfume for our new life together," he says, his face filled with hope.

I look doubtfully at the tablet. This may solve one of my fears, but it now seems such a small fear compared to the others that beset me at every turn. "If it ends peacefully for us all," I say.

But Nurmat's eyes are full of the happy future he is envisioning, a future he thinks is coming closer every day. He pats my hand. "Soon it will all be over," he promises me as he leaves. "Ask the questions and when Iparhan has the answers she needs this will all be over. We will be free of this, Hidligh.""

I try. But I do not want to ask the Emperor questions when I am lying in his arms. Later, I think, later. When we eat, perhaps. But when he selects choice morsels from his own plate and offers them to me I am too hungry for the touch of his fingers on my mouth to remember what questions I should ask. When we walk in the gardens I am distracted by the touch of his hand and his laughter when my dogs shake their paws at the first hard frosts underfoot.

"You said you had a question for me," he reminds me as we watch the birds at their evening flights.

"Did I?"

"Yes," he says. "Something about Xinjiang's borders."

"It doesn't matter," I say.

I begin to ask for particular eunuchs to guard me, often Jiang or Huan, sometimes others, but I ask for them by name, rather than allow Nurmat to take his turn as my guard. Night after night different eunuchs guard me but it is never his turn and so I am left alone, free to enjoy the Emperor's attentions.

He doesn't call for me every night, for Imperial Noble Consort Ling and others are still favoured. Nor on those nights when I'm called may I always stay by his side till morning. Sometimes he will kiss me and send me away in the darkness. But I find myself smiling more often and sleeping more soundly. Huan tuts proudly as my waistcoats and waistbands have to be adjusted. I'm not grown plump yet but my curves are more shapely and I walk more freely, hold my head higher. The Emperor favours me and my place at court is assured.

His gifts are made yet more lavish by our caresses.

By the south-western red wall of the Forbidden City a new building is erected. The Tower for Gazing at the Precious Moon is two stories high. Inside its upper level the walls are lined with mirrors, which Giuseppe tells me is like a great hall in a famous European palace. When I first ascend the steps of the hall and find myself in the room I'm startled by the view.

Beyond the moat is Beijing. I've grown so unused to thinking of there being another city surrounding our own that I step backwards, which makes the Emperor laugh.

"A window on your homeland," he says. I step forward again and realise that the tower has been built so that we can look out at the Muslim quarter, which the Emperor has encouraged to flourish since my arrival.

"I had not realised there were so many…" I say.

"So many of your own countrymen?" He nods. "Your family, of course, amongst them. But many more people from Xinjiang are coming to the capital now."

I look across the waters to the bustling streets, a little wary that someone – Iparhan – might see me. But the figures are too far away to make out their features in any detail, although I can see by their styles of dress that they do indeed hail from my own land. There is a lot of building work going on.

"It is growing day by day," I say.

"It is," the Emperor agrees. "And there is one building that will truly remind you of home. But that is a secret for now."

It's not a secret for long. I hear a wailing cry one morning whilst entering the bathing house close to the Tower and afterwards, curious, I direct my chair to the Tower, for the sound was familiar and yet I can't quite believe I heard what I did.

In the Muslim quarter a mosque has risen, with its own minaret, echoing my own tower. The sound I heard earlier was the call to prayer, and it can be heard in much of the Forbidden City, although most clearly from the Precious Moon Tower. I go there often now, looking out at the bustle of the streets and bringing out my little prayer mat to join in with the prayers being said when the call sounds.

The Emperor however, is not satisfied with the tower, the calls to prayer, the viewing platform he has created for me. "You would like to be amongst them, would you not?" he asks.

Quickly I shake my head, although I keep a smile on my face. Not only do I know it to be an impossibility, but I'm afraid that Iparhan might reach me if I walked those streets. Or that my 'family' would see me. They are not allowed to come and see me here but if I were to go out they might catch a glimpse of me. I've no desire to walk amongst them, indeed, the thought horrifies me.

"You must!" he says. "I will arrange it."

I try to continue smiling, for I've no choice in the matter.

But I've underestimated his plans. "I will make you a bazaar," he promises. "Within these very walls."

"How?" I ask.

"You will see," he says, and is gone.

And so it's decided. There's to be a bazaar, modeled on all that I've told him of Kashgar and its marketplace. It will be created and made to disappear again in only a few short days; a gift of illusion.

All of the court is invited to attend and they're curious to see this, my latest gift and a taste of a far-off region of the empire.

It's Lady Wan, of course, who most enters into the spirit of this pretence. She calls for Huan to show her own hairdresser how to arrange her hair "in the Xinjiang style" and her interest sparks more of the ladies to take part. On the first day of the bazaar, a cold autumn morning, she arrives early, her wig in the form of two long plaits laden with gems.

"You look lovely," I tell her and she blushes as though I were the Emperor himself.

"What a wondrous spectacle," she says. "Do all the sights and sounds take away your homesickness?"

I want to tell her that this illusion, this multi-coloured lavish display of how the Emperor imagines Kashgar to be is hardly how my 'home' was. Here I am an Honoured Lady, chosen companion to the Emperor, dressed in my finery and walking amongst a perfect tiny world rather than dressed in ragged layers for warmth, begging or stealing food, worked too hard or going hungry. But innocent Lady Wan, who has lived within these sheltering walls for decades, would not understand and so I nod and smile. "His Majesty has been so kind," I say, which is true. "It is just like home." Which is a lie, but it pleases her and she darts forward and gives me a quick impetuous embrace before stepping back, as though she had done something very daring. I act without thinking, reaching out my arms to her so that she clasps me to her again. I breathe in her perfume, her warm smell of kindness and tighten my arms about her. Faint memories of my mother's hard life rise up in me and when I leave Lady Wan's embrace I have to draw her attention to my little dogs who are pawing at her skirts so that she will not see that my eyes are glistening.

Other ladies arrive with their hair arranged in variations of my own style and many have dressed in versions of the clothes I wear. I know that the dressmaker I use has been much in demand for they've learnt how to make my clothes and have been able to replicate them to suit the other ladies. The ladies walk oddly, conscious of their tight waistcoats outlining their figures. My high-heeled shoes, however, come easily to them. They are used, after all, to walking in shoes raised on platforms the height of a hand. Perhaps they hope that by dressing like his new favourite they will draw the Emperor's favourable attention to themselves, but in this they are mistaken, and I see Lady Wang's face grow dark when she is not even glanced at. Meanwhile Empress Ula Nara is notable by her absence. Word is given out that she is unwell and has asked for the Emperor to attend her. He does so, but briefly. She is not seen again until the festivities are ended, whether by her own choice or his command I am unsure. But something new in all our lives is to be welcomed, and soon there's a festive air, even among the most ambitious ladies.

The bazaar itself, starting at the base of the Precious Moon Tower and stretching across the courtyards of the Forbidden City, is extraordinary. It is huge, once in it one can walk for many minutes before catching a glimpse of its boundaries. There are stalls everywhere, tightly packed to create small walkways between them. Fruits, vegetables and eggs are stacked so high one fears a single item plucked from the towering heaps would bring all crashing to the ground. Sweet raisins and round melons tempt the tongue. Cones of coloured spices and sugars can be cut or scooped to measure. There are stalls with food that can be eaten there and then – hot noodles, stuffed breads, dried melon strips, roasted meats and piles of sweets made with nuts, sugars and honeys. Much of the food has been made under Nurmat's command using an army of cooks and he is here, overseeing the stalls, ensuring foods are offered to all the visitors while he explains what they are and how best to enjoy them. There is a stall of knives with elaborate handles and one of jade. Hats, scarves and shawls made from every kind of fabric and in every colour imaginable flutter in the breeze. The younger women try them on in endless combinations, giggling at themselves as servants hold up mirrors for them to admire the effect.

The stallholders are all eunuchs, those who usually give performances for festivals or in the Emperor's own theatre. They are dressed in traditional clothing, although far too lavishly. It makes me laugh to see stallholders dressed in fine velvet waistcoats, sporting fancifully embroidered felt caps on their heads.

There are animals, too. Camels have been brought here. Goats, sheep, geese, mules. We might be at the trading fairs where the men barter, except here even the animals must be luxurious and so they are brushed and gleaming, some dyed bright colors while others toss their heads at the fluttering of cheerful ribbons woven into their manes, tied about their horns.

Nothing has been overlooked. When the call to prayer sounds from outside the stallholder-eunuchs pull out newly made prayer mats and say prayers they learnt only two days ago. I join in, although I am the only one who understands the words being recited. The ladies and courtiers stand and stare. My praying is usually done behind closed doors and although they have seen many altars and temples, many forms of prayer in their time, this is something new to most of them. I rise a little flustered, but there are so many sights that soon their attention is diverted elsewhere. Performers have been brought in from the Muslim quarter outside. Singers croon the traditional song cycles of the twelve *muqams,* wrestlers and acrobats vie with one another for ever-more daring feats of physical prowess and dancers swirl, the rhythms of their feet growing faster with the clapping of the spectators.

The bazaar lasts for several days, enough time for all those who wish to try their hand at bartering (although the goods on the stalls are theirs for the asking), to ride on camels, to clumsily learn the secretive trading codes of the men. Even some of the little princes and princesses join us and squeal at the unfamiliar sights and sounds. Consorts Qing and Ying are hard-pressed to keep Yongyan in sight as he darts about the stalls. The street foods are popular, though I see to my amusement that even these are protected with the omnipresent silver strips, which look odd amongst sizzling kebabs and stuffed breads laid out on rough platters and grills rather than the dainty porcelain dishes more generally used in the palaces. The Emperor visits every day, striding about greeting his ladies and children, well pleased with the success of his plans. We walk the length of the bazaar together, his arm tight about my waist. He stops to kiss me sometimes and I wrap my arms about his neck and return his kisses under the gaze of his courtiers, insatiable for his touch, the taste of his mouth. I laugh at his antics as he eats from the stalls, tries on hats and plays with the younger children. He feeds me sweetmeats from his favourite stands, so that I have only to see his outstretched fingers to think of honey in my mouth.

Winter comes to the Forbidden City and the winds are unforgiving even within our high red walls. Sparkling icicles dangle down from the edges of the golden roof tiles, adding to their splendour. I'm wrapped in furs and thick velvets, double and even triple layers of silks make up my skirts. The *kang*s of the palace are heated day and night and even Fury doesn't venture out into the snowy gardens.

Sometimes I invite Lady Wan to my rooms and we play drinking games, although I don't drink alcohol and she cannot hold her drink at all – I stumble over the words of poems in my poor Mandarin while she grows pink and flustered, giggling over innuendoes that don't even exist. But I enjoy her company.

Giuseppe asks me to pose for him and I accept willingly. Any indoor pastime is welcome in the cold. After many days of sitting, a servant arrives, with the picture wrapped in silk. I step back, surprised. The face is my own, for Giuseppe is a fine painter. But once again he has disregarded the clothes I wore whilst sitting. Instead, he's painted me in a dark red Manchu dress, my hair in the Manchu style, like a court lady rather than the way I've always been dressed here, in my Altishahr style.

"Why am I dressed as a Manchu?" I ask Jiang, who is peering over my shoulder.

He is unsure and I am puzzled. But I find as the days go by that I'm beginning to like the portrait. I imagine wearing court robes at the big banquets and court events, being a part of the Emperor's entourage rather than the odd one out in any crowd, unable to take part in court life without being noticed and commented on, even after all this time.

When I do meet Giuseppe again he asks if I like the picture.

"Yes," I say. "It is a lovely likeness."

He tilts his head. "And the clothes?" he asks, with mischief in his eyes.

I mimic his tilt of the head. "What about them?" I ask, and he smiles.

I awake in the darkness, a figure standing over me. I wait, silent, trying to keep my breathing steady as though I were still asleep. But Nurmat is not so easily fooled.

"You are in his chambers often now," he begins without preamble.

I sigh. I have escaped Nurmat's questioning for a long time and now I can tell he will not be pleased with me. His hopes of a happy life with Iparhan rest on my ability to provide whatever information she needs. I try to avoid the chastisement I am about to receive. "Where is Jiang? It is his turn to guard me."

"He swapped with me willingly enough. He would rather sleep elsewhere."

"Go away. If they find you…"

He holds out the drinking bowl and lets a few cold drops fall on me. "Water. Your ladyship was thirsty."

I push him away. "Go."

"I have questions for you. I need answers."

I sigh and sit up in bed. "Go back to her, Nurmat. Tell her I am a clot and a useless girl who can't even ask simple questions of the Emperor. Tell her she should give up and go away with you to be married. Or find some other way of raising a rebellion."

He ignores me and sits heavily on my bed, head and shoulders slumped.

"Do you have questions for me, then?" I ask impatiently.

"Is he gentle to you?"

"What?"

"You heard me."

"What do you care?"

"She wants to know."

"Why would she want to know that?"

"Just tell me," he mutters, his face turned away from me.

I frown. "Yes."

"And his rooms – do you stay in them all night?"

I don't understand this line of questioning. "Not always."

"Does he favour darkness or light when you are in his company?"

I blink. "There are lanterns," I say. "But they are only a soft light. Why?"

He shakes his head but doesn't answer.

I wonder if he enjoys thinking of the Emperor and I together in his chambers and shift my feet away from his perch at the foot of my bed. "I am tired now, Nurmat," I say, my voice cool. "You should leave."

He gets up and stumbles, catching himself on the edge of the bed close to me. When he breathes out I catch a strong smell of alcohol. "Are you *drunk*?"

"Mind your own business," he mutters.

I catch hold of his arm and put my face close to his, sniffing. He reeks of drink. "You idiot," I hiss.

He keeps his face close to mine, inhaling my scent and slurs his words. "Kiss me, Iparhan."

I push him away, hard. "I'm not Iparhan, as you know all too well," I snap.

"I wish you were."

"What do you mean?"

He sighs. "Look at you, Hidligh," he says. "Full of love for the Emperor. Making friends even with the other ladies. Playing with your pet animals. You have a gentleness that I would wish for in Iparhan. If she were more like you she would have turned away from all of this, she would have come to me when I begged her to, rather than chasing this dream."

"It's not a dream, it's a nightmare," I say.

We sit for a moment in silence before he sighs again. "I have questions," he says. "Questions that have to be answered."

"What are they, then?"

"When you are with the Emperor, does he like to fondle your breasts – or does he prefer your buttocks?"

I gape at him in the darkness, then feel rage boil up in me. "Go and drool over that album of paintings I was forced to enact with you if you want to know what a man and a woman do together. It's not seemly to ask me."

He laughs. "The street girl is growing modest," he says with a jeer in his voice that I don't care for.

"I was always modest, even when I was on the streets, Nurmat," I spit back. "I was penniless, not a whore. Leave, now."

"Show me what you do with the Emperor," he says, coming closer to me.

The slap I give him is loud enough to make him back away. "Get *out*," I say as loudly as I dare. "And take your filthy suggestions with you. What would your precious Iparhan have to say if she heard you propositioning me?"

He stands, swaying, above me. "She asked," he says. He sounds sad, but there is anger underneath. "She asked."

"Asked what?"

"What you do with him."

I frown, afraid now rather than angry. Why would Iparhan ask such a question? "I don't believe you."

He shrugs, sets the water bowl down unsteadily and shuffles towards the door. "She asked," he mutters.

"Wait!" I hiss at him, wary of making too much noise. "Why would she want to know such things?"

He pauses in the doorway without turning to me and takes a breath as though about to speak, but instead he exhales and shakes his head. "Better you not know," he says wearily. "Go back to sleep, Hidligh."

I lie awake throughout the rest of the night although my eyes ache with tiredness. Something has changed. Nurmat knows something about Iparhan's plans, something that has taken away his hope of a happy future, something that has made him full of despair. I reach out for the answer but it will not come to me and by dawn I give up. No doubt Nurmat will come to me again and I will ask him then.

But he does not come at night and he avoids me during the day. If I try to catch his eye he looks away. I think of calling him to me and demanding an explanation but I cannot bring myself to do it. I want to enjoy this freedom from his questions and so I pretend all is well, although I know I am lying to myself.

We celebrate the Emperor's birthday. It's an occasion of lavish gifts, good wishes, elaborate clothing and rituals carried out to perfection. In the evening we make our way to the palace theatre, where giant floats are paraded by hundreds of costumed officials and actors, waving banners while loud music is played. Twisting imperial dragons dance while giant peaches – symbols of longevity – split open to reveal colourful carved flowers, Buddhas and gods hidden within. Princes and nobles make their obeisances and all is joyfulness. The servants chosen to accompany me include Nurmat and he presents sweetmeats made to my orders, which are offered by the Emperor to those closest to him. Nurmat carries the dishes of sweets from one lady to another while I keep a wary eye on him.

The Empress arrives, causing a flurry of bows in her direction. She looks about her and her eyes alight on me. I bow and send Nurmat to her with the sweets. She looks down at the platter and I think she is going to refuse but then she chooses one and lifts it to her mouth. Nurmat bows again but she holds up a hand to keep him by her side.

"Are you happy here?" I hear her ask. "So far away from your homeland?"

Nurmat blinks a little at being addressed directly. "Yes, Your Majesty," he answers.

She gazes at him in silence before selecting another sweet, her golden nail tips holding it as though in a bird's beak. "These are good," she tells him. "You will stay by my side while I eat."

I frown as I watch her eat one after another without any apparent enjoyment. Her mouth opens to speak but a new float arrives and the gongs and cymbals accompanying its shower of sparkling fireworks prevent me hearing what else she says. I see her mouth move and Nurmat's mouth responding but I cannot make out what they are saying. I watch them, wondering at her interest in him, until the Emperor waves me over to him. He offers me a slender pole from which dangles a giant pearl carved from white jade. He points to a writhing dragon and shows me how to offer the pearl, his hands on mine, our bodies pressed close together. I forget about the Empress and enjoy the warmth of his touch and his laughter in my ear while below us the dragon roars and bites at the pearl.

"Come to my rooms," murmurs the Emperor in my ear and I nod, feeling a sudden heat rush through me.

I stand impatiently as I am undressed, my feet twitching, ready to walk behind the eunuch to the bedchamber. Once there, instead of making my way to the bed I stand before the strange chair, my feet on its padded base, my hands resting lightly on its absurdly long arms. I cast my mind back to the dunes. Was there a painting with such a chair depicted?

"Kneel," says the Emperor's low voice behind me.

I don't turn to face him. Instead I lift up one leg and then the other, kneeling on the silken seat, my knees spread apart. From behind me the Emperor lifts up each of my hands and places them on the high, upholstered headrest. The position tilts me forwards, my own weight pinning down my hands, my backside lifted towards the Emperor. I find my breath growing short as I feel him caress me, hear his own breath growing quicker. His fingers slip between my parted thighs and when he finds me wet to his touch he groans my name. In a moment he is inside me and I cry out with the suddenness of it, with the urgency of his desire.

On my return to my palace I find the servants waiting anxiously.

"The Empress has sent for you," says Huan, and seeing my face turn white he pats my hand to comfort me, but he cannot countermand her order and so I am forced to step back into my chair and feel the lurch in my stomach as I am lifted.

I'm shown into her palace and taken once again to the room with the black screen, but this time she is standing by the golden table, staring at her four *ruyi*.

I perform my kowtow to her and she waits until I rise, then dismisses the servants from the suddenly empty room.

I shift from one foot to the other, too aware of the wetness between my thighs. I did not have time to wash before I came here. Can she smell the Emperor on me?

"The Emperor shows you favour," she says.

I feel my heart sink. "Yes, Your Majesty," I say. "He has been gracious to me – as he is to all his ladies," I add, hoping to divert her attention to those other women whom he also favours, such as Imperial Noble Consort Ling.

She ignores my ploy. "I am concerned."

I bow my head, waiting.

"I have heard rumours," she says.

I look up, frowning. "Rumours?"

"I have heard that the cook that His Majesty gave you is of your own country and that you speak often with him."

"He comes to me for his orders," I say, too quickly. "To agree on the dishes he should serve at my table." *Does she know?* I think to myself. *Does she know somehow that he is not a eunuch?*

Her smooth calm face does not change. Her steady eyes meet mine. "At night?"

I feel my skin grow cold. I try to keep my eyes on hers but can feel myself fail under her gaze. "He is a eunuch," I say and then curse myself for bringing attention to something over which there should be no doubt. "There can be no harm in his attending me."

She tilts her head slightly. "There are many ways in which a eunuch may please his mistress," she says quietly. "It has been known before."

I gape at her. Such a thought had never even occurred to me. "I – such things – how?" I stutter at last.

Her lip curls. "Perhaps when you are older you will understand more of what can be between a woman and a man – or even a eunuch," she says. "You are still a child who believes the storytellers' lies of true love."

I wait. She could have me demoted, stripped of my title, even, perhaps, executed, if she can prove wrongdoing.

At last she turns away. "Thank you for your visit, Lady He," she says.

I kowtow to her back and when I am done I back nervously away, expecting her to turn on me at any moment. She keeps her face turned away but speaks softly just as I reach the safety of the doorway. "Lady He?"

I hold onto the doorway for courage and turn back. "Your Majesty?"

"I will not fail to undo you if I find you are betraying the Emperor."

Back at my palace I call for Huan. I'm shaking with fear and anger. "I have a spy amongst my servants," I tell him. "Someone who reports on me to the Empress. I will not have such disloyalty."

Huan is devastated. He orders a search of the servant's quarters and when a maid is found with a jade hairpin and a eunuch is found with several large coins, more than most servants might have, they are dragged before me, each protesting their innocence.

"Whip them," I say, my fear overriding their tearful faces and protestations.

I've never ordered a punishment before, but then I've never been so afraid either. But I can't watch for long. The eunuch gets only a few lashes before I put my hand on Huan's sleeve and beg him to stop. The sight of the red wheals rising on his back make me feel sick. Huan tuts at my softness.

"A spy in your household is a dangerous thing," he says. "They must be punished."

I shake my head. "How do we even know they are the right people?" I say.

Huan is stubborn. 'Well, the maid has not been whipped yet," he says, "But she will kneel in the courtyard throughout the night tonight, in the cold, as a warning to any of your servants who might be disloyal."

I let her begin the punishment but that night, when all the servants are asleep, I make my way outside and pull the weeping girl up by her arm. She staggers, for she's already been kneeling for some time, but follows me back to the palace, sobbing her thanks for my kindness to her.

"Be quiet," I tell her. "You will wake Huan and he will send you back out to the courtyard."

She manages to stifle her sobs but the next morning she is brought to me by Huan. She is carrying a stick.

"Don't beat her, Huan," I say, weary from a night spent unable to sleep. "I will not have her beaten when I do not even know she is a spy."

The girl falls to her knees before me, her face pressed to the ground. "I *am* a spy," she sobs. "But not for the Empress."

Huan pulls her to her knees. "Tell her ladyship what you just told me," he demands.

"I was sent to work for you by Lady Ling," sobs the girl.

I rub my eyes, which are aching. Nothing makes sense. "Lady Ling? Why would she want to spy on me?"

The girl holds out the stick to me. "For this."

I take the stick. It's nothing special, a plain piece of wood, shaped into a long flat stick. It has notches on it, roughly etched on its surface. I turn it over in my hands. "What is it?"

The maid points to the notches. "Lady Ling wanted to know when you bled and for how many days, how much blood. Which days the Emperor summoned you. If you were to fail to bleed, if you were to fall with child, I was to tell her at once."

I look down at the notches, which tell me what I know anyway, that my courses are erratic and short. Perhaps the years of poor food and cold as a child and young girl damaged me inside, but certainly I do not expect to bear children. I shake my head. Huan's fists are clenched; he will beat the girl himself if I do not stop him.

"Why did you confess to me?" I ask.

The girl looks up at me, tears still flowing. "You stopped my punishment," she says.

I sigh. "You will stay here and serve me," I say and Huan tuts under his breath. "You will be loyal only to me."

"Yes, your ladyship," breathes the girl. "But Lady Ling? I am afraid of her."

I turn the stick over in my hands. "Wrap this in silk and take it to Lady Ling," I say to Huan. "Give it to her and tell her that her children have little to fear from me. Tell her to keep to her own path and that I will keep to mine. Our paths will not cross."

Huan is reluctant but he does as he's told and the maid is sent back to the servants' quarters, her eyes shining with new-found devotion to me.

The bitter cold continues and now the Kitchen God must be sacrificed to. This year, being in favour with the Emperor, I see many of the rituals in person. The altar is loaded with fat sheep, cakes, tea, soups as well as fruit and vegetables. I pour sugar on when it's my turn to make an offering. There are firecrackers everywhere and I clutch at my furred skirts to make sure none might set me on fire, so wildly are they thrown about. But in all of the chaos it is the Emperor himself who holds my attention. He enters into the celebrations with gusto, banging on a little drum and singing a song that sets the courtiers laughing, called 'The Emperor in Search of Honest Officials'. His face grows flushed with the performance and I find myself laughing. He laughs back and carries on with his song, his drumming growing ever louder to compete with the din of fireworks. Afterwards he takes my hand and leads me to the main gates, where mighty fireworks rise over the walls into Beijing itself.

"Happy?" he asks and I only nod, my cheeks pink from the cold and excitement, my hand warm in his. He chuckles and then leaves me to make his way to yet more altars, for the New Year celebrations require him to undertake many rituals and ceremonies.

I watch him go before turning back to my chair to be carried home. I wish I could go with him.

Mid-afternoon and Huan almost runs into the room. "My lady! My lady!"

I look up from a board game, my piece still held in my hand. "Yes?"

"You are to be promoted!"

I feel my heart swoop. "Promoted?"

He kneels before me, his face flushed with happiness. "Yes! You are to be made *Pin*!"

"Pin?"

"An Imperial Concubine, not just an Honoured Lady. Only six of that rank are allowed within the palace at any one time. Whereas there can be any number of Honoured Ladies! Your rank rises to fifth."

His pride in me is touching. "And this is because the Emperor has…" I blush.

He shakes his head, beaming. "It is because the Emperor is *pleased* with you," he is keen to clarify. "Not all the ladies who are called to his rooms are promoted."

I blush more deeply, but I'm happy. My only fear is the Empress. Will she use this as an opportunity to expose me, to humiliate me? Or has her unknown spy told her that Nurmat no longer comes to me at night?

My clothes, as ever, are magnificent, rich pinks and golds, silk flowers pinned in my hair and gold earrings that drip with pearls.

"The Lady He is promoted: she is made *Pin*, Imperial Concubine!"

Lists of my new privileges are read out. New allocations of taels of silver, bolts of cloth, servants and more will be given to me. I am also presented with a new *ruyi*, this one of delicate white jade inlaid with many coloured gems which take the shape of a garden of flowers.

I look about me and see the ladies of the court watching me just as they did on my arrival here. Now I see the friendly faces of Lady Wan, Consorts Qing and Ying and I smile at them, but I am also aware of the less friendly gazes fixed on me. The Empress, Lady Ling, Lady Wang. Their eyes travel over my face and the precious *ruyi* clasped in my hands, symbol of my promotion. Lady Wang's scowl is quite terrifying, although I don't believe she holds enough power to be a real threat to me. Lady Ling is only interested in her children and as the months pass and still I am not pregnant I must surely become less of an enemy to her. But the Empress…

I move to leave the room, hoping that my absence will mollify her but the Emperor holds up a hand. "I have another gift for you," he says, smiling. "Something to mark the anniversary of you joining my court."

All heads turn towards him. His lavishness in my regard sometimes creates jealousy amongst his ladies, but the nature of his gifts is intriguing to the courtiers, for they're often unusual.

I smile and bow. "I am honoured, Your Majesty. You have done more than enough."

He's pleased, but his eyes still twinkle with the thought of his new gift. "I believe your cook has been satisfactory," he says. "I have enjoyed good meals at your palace and I even hear your clothes have been altered to ensure you can continue to eat your fill." He chuckles.

My eyes slide to the Empress, whose face is motionless, then back to him. I try to smile as though amused and a little embarrassed by his reference to my new-found curves. "Yes, Your Majesty. He is a most excellent cook."

"Very good," he says. "Now I have brought you a new servant. A maid."

My eyebrows twitch towards a frown although I try to keep a pleasant expression on my face as he watches me, beaming. *A maid?* I think, *I have many maids. Why another?*

"A maid," he clarifies, "from your own lands. One who will remind you of Xinjiang and help you to feel more at home here."

I feel my legs begin to shake beneath the heavy folds of my skirt. *No*, I think. *It's not possible. Please.* I feel Jiang by my side, discreetly placing a hand against the small of my back for support, for he's seen my colour fade and can sense my distress, although he must be unsure as to what's causing it.

But the Emperor has already waved his hand towards someone behind me. I turn very slowly and there on the floor, prostrate in a bow, her hair tied back into a plait with a small red ribbon, her robe a humble blue cotton, is Iparhan.

I know it's her, before she even lifts her head. I know her too well to be fooled. She kowtows to me, her face, as it lifts up towards me, a picture of submission, then stands and makes her way into the shadows by the door to await me. She is limping, her right leg drags a little behind her.

I look back at the Emperor and lock my knees so that my legs can no longer shake. I wait for the truth to appear on his face, for him to have seen what I know is there to be seen: how Iparhan and I are so alike. I wait for his face to grow puzzled at our similarity, for the whispers around the court to begin, for the Emperor to command us both to stand before him so that he can see our faces more clearly and then… and then demand to know what is going on here, how it can be that a humble maid should look like her mistress, how…

He is waiting for my thanks. His smile is beginning to fade, for I am standing staring up at him as though mute. I wait a moment longer. Can he not see us, I think? I glance over my shoulder and see Iparhan's outline in the shadows. I would know her for a palace maid anywhere, I think. The pale blue robe, the little red hair ribbon holding her single plait...

And now I see that it is our clothes that have saved me. How could anyone look at this maid, in her humble cotton robe in the Manchu style, and then at my glorious pink and golden silks in the Altishahr style and think us alike? I may be safe if I can keep her as hidden away as possible.

I swallow and wet my lips. "Your Majesty's generosity knows no bounds," I say. "Thank you."

His smile returns. He enjoys giving gifts and in me he has found a supposed reason to give even more of them. My 'homesickness' allows him to be inventive, to give gifts which are not just tokens or commonplace priceless items. He is enjoying this chance to woo me in a different way. "You should go back to your palace now," he says cheerfully. "Your maid can tell you of life at home. You will enjoy her company and forget your longings for Xinjiang."

I kowtow to him and then stand, making my way to the door. At the door Iparhan steps to my side. She is all demureness and respect.

"Are you mad?" I hiss to her, moving away from Jiang who might overhear and understand us. "What are you doing here?"

She smiles and dips her head to me in a parody of obedience, which from a distance must look convincing. "I am here to take your place," she says as she helps me into my chair, her voice so soft I cannot be sure I heard her correctly.

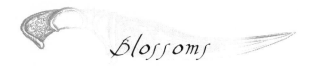

Blossoms

I DON'T ENTER THROUGH THE IMMENSE red doors, of course. I am led into the Forbidden City by means of the side gate on the western wall, surrounded by the crowds of beggars and street vendors who are unceremoniously kicked out of the way by the guard who leads me here. I keep my head down and my limp heavy. Past the endless walls we walk, across the bridges where the water lies frozen beneath us and at last up the many many steps to the huge receiving hall.

There was once a great orchard estate outside the walls of Kashgar. In spring we children ate mulberries, the first sweet taste of sunshine yet to come. In summer we ate cherries and apricots, crammed our greedy mouths with juicy figs before autumn's sunshine brought us sweet new almonds and pistachios, fresh pears and crunchy apples, icy pressed grape juice and bejeweled pomegranates. We ate until we were full, refused the meals our servants had prepared, ruined our clothes with the dark juices of fresh fruits and climbed the trees, standing swaying in their tops to allow the breeze to caress our flushed skin.

Then the newly-appointed officials of the Emperor decreed that Kashgar was too congested for their liking. The blossoming trees were felled to make way for the barracks, the armoury, the granaries, treasuries, the Imperial Hall and Temple. Where once fruits and leaves reached out to the sun, now there are only soldiers and officials and scribes, the Emperor's men, doing his business, securing his conquest.

At first I barely recognise her. She is dressed more magnificently than we were ever able to clothe her, her dark hair shining with silk flowers, her whole body richly adorned with pink and gold silks. Strings of pearls fall from every part of her – her hair, her ears, her throat.

But it is happiness that has truly changed her. She stands taller; she is more graceful. As she rises from her kowtow she looks into the Emperor's face and the smile she gives him is for him alone, as though they were in their bedchamber together.

Standing in the shadows of the cavernous receiving hall I too look at the Emperor's face, for the first time. This is the man who has taken my country, my family, my home. He took my family's power and crushed it; his men have taken the blossoms of our orchard and trampled on them. Because of him I have lost everything. I want nothing more than to see him dead.

He holds out a hand, indicating me with a smile. I strip my face of my true feelings and fall to my knees, ready to be presented to Hidligh.

Five Hundred Oleaster Trees

I SIT IN THE GLOWING ORANGE-TINTED interior of the chair as it rocks back to my palace. I can think of nothing except pulling air into my lungs and releasing it. Each breath is a struggle. I pull aside the curtain at the window hoping that cooler air will help me but by the side of my chair trots Iparhan, her eyes looking ahead, one foot dragging a little. I close the window again and gulp the air although it does not seem to reach my lungs.

Once we reach the courtyard Iparhan's hand appears in the doorway of the chair to help me out. I ignore her and step out alone, then walk swiftly into the palace, making my way to the bedroom. I call for Huan, who is all happiness at my promotion and is busy instructing my new servants in their duties.

"I need tea," I say, "and rest."

"Of course," he says. "It has been a busy day. I will send your new maid to you."

I open my mouth but it is too late to refuse, he has already left the room. I sit on the edge of my bed, my shoulders hunched until she arrives. "Why did you come?" I ask.

"I have come to do what must be done," Iparhan says. She keeps her voice light and pleasant, so that anyone hearing her and not understanding our language would think her a well-spoken serving girl with a cheerful demeanour. While she talks she busies herself tidying the room, as though dusting the playing pieces of my board games were her only concern in life.

I try to keep my voice from trembling so that anyone listening will not know that I am in distress. I have to lie back on my bed as though at rest, although I'm finding it hard to lie still. "You are putting me at great risk. You said all I had to do was live a life of luxury and tell you what you wanted to know. I told you all about the eunuchs and you sent a fake eunuch to live within my palace, risking his life and mine. I was encouraged to become the Emperor's favourite which I have done and now you are here to carry out some plan of which I know nothing and which is probably risking my life even further. We look like each other! Someone will notice. I can't believe they have not seen it already."

"They all look the same to me," she says. "No doubt we all look the same to them."

I think of Huan's worried wrinkles, Jiang's gentle smile. My maids, the one with the round plump face and the one with the surprised eyes. "They don't look the same to me," I say.

She shrugs. There is no one to see her but me. "There's no need for you to fret about what your maids look like," she says brightly. "Carry on living your life of luxury. Meanwhile your people are oppressed by a greedy Emperor who drains our country of its goods and its pride."

"You think he is a monster," I say. "He is a kind man."

"A kind man when he gets what he wants," she says, still with a smile on her face.

"Stop pretending to be pleasant, Iparhan," I say. "There's no one here to see you except me and I know better."

"I will speak with you tonight," she says, her voice still light, her smile still fixed. "Appoint Nurmat as your guard in the bedchamber and ask for me to wait upon you. You can tell Huan that you wish me to talk to you of your homeland." She snorts. "I am sure he will believe you, the fool dotes on you."

I don't answer her. I think for a moment of asking for someone else to guard me, of telling Huan that Iparhan is not to attend me at all, but I know this will only seem odd. A heavy weight settles in my stomach as I carry out Iparhan's orders.

The lights are dim in my bedchamber. Huan checks that all has been done according to my stated wishes – that Nurmat is ready to lie on his bedroll just inside my door, that Iparhan is standing, the very model of duty and good behaviour by my bed – then he wishes me good night. I want to ask him to stay by my side but I cannot and instead I force a smile onto my lips. "Good night Huan," I say, and he leaves the room, satisfied.

I pull my legs up tight to my chest and sit huddled among my silk covers. "Well?" I ask. "Are you going to tell me now what your plan is?"

Iparhan is already busy. She has collected my discarded clothes, as a good maid should, and now she lays them on a small table and begins to undress.

"What are you doing?" I ask.

"Be quiet," she says, her movements quick. Nurmat sits on the bedroll by the door. He does not watch her. He seems to know what she is doing already. He keeps his eyes lowered, fixed on her blue cotton robe, now lying crumpled on the floor. She pulls on my clothes, and busies herself with the buttons. She is now dressed in a magnificent skirt in a vibrant blue, embroidered in gold vines and pale pink blossoms with a waistcoat in rose, a shirt in sheerest cream.

I swallow at the sight of her, at the fear rising in my gorge. "Why are you here?"

"To take your place, as I told you."

"I don't understand."

She speaks as though to an idiot. "I will play your part. You will play mine. You will be the maid. I will be the concubine."

I blink. "That's not possible. The people here at court know my face."

"Don't be a fool, Hidligh," she says, stepping into my shoes. "You must have known the first time you saw yourself all dressed up in a mirror that we look alike. Didn't you ever wonder why you of all people should have been chosen? A dirty little street girl with the manners of a peasant? To be made into a concubine fit for an emperor? An ignorant child, who knows nothing of my plans, nor understands the troubles of our homeland, to be made into a spy? Come, you are not so dim-witted as all that."

And then I know. And I know how stupid I have been from the very beginning. Iparhan wanted to enter the Forbidden City but her scar stopped her from doing so. A concubine must be perfect. But when she saw me in the market and the resemblance I bore to her, she knew that her plan was not ruined on the day Nurmat scarred her. By having me enter the Forbidden City in her stead and endear myself to the Emperor, she could then take my place in the palace and in the Emperor's bed. She could find out whatever she needed to know. Her stories about how I should spy for her were only stories. All she needed was for me to arrive at court, to be known to my servants and favoured by the Emperor. I think of Mei's instruction to look in a mirror. I curse myself for being a fool, for pushing away my fears and believing in the possibility of a happy life here. But still I find myself groping for a reprieve. "Your scar…"

She finishes the buttons and nods as though I have been helpful in reminding her. Seating herself at the table where Huan does my hair and makeup she unfastens the small red ribbon holding her hair in its humble plait. Unbound, her hair is a river of black silk, still rippled from its former bindings. From Huan's small bags she extracts various little pots and boxes, before carefully applying creams and powders, slowly covering her scar, now grown white with time. I watch as her face changes to how it must once have been, her skin smooth and even. Once her scar fades away her eyes shine out, large and dark. She paints her lips a dusky pink and outlines her eyes. Once or twice she glances at me, then looks back into the mirror, making changes to her face. She adds a deeper blush to her pale cheeks, darkens her chin to give the appearance of a dimple, which she does not have. I do. She adds paler powder to the sides of her slender nose, making it seem a little wider, like mine. She is making herself look as much like me as possible.

I feel myself beginning to breathe faster, although each breath is too shallow to give me enough air. I try to think about how I look. Does she look enough like me? The dim light in the room is aiding her disguise.

"Light more lanterns," I say to Nurmat.

He looks up at me and I stare back at him. "Do it," I say, and my voice is hoarse.

He looks to Iparhan for confirmation and she shrugs as though my request is of little consequence. She is busy rebraiding her hair into my customary two plaits, entwining them with ribbons and gems. She is quick and certain. She must have practised this many times. "Do it," she echoes.

Nurmat stands and slowly lights another lantern.

"And another," I say. "Light them all."

It takes some time and while he lights the lanterns Iparhan examines herself in the mirror. Satisfied, she stoops briefly, then stands. In her hand are the blue cotton robe and the small red ribbon that bound her hair. She throws them towards me. The faded blue and red drift lightly through the room, landing on the edge of my bed.

"Put them on," she says.

I shake my head although I know already that I will do as she says. But I feel as though I must oppose her, if only briefly, if only so that she knows that I am unwilling. It seems so important that she should know that I am unwilling.

"Put them on," says Iparhan.

Slowly I reach out my hand and pick up the cotton robe. I let the silk sleeping robe I am wearing slip from my shoulders and pull the rough cotton over my head. I swing my feet to the floor and stand, unsteady as though I have been drinking. The robe falls nearly to my feet, its colour dimmed with many years of washing. The red ribbon slips from the bed and falls to the floor. I bend over automatically to pick it up. As I stand I find Iparhan behind me, her hands already in my hair.

"Keep still," she says. She braids my hair, her hands moving at speed while I stand motionless, one hand clutching the red ribbon. She pulls it from my grasp and ties the end of my single plait. "Now come here," she says.

I stumble as she leads me to the table, then sit, eyes lowered, unable to look in the mirror. Beside me, Iparhan rummages in the bags and begins to apply makeup to my face. The room grows brighter as Nurmat lights lantern after lantern.

"Look," says Iparhan. Her hands are still at last.

I stay still.

"You said it was not possible," she says. "Now judge."

The room is now so bright with light, it might almost be daytime. I lift my head and look into the depths of the mirror. Behind me, in the far part of the room, still holding a darkened lantern, stands Nurmat. At my side, Iparhan.

In the mirror are reflected two women. One richly adorned in fine clothes, her hair bound with gemstones. The skin of her face is smooth and pale, with flushed cheeks and pink lips. Her eyes are large and dark. By her side, shoulders slumped, sits a maid. Her dark hair is pulled back in a simple plait, tied with a worn red ribbon. Her skin is pale, although its smoothness is interrupted by a scar, which runs from the tip of her eye down across the whole of her cheek, marring any good looks a girl of her lowly stature might have been blessed with. Her rough cotton robe is a pale blue, the dye worn away by many years of service.

I reach up a hand to the scar painted onto my face and try to wipe it away but Iparhan's hand is already on mine, her grip so hard her nails dig into my skin.

"You can have it painted on or carved on with a knife, Hidligh," she says. "You know I will do it. Which is it to be?"

I let my hand go limp in hers and she releases me. I sit with my hands in my lap. Iparhan nods her approval.

My voice comes out as a whisper. "The servants may be fooled," I say. "But I have lain with the Emperor. He…"

Abruptly Iparhan holds out her hand. I flinch, expecting a dagger, but she places one hand over my eyes and the other close to my face. "Breathe in," she commands.

I breathe in and the perfume we are both wearing washes over me.

"In the darkness there are only two senses," says Iparhan. "Touch. And smell."

I sit, silent and blinded, the scent filling my nostrils. The perfume I've worn with such care and growing pride since I came here, the perfume that was first Iparhan's and then mine, is being turned against me. The whole world by now knows that the Emperor's concubine from Xinjiang is scented with a magical fragrance emitted from her very own skin. The court perfumer has been unable to replicate it. In the darkness, that fragrance *is* Lady He. Any suspicions would fall away in the shadows of the Emperor's bedchamber, once he smelled that scent. Besides, there is only one woman in all of the palaces who dresses in these foreign clothes, whose hair is arranged like this. I am unique at court and this uniqueness is Iparhan's greatest weapon.

Hot unbidden tears trickle down my cheeks and neck.

Iparhan pulls away her hand and wipes my tears off on her silk skirt. "You are beginning to care for him," she says. "You fool. You are nothing to him, just another woman at his beck and call. You are favoured now because you are still new and every time he sees you he thinks of his conquests and he feels desire rise up in him. But in time another girl would come along, another pretty face from some other conquered land. And then you would be a nobody. Waiting, like bald, wrinkled Lady Wan, for a call that never comes. Playing with your little animals in your gilded world. Theirs would be the only caresses you would ever receive."

I turn my face away from her.

Iparhan looks back into the mirror. "So," she says. "You believe me now. You have seen that it can be done."

I sit in silence.

"I will not take your place all of the time," says Iparhan. "Only when it suits my purpose. It does not suit me to spend my days being fawned over by those mincing eunuchs. And it would be difficult for me to hide my scar all the time when I must be bathed by others. For the most part, you will continue your life as it was before I arrived here. But when you are due to meet with the Emperor, or any other person whom I deem to be of use to myself, I will take your place and you will take mine. You will not argue with me when I order you to your room so that we can effect this change. If you do, I will see to it that you lose your life."

"Then you would lose your place here," I say quickly.

She shakes her head and stands. She begins to strip off my clothes and I feel myself slumping with relief that she is about to give me back my place. "I would take your place once you were dead, Hidligh," she says, the clothes slipping to the floor. "It would be difficult to hide my scar, but not impossible." Suddenly she raises her voice. "Huan!" she calls loudly. "Huan! Nurmat – go and fetch Huan for me."

Nurmat leaves the room and I turn to her. "Iparhan," I begin, but she waves me into silence as footsteps return. Huan has come at a trot, anxious to know why his mistress should be calling for him in the middle of the night. I stand up, uncertain of what will happen now, whether I should be preparing to run or plead my case. I find myself holding my breath, waiting. Huan knows me too well to be fooled by some makeup.

Iparhan has already darted across the room, grabbed my sleeping robe and thrown herself on the bed. She lies with the covers strewn about her. As soon as Huan enters the room she reaches out her hand to him. "I do not feel well," she says, and the voice that emerges from her mouth is so like mine that I blink. I think back to the dunes, how she mimicked Mei's voice. Now she has taken mine.

Huan is all attentiveness. "What ails you, my lady?" he asks.

"I have a stomach ache," complains Iparhan and I see Huan's eyes widen with fear that she has been poisoned. She reassures him. "A... a *woman's* ache," she modifies, lowering her eyes as though embarrassed at revealing such an intimacy.

Huan's anxious demeanour changes. I wait for him to say something, to realise the deception, but he is all comfort. He arranges the covers about her, settles her back on the pillows. Then his eye falls on me. "Don't just stand there, girl," he admonishes me. "Pour her ladyship some water."

I stand and stare at him. I cannot believe that he has been fooled, that he looks at me and does not see me, sees only the blue robe of a maid, any maid, but he is already searching through a box for some medicine from the physician. "Here," he says with tenderness to Iparhan. "It will help you sleep better."

Iparhan takes the proffered remedy.

Huan turns back to me. "Girl!" he says, annoyed. "Water! Now!"

I fumble with the water jug, slopping water over the table as the little bowl overfills. Huan strides over to me and cuffs me sharply round the head, the blow stinging my ear. He fills a new bowl and takes it to Iparhan. "Drink this, my lady," he says. Over his shoulder he snaps at me. "Clean up the mess you have made."

Iparhan pats his hand. "You are very good to me, Huan," she says, all but simpering. "Don't mind the girl. She has a good deal to learn. I am sure you will make her into an excellent maid. And I feel better now. I shall get some sleep."

Mollified, Huan arranges the covers one more time and nods to Nurmat to put out the lanterns. "Good night, your ladyship," he says, then turns to me. "Come along girl, back to your sleeping quarters."

Iparhan intervenes. "I will keep her with me until I am asleep," she says. "Then she will return to her bed."

Huan nods with satisfaction, bows to her and leaves the room.

I stand in silence while Iparhan slowly climbs out of my bed. She is smiling. "Your chief attendant is not very perceptive, is he, Hidligh? The room so bright, his face a mere hand's breadth from mine, and still he cares for me like a child while he cuffs you for being a lazy maid." She stands, removes the silk robe and holds out her hand. "Take off that robe," she says. "And wipe your face. You don't want to wake up with a scar, now, do you?"

I stand naked and watch her braid her hair. When she is done she heads for the door, her bare feet silent.

"When will you take my place?" I ask her.

She pauses for a moment by the door and answers without facing me. "Whenever I so choose," she says. "Goodnight, Hidligh."

I wait, dreading Iparhan's next move, but she plays her part to perfection for days. She does not speak much, she limps, her scar is clearly visible. Huan grows to like her.

"She is so helpful and reliable," he says to me. "So compliant. I believe she has learnt our ways more quickly than I expected after her first clumsiness."

I find even talking about Iparhan difficult. My hands ball into fists and I struggle to keep a smile on my face.

"Are you pleased to have her here?" asks Huan. "Does she talk to you of your homeland?"

I shake my head. I don't want to encourage Huan to send her to me more often. Just the sight of her makes my heart beat faster, my breath grow shallow in my throat. "She is a good enough girl," I say. "But her memories of home are different from mine."

"Of course," agrees Huan. "She is only a poor girl, not from a well-to-do family like your own. She would know little of the life you led before coming here."

I nod, thinking of how even her hideaway was luxurious whilst my own life was lived in the streets and stables of fine houses like those her family would have owned.

"I believe there may also be a little romance blooming," says Huan coyly.

"Romance?"

"Between your cook and the girl," says Huan, now happily gossiping. "I saw them talking together and he stroked her face. She turned away, of course, as a good girl should, but…"

I think about the parts they're playing and frown. "He's a *eunuch*," I say.

Huan shrugs. "Sometimes the eunuchs are permitted to take a wife. And besides, the poor girl will not have many offers, with her face scarred and that limp. But she is a kind girl and no doubt she would make a loving wife."

I nod, distracted. If Iparhan and Nurmat are seen together perhaps it will take away suspicion from myself and Nurmat, which can only be a good thing.

"Well, they have my blessing," I say, hoping that by doing so I will lend credence to their play-acting. "Although it does not seem much of a marriage for a maid."

Huan nods. "It can be difficult," he agrees. "But there have been many such marriages and she would be cared for at least. She might even adopt a child."

I try to imagine Iparhan dandling a baby and fail. "Enough chatter about servants' matters," I say, forcing my hands to unclench. "Tell me some court gossip," I add, hoping it will turn Huan's mind away from Iparhan and Nurmat.

Huan leans in to me. "Lady Wang is in trouble," he whispers. "She beat a servant to death. She is in disgrace and has been demoted."

I find myself wondering whether it would be worth a demotion to have Iparhan beaten to death but I know I don't have it in me to order such a thing, whatever crime I could invent for her to have committed. My fingers creep to my throat and the little rough red mark I'd thought gone returns with my nervous habit.

I am sitting with Lady Wan, drinking tea and playing a board game, when a servant appears at the door. "His Majesty requests your company this evening," he says.

These words always lift our spirits but I am a little embarrassed, for Lady Wan has not been called to his rooms for many years. But she is smiling. "Huan," she calls. When he joins us she pulls from a little purse at her waist a golden-wrought lotus flower. "For her hair," she instructs him.

"Thank you," I say as she rises to leave us.

She pats my hair. "Such fine hair deserves fine jewels," she says. "I will see you soon."

As soon as she leaves us there are plans and preparations. Clothes are selected, Huan mulls over hairstyles to incorporate the new golden flower, servants rush about. It's mid-morning and I say that I will eat and then sleep, so as to be fresh for the Emperor this evening. I've found this to be a wise course of action, for aside from his bedchamber we spend many hours eating and talking, looking at works of art and playing board games together. Sometimes, too, I am sent back to my rooms after we have lain together, so that it's often very late before I can sleep.

I awake to find Iparhan seated at my mirror, already dressed in my clothes, painting her face with great care. Nurmat guards the door, his face sullen. I leap out of the bed.

"No," I say.

"Be quiet," says Iparhan, slipping on my shoes and standing. As I am in bare feet and she is in heels she looks down on me.

"Don't do this," I say, my voice breaking a little. "I beg you."

"I am here to spend time with the Emperor, to understand his plans," says Iparhan, implacable. "And how fortuitous that he should call for me so soon."

"He called for *me*," I say.

"I doubt he will know the difference," says Iparhan. "I'm sure all you women are alike to him anyway."

"Please," I say. "He will not talk of military strategy, Iparhan. He will only want to – to – "

I see Nurmat's jaw tighten, but Iparhan ignores us both. "Sit down, Hidligh. I need to do your face. Put on the robe," she adds, passing me her maid's robe and hair ribbon.

"No," I say.

Iparhan sighs. "Do not try my patience, Hidligh," she says. "Dress quickly and keep your mouth shut. I am taking your place because I must be certain that the Emperor will not notice the difference between us. If he does not, you can be certain that I will not take your place too often for such moments. Why would I want his hands on me? I wonder you can bear it at all."

I stand motionless.

"Dress," says Iparhan. "Or I will kill you now and go to the Emperor anyway."

Slowly I pull on the robe and braid my hair into a scruffy plait, unlike the smooth gem-laden plaits that Iparhan's hair is bound in.

"Good girl," says Iparhan. "I knew you would see sense." She addresses Nurmat. "Go and tell Huan that I have dressed myself but that he must put the finishing touches to my hair before I leave."

Nurmat does not meet her eye. His hands are clenched in tight fists. He turns and leaves the room. Iparhan watches him go and then straightens her back. "I will see you later," she tells me. "When I return you will be waiting for me. You will tell Huan I requested that you wait up for me and help me to undress."

I'm shaking. I reach for something that will hurt her as she is hurting me. I wait till she's almost gone before I ask, "And Nurmat?"

She pauses without turning. "What of him?" she asks and her voice is low.

"Does he know you are willing to give yourself to the Emperor when you won't give yourself to him?"

She keeps her face turned to the door so that it is hidden from me. "He has made his peace with it."

"Really?" I ask. "Is that why he has started to drink?"

She does not answer, only pushes the door open and leaves the room. As her footsteps die away I sink slowly to the floor and begin to weep.

Huan finds me. "Get up, girl," he says. "What are you sitting there whimpering for?"

I daren't speak, only shake my head.

"Well up you get, then," says Huan. "Tidy this room, then lay out her ladyship's bedclothes. You will wait up for her. Then get something to eat," he adds, more kindly. "You may have to wait up till late, we cannot know when she will return."

I nod. I have no choice. I carry out Huan's orders, then make my way through the rooms of the palace. I know where the entrance to the servants' quarters is, but I have never entered them. I hesitate outside the door, uncertain of what to do, how to conduct myself. Jiang, who is hurrying that way, finds me.

"Is there something wrong?" he asks, seeing me standing motionless before the door.

I shake my head. Jiang pushes the door open and I follow him, remembering as I do so that I must limp.

The room I enter is large, but its plainness, after so many months living in splendour, is startling. The muted paints used on the walls are faded and peeling, there is little furniture and what there is looks very plain to me. Over twenty people are in the room: maids who are mending and embroidering clothes, eunuchs polishing silverware. From the smells I can tell that food is being prepared in a room close by. Some of the youngest maids come and go with foodstuffs to be used, or carrying heavy buckets of water, their little frames bent over with the weight. I've barely stepped into the room when one of the maids hands me the shoes she is holding. "The soles need cleaning," she says. "Her ladyship has been walking in the gardens and they're dirty."

Slowly, stupidly, I manage to find a little pot of water and a small brush, which I use to clean my own dainty shoes, their pale cream silk marred by dirt that has soiled them during one of my many walks. I hold the little shoe and look at it as I have never done before, my efforts at cleaning it so useless that the same maid tuts and takes the pair back to do a better job herself. I excuse myself as quickly as I can and make my way back to the bedchamber, forgoing any food.

It is fully dark and the Forbidden City has been closed up for the night before Iparhan makes her way back. Her face, in the dim light of the flickering lanterns, is drawn. She does not meet Nurmat's eye, only walks past him with such care that no part of her even brushes against him. She undresses so fast I hear a ripping sound as she pulls off her shirt and she wipes a wet cloth over her face with a roughness that turns her skin a livid red. Seeing how anxious she is to take back her place I hurry to remove the painted scar and the cotton robe I am wearing. The cool touch of silk on my body again is like a retreat to a place of safety. I sit on the bed, watching her replait her hair and tie the red ribbon in it.

"Did he..." I begin, unsure of what question I want to ask and whether I want to know the answer.

"Oh he did not miss you, have no fear," she spits back at me. "He could barely keep his hands off me. It was disgusting."

I feel my throat grow tight and gulp back a sob. "Get out," I say.

Iparhan pauses, looking at me in surprise. "Do not tell me what to do."

"Get *out*!" I cry at her, unable to contain myself.

Too late I hear footsteps come running and Jiang's anxious voice on the other side of the door. "Is all well?" he calls.

"Yes, yes," I answer.

I hear him walk away and turn to Iparhan. "Get out," I say. "And do not speak to me again of what you do with the Emperor."

She looks at me, gives a mocking bow and leaves the room.

I look at Nurmat and see my own tears reflected in his eyes. "What is to become of us?" I ask him, but he does not answer, only lies down on his bedroll by the door and turns his back to me.

In the darkness, our muffled sobs continue for a long time.

When I see the Emperor again I cling to him and he smiles down at me. "So full of desire?" he asks. "When I last sent for you it seemed you were not so willing."

I leap at this sign that he saw a difference between Iparhan and I. "Was I not myself?" I ask, filled with hope.

"A little reluctant, perhaps," he says. "Not so eager as you seem now," he adds, laughingly picking me up and flinging me onto the bed.

I hold out my arms to him. "I am eager for you," I say, my voice choked. "Come to me."

He climbs onto the bed, crawling slowly up my body until I seize his arms and pull him to me, twisting and rolling until I am seated above him, my legs straddling his body. He looks up at me and his hands reach up to stroke my hair where it covers my breasts. "I prefer you like this," he smiles, and I fall onto him, my body pressed against his, trying to make our flesh one.

Spring is coming. Consorts Qing and Ying are visiting me. I'm playing a game with little Yongyan, herding his carved wooden animals, when Iparhan, making tea close to us, speaks in our tongue, her voice humble, as though asking for instructions.

"Ask the Emperor for a grove of oleaster trees, to be brought here from Kashgar," she says.

I freeze for a moment but then continue the game although my hands tremble. Ladies Qing and Ying continue their chatter, talking of inconsequential matters, uninterested in whatever my maid is saying to me.

"No," I say. I don't know why she would want such a thing but all her requests make me suspicious.

"Ask for them," she says. "Or I will take your place again and do the asking myself when I am in his arms."

I turn my face away and don't answer her, but I cannot bear for her to take my place if I can prevent it. Reluctantly, I make the request, spouting some garbled nonsense about how they remind me of home.

A few days later the Emperor calls me to his gardens and we walk together. He slips his arm about my waist and I lean against him, feeling the heat of his body through the silk of his robes. "I am thinking of planting the trees here," he says. "And in your garden as well, of course."

"Trees?"

He frowns. "The oleasters. From Xinjiang. You asked me for them the other night."

I nod. "Of course," I say, trying to sound excited. "How many of them will there be?"

"Five hundred saplings," he replies, reassured. He walks a little ahead of me and points to a few places where he thinks oleaster trees will look well. "I liked your description of them," he calls over his shoulder. "Silver leaves and golden fruit. Very poetic."

I stand and watch him. Through me Iparhan is making demands of him but I don't understand their meaning. Why would she want oleaster trees?

I lose my appetite and barely touch my food. It grows cold before I finish. Fat congeals on plates, broths cease to steam, breads lose their fresh-baked softness.

Huan frets. "Why will you not eat?" he asks.

I shake my head and mutter something about being too hot, or too cold, or whatever other poor excuse comes to mind.

I lose my pampered curves and grow a little thin. The spot at the hollow of my throat grows coarse with my touching of it and Huan tuts and has my clothes altered, applies unguents to my neck.

Then news comes from Altishahr.

"There has been a rebellion," says the Emperor. His face is stern.

"What set it off?" I ask, wondering if Iparhan has had any hand in it.

"Your trees, it seems," he says.

"My trees?"

"The oleasters you asked for. It seems the porters rebelled against transporting them here. Two hundred and forty men were requisitioned to carry them here. They rebelled and used the trunks as clubs to attack their escorts, then went on to kill local officials and install their own leaders."

"I am sorry," I say, horrified, cursing Iparhan in my head. "I would not have asked for them if I had known they would cause so much trouble."

He shakes his head, stubborn. "You shall have whatever you desire," he insists. "It is not for porters to tell their Emperor what he may or may not command of them."

Sure enough more oleasters are sent for.

"All you have done is make him angry," I say to Iparhan when no one is nearby. "You are a fool. Now he will not withdraw troops from Altishahr for many more years."

"I have shown our people what can be done when men rise up

313

together," says Iparhan, her head bowed while she brushes my dogs. "They are sick of his demands. Now they know what they can do they will rise again and again."

"And cause more bloodshed?"

She shrugs. "Whatever blood is shed is shed for the glory of Altishahr and its future," she says and I stop talking to her, knowing that my words go unheard.

The oleaster trees arrive, their silvery leaves rustling, yellow flower buds shining. Hundreds of saplings fill the courtyard while they wait to be transplanted into their new homes, each housed in its own crate filled with soil from Altishahr. I touch a little handful of it, let the dark earth trickle through my fingers. I stroke the leaves and smell the buds. This autumn there will be fruits, if the trees recover well from their journey. I wonder if I will be here to see them.

I know that their presence here is a triumph for Iparhan. She has created unrest in Altishahr through a simple request of the Emperor. There are many more such requests she might command me to make. I must make them or Iparhan will take my place to do so and the Emperor will fulfill them because he believes he is assuaging my homesickness. If they lead to greater unrest, so much the better for Iparhan's plans. She could ask for many things from our homeland – jade, cloth, fruits. She can stir up unrest through the petty demands of a favoured bedmate. Such power she can wield through me.

Jiang, always seeking to learn new things, inspects the trees, following one step behind me. "Is it true that their blossoms can be eaten? They are saying that you ate the blossoms as a child and their scent was transferred to you."

"You listen to too many stories, Jiang," I say. "Where do you hear such nonsense?"

"Everyone has stories about you, Lady He," he says with a happy smile. "About your perfume and the Emperor's many gifts to you."

I shake my head and walk away from the trees. "Stories, Jiang. All stories."

"He gave you the bathhouse," he says. "And the Moon Tower. The bazaar. Your prayer room. The melons, the sweets for your birthday. The cook and…"

I stop him before he can mention Iparhan. "Enough, Jiang. My life is not a fairytale."

He is delighted with the notion. "But it *is*," he says.

The Emperor walks with me in the gardens, through the groves of oleasters, now planted and rustling in the breeze. "You've grown thin," he says, disappointed that I'm not more impressed with his latest gift. "Are the trees not pleasing to you?"

"They are beautiful," I say quickly.

"But?"

"But nothing," I say. "I am happy, Your Majesty."

"You are thin and pale," he says. "And I know why."

I wait, my heart beating too fast. If he ever knew why I am thin and pale my life would be forfeit.

"You are missing your riding and travels," he says, smiling. "The hunt seems long ago. But that can be cured. We are going on tour."

"On tour?"

"It is part of my duty to travel around the empire," he explains. "And my mother much enjoys such travels."

I know by now that his filial duty is an excellent excuse to fulfil his own restless desire to travel. "Your mother is lucky to have such a caring son," I say, anxious to lift his spirits.

He smiles. "So! We will go on tour. You can ride, see the countryside. Get some colour in your cheeks and eat good food."

I can only smile and agree with his plans, but I'm wondering what new opportunities our travels will give Iparhan.

"A Southern Tour!" says Jiang excitedly. "I have never been on one."

"Where will we go?"

Jiang is all too keen to recite our route. "We will begin our journey overland through Zhili and Shandong to Qingkou in Jiangsu. There we will cross the Yellow River and continue our journey on the Grand Canal. There are many cities that we will visit in this way: Yangzhou, Zhenjiang, Danyang, Changzhou and then Suzhou. After entering Zhenjiang, we will also go on to Jiaxing and Shimen to Hangzhou, our last stop, on the Yellow Sea. On our return the Emperor will inspect the troops at Jiangning. All in all we will be away from court for four or more months."

I gape at him. "So long? And so *far*?" I have grown used to the Emperor's constant desire for a change of scenery but so far all our travels have been short. I try to think in Chinese distances. "More than five thousand *li*?"

Jiang nods. "The Emperor is keen to ensure that the Yellow River is well maintained so as not to cause floods. I believe he wishes more barrages and ocean levees to be built to avoid such disasters. He will inspect the works."

"It sounds like a building project rather than a tour," I say.

"Oh, there will be processions and so on, of course," says Jiang. "There is special permission granted that the people may look upon the Emperor's face as he passes by, unlike here where we travel with the bamboo screens. There will be thousands who come to gaze upon him – and all of the court."

Iparhan, of course, has other views on the Emperor's tour. "How good of him," she mutters. "To allow his subjects to catch a glimpse of his luxury. The only reason he goes to the south is that it is one of the richest parts of his empire and he must keep it loyal to him. All the grain and silk comes through those parts. And every city that he visits will have its taxes cancelled out of his generosity but they will pay far more than taxes to ensure his comfort – and yours, of course," she adds. "They will have to refurbish palaces and lay on entertainment. It will drain them. He was only there three years ago, they will barely have recovered since then."

"Be quiet," I say, for Jiang is entering the room and she risks a beating to be heard speaking so of the Emperor.

"I could leave Nurmat and Iparhan here," I tell Huan, waiting to see his reaction. "There is no need to take many servants."

He looks shocked and my heart sinks before he even speaks. "His Majesty might be offended," he says. "He may think you are disparaging his gifts to you. Besides," he adds, "we need Nurmat to manage your kitchen while we travel and Iparhan is a most helpful and reliable maid."

I curse Iparhan for having made herself indispensable to Huan. "Very well," I say. "They will accompany us." Before we leave I give orders that the servants' quarters of my palace are to be repainted and put into good repair for our return. New robes are to be made up and issued to them all. My own shoes are to be modified, adding a thin layer of bamboo wood to their soles, making them easier to clean. And only the older maids or eunuchs are to carry the water buckets, not the newly arrived child-maids who reminded me too much of myself, struggling to earn a living in the streets of Kashgar.

As ever the court on the move is an extraordinary sight and one I'm not yet used to. Not all the court will come with us, however. Those in favour are taken along. The Empress, of course, as well as myself and other ladies. Others are not so fortunate. Lady Wan remains at home and bids me farewell with tears in her eyes.

"It is a little lonely here when the court is away," she admits and I wish I could ask for her to accompany us, but I know that many ladies are being left behind. Instead I embrace her and beg her to look after my dogs while we are away. She looks doubtful at first, but once they've greeted her, tails wagging and eager tongues licking her proffered hands, she gives way and I can see that they'll be spoilt in my absence.

"Be careful," she whispers, as I take my leave of her.

"Of what?" I ask.

"The Empress."

"Why?"

"She asked the Emperor not to take you on the Southern Tour," murmurs Lady Wan. "He refused her request and she is known to have wept in her rooms for many days. Now she is angry. You must know that she is jealous of you," she adds.

"I am only an Imperial Concubine," I protest. "She is the Empress, and nothing will ever change that."

Lady Wan smiles. "You are a beloved concubine," she says. "And she is not a beloved Empress, although she craves the Emperor's favour."

"Why doesn't she turn her jealousy onto Imperial Noble Consort Ling? She more highly ranked than I am and has many children by the Emperor. She is often in his chambers."

Lady Wan looks at me for a moment. "Lady Ling is favoured," she says. "But her love is all for her children and their future. She does not crave the Emperor's love."

I look at her. "And I do?"

She pats my hand. "I believe Ula Nara looks at your eyes when you behold the Emperor and she sees something she recognises," she says. She tilts her head. "Is it so?"

I shrug and look away, unable to meet her steady gaze. "He is a kind man," I say. I try to form more words but stop, unsure of what they might be.

Lady Wan smiles and strokes my hair. "Enjoy the tour," she says. "But be careful. She may not be in favour but the Empress has great powers and she can command whomever she wishes to serve her."

I embrace her again and make my way back to my own palace, where the servants are hurrying about, for we must be ready to depart in the morning.

We're almost ready to set out and everywhere are chairs, servants, officials and courtiers, ladies of the palace, children. I stand stroking one of the horses, which the Emperor has promised I may ride sometimes. I would prefer horseback to the endless swaying of a palanquin.

Prince Yongyan runs across my path, having once again escaped the ministrations of Consort Qing. He is dressed in bright orange silk, with painted dark stripes that have convinced him he is a tiger. He roars at a younger sister, leaving her whimpering until a nursemaid rescues her from the terrible beast.

I laugh at him and he bares his teeth. I cower. "Have mercy on me, noble tiger," I plead.

He roars again but giggles halfway through at the sight of my pretended terror, spoiling his fierce demeanour. I pick him up and allow him to sit on my horse for a moment. He clutches at the reins, then, remembering his training, composes himself more proudly, back straight and chin up as though he were posing for a portrait.

"Very good, Your Highness," I tell him. "Your father will be proud of you."

He beams. "I am a true Manchu," he says grandly and as I let him down he rushes away to boast to his siblings.

The palanquins assemble by rank. There is much confusion as each lady and her retinue takes her proper place. Soldiers and courtiers mill about us. For once the giant open spaces of the Forbidden City's Outer Court are not large enough. In the chaos my palanquin comes close to a chair draped in yellow silk. A hand emerges from the silken folds, its golden nail shields flick in my direction and I hear the voice of the Empress Ula Nara. "The dogs should be at the back of the procession," she says. "Especially that mongrel cur." Her voice lacks her usual slow, elegant delivery, it trembles a little. Huan quickly gestures to my bearers and my palanquin moves out of her sight. Jiang leans through my drapes and fans me a little, as though to blow away her words.

The travelling is tedious and I soon grow heartily sick of it, as do most people in the court. No sooner do we reach one place, then we are on our way to the next, our resting places changing from one night to another. The servants grow harried with the constant packing and unpacking that must be done.

Anywhere that dykes, levees and barrages have been built there must be inspections. We soon tire of the endless discussions regarding stone versus earth banks and the Emperor's insistence on arguing over the finer details of their construction. Fewer and fewer of the ladies attend such sessions, pleading exhaustion or even the effects of the 'Southern heat', although we're still in the early part of the summer. But the Empress seizes the tour as her opportunity to prove her devotion to the Emperor.

In every city there are rituals to be performed at temples. There are those dedicated to particular deities, great sacrificial ceremonies at the mausoleums of ancestral emperors as well as commemorations at the graves of local historical personages and officials, to honour their deeds and memory. The Empress throws herself into these obligations, whether by the Emperor's side or on her own, carrying out one rite after another. Her days are an endless round of ascending and descending the steps of temples and memorials, kowtowing to the gods and ancestors, breathing in the overwhelming clouds of incense smoke. Once she stumbles on the steps and falls, a rush of monks and servants failing to catch her in time. Back on her feet she stands, shaken, for a moment, looking down at the soft palm of her right hand, which has been scraped and is bleeding. For that day, at least, she is hurried back to her rooms and tended to. But the next day she sets out again. She begins to look tired, her face seems more lined and her movements become a little slower. She looks thinner, as though the constant movement is stripping away her former slender curves. But she does not rest.

I see little of Nurmat. He manages my kitchen as he has always done but when I catch sight of him he looks weary.

"Are you well?" I ask him directly, when I see him passing one day.

He turns to look at me and I see his eyes are bloodshot, either from too much drink or too little sleep. "Your ladyship is kind to ask," he says, although each word is heavy.

"There's no one here to understand us," I say. "Are you well?"

"Ah, Hidligh," he says and his eyes fill with tears for a moment. "Do not ask such questions. Keep to you own life and let what is to be, be."

I want to question him further but he is already making his way from the room, his steps slow.

I call for Iparhan and she comes and stands before me.

"What is wrong with Nurmat?" I ask her.

She bows. "Your ladyship?"

"Don't seek to fool me," I say. "If Nurmat is unhappy it is you that are the cause. What are you planning now?"

"Do not question me," she says, her face still holding its pleasant expression. "Enjoy your pastimes and forget about Nurmat. His woes are not yours."

I dismiss her and she leaves me, her steps quick and light despite her pretended limp. I sit for a while thinking of Nurmat's unexpected tears but I know neither of them will tell me the truth. All I can do is continue to ensure that Iparhan does not take my place when I am called to the Emperor's side.

In Yangzhou we ride down the Grand Canal in the imperial barges, flying banners and flags of bright colours. On either bank silk-draped makeshift theatres have been erected. As we pass one and then another performers compete to out-do their rivals on the opposite bank, so that opera songs intermingle and dancers' rhythms blend into one cacophonous sound, neither harmonious nor pleasing.

I wake to find Iparhan standing at the foot of my bed, already dressed in my clothes, her face painted as mine. She throws the cotton maid's robe at me. "Get up," she says. "Today I am taking your place."

I'm immediately wide-awake. "Why?" I ask.

"I want to speak with that painter of the Emperor's," says Iparhan.

I feel protective of Giuseppe. "Why?" I ask, putting on the maid's robe as slowly as I dare.

"He knows more than you have ever bothered finding out," she says. "He has been at court throughout the reign of three Emperors. He knows every building, every palace. He was here when they planned the campaign against our country."

I watch her as she leaves the room but at the door she turns back to me. "Today you will accompany me," she says.

And so I find myself trotting alongside the orange palanquin that I am used to sitting in as Iparhan is carried through streets and courtyards to the house where Giuseppe is staying.

He comes to greet us and I have to stand still rather than advance to meet him. Iparhan emerges from the chair's depths and makes her way to him.

"You will paint my portrait," she begins without preamble, and I see Giuseppe's surprise at her tone, so abrupt compared with how I speak with him. I have never demanded a portrait. He has offered or it has been the Emperor who has commanded him.

He bows, matching her formality. "It will be an honour, Lady He," he says. "I have mostly been requested to paint the building works. It will be pleasant to paint something prettier." He offers a warm smile, but Iparhan does not return it and he looks a little sad, as though he expected better of her – of me.

I feel my hands clench into fists by my side, but I have no choice but to stand here, silent by her palanquin until I am commanded to do otherwise.

Giuseppe bows again. "I will request that my materials are brought to me," he says. "Perhaps you would care to pose out here, in the garden. It is a pleasant day."

Iparhan nods indifferently.

Giuseppe calls for a eunuch and gives his orders. He turns back to Iparhan. "May I offer you some refreshment?" he asks.

Iparhan shakes her head without bothering to answer, as though he were a servant. I want to speak out, want to tell her to be civil to this old man who has been nothing but kind to me, who has treated me like a granddaughter since I came here, even reminding the Emperor of my very existence when I thought he would ignore me forever.

Giuseppe seems to see that no further conversation is forthcoming and in the ensuing silence he arranges his materials, asks Iparhan to take a seat before him and begins his work. But after only a short time Iparhan leans forward.

"You were here when the Emperor planned the campaigns for the conquest of Altishahr, were you not?" she asks.

Giuseppe keeps his gaze on the stretched silk onto which he is painting. "I have been at court since I was a young man," he says.

"The formations of the army are very particular," says Iparhan. "Are the archers always at the front? Their armour does not seem very protective."

Giuseppe pauses in his work and looks up, his face puzzled. "An unusual question," he says. "Are you very fond of military strategy, Lady He?"

Iparhan does not draw back. "I saw many battlefields as a child," she says. "My homeland was conquered. Such images stay long in the memory."

Giuseppe nods, a slow nod. He looks at her face for a long moment and then back down at the silk. "And as an innocent child, who watched those she loved die in battle," he says, with great gentleness, his voice so low that I have to strain to hear it. "Did you swear vengeance on the man whom you now call husband?"

Iparhan's face grows still and she sits back in her chair. "Yes," she says, when the silence has grown too long. Her voice is very low. Suddenly she rises. "I have sat here long enough," she says. "You are well enough acquainted with my face, I believe. You can paint the rest from memory or from the portraits you have already made of me."

The guards and servants quickly arrange themselves about her as she makes her way back to the palanquin. I turn to look at Giuseppe as we depart. He stands alone, in his little garden, looking down at the silk painting, his eyes not seeing what is before him, but something else.

I lie awake at night worrying about what Iparhan might be planning. One night I slip from my bed, past the sleeping eunuch on guard and through my own lavish rooms to the small lodging that houses the servants. I want to know if she leaves the grounds at night.

In the half-light of a lantern carried from my room, I see the kitchen, a washhouse and at last the rooms where the servants sleep. The smells here are of soap and food, of sweat and sleeping breath rather than the rare woods and incense that scent my own rooms.

I stand at the threshold of a room where many bodies are stretched out, wrapped in rough blankets and lying on bedrolls. I look them over, naming them in my head, the maids, the eunuchs. I see Nurmat, who is snoring, probably drunk. Then I spot Iparhan and my heart, which had been racing, slows. She is here, and asleep. I take a deep breath and step away, then move towards the kitchens to find some water for my dry mouth.

The kitchen, when I find it, is dark. I hold the lantern higher but then stumble against something soft at my feet. I lower it and see two bodies. Jiang and Huan. Their bodies are intertwined, Jiang's head resting on Huan's shoulder. They stir in the light and then spring apart.

"My lady!" gasps Jiang. Huan is on his feet already.

I back away. "I only wanted water," I say in a whisper.

Jiang cowers on the floor while Huan, clutching a sleeping-robe about him, hurries past me, head lowered. He is back in moments with water, his bare feet soundless on the floor. He gives me the little bowl and then both of them crouch on the floor before me, heads bowed.

I stand, awkward. I drink a little water and then turn to go. "Thank you," I say. "I am sorry to have disturbed you."

Huan looks up and his face is white in the darkness. "Forgive us," he whispers.

I turn back. "What?"

"Forgive us," he says a little louder and I hear someone stir in the other room.

"What is there to forgive?" I ask.

Huan's head rises a little higher. "Our… we…"

I shake my head. "I'm glad you have found comfort," I say, miserably. "I wish I could." I turn and walk away, back to my own rooms. When I climb into my bed I realise Huan and Jiang have followed me back. Silently, they tuck me back into the bed and when I seem comfortable, they leave me alone in the darkness.

We do not speak of what I saw again but the next day I order that from now on Jiang and Huan, as senior servants, will have a room allocated apart from the others, both here and when we return home. For now, we travel onwards.

Nurmat

HE KNOWS NOW, EVEN IF she has not yet understood.

I see it in his eyes when I sit at the mirror, painting my face into Hidligh's. I see it in the trembling of his hands as he reaches for more drink, something to drown out the sound of my footsteps leaving him. I hear it in his breath when I we take our places in the servant's sleeping quarters each night, how he lets it go in a sobbing rush when he thinks we are all asleep.

I try to speak with him, to draw him to me so that he can help me but he turns away from me when I approach and shakes his head when I speak with him. I have lost him. He has lost his love for me, I am sure of it. He no longer wants to be by my side.

He does not love Hidligh. I was wrong in that. He saw me in her and loved what he saw, but now he sees that she has changed. She is no longer merely my reflection. She has her own love growing inside her; it is plain to everyone except her. She wants to be free of us – of me. She is afraid of me not for herself but because of what I might do to her new-found happiness and the one she loves.

Our betrothal took place with much celebration. Music was played and all around us people danced. Nurmat's face was full of joy and I was impatient for the fifteen days to pass so that we would be married.

On the tenth day, we saw the Emperor's banners approaching. My father promised us that the delay to our wedding would be short. We *would fight off the Emperor as we had done before and our wedding day would be a day to celebrate our victory.*

He was wrong.

I have broken Nurmat. I see that now. He was mine, body and soul, heart and mind. Until my plans began to break him. That quick blade in his hand should have warned me that he was breaking, even then. But I pressed on. Hidligh confused him. That one night when I welcomed him into my arms and then turned from him once more broke him as surely as if I had never lain with him. I made him play the part of a eunuch and then when he had proven his loyalty over and over again I showed him my true plans and took away all he had longed for.

Now he is alone in his misery. He cannot turn to Hidligh, for she believes him still mine. He cannot turn to me, for I have broken him. My desire for blood has ripped him apart.

To whom can he turn in his misery? Perhaps only to drink and oblivion.

Ula Nara

THE CITY OF SUZHOU BRINGS us close to the end of our journey. Criss-crossed with waterways to be navigated on boats or over tiny bridges, it is a beautiful place. The Emperor is fond of its famous gardens.

"You must see them," he says to us all as we enter the city. "Although they have all sorts of fairytales to tell you about them – rocks split by swords and other nonsense. But they are certainly beautiful." He leans closer to me, so that he can whisper his next words in my ear. "There is even a maze in the Lion Grove Garden," he says, his warm breath against my throat. I laugh and blush, thinking of our first night together, and he leans back in his seat, smiling. "It winds through dark twisted rocks made of *taihu* stone which seem to take on every kind of shape," he adds.

"Like lions?"

"Lions," he agrees. "But many other forms too. You must see it for yourself."

We enter the city on our decorated boats, sailing down the Grand Canal, so that the people may see their Emperor. The canal is lined with his subjects and music is played on the banks. Singers compete to draw our attention and everywhere are hung lanterns in bright reds and oranges. The ladies of the court add their own decorative styles to the boats, each competing in her lavish robes to outdo the next. The onlookers gape at our hair, our jewels, our clothes. They throw themselves on their knees and kowtow to us as we pass by. Even in a city known for its fine cloth and embroideries, we stand out.

Sitting close to the Emperor is the Empress Ula Nara, today resplendent in her imperial yellow with a diadem of towering golden birds and dangling pearls. Her face, though, is set and pale. Despite the bulk of her robes she seems still thinner than when I last saw her. Her hands are growing bony and they twist in her lap as though in pain.

"Are you sick? Smile," commands the Empress Dowager. She's bad-tempered today, weary of the constant traveling which apparently is all for her benefit. She is more than seventy years old and would probably prefer to stay at home but her son has wandering feet and the constant journeys – to the Summer Palace, the hunting grounds, the Southern Tours – are beginning to put a strain on her, although according to him they are all done for her benefit. She indulges him by pretending it's so. She chastises him for his gifts to her, which are many and priceless, but he doesn't listen. It makes him happy to be generous.

Ula Nara bows her head and when she raises it her lips are curved in an unhappy mockery of a smile. She stretches out a trembling hand and places it on the Emperor's sleeve, as though to draw his attention, but at that moment he sees ahead a group of local high ranking officials waiting for us to arrive and stands, ready to step ashore, causing her small gesture to go unnoticed. As I step out I see her watching me, her eyes narrowed. I bow my head but she only continues to gaze at me as though I were doing something that requires all her attention. A bowing official indicates which way she should walk and at last she turns to follow him, her steps a little unsteady as though her mind is elsewhere. I watch her go and feel a shudder pass over me. There is something growing in her, an anger or a pain that needs to be appeased, and I am afraid that only my own destruction will bring her relief.

Two days after our arrival, as the lanterns are being lit, I make my way from the garden of my allotted palace to my bedchamber and come across Jiang in the walkway, who has just left the room. He stops and regards me with something approaching horror.

"What is it?" I ask, concerned.

"I – you," stammers Jiang. He looks back at the closed bedroom door. "I just left your ladyship in your room and yet – you are here."

I feel my stomach drop. Jiang turns back towards the door, his outstretched to open it. "Jiang!" I say, as loudly as possible. "What is the *matter* with you?"

The door swings open and reveals an empty room. I feel the air come back to my lungs. Jiang looks about the room, confused. My tone of hysteria is not forced. "Are you *drunk*, Jiang?"

"No, my lady! I swear!"

"I will have you beaten if you are," I say, unforgiving.

"I swear, my lady!"

"Huan!" I call, at the top of my voice. Jiang turns back to me and behind him, in the room, I see Iparhan, dressed as me, drop down from her hiding place – she had been pressed flat against the ceiling, as she once did in the house in the dunes. Now she slips behind curtains of my bed and waits.

Huan comes at a run. "My lady?"

"Jiang is drunk or seeing things. Tell him, Jiang."

Haltingly, Jiang explains. "I – saw her ladyship in her bedroom, she was dressing. Then I left her room and then – and then I saw her again, in front of me, here on the walkway, but dressed differently."

Huan sounds concerned. "I recall when your ladyship first came

331

to us," he says, "You mentioned a dead sister whom you resembled. Perhaps her spirit is unhappy."

Huan has given me a way out. "Perhaps," I say slowly.

Huan takes charge at once. "We must perform an exorcism," he declares.

"An exorcism?" I repeat – but I'm talking to the air. Huan has already left the room to arrange matters, Jiang trotting anxiously behind him.

I enter my bedchamber and close the door. Iparhan emerges from her hiding place.

"We were nearly found out!" I say. "Why would you take such a risk?"

"I was in a hurry," she says, calm. "Hurry up and change before they catch us again."

I'm aghast at her lack of care. "They shouldn't have been given the chance to catch us at all!"

"Nurmat should have been guarding the door," says Iparhan, helping me to change.

"Why wasn't he?" I ask. "Is he turning against your plans?"

She does not answer.

The exorcism lasts three days. Altars are constructed in the garden and are surrounded by representations of what appear to be hundreds of benevolent spirits. There are monks everywhere. There is so much incense I can barely breathe and the interminable chanting and ringing of gongs begins to grate on my nerves.

I find my own way to punish Iparhan by insisting that the exorcism is so frightening that I must have her by my side, to fan me and offer me sips of fortifying teas. She glowers at me. Her eyes are red from all the incense. They make her look exhausted.

"Look at what you are doing," I say to her under cover of the endless chanting around us. "You are drawing attention to me. You are risking being found out. Whatever you have planned I'm sure it doesn't involve being discovered?" I try to stop my voice sounding pleading. "You surely need to keep me alive?"

She looks at me but her eyes are unsteady, as though she can hardly see me, although our faces are only two hands apart. "What good is your life to me?" she says. "I should throw you out on the street where you belong." She fans me, her hands poorly coordinated so that the fan moves erratically.

"I've done nothing to you," I say. "Think of what you have done to me."

She pauses in her fanning. "Brought you to a place where you are well cared for," she says. Her words sound almost slurred, as though she has repeated them so often in her mind that the words all run into each other. "A place where you are fed, watered, dressed, served. Befriended. Loved, even."

"A place where I am controlled," I say to her. "Threatened, put at risk, kept in the dark."

The chanting rises to a crescendo and Iparhan lowers the fan. "Loved," she says very slowly. "What is it like to be loved, Hidligh? Not as your lover wishes you were, but as you are?"

"As *I* am?" I repeat. "An actor playing a part? A puppet controlled by a madwoman? I cannot be myself until you are gone from my life, Iparhan."

She looks away. "I hope it will not be long, then," she says. "I am ready to go."

I take a deep breath and nearly choke again. I feel sick enough, miserable and afraid enough to ask the question to which I do not really want to hear the answer. "Will I be alive when you do?"

She shrugs. "Who knows," she says, her eyes blinking against the clouds of incense, her voice unsteady. "Who cares?"

I call for Huan then and tell him that despite the warm summer evening I feel cold, that he must bring me a thicker jacket. And that Iparhan can go back to her quarters.

The Emperor is still caught up in endless tours of inspection and rituals to be performed. The vermillion ink used only by him marks hundreds of documents presented to him by black-inked scribes, detailing local taxes, noble houses, military ranks and endless, endless petitions.

"He has the Empress with him, anyway," I say to Huan sadly. "He will not miss me."

Huan shakes his head. "The Empress has not accompanied him since the first day we arrived in Suzhou," he says. "She is pleading illness."

"Maybe she'll leave me alone then," I say.

I spot Giuseppe again in a crowd of courtiers. "How are you?" I ask.

He bows but does not smile. "I am well, your ladyship."

I want to beg his forgiveness for how Iparhan behaved – how it must appear to him that I was rude and vengeful, but there is nothing I can say. " I would like to see the portrait," I say, smiling.

He looks at me for a long moment. "There is still work to be done on it," he says. "My memory is not as good as it once was."

"Should - should I sit for you again?" I ask, hoping to spend time with him again so that I can erase his memories of Iparhan.

"It is not necessary, my lady," he says, "and if you will excuse me I must speak with that gentleman." He leaves me standing alone and makes his way over to a court official.

"You are destroying my friendships," I say to Iparhan. "Giuseppe barely speaks to me now."

"Why would you want to speak with him?" she asks. "He is a doddering old fool."

"He has been like a grandfather to me," I say, unguarded.

She turns on me. "You don't have a grandfather, Hidligh. You have no family at all. Your supposed family wants only the favours and riches that your position brings. No one cares whether you are dead or alive. Remember that."

I turn away from her and do not speak to her of Giuseppe again.

Remembering the Emperor's enthusiasm for the local sights I set out late one morning to see some of the better known ones. The Garden of Books proves beautiful, as promised, with scenes arranged around a central pond, designed to recreate fairy tales. My guide, a stout local official, is delighted to have a favourite of the Emperor's as his guest and he tells one tall tale after another as the sun reaches its peak.

"And Tiger Hill," he says. "Have you visited that yet?"

I shake my head.

"Oh, but your ladyship must go there!" he cries. "It is said that to visit our city and not to visit Tiger Hill is not to have visited at all."

Once at Tiger Hill my guide enthuses about the Sword-Testing Rock – the one the Emperor dismissed as nonsense; a huge, perilously leaning pagoda that I decline to climb, fearing for my safety; as well as the Pond of Swords.

"There is a great treasure buried beneath those waters," my guide assures me. "Three thousand swords, each of legendary sharpness and with jewel-encrusted handles."

I nod, as though impressed, although I can't help thinking they must surely be covered in moss and mud by now. The afternoon is warm and before we leave he dips a bowl of water for me from the

Spring of Simplicity and Honesty whilst telling me of its appearance to a water-carrying monk.

"And now the maze of the Lion Grove Gardens, your ladyship," he says, as twilight approaches. "We can be there in only a short while."

"May I walk in it alone?" I ask. He's a good-natured man and means well but his constant chatter is beginning to weary me.

The official is disappointed but he can't disagree with me. Once we reach the gardens he positions himself at the entrance. "I will wait here for you," he promises.

The garden has been cleared so that I can have it to myself, and it seems very silent. Lanterns have already been lit, although dusk has not yet fallen. I enter the maze.

It's made up of nine paths, which twist and turn through twenty-one caves, set on three different levels. It's not like the flat, easy walkways of the maze at the Summer Palace. I have to keep a hand on the walls to ensure I don't slip, for the path itself is rough in places and its changing levels, together with my high-heeled shoes, threaten the wellbeing of my ankles. But the rocks seem alive, misshapen and molded like no other rocks I've ever seen. You don't need a fanciful imagination to see creatures, people, trees, both commonplace and those escaped from some twisted storyteller's mind or the realms of the Immortals. Tiny lanterns cast flickering shadows in the darker areas, making the shapes come to life.

The silence, which I'd thought would be a relief, becomes eerie when I've walked for some time. I can hear water from the various pools and waterfalls, occasional birdsong and the breeze in the trees above me but nothing else. I'm unused to being so alone now, and find it a little unsettling. I'm about to turn back when an unexpected sound startles me. A whistling followed by a thump, like no bird I have ever heard before, followed by another and then another. Once I listen to it closely, it's oddly familiar although I can't place it.

I step through an archway of crooked shapes and make my way down a new path, wondering whether I will, in fact, be able to find my way back out of here. I suppose if I called out loudly enough the eager official would come rushing to my aid. Meanwhile I follow the source of the sound through the maze until I step past a little curve in the rocks and see before me an open area, still filled with the twisted rocks, but looking out over a pond and trees. The sound comes again and suddenly I know what it is and have to stop myself from ducking.

"Missed you," says Iparhan. Another dagger flies close by and embeds itself in a tree in the middle of the pond, its trunk studded with daggers. She's wearing my clothes, hairstyle and makeup and to see myself, or what appears to be myself, throwing daggers with such accuracy is frightening. By her side is a small heap of daggers and a thick jacket, which she's taken off and thrown carelessly to the ground.

"Stop that," I say.

She lowers her hand and looks at me. "What's the matter, Hidligh?" she asks in a mocking tone.

"You did not tell me we were swapping places today."

She shrugs and another dagger goes flying. "I heard that the Emperor was on his way here. It seemed too good an opportunity to miss. You were nowhere to be found."

I look quickly over my shoulder but the garden is deserted except for us. "How do you know the Emperor is on his way here?"

"I make it my business to know," she says.

"Why don't you make it your business to be more careful?" I ask her. "You are growing careless, Iparhan. Jiang has already seen us together. Now you are wandering about the city, dressed as me when

I do not know you are doing so – what if others see us? How many times do you think we can be so lucky?"

"Ah, Hidligh."

I look up to see Nurmat emerging from the rocks behind me. His eyes are bloodshot and his walk is slow.

I look at him and shake my head. "You're drunk again."

He shrugs and sits down on a sleeping lion rock a little way off, pulls out a bottle and drinks. Iparhan ignores him. She stops throwing daggers and begins to pace back and forth like a beast caged for too long, her face twitching and her mouth moving silently, perhaps reciting a long list of the Emperor's wrongdoings to her family and country.

"Stop that," I say. "Be quiet. I can hear something." I stand, then grab hold of a rock and pull myself up so that I can see across the gardens. My shoes slip and I break a nail shield in the process. An imperial yellow palanquin is making its way into the gardens, some way off. I slip back down.

"Is he here?" asks Iparhan, Her voice is too keen for my liking, her eagerness is making me nervous. I am afraid she is growing less and less cautious, throwing all of us into danger.

"No," I say, playing for time. "I was mistaken."

She turns back to her heap of daggers and throws another. The thud it makes when it hits the tree brings a cold shiver down my back. I sit down next to Nurmat. He reeks of alcohol, his breath is sour with it and his breathing comes heavily from his half-open mouth.

"Why does she want to see him so urgently?" I mutter to him.

"Probably wants to make love to him," he slurs. "Whore."

I want to slap him for saying what's in my mind. "Shut up," I spit. "Take that filthy bottle out of your mouth and dunk your head in the pond. You need to be sober."

"What for?" he asks. "She's going to be off there shortly, rubbing up against him, whispering sweet words – you know it as well as I do."

"Do you know what will happen if we are found out?" I hiss.

"She'll be killed," says Nurmat. He drinks again from the bottle. "She'll be dead, I'll be dead. You'll be dead. Inevitable, don't you think? Nothing left to do now but wait. And drink," he adds, lifting the bottle once more.

I knock the bottle out of his hand and press my face close to his, the stink of his breath hot on my cheek. "We need to get her away from him." I whisper urgently, while Iparhan throws another dagger. "Neither of us wants things to end this way; this was never the plan. You were supposed to be here to help me get whatever information she wanted. Then you and she were going to go away and leave me to a peaceful life. That's what you wanted, isn't it? A life with her? If we are found out…" I can't even finish the thought. "Help me, Nurmat," I beg, kneeling in front of him and shaking his shoulders. "Think of something we can do."

He tilts his head back to look at me, and laughs out loud. "Like what?" he asks. "Like what, Hidligh? Like what? You're still clinging to what you believe is the plan. You're a fool, girl, as big a fool as I am. Iparhan lied to me. She lied to you. She told us both a fairytale, that all of this would lead to glory for our country and love for me and her together. That you would be left with a full belly and a warm bed." His voice grows louder and more ragged. He is half sobbing. "The night you entered the Forbidden City she took me into her bed and gave me her maidenhood. And she whispered such lies, Hidligh. She said it would all be over soon." He puts his head in his hands and for a few moments he sobs. Iparhan, further down the path, does not turn towards us, though she cannot fail to hear him. She throws one dagger after another, faster and faster, as through to drown out the sound of his grief.

I watch him with pity. I can't help remembering him as he was when I first met him, full of hope for his future with Iparhan. I sigh and squat down beside him. "It can still be over," I say, although I'm not sure I believe my own words. "If we can just…"

Nurmat looks up at me. His eyes are filled with tears. "Do you know why she took me to her bed that night, Hidligh?"

"Because she loves you," I say.

He shakes his head. "You're still clinging to hope, Hidligh," he says. "She took me in her arms because she was still a virgin and she believed you were about to be deflowered by the Emperor. She knew she would take your place one day and she could not be a virgin if the Emperor took her to his bedchamber. She used my love for her, my desire for her, to make herself more like you. Do you know how angry she was when she found out he had not yet taken you to his bed? She could not take your place until you, too, had lost your virginity. That is the only reason why she arrived at court so late."

There's a sound nearby and both of us spring to our feet and look about for the source of it. Without our having noticed, a palanquin has made its way down our path. It's decked out in imperial yellow silks and I freeze, expecting the Emperor to have somehow arrived from a different direction. I try to dab my face with my sleeves while Nurmat kicks at the smashed bottle with his toe so that the broken shards enter the lake. The bearers, faces blank as though our presence here were expected, set down the chair so that the occupant can climb out. A shoe entwined with pearls emerges and my heart sinks. This is the chair of the Empress Ula Nara.

Once out of the chair she stands blinking, as though she cannot see us, even though it is not yet fully dark and there are lanterns all around. She gestures to the bearers and they disappear behind the bend in the path, out of sight and hearing.

I try to think how to present myself to her but I know that I'm ruined. I'm in a deserted garden with my cook, who is drunk. By my feet lie daggers and a crumpled jacket that appears as though I've removed it and lain on it. I might as well have been in Nurmat's arms. A little way beyond us is Iparhan, who has slowly turned to face us, presenting the Empress with the extraordinary vision of my double, a woman alike to me in every way except that she is holding a dagger in her hand.

Suddenly Iparhan drops the dagger and runs. She moves fast and in a brief moment she is gone. I am alone with the Empress and Nurmat.

I fall to my knees in the dust and kowtow to her, as does Nurmat. While he remains kneeling respectfully on the path as befits a servant, I rise and face her.

Ula Nara is very pale and thin, the pink painted on her cheeks making her look fevered rather than flushed with health. Her robe hangs loose on her and her neck and hands are beginning to look skeletal. She looks at me and at Nurmat, at the crumpled jacket on the path, the daggers. She looks beyond me to where Iparhan has fled.

"How can there be so much treachery in one place?" she asks at last, and her voice is broken, hoarse.

I look down. I don't know where to begin to answer her – I cannot even think what plea would be strong enough. What am I to explain to her? Everything? Nothing? The truth? A lie? There can be no lie that would account for what she has seen.

When I look up the Empress is still standing there, swaying slightly as though she too were drunk. Then she speaks, slowly. "You have been loyal to me," she says. "I will not forget it."

I frown. "Your Majesty?"

But her eyes are on Nurmat and it's Nurmat who answers from his place on the dusty path. "I live only to serve you, Your Majesty," he says, his eyes bloodshot from the drink.

I stare at him. "Nurmat?"

He returns my shocked gaze with a righteous glare. "Now your ladyship will be punished for your transgressions," he says. "For attempting to seduce a eunuch servant of your household. For having treasonous intentions towards the Emperor, spurred on by traitorous rebels from Xinjiang with whom you secretly corresponded in Beijing. Her Majesty the Empress will see to it that you forfeit your life for these crimes."

I gape at him and then look to the Empress. "I—" I begin, but she holds up a hand to stop me.

"You traitorous, lust-ridden bitch," she says to me. She's angry but I can feel her pleasure and relief, too, at being able to accuse me at last. "I will have you killed for this and then the Emperor will see how wrong he was to care for you. He will reward those who are loyal to him."

"Your Majesty—" I begin.

"You can deny nothing," she says. "Your own servant has testified against you."

I put out a hand but she steps away in disgust and fear. "Don't touch me," she says. "Or I will scream."

I draw back and she makes her way, unsteadily, to her palanquin. Before she climbs into it she pauses, her thin hand clutching at the yellow silk curtain of her chair. "Your country is a treacherous pit of mongrel dogs," she says. "It does not surprise me that we have been sent two of its bitches to commit treason against the Emperor. You will all die for this."

She dips her head to enter the chair and then the bearers, still blank-faced, lift her and are gone.

I turn on Nurmat. "You two-faced bastard," I hiss. "*You* were her spy. You were supposed to help *me*, Nurmat. I trusted you. I thought you wanted what I wanted, for all of this to be over."

"I wanted the Empress to send you away," he says, his face still hidden from me, his forehead resting in the dirt. "If she sent you away Iparhan could not come into the palace in your stead, could not go and whore herself with the Emperor."

"Send me *away*? The Empress will have me killed!"

At last he looks up. His shoulders are slumped. He shrugs. "You're a dirty little street rat," he says. "If you hadn't been born she would have lived a happy life with me after I scarred her. You made her obsession rise again. If it wasn't for you we could have been happy. Who cares what happens to you?"

I slap him hard across the face. "You deceiving piece of filth," I say. "I hope the Empress finds Iparhan right now and has her executed."

He's on his feet in a moment although he stumbles. "I must get her away from here," he says.

I pull at his clothes. Despite everything I've just learned, after all that we've been through, I still can't help thinking of Nurmat as my ally, my friend. "What about me?"

He pushes me away so hard that I fall on the path. "Get out of my way," he spits. And he's gone, running down the path and then through a small entranceway in the rocks.

I lie in the dust and let my body go limp. Slowly I finger the silk of my skirt. I try to think. If I can remove some of the more elaborate items, will I pass as a rich young woman rather than a concubine? Could I escape into the streets again? I shake my head, my braids rolling in the dirt. Every item of clothing I now possess is too magnificent even for a rich woman. And everything I wear marks me out as a foreigner.

"Your ladyship!" A shadow falls over me and I look up into the eyes of the eager official, who is white with fear. "Your ladyship! Have you been taken ill?" He bends over me, half afraid of touching me, more afraid of leaving me there in the dirt of the rocky path. At last he tentatively holds out a hand to me, which I take, then carefully lifts me to my feet. I stand and wait for him to call for the guards, for the Emperor to appear. Instead he stands and stares at me, at a loss for words.

At last I speak. "The Emperor," I begin.

"His Majesty is waiting for you," says the official, relieved to have something to say to me. "He said he would like to see you, to walk with you in the gardens. I – I should have come sooner – is it the coldness of the evening after the warmth of the day that has affected you, or…?"

I frown. No mention of the Emperor's wrath, no mention of Iparhan. No mention, either, of Empress Ula Nara. "The heat, I mean cold, yes," I say. "I felt a little faint…"

Now the official is all action. Tenderly he makes me sit on a rock, rushes away to call for my bearers and in moments I'm seated in my chair and heading along the little paths to the main gardens, whether the Emperor awaits me. Along the way I'm passed water, fans, even tea by the poor man and I thank him with tears in my eyes. He may be the last person to treat me with such care. For his part, his relief in having found me is tempered only with fear that the Emperor will hear that he has failed in his duties towards me, that he will be punished for returning me in so poor a state. I should comfort him better but I do not have the strength for it.

We round a corner and my palanquin comes to a halt. I put out my hand through the curtain to the official but a larger hand takes mine.

"Were you lost?" asks the Emperor, smiling, as he helps me out.

I stand before him, my legs trembling. I lock my knees so that I will not fall. I try to smile. "A little," I say, unable to think what else to reply.

The Emperor chuckles. "I thought you were an expert at

navigating mazes," he teases. He sees the official hovering and nods to him to leave, which he does with much bowing. "Let us walk," he says to me. "Have you enjoyed the gardens?"

"Yes," I say. I can't think of any more words.

We stroll through the gardens, past flowers of all colours and pools of water. The Emperor seems happy to be silent and my mind is in so much turmoil that I can think of nothing to speak of. I wonder, for a mad moment, whether I should confess all and beg him to protect me, but why should he believe me? Iparhan would no doubt claim that she was the 'real' concubine and perhaps the family would be brought in to verify my – our – identity, which can only lead to certain death for us all. We walk on in silence, the servants following along behind us at some distance.

At last we come to a little clearing, with a tall tree surrounded by banks of flowers. The path from here leads to the exit of the gardens. The Emperor pauses to admire the flowers, then looks up as a eunuch enters the clearing. "Yes?"

The eunuch bows. "Her Majesty the Empress is unwell. She requests your presence."

I freeze, feel my hand clutch the Emperor's. But he does not seem unduly worried. "Tell Her Majesty that I will join her shortly," he says. He pulls me closer to him. "I must leave you," he says. "But I will call for you as soon as I can." He smiles down at me, then kisses me lightly and releases me.

But I am overcome with a desperate desire. I reach out and grab at his sleeve as he turns from me. Surprised, he turns back, and I press myself to his chest. "Kiss me again," I say. I cannot bear the thought that the last kiss he ever gives me might be one so lightly bestowed, a gentle kiss. I need a kiss that I can take with me when I die, a kiss to comfort me from the torment of being wrenched away from him.

He laughs at my ferocity and crushes me to him, his arms tight about me. He kisses me, at first gently and then with a growing desire. I allow my hands to move down his robe, below his jeweled belt and fumble with the folds of thick silk, lifting them so that my hands can slip beneath and touch his skin. He pauses in kissing me for a moment, his eyes grown dark. He makes a gesture with one hand behind me and I hear the shuffle of feet as the servants back away, rounding a corner where they cannot be seen nor see us. They will hear us, but I find I do not care. The Emperor has backed me against the tree and I push back against it as he lifts me up, so that my legs are wrapped about his waist while he holds me, his arms crushing me, my hair catching in the bark. I don't feel the pain, I am too caught up in the pleasure as he enters me, my skirts pulled up, my waistcoat ripped open so that he can see my breasts through the gauze of my shirt. He buries his face in them while I grip his shoulders and cry out.

It's over too fast. I want the moment to go on forever, to stay in this clearing, where we are alone and suspended for this moment in time where I have yet to be found out.

He laughs, a little breathless. "What are you doing to me?" he says. "I have never done such a thing."

"Never?" I ask. "

He looks down at me and brushes bits of bark out of my hair. His eyes are very dark. "I have never been so overwhelmed with desire for a woman," he says, his voice low. "You have bewitched me."

I press my face against his chest, hear his heart beating fast beneath the yellow silk. "Let us stay here forever," I say, my voice breaking a little.

He smiles as he pulls away from me. "I wish we could," he says. He is regretful. "I must go to Her Majesty and see that she is well taken care of," he says. "But I will call for you very soon."

I try to think of some way to keep him with me but there is

nothing I can say. He walks away from me and I watch him go and have to bite my lip hard to stop from crying out to him.

Inside my palace the servants are gathered, expecting me. Among them stands Iparhan in her plain blue cotton robe, her face now scraped clean of makeup, her scar fully visible. I look at her but she looks away.

"The Emperor sent word that you are to join him this evening," says Jiang, looking worried at the state of my clothing and hair. "We must hurry, there is hardly any time to prepare you."

I begin to shake. The Empress has already spoken with him. I will be sentenced to death for adultery, impersonation, treason...

I eat nothing; drink nothing. I don't speak whilst I'm prepared. When I climb into my chair to be taken to the Emperor's palace, I clutch hold of Huan's hand for a moment.

"Goodbye," I say, struggling to keep my voice steady. I want to thank him, to tell Huan how much his care and kindness have mattered to me. I want to tell him that he has been a father to me, a shrieking, fussing, mother hen of a father that I have grown to love as a daughter. But I cannot say any of this even though it's likely that I will never see him again. "Goodbye," I repeat, holding his hand more tightly in both of mine.

He looks puzzled but pats my trembling hands with his free hand. "Good night, my lady. I hope your evening is enjoyable. I will wait up for you should you return to us this evening."

Tears well up in my eyes. I let go of his hand and turn my head away, gesturing for the drapes to be closed around me.

The journey across the city is too quick. I'm not yet ready to face the Emperor and I call to the bearers to take a longer route. They ignore me. I may be their mistress but the Emperor cannot be kept waiting.

I find him in the gardens of the palace in which he is staying, accompanied by Giuseppe. He's beaming. "I have been telling Lang Shining about our walk," he says, a mischievous smile on his lips suggesting that he has not told the old man the truth of our time together. "The gardens are pleasant, are they not? It is a shame the Empress was taken ill and we had to interrupt our time together, but here we are again."

"Is – is she better now?" I ask.

He nods, dismissing the topic. "The heat, I believe," he says. "She was weeping when I arrived and I ordered that she should be taken back to her own palace to rest before we speak together." He turns back to Giuseppe. "And Lang Shining has been painting you again," he says, full of interest. "You must be his favourite subject – with all the travels we have made he still finds time to paint you rather than the scenery. All these days whilst I have been busy he has been painting you. Come and see the finished work."

I make my way forwards, wondering if this is a trick. Will guards rush out to seize me? But he's still smiling and as I join them he holds out his arm to me.

I daren't look him in the eye and so I address Giuseppe as I reach the Emperor's side and try to keep my voice steady. "Are you well, Giuseppe?" I ask.

He looks up at me. "Yes, my lady," he says, although he does not sound as warm as he usually does. "The portrait you requested is complete."

The Emperor laughs. "Giuseppe says he has chosen another unusual costume for you," he says.

Giuseppe turns the large portrait so I can see it. I step back.

The portrait shows a woman in full armour, her face filled with military fervour. Her broad high cheekbones and full lips are encased within a helmet topped with plumes. Long dark hair peeps out from the back of the helmet. One hand rests on her sword, the other on her hip. It's a portrait of a warrior woman posing victorious after a conquest.

It's a portrait of Iparhan.

We may look alike to those who don't know us well, but there are differences, of course; we're not twins. Looking at the picture I see how the woman's nose and chin are shaped differently to mine, how her neck is a little longer. There's a dimple in the chin like mine but I have watched Iparhan recreate that dimple with powders. There's no scar, but this is Iparhan's face.

The Emperor is delighted. "Here you are as a warrior," he says, chuckling. "Like a Manchu of old! It is all the riding you like to do." He puts an arm about my waist and pulls me closer. I try to move into his embrace, to feel the warmth of it, but I'm too much afraid. I turn towards Giuseppe, who is looking at the portrait and then at me, as though something is bothering him.

"I have seen a new side to Lady He of late," he says slowly. "She spoke of many things with me while she sat for this portrait. Of battles, of the Emperor's armies and their tactics."

The Emperor is still contentedly examining the portrait, ignoring Giuseppe's words. "She is happy here," he declares with satisfaction. "It has made her look more confident. Why, I remember her arrival. She was barely a girl and trembling with fear. I thought she was nothing but a child the first time I saw her." He chuckles. "Now she is a warrior. I will have it hung in a place of prominence when we return to the Forbidden City."

I smile politely. There seems to be no trick. The Emperor is happy. The Empress has not yet spoken with him but she may do so at any moment and my life here – my life anywhere – will be over when she does. I take the Emperor's hand in mine and feel his warmth and strength. I squeeze it tighter, hoping somehow to keep that feeling with me for the future. He clasps my hand in return, smiling down at the portrait.

Giuseppe stands behind me. "Is all well with you, Lady He?" he asks. He looks at me and then turns back to the painting, then back to me, waiting for an answer.

There is nothing I can say to him that can be said. "Yes," I say. "It is a fine portrait. Thank you."

"Come, it is time to eat," says the Emperor and I go with him, leaving Giuseppe standing there with the portrait of Iparhan, looking from the image to my departing back, a confused old man.

Huan comes running into the sitting room. He's shaking and his face is white. "The Empress Ula Nara," he gasps.

Iparhan, squatting over a tea that she is brewing, rises to her feet.

Slowly, I set down my fan. "What about her?"

"She has gone mad."

"What?"

Jiang joins us, his usually neat robes crumpled, sweating from running. "The Empress has cut her hair."

I frown. "Her hair?"

They nod, their faces pale.

I fumble to understand the meaning of this news, thinking of all the times Huan has cut my hair, to keep it smooth and fine and its thickness even. I glance towards Iparhan but her face tells me nothing. "Is she... not allowed to cut her hair?"

Huan shakes his head. "She has cut it *all* off."

I try to imagine any lady of the court without their towering hair, shimmering with flowers and gems. Even bald Lady Wan is never seen without her magnificent wigs. "None of the ladies has short hair," I say at last. "Why would she want short hair?"

Huan is frantically waving his hands. "Your ladyship does not understand," he says. "It means the Emperor is dead."

I feel the air leave my body and find myself half-standing, my hands clutching the arms of my chair, my legs trembling. "The Emperor is *dead*?"

They realise their mistake and hurry to reassure me. "No, no!" says Jiang. "The Emperor is alive and well. But when an Empress cuts off all her hair it means the Emperor is dead. It is done only when a senior member of the imperial family dies, and senior to Ula Nara are only the Empress Dowager or the Emperor. She has gravely insulted either the Emperor or his mother."

"So you see," says Huan, "the Empress Ula Nara has gone mad. There is no other possible explanation."

I sink back down into my chair and try to think while I catch my breath. The Empress saw Iparhan and I in the Lion Maze, and became ill, fainted. She has not been seen until now.

"Perhaps she is still unwell," I say, wondering whether I can blame anything she may say against me on hallucinations brought on by a fever.

"*Yes*," agrees Huan, vigorously nodding, relieved that I have at last grasped the severity of the situation. "She has gone *mad.*"

Whispers fly through the city and our departure is delayed for days while the court awaits the Emperor's punishment. It comes sooner than expected. I've barely risen, the day is still cool and the sky still pale when Jiang comes to me, Huan hovering behind him, anxious. I'm pulling on a thick blue silk jacket with wide sleeves over my clothes.

"What is it?"

Jiang's voice barely rises above a whisper. "The Empress is to be sent home," he murmurs.

"Home?"

"Back to Beijing."

"Alone?"

"With a small retinue of guards."

"Did the Emperor order this?"

"Yes."

We're silent for a few moments. Such an action is unheard of – although so was her cutting off her long hair in defiance of every protocol.

"Has he said why?"

"He says she insulted his mother."

I frown. "Empress Ula Nara insulted the Empress Dowager? How? Ula Nara is her favourite."

"It is not known."

I shake my head. "You have to do better than that, Jiang. What is being said?"

His voice drops so low I have to lean forward so that he's almost whispering in my ear. "It is said that she was jealous of the Emperor's love for another woman. The Empress Dowager and she argued and Ula Nara struck her."

Despite the shock of the Empress striking the Empress Dowager all my focus is on the other thing he said. I try hard not to be jealous but... "What other woman?"

Jiang draws back a little and looks at me. He does not speak but makes a small gesture forwards with his chin towards me.

"Me?"

He nods.

I can't help it. My lips curve into a smile although it fades quickly. "And why would she cut off her hair?"

Jiang hesitates and my heart sinks. "Well? Tell me."

"It is only rumours."

"Talk, Jiang."

He is careful. "The Empress Ula Nara made... accusations."

"Of what?"

"That – that the Emperor's life was in danger from you. She cut her hair to warn him that he was about to die. She said she had seen ghosts and warriors with daggers and..." He makes a face. "She is mad."

Suddenly I am calm. This, then, is the moment I have been dreading. This is the moment when the Emperor will find out all there is to know about me, for who knows what Nurmat has told the Empress and what she in turn, after those moments in the Lion Maze, has said to the Emperor. This is the moment when I may lose my place here – lose my life, even. But I will not sit here, waiting to be summoned. I will fight to live; fight to stay here. I think of Lady Wan, Huan and Jiang, my animals, Giuseppe, Consorts Qing and Ying and the little prince. I may have come here to fill my belly, but time has passed. I want to stay here now, even if I were to starve. I think of the Emperor's face, think of his arms about me, the smell and warmth of him and stand up. "Where is she?"

Jiang and Huan step back, alarmed. "You cannot go near her!"

"I have to. Fetch my chair."

Iparhan, who has been listening in silence, approaches me "I will go," she says, low enough for Jiang not to hear her.

I don't pause. "No," I say loudly. "Stay here, Iparhan."

The three of them walk backwards before me, trying to change my mind but I make my way past them into the garden of my palace and wait until my chair is brought. Then I give directions and Huan and Jiang, unable to disobey, are forced to trot alongside me along with a few other servants. I look out of the window and see Iparhan standing at the gates of my palace, watching us depart. The speed of my departure has wrong-footed her. We make our way across little bridges and down tiny lanes towards the Empress' allotted palace.

I arrive to find three imperial yellow chairs set down amongst the blazing scarlet flowers of her courtyard. The Emperor and Empress Dowager are here. The courtyard is full of servants – mine, the Emperor's, the Empress Dowager's, Empress Ula Nara's. They stand about, awkward and desperate for orders. I step from my chair and hold up a hand to forbid anyone from following me then make my way, unannounced, into the palace. Inside a maid sees me and backs away, helpless. She's too young and lowly to know what to do about my approach, neither announcing me nor preventing me from entering. I follow her terrified eyeline and walk into the receiving hall.

The Emperor is seated on a carved throne and the Empress Dowager is standing by a window, her face turned away. They look strange before I realise I have never seen them alone before. Always, there are servants present. Now there are only the three of us in the room.

Four of us. A strange gasping sound comes from a corner of the room. I turn that way and see Ula Nara, half lying on the floor.

She's wearing imperial yellow but her robe is dusty and unwashed. It hangs badly on her, for she's lost weight even since I last saw her and her belt has been pulled too tight trying to correct the difference in size, making crumpled folds instead of smooth lines. Her feet are bare, with dirty soles. Her skinny hands protrude from the wide sleeves of her robe and her golden nail shields are broken to different jagged lengths. But for once protocol is correct, for more shocking than all of this is her hair.

It's been cut raggedly, by her own hand, so that one strand of shoulder-length hair falls lop-sided, behind her left ear. The rest is cut very short, but in clumps, with some parts of her skull now all but bald and others clad in thick chunks of dark hair, like a moulting black camel. The hair itself is dirty, lank where it's long and stiffly greasy at its shortest. Her white scalp shows through in patches, giving her a mangy appearance.

I stop when I see her but as soon as she spots me she lets out a wail and points towards me. Her voice is hoarse with crying and I step back.

"They want to kill you," she screeches at the Emperor. "I swear I am telling the truth! She has a twin, a sister! I saw them – first one with her lover the cook, both of them with daggers, embracing. And then the other one – walking with you. There are two of them and they mean to kill you!"

I look towards the Emperor and his eyes meet mine. His face is stern but his eyes are sad. "The Empress is unwell," he says slowly. "She has been making accusations which I cannot believe are true. She says you are two different people, she accuses you of wishing to kill me, of drawing me close to you so that you might use these... daggers... to assassinate me in the Lion Grove."

I stare at him and try to find my voice. "And you believe her?"

He shakes his head wearily. "She is unwell, as you can see," he says quietly. "I walked with you in the gardens and all was well between us, as you know. There is only one of you. She is hallucinating."

"She will have hidden daggers in her clothing. Make her show you!" screams Ula Nara and throws herself at me, grabbing at the sleeves of my jacket. Her face comes very close to mine. Her breath is rank and she smells of sweat. I can hardly stand upright against her fury. She pulls at my jacket and I step away from her as she rips it off me, then stumbles and falls to the floor at my feet with the heavy silk in her hands. She frantically turns it inside out, then, seeing no daggers embedded in the cloth, sets about the sleeves with her ripped nails and uncleaned teeth. She writhes on the floor as the silk rips and the wadding is revealed, but still no daggers. I stand above her, my breathing almost as fast as hers. What if Iparhan has indeed left daggers in my clothing? But there's nothing there and Ula Nara puts her head to the floor and weeps, rocking back and forth, still clutching at the torn silk with her bony hands. I turn, helpless, to the Emperor.

But he's changed. I'm used to seeing him in good humour, smiling and calm. I've even seen him laughing and joking – with his children, with me. At the most I've seen him looking important and officious as he works his way through documents of state or the daily rituals of sacrifice and prayer.

Now he is terrible. He stands at his full height, making him a head taller than all three of us women. His robes of state add splendour and breadth to his stature and his face is angry. This is the wrathful lord of an empire and suddenly I'm afraid of him. *If he ever knew my story*, I think, *this is how he would look at me.*

"You will be sent back to Beijing in disgrace," he tells Ula Nara. His voice is low but carries as though he were shouting.

Ula Nara doesn't raise her head. Instead she twists towards the sound of his voice and begins a terrible parody of a kowtow. Where I've always seen her perform the reverence with the grace and poise of many years' practice and breeding, now she stumbles and pitches her head forward too fast, knocking it hard on the stone floor. Her eyes are glazed when she raises her face and for a moment I think she's going to faint.

"Do not punish me, my lord," she begs, and her voice is so weak and broken that I lower my eyes. "Punish her and her twin. They are treacherous bitches. I am your Empress and she is a nobody, a prisoner of war from a land ridden with mongrel curs." Tears roll down her cheeks. "I have been loyal to you," she whispers. "I have bound myself to you since I was chosen and I have done everything in my power to deserve your favour. Do not punish me."

I look at the Empress Dowager but she seems to know what's

coming, for she raises her head to meet my eyes. I see that her cheek is marked by a long red scratch, reminding me of Iparhan's scar. I can only guess that Ula Nara attacked her before I entered the room. She holds my gaze for a moment and then with a minute shake of her head turns away again, towards the Emperor but without meeting his eyes, which remain fixed on Ula Nara.

"You will return to Beijing under guard," he says.

My legs begin shake. His voice is terrible but what he's suggesting is worse. An Empress, under guard rather than guarded? But he's not finished.

"You will remain there until my return and then you will be taken to the Cold Palace where you will live until the end of your days. You will no longer live within my presence."

Ula Nara's bloodshot eyes roll up. "*I am the Empress*!" she shrieks. "You cannot do this to me!"

"You are no longer my Empress," says the Emperor. "From this moment you are stripped of your titles and privileges."

I wait for his mother to protest. She herself chose Ula Nara as his Empress. Surely there will be some more discreet punishment? Perhaps she could be sent away to become a Buddhist nun or kept under house arrest without being demoted, with some mysterious illness as an excuse? But the Empress Dowager stays silent and I realise that I've witnessed something unspeakable.

There's a long silence, broken only by Ula Nara, who is lying on the floor moaning as though in pain. I want to comfort her but I'm afraid of her anger towards me and I don't know how a demoted Empress should be treated. I look at the Emperor but he stands motionless, looking down at her. His face is still angry but his eyes are glistening and I can see he, too, is shaken. I want to find a way to get out of the room, to remove my having been here at all, but there's no easy way to do so. So I stand, waiting, until at last his eyes turn to me.

"Call the guards," he says. "And a maid."

I nod and back away. By the doorway to the courtyard I grab the arm of the terrified maid who is still lingering, unsure of whether to go outside. "Go to your mistress," I hiss at her. "At once." She nods and scurries towards the receiving hall. I look out into the courtyard and every face turns towards me. They will have heard Ula Nara's shrieks, but nobody has stirred, fearful of what they might find on entering.

I look about me and spot Huan. "I need guards," I say.

He nods, unquestioning. "How many?"

I don't know. "Several," I say and he hurries to where the guards stand. Soon eight of them are making their way into the palace behind me.

"Stay here," I whisper to Huan and he stays by the doorway, preventing any other people from entering.

Inside Ula Nara is still on the floor and her maid is holding an armful of clothes.

"Something plain," says the Empress Dowager, who is directing her, although she has half turned away so that her damaged face can't be seen.

The maid hovers, uncertain. The Empress of China has very few clothes that might be called plain. She holds up a few robes but even those that are not official court robes are exquisite in their use of fine materials and embroidery. I see the Emperor shift his feet in growing impatience. The Empress Dowager, aware of this, waves her hand without looking. "A maid's robe," she says.

The maid gapes at her.

"Fetch one!"

The maid hurries away and returns with a pale blue cotton robe, cleaned so many times that it's faded, still crumpled from its latest wash. The guards, standing behind me, are silent as the maid holds it up. The Empress Dowager nods and turns away.

"Dress her," she says over her shoulder, her scratched face hidden.

The maid tries, but Ula Nara's body has gone limp and I have to kneel beside her. Together we strip off her outer robe of imperial yellow silk and cover up her sweat-stained inner robes in the faded blue cotton. She doesn't protest, only lies like a rag doll as we finish dressing her. I look up at the Emperor. He has not turned away while his Empress, in a few short moments, has been transformed into a lowly maid.

"Take her back to Beijing," he says to the guards.

They daren't gape nor disobey but they hesitate before laying hands on her. Carefully, three of them lift her up and make their way to the door. I follow behind as they carry her down the steps towards her yellow palanquin, topped with golden phoenixes and shielded from curious eyes by silk drapes.

"Stop!"

At the Emperor's voice ringing out behind us, every servant falls to their knees, face down on the ground. I stand still, surrounded by prostate bodies.

"She is no longer permitted to ride in that palanquin," he orders. "Fetch a red chair."

There's a disbelieving pause before one quick-witted servant jumps up and dashes out of the courtyard, returning a few moments later with an intercepted red chair and bearers, its bewildered owner unceremoniously evicted somewhere just outside the palace gates.

The whole courtyard watches from half-crouched positions as the once-Empress Ula Nara is led out in a faded blue cotton maid's robe, to a plain red chair such as is used by any lowly courtier or even a high-ranking eunuch. Her own imperial yellow palanquin sits nearby, discarded.

I stand still for a moment and then run down the steps to where the guards are trying to manhandle Ula Nara into the chair. She is not fighting them but her body is limp, like a sack of rice and just as unwieldy.

I crouch in front of her, aware that behind me the Emperor is watching. "Give me your hand, Your Majesty," I say in a whisper, so that no one else can hear me address her by her former title. "Let me help you into the chair."

Ula Nara looks down at me. Her eyes have become glazed over. "There were two of you in the garden," she says in a croak.

My heart hurts for her. Her jealousy has led her partway to the truth but I cannot save her now. "There is only one of me here," I say. "Will you give me your hand?"

She gives it to me as a child might offer their hand. I take it and help her into the chair. The jagged edges of her broken nail shields dig into my skin. When she is safely inside I straighten up and gesture to the bearers to lift her. I look through the little window at her confused face, the tracks of tears on her cheeks and pull the gauze curtain across, shielding her from the view of onlookers, the only protection I can offer her without risking my own life.

We wait as the red chair makes its unsteady way out of the courtyard and the Emperor steps over the bodies between him and his own yellow chair. Behind him comes the Empress Dowager. The bearers lift the two chairs and turn towards the gates of the courtyard. Slowly the servants get to their feet and trot uncertainly after their masters' chairs. Those left behind, surrounding the abandoned yellow chair and my own orange palanquin lift their faces cautiously from the ground and look towards me as I stand on the threshold of the Empress' palace.

"Go back to your quarters," I say and enter my own chair where the darkness of the drapes hides my trembling as I'm carried back to my own rooms. In my mind is only one thought, which fills up every part of me and circles round and round in my thoughts until I begin to sob. If the Empress has been banished for making accusations that the Emperor does not wish to hear, even though she had almost perceived the truth – what would happen to me – what would he do to me if he found out they were true? Would he turn his wrath towards me, would he look at me as though I were nothing to him?

When I arrive I run to my bedroom and only Huan is brave enough to follow me. He finds me rocking back and forth, tears rolling down my face.

"Your ladyship," he murmurs. "What is wrong?"

I try to wipe my nose with my silk skirt. Huan reaches out very gently and wipes my face with the sleeve of his own robe. "Tell me what is wrong," he says.

"I thought my time here was over," I sob. "The Empress – Ula Nara said – things. She wanted me – gone."

"And the Emperor?" Huan asks.

"He was so angry. He – he sent Ula Nara away – he said she is no longer the Empress." I look up at Huan. "Can he do that?"

"The Son of Heaven can do anything," Huan says. "All things are in his power." He is silent for a moment. "And now?" he asks. "Are you afraid of him? Or do you no longer wish to be here now that you see what punishments may befall a lady of the court if she falls from favour? Is that why you are crying?"

I look up at him and the tears fall even harder. "No," I say between sobs. "It's because now I know how easily any of us could leave this place if we are found – if we are found wanting. And I – I want to stay. I did not know how much until now."

Huan almost smiles, as though he has known this all along. "And why do you wish to stay, my ladyship?" he asks, as though what I feel must be said out loud, as though my next words are an incantation that will protect my future here.

"Because I love him," I say. "I love the Emperor."

Iparhan

I CANNOT SLEEP. MY EYES BURN *with exhaustion and yet I cannot sleep for more than a few moments at a time. I sleep and then wake and see it is still dark, over and over again. I lie awake and my fingers slip beneath my bed and seek out the daggers where they lie hidden. I caress them and feel their sharp blades. In the mornings I examine my hands and see on each fingertip the skin shredded, sometimes too pink where I have almost cut through to where the blood runs, despite my gentle touch on their blades. I have to hide my hands inside the cuffs of the robes I wear to avoid comment. My eyes are so tired during the day that the sunlight hurts them. I blink too often and objects before me blur and change their shapes.*

I cannot eat. I grow thinner, my bones slowly revealing themselves through my skin, one after another – my collarbones, my cheekbones, the gaunt shapes of my fingers, my hip bones jutting out beneath my clothes like the hilts of my daggers. I try to force down food although there is no taste when I chew. I must not grow too different from Hidligh. I must be her reflection.

I do not hear. Huan tuts because I do not heed his commands. I emerge from my dazed thoughts and try to understand him, although his voice seems far away. Nurmat watches me and when I refuse to speak of an uprising, when I tell him to send away possible allies his eyes grow wary.

Always in my nostrils is this smell. The perfume that once adorned me now adorns the Emperor's concubine and its scent chokes me. It has become a stench, pervading every part of me, released with every gesture. I have come to associate it with the Emperor himself and it makes me want to retch. But still I must smile, must carry myself with grace when I take on her form.

I must gaze upon him as though he were my beloved, when he is the reason for all my suffering. I must speak to him with a soft mouth when I can feel my hand reaching for a dagger that is not there. My life grows more painful with every hour of this pretence and I do not know how much longer I can bear it.

I no longer wish to lead my people against him. Even his defeat in battle would not assuage my need for revenge.

Rong Fei

SLOWLY WE MAKE OUR WAY back north. In our procession there are still three imperial yellow palanquins, but the third is empty. Its bearers carrying nothing but rumours and whispers in the air around them, the heavy weight of sadness and fear inside its yellow silken folds.

Now Iparhan stays away from me. She does not ask to take my place. She does not spend time with Nurmat. She is a maid, nothing more. This frightens me more than her shape-shifting. Why would Iparhan lose all hope, all her obsession with revenge now, when she is where she has planned to be all along? She is here at court, at the very heart of the Emperor's world. She can take on my shape to do her spying and yet she does nothing. I watch her when she is close to me and try to catch her eye but she keeps her gaze on the floor and slips away as soon as she can.

Her behaviour convinces me that my days here are numbered. There is an ending coming. I can feel it. I do not know what ending it will be – whether it will end a part of my life or my life itself – but meanwhile I cling to my time here. The Emperor laughs at me, for I beg to stay close to him, both in his bedchamber and on his tedious building expeditions and visits to temples.

"What is it you want of me?" he asks, chuckling. "Are you about to beg a great boon of me? There must be something you want very dearly to follow me about like a lost lamb."

"I only want your company, Majesty," I reply and he smiles and wraps me in his arms. I inhale the scent of him, warm and masculine, and let my fingers stroke the back of his neck, his cheekbones and his lips until he kisses me with ever-growing desire and leads me to his rooms. The endless temples and incense, the great building works, fall away from me as he strokes my skin until I pull him to me and he smiles at my eagerness.

Iparhan does not smile. Her hair is unwashed. It hangs limp and greasy in its single plait. Her clothes look crumpled and I hear Huan berate her more than once for not attending properly to her duties. Her mask of the consummate maid is beginning to slip, her anger too strong below the surface to be properly hidden. I keep her in my sight when I am in my own rooms. I tell Huan to watch over her when I go out, telling him in front of her that I am worried for her health, that she has not enjoyed the 'Southern climate'. She can say nothing but I know that she will not submit to such restrictions for long.

Nurmat's drinking is by now common knowledge. He rarely cooks any more, since my other servants have learned to make the dishes from my homeland and so he is often to be found asleep or slumped in a corner of the servants' quarters. Huan despairs of him. "But we cannot dismiss him," he says. "He was a gift from His Majesty. It would be an insult."

"Leave him be," I say. I know that whatever Nurmat's fate is, it rests in Iparhan's hands, not mine. I wish I could still believe in him as my ally in this folly but I know now that his loyalty will forever be with Iparhan. He is hers, as he always was. I am left to find my own path and fight my own battles.

We return to the Forbidden City in time for the Mid Autumn Moon festival. As soon as we're installed back in our palaces the servants busy themselves with preparations. The whole city is hung with lanterns – from trees, rooftops and down every alleyway. Tonight we gather in the Emperor's private garden to gaze at the fullness of the moon and celebrate the harvest that she brings.

My chair makes its way through the tiny passages between palaces on its way to the gardens. Each palace glows with lit lanterns and every courtyard is full of people preparing for the celebrations. Other ladies' chairs join mine along the way so that we begin to form a procession; one filled with laughter and accompanied by many servants carrying lanterns hung on bamboo poles which light up the way ahead. Even the little children will attend tonight's festival, and their high-pitched squeals of excitement make me laugh.

Just before the gardens come into sight we pass one more palace and our procession, so noisy and bright a few moments ago, stutters into silence and our festive pace becomes a shuffle.

The palace of the now-deposed Empress Ula Nara, a building that once sat majestic among our lesser dwellings, now hides in the flickering shadows of our chairs as we pass by. No lanterns shine out, there is no sound from her courtyard. As the Emperor threatened, on our return from the tour Ula Nara was sent away from Beijing with a handful of her servants. The rest were redistributed amongst the other palaces and women of the court. I myself received a eunuch and two maids from her palace. Humbled by their mistress' fall from grace, they obey Huan without question, go about their tasks in silence and creep away to their quarters when they are not needed.

Once past this silent reminder our procession increases its pace and gradually the sounds of revelry rise again as we reach the Emperor's gardens.

Trees rise up above delicately balanced rockeries and deep pools of water, reflecting the hundreds of lanterns hung on every available surface – perched on rockeries, hanging from trees, suspended from tall bamboo poles. An altar has been set up in the open air and each lady's chair makes its way towards it as she arrives. A flute is being played somewhere close by.

I climb out of my own chair and Huan places in my hands an open carved casket containing mooncakes, each the size of a small peach, their golden pastry marked with gilded characters, their soft insides filled with sweet lotus bean paste. I approach the altar, place my offering with care among the many other cakes, light sticks of incense and then bow. As I do so the Chief Eunuch announces my name.

"The Lady He's offering! May the Mistress of the Moon grant her honoured daughter eternal beauty!"

As I stand to make way for another lady's offering one hundred sky lanterns are released around me. Each one a delicate white orb, painted with the characters of my own name, they rise above us to join the hundreds more already floating towards the full moon. I make my way to join the Emperor and the rest of his family. He's surrounded by his children as well as by those ladies senior to myself.

"Tell the story!" pleads one of the princesses, tugging at his robes. Her cry is taken up by the other children. "Yes, tell the story, tell the story!"

The Emperor laughs. "There are still ladies who must join us," he remonstrates.

We wait and watch as more ladies arrive. Each makes an offering and for each more sky lanterns are released. The sky above us is full of them, our names shining high above us, the characters illuminated by the fires within. The air grows thick with incense as hundreds and hundreds of sticks are lit.

Servants pass us platters heaped with peeled segments of citrussy pomelo fruits and mooncakes – some sweet, others filled with salted egg yolks. Close by fires are lit to boil water for tea. We eat and drink while admiring the spectacle before us.

I notice the children of Ula Nara, sitting as proud as the others, but perhaps a little too upright, their positions now threatened by their mother's shame. They may have seen little enough of her, being cared for by other ladies of the court as well as their nursemaids and wet-nurses, but to be the children of the Empress was a position of privilege. Now their faces may remind their father of her disgrace and they are anxious to please.

I touch the Emperor's sleeve and he takes my hand in his and caresses it. "My Lady He," he says smiling. "My fragrant concubine."

I smile back but point towards the children. "They are longing for your favour, Your Majesty."

The Emperor follows my eyes and gestures to them to approach. They do so timidly and he strokes their hair. "I believe there are dragons out there," he says laughing as a clashing of gongs heralds the arrival of the Fire Dragon dancers. The children, reassured, run to join their siblings.

At last every lady and child has arrived and the children cluster around the Emperor again.

"The rabbit!" shrieks Yongyan. "Tell about the rabbit!"

"Rabbit?" asks the Emperor, bewildered. "What rabbit?"

"The *rabbit*!"

"*This* rabbit?" From his robes he pulls out a tiny jade carving of a rabbit.

"Yes, yes!"

The Emperor laughs and nods to a eunuch at his side, who hands out a tiny carved jade rabbit to each of the princes and princesses, each one carved from a different shade of the precious stone. The tiny ones grab for them, the older ones incline their heads and examine the carvings with studied poise and appreciation.

The Emperor begins a tale of a moon-dwelling rabbit, but a eunuch is hovering at my side. "The Empress Dowager wishes to speak with you," he murmurs.

I rise and follow the eunuch to where she sits. I kowtow and open my mouth to address her but she holds up a hand and I fall silent, waiting for her to begin.

She doesn't take her eyes off the glittering dragons as they writhe before us. "Lady He. I wish to thank you for your management of the unfortunate... moment... with Ula Nara."

I don't know what to say so I say nothing, only bow my head.

"It is good to see that you understand how to behave in moments of difficulty," she goes on. "Despite your – " her eyes flicker over my clothes " – *foreign* ways."

I bow my head again.

"I know that my son is fond of you," she says. "I have cautioned him against becoming too fond of a woman from a country whose loyalty to us is yet in doubt. However, it seems your personal loyalty is strong and we must hope this bodes well for your country's future. You will be rewarded."

I don't know what she means but I bow my head for the third time and make my way back to my seat without having spoken a single word. The children have dispersed, running about the gardens shrieking.

I hold out my hand to the Emperor. "Come to my bedchamber," I say.

He raises his eyebrows. It is for the Emperor to make the first move with his ladies. "Are you wooing me, Lady He?" he asks, amused at my boldness.

"Yes, Your Majesty," I say.

He chuckles and stands, taking my hand. "How novel," he says.

In my bedchamber I wait patiently for the servants to finish undressing us both. Once they are gone I indicate the bed. "Lie back," I say, and he grins at the reminder of our first night together. Obedient, he does as he is told and I sit as he did that night, holding his smooth feet in my bare lap, caressing them softly.

"Am I to ask why you did not call for me before?" he asks me and I smile at the knowledge that he remembers every word and gesture of that first time.

"Oh," I say, allowing my hands to slip further up his legs. "You seemed so shy, Majesty, when I first met you. I thought perhaps you should grow in confidence, feel at home, feel yourself the master of your own palace before I called for you." And we are giggling like children as I fling myself onto the bed beside him. He takes me in his arms and our kisses, sometimes so urgent, now are slow, sweet and gentle. I close my eyes as he caresses me and as we move together I shut out all my dark thoughts and focus only on his scent and our skins touching, the sounds of our lovemaking. But when we are spent and he falls asleep, I hold my body very still so that he will not feel my sobs and press my face against his chest so that the silk coverlet will soak up my tears of fear.

The next morning I wake to an unexpected clamour in the room outside my bed. Fumbling, I pull back the curtains and find that the eunuchs and maids are all crowded into my bedroom, accompanied by what appear to be all my animals. The servants are bursting with pride and their suppressed excitement has made the dogs go wild, yapping and jumping up and down, their tails wagging and tongues lolling. Huan pushes through, slapping this way and that impatiently to make them part before him.

He hurries to my side as I draw a robe about me and try to fully open my eyes. "You're to be promoted again, my lady. You will be a *Fei*! A Consort, not just a concubine. Fourth-ranked! And," he says, his voice dropping conspiratorially while all the servants lean forward to hear him better, "of course now that there is no Empress, and the Emperor has said he absolutely refuses to appoint another as long as he lives, *really*, you will be third-ranked." He beams.

I look to the back of the crowd where Iparhan and Nurmat stand. Nurmat's eyes are bloodshot from his drinking while Iparhan's suddenly shine too brightly in her drawn face. If any of us live long enough to see this promotion, I think. "The Emperor is too kind to me," I say out loud, although I'm thinking of the Empress Dowager and Ula Nara's disgrace, through which it seems I have earned this promotion. "I am not worthy of the honour he shows me. When is the ceremony?"

"Tomorrow afternoon," says Huan. The eunuchs shush the gasping maidservants.

I stare at him. "Tomorrow afternoon? But last time it took so long to prepare for it!"

Huan waves away my concerns. "I have already sent for the dressmakers," he assures me. "You will need new clothes for the ceremony of course." He thinks. "At your last promotion you wore a pink skirt, with gold embroidery on the waistcoat and your cap was—"

I hold up a hand, interrupting him. "I will wear court robes," I say.

He gapes at me. "Not your Xinjiang clothes?"

I shake my head. "Manchu style. Court robes in the orange silk. And my ears need piercing for the triple pearl earrings."

He wants to make sure of his orders. "Just for the ceremony?"

I look into Iparhan's eyes. Slowly I shake my head. I know that my choice will trigger her rage but I can no longer live my life waiting for her moves. It is time I played my own game. "No. After the ceremony

371

I will always wear Manchu robes." I pull the bed drapes about me and lie down on the bed. Outside I can hear Huan and Jiang shrieking at the maidservants. They sound cross but really they're excited. So much to do. So many wondrous new clothes to prepare. Their status, like mine, will rise again as I become a Consort, and there will be whole new wardrobes to arrange for me. If I wear court robes in the Manchu style I will be competing directly against the other ladies, no longer set apart by my clothes. I hear them squabbling over how my hair should be dressed for the important day – in the Manchu style of course but which ornaments? What kind of nail shields should I have? One thing they are all agreed on and that is that I should retain the lotus as my signature flower, an echo of my first court name, a reminder of my precious scent.

"It has brought good luck to my lady," opines Huan, and the other servants murmur agreement and then shriek over new details to be considered. They can barely list all the things that must, simply *must*, be done at once, now, this *minute*.

I leave them to it and make my own plans. I send alms to the beggars by the gates of the Forbidden City and hair ornaments to Consorts Qing and Ying. I send a nest made of golden twigs filled with silk feathers to Yongyan for his favourite toy, the little jade duck. To Lady Wan I send a puppy, a longhaired, lolloping creature with floppy ears and an eager wet tongue to lick her hands and warm her heart. To Giuseppe I send a gift of costly paints and a message saying that I was unwell when we last spoke and that I beg his forgiveness for my rudeness. I tell him I was not myself. Formal gifts to celebrate my forthcoming promotion will be chosen by Huan and sent to other important members of the court and the more senior ladies, but these gifts I choose myself.

The Emperor sends word that he will dine with me tonight, ahead of tomorrow's ceremony. This news very nearly reduces Huan to tears. He already has a room set aside for the dressmakers, who are frantically preparing my court robes for tomorrow's ceremony. He had hoped for no further interruptions, but now has to ensure that a lavish dinner is prepared, as well as readying me to receive the Emperor.

"You," he addresses Iparhan. "You will bathe your mistress and then take her to the bedchamber and dress her. I will arrange her hair and makeup when she is ready. I cannot spare any maids to help you beyond bringing the water, you will have to manage by yourself. Can you do that? I am giving you this task because I believe you to be trustworthy," he adds. "Do not fail me."

Iparhan bows her head and makes a small gesture to me. "My lady," she says, "Please come with me."

I follow her with some reluctance. I don't wish to spend so much time alone with her and she seems too eager for this menial task. I wonder whether she will command me to switch places with her and I linger in the doorway, thinking to back out of the door and call Huan, ask for a different maid. But Iparhan is silent. She behaves as any senior maid would, testing the water, undressing me when I slowly step forward, then helping me into the large tub, shooing away the last of the other maids when they have finished bringing hot water. When we are alone again she turns away to place my clothes out of the way of any water. I have my back to her and cannot see her, only hear her humming tunelessly. It makes me uncomfortable but I try to ignore her. I concentrate on my promotion ceremony tomorrow. I hope that by switching to court robes I will wrong-foot Iparhan. If I am dressed the same as any other woman at court I will take away part of her disguise, for my 'foreign' clothes mark me out against the other women. If my hair and clothes look like the others, perhaps more attention will be drawn to my face – or Iparhan's. It is a small step, but for now it is all that I can think of. I rest my face in my hands for a moment as I try to think and feel something brush against my fingers. "I still have my earrings in," I say to Iparhan. "Huan does not like them to get wet."

Behind me, Iparhan unplaits my hair and sheds its gemstones and ribbons. "It won't harm them," she says. She begins to replait my hair into a single plait. "Your hair is clean," she says. "I will not need to wash it but I need to keep it out of the way of the cream for your face. Close your eyes."

Reluctantly I close them and feel her hands on my face, her movements quick and light, rubbing in a cream that Huan swears will keep me wrinkle-free until I am older than the Empress Dowager herself. I'm not sure I believe him but I've grown used to it and it has a pleasant enough smell. Iparhan's fingers move over my skin until she is done. She takes longer than Huan but then it is not usually her task to perform. I open my eyes and stare at the wall as she bustles about behind me. I am trying so hard to think that I feel almost dizzy in the heat and steam of the room.

"Stand up," she says, and I do so. She pats most of me dry with a towel. "Put your arms up," she says.

I raise my arms and a robe slips over me.

In the brief moment I feel it fall about me I know something is wrong. What I am feeling is rough cotton, not silk. I look down and see blue, then turn my head just as Iparhan screams.

"Huan! Huan! Help me!"

I almost fall into the tub as I try to climb out, clutch at the sides and hear feet come running. As my bare feet touch the floor I twist my head to see Iparhan, fully dressed and made up as myself. She has her back pressed to the wall in an attitude of fear, while her face, turned to me, wears a triumphant smile. I don't even need a mirror to know that she has painted the scar onto my face while she told me she was applying Huan's miraculous cream.

The door bursts open and Huan stands panting, two eunuchs by his side, three maids peering out from behind him. "My lady!" He looks from Iparhan, her face now a mask of alarm, to me, standing frozen and barefoot by the tub. His eyes shift back to Iparhan, who motions, wordless, at my feet. I look down as Huan does. A dagger lies by my right foot, as though dropped from my hand.

Slowly, Huan steps forward. While I stand, unable to move, he walks with care until he is standing in front of Iparhan. Then he kneels, still with infinite caution, and stretches out until he can reach the dagger, all the while looking up at my face, to see if I will attack. I look at him, keeping my eyes on his, praying that for once he will see the difference in us.

Huan reaches behind him with the dagger and carefully lets Iparhan take it. Then he advances on me, his hands ready to grab. Behind him, Iparhan whimpers. "Be careful, Huan. She stole my earrings and then she attacked me. She had this dagger concealed on her. What if she has another?"

Huan reaches me. In one swift moment he grasps my wrists and forces me to the floor. For all his usual elegance in bearing, he is a strong man and I sink down to my knees without any attempt to fight against him. Held in a tight grip, my face pressed to the floor, I begin to weep.

"I will beat you myself," says Huan. "And when I am done beating you the Emperor himself will hear of this and you will forfeit your life."

"No," says Iparhan above me. "I do not want him to know of this matter. He will feel affronted that this girl, his gift to me, should be such a disappointment. Better that we manage this between us, Huan."

Huan sounds uncertain. He shifts his grip on me. "You cannot keep her," he says. "She attacked you. She should be executed. She can never be trusted again."

"You are right," says Iparhan. "I want you to take her to the gates of the Forbidden City and cast her out."

"Out?"

"Into the streets of Beijing," says Iparhan. "There she can live or die. She will no longer be a threat to me."

I feel my neck muscles wrench as I twist my head against the floor to try and look up at her but Huan reinforces his hold on me and presses my cheek back to the floor. "It is not usual…" he begins.

"It is what I command," says Iparhan. "Do it now."

I feel another hand come down on me, holding me in place, as Huan loosens his grasp, pulls out each earring from my ears with ungentle hands, then stands. "As you wish, my lady," he says, then addresses the unseen eunuch holding me down. "You will take her to the gates and have her thrown out. Now."

Until this moment I had not believed what was happening. Now I reach out an arm and clutch Huan's ankle as he moves away from me. "Huan! Please don't do this to me. I did not harm her!"

The eunuch pulls my hand away from Huan so hard that for a moment I believe my arm has come out of its socket. I shriek with pain. Huan moves further away. I twist my head again so that I can look up at him. He has gone back to Iparhan's side. His arm is about her shoulder and he is guiding her out of the room. He does not even look down on me.

I scream. I have nothing left to lose. "Huan! Help me! I – she – she is not who she seems to be! Her name is Iparhan! She comes from a family who fought against the Emperor and lost! She means to lead a rebel army against him! She – she found me on the streets Huan! I was a beggar girl, nothing more. But she had a scar and – "

Huan has almost taken Iparhan from the room but now he pauses.

I stop screaming, half-believing that he will ask questions, that he will ask me to repeat my claim. Instead he addresses the eunuch. "Get her to the gates quickly," he says. "And bind up her mouth. She cannot say such things while you take her there. Someone might hear her ravings." The eunuch jerks me to my feet in one hard movement. I stagger and try to find my footing as Huan turns and leaves the room.

The voice I hear from my mouth is not my own. It is a terrifying shriek of fear and pain. "Huan! *Wipe her face!* Wipe her face and you will see her scar! I beg you. I beg you! Huan! *Huan!*"

But he is gone.

I struggle against the eunuch who is holding me. I hope that I might wipe the painted-on scar from my own face, that when I do so it might give him pause. But he is too strong for me and my hands are pinned so tightly I can do nothing. A maid gives him a cloth and he gags me. When I struggle harder he binds my feet and hands as well, limiting my movements. Then he picks me up and slings me over his shoulder, so that I am hanging upside-down. I can no longer speak clearly. I can only scream.

I scream. I scream and scream as he carries me down the steps of my palace. I scream as he carries me through the little streets of the Inner Court and as we pass into the Outer Court I scream. My voice echoes off the paved courtyards, the red walls, the golden rooftops. I grow hoarse long before we reach the Western Gate. Still I scream, although my voice grows quieter and quieter, its strength fading with every step the eunuch takes. I see guards, eunuchs and courtiers passing. Some glance my way, many ignore me altogether. A maid is of little interest. A maid who has committed some misdemeanour and is to be punished is of even less interest. Only the maids we pass turn their heads to watch me. Their fear of my unknown misdemeanour and punishment makes them walk faster, keen to avoid a similar fate.

They scurry away. My screams will be in their nightmares for many days to come.

I am released, dropped abruptly to the ground, my ankles and wrists roughly unbound. The gag is pulled away. I struggle to my feet, dizzy from having been upside down for so long. I stagger, then straighten up and look about me just as the towering red doors of the West Glorious Gate slowly swing shut against me, the eunuch already making his way back to Huan.

I rush at the gate, my hands outstretched. The impact as I slam into the unyielding wood is so hard I feel the pain shoot up both arms. My torn throat releases a cry that is barely audible as I sink to my knees, holding my shaking arms against my chest. Through my tears I look up at the red door, patterned with row upon row of gilded brass studs. Quickly I move to the outside of the arch that contains the door. There is a low panel of white stone, carved. I try to climb onto it, my hands reaching up the perfectly smooth red wall, a mad thought of trying to climb over it in my confused mind. For one precarious moment I stand pressed against the red wall, my arms reaching up to its endless summit, before I fall, my knuckles scraping against the stone as I try to save myself. My fingernails are broken, my hands are bleeding where the cool stone has ripped the skin from my flesh. I rock back and forth, my bare feet pressed hard against the cold paving, my tears dripping slowly onto the stone. The moaning I can dimly hear is coming from my own mouth. There is no other sound for the gate remains closed and there are no other people nearby. The late autumn day is already turning to dusk.

Dusk. I struggle to my feet and begin to run. To my left, the endless red walls of the Forbidden City. To my right, the dark waters of the moat. I run and run. My feet, grown soft in my silken shoes, hurt with every step but I only run faster. Finally I see where the wall ends and I turn the corner to my left, heading for the Meridian Gate, the great southern gate that is the main entrance to my former home. Here there is no silence. Here there are crowds of people. Beggars, street vendors, petitioners, guards. Courtiers, their servants pushing the beggars out of their way as they leave the Forbidden City. The beggars push their hands into the palanquins, their grimy fingers reaching for alms and being slapped away. There is a hubbub of voices all about me as I press through the crowd, my ears filled with only one sound.

"Draw the bolts, lock up, careful with the lanterns. Draw the bolts, lock up, careful with the lanterns."

The call is coming from very close inside the main gates and already, as I fight my way through the oncoming crowd I see the guards move to grasp the great red doors and swing them close. I try to move faster, but I am heading towards the gates and everyone else is moving away. Again and again I am pushed back, and I hear Jiang's voice in my head, from the day I first came to the Forbidden City, was frightened by the call and asked its meaning. *All those who had business in the Forbidden City today have left. The gates are to be locked up now; only the Emperor and his family and servants will remain.*

The gates are to be locked up...

I shove a street vendor aside so hard he stumbles. "Watch yourself, you stupid girl," he shouts, his little cakes falling to the ground, but I am already closer to the gates and a dark dread makes me push harder. I hear curses from all sides as I finally reach the red gates, but they are already closed. I throw myself at the feet of one of the guards.

"Let me in," I half-sob.

"What?" asks the guard.

I've forgotten to speak Mandarin. I try again, my voice coming out tight and ragged from my throat. "I serve as a maid to Lady He," I say. "I – I was running an errand for her and I returned later than I expected. Please let me in. She will beat me if I do not return tonight."

"Tally," says the guard, his hand outstretched, his voice bored.

"Tally?"

"Where's your tally?" he demands more roughly. "No servant leaves the Forbidden City without a tally. Otherwise how would we know who is a real maid and who is just –" he looks at my dirty feet, damp crumpled robe and disheveled hair, "– some beggar girl from the streets?"

"I dropped it," I say quickly.

"Then you'll have to wait till morning," says the guard, bored again. "A senior eunuch of your mistress' household will be sent for, to identify you before you are allowed to enter. And I should imagine you'll get a sound beating for being so careless," he adds.

"Please," I say, my tears beginning to fall again. "Please let me in."

"No," says the guard, and it is clear from his tone that no amount of begging and pleading will make him reconsider.

I fall back and let myself be swept away by the crowds around me, all flowing in one direction: over the bridge that crosses the moat, into Beijing itself. I hardly think, hardly even feel myself walking, only let myself drift along amongst the voices and elbows. Only when we reach the other side of the bridge and the crowd disperses in all directions, freed from the bridge's constraints, am I released from the flow. I stop. Motionless, I stand at the corner of the bridge, looking back at the red walls of the Forbidden City, now more than fifty paces away from me, protected from intruders by its cold dark waters and high walls. I have not been without the protection of those waters and red walls for almost two years. The warmth of the bodies about me fades and the cold of the approaching night creeps up my bare feet and into my bones.

Only when my teeth begin to chatter together do I move again. I turn around on myself, dazed by the cold. It's growing darker now and slowly the reality of what has just happened seeps into me. I am alone. Outside of the Forbidden City, with no way to return inside its walls. I am cold and poorly dressed for a night or indeed a life on the streets. My past life as a quick-witted girl fending for herself on the streets seems a long way away – and besides, that was in a city that I had known since birth. I know nothing about Beijing – I have never even seen it except from the upper stories of my own tower or snatched glimpses through bamboo screens and the shimmering silk curtains of a palanquin.

I try to think through the cold fog that has crept up from the soles of my feet and filled my mind. I have two choices – to get back inside the Forbidden City or to accept a life back on the streets. I cannot think how to get back inside the Forbidden City, unless perhaps to steal one of the tallies carried by the servants – and how carefully they must guard them, wary of the fate that has befallen me tonight! The guards will not let me slip inside, their lives depend on not allowing such things to happen. I stand on one foot and then the other, pressing the lifted foot in turn against my cold legs, hoping for some residual warmth to take away the now-painful chill of the ground.

I will have to live on the streets again. I have done it before. Iparhan is now stuck inside the Forbidden City. Without me there to swap places with she will be forced to play the part of a concubine until she dies, so perhaps she will leave me alone. In a city the size of Beijing there will be more opportunities for work. But there will also be more dangers and I will not know where they are until they find me. I try to think about how to begin.

I need to be warm. The remnants of the old days come back to me. Above food, above hunger, comes the need for warmth. If I continue to stand here like this, shaking with cold, my teeth clenched to stop them from breaking one another, my feet growing numb, I will lose the ability to think, to move. I will die here, on the corner of the bridge leading to the Meridian Gate of the Forbidden City. I need to move and I need to seek out some warmth – through clothing or shelter and preferably both.

Then I will have to find food, although I know that I can go for many days without a full belly, no matter how much my stomach rumbles and begs for nourishment. I have been fattened up these past two years, my pampered curves will sustain me until I find a way to feed myself. My shoulders slump. If all else fails I know full well that there will be women's lanes here, whatever they may call them in Beijing. I am no virgin now and so what is to stop me? I would be fed and clothed, after all, and isn't that what all of this madness, this pretence, was for?

But my head rises up as I think of what a life on the streets will really mean. It is not the hunger or the hard work that I am afraid of, nor the dangers from unknown men in the darkened streets and back rooms that frightens me. It is not that I will never wear silks again, nor be served a hundred plates of food at every meal. I will not miss the luxuries I have risked my life for every day these past two years. A flood of images comes to me as I stand shaking on the bridge.

I will never again see little Prince Yongyan running away from his guardians, Consorts Qing and Ying in hot pursuit of him, promising sweetmeats if he will only obey them, just this once.

I will never again sit in my rooms, surrounded by dogs and cawing birds while Huan frets over my hair and Jiang peers worriedly out of the windows as Fury attacks another snake.

Giuseppe will not be by my side in these dark cold streets with his words of advice and his portraits that show me another side of myself.

Lady Wan will sit alone in her rooms with only her towering wigs for company and no one to play her silly drinking games.

And I will never be held in the Emperor's arms again.

I will not do it.

I will not turn and walk into the dark streets of Beijing and be swallowed up by my old life. I will find a way to make my way back to the life I have unwittingly made for myself, the home and friends I have created out of a crazed plan, the love I never expected to find while playing the part of a spy. I look about me. I have to think quickly and I have to move before I freeze to death. Who can I trust?

Giuseppe.

He is the only person I know in Beijing. If I can find Giuseppe and tell him my story he may believe me. He is a kindly man. More, he is a painter, he has stared at both my face and Iparhan's over and over again. He knew something was not right when she sat for him, when she spoke abruptly to him and asked too many questions about war. I saw in his face that he was confused, that he saw something in her face but could not give what he saw a name against the too-obvious clothes, hair, makeup, status. If I can find him now I can tell him everything and pray he believes me, that he can find a way to help me. I don't know whether he can, whether this has all gone too far to be made right again. But I have to try.

I move my numb feet eastwards. I know that each night, when he leaves the Forbidden City, Giuseppe makes his way to the Jesuit Church. He calls it St Joseph's, but the local people know it as Dong Tang, the East Church.

I have to ask over and over again for directions. Some people don't know what I am talking about. Some point vaguely this way or that, seeming to contradict one another. But finally I see it. A towering building, thick grey stone rising above me. In front of it, a great gate rises. I press my face against its bars and look through. Three domes top the building, three doors pierce its facade.

"What do you want?"

A lantern shines too brightly in my eyes and I draw back a little. A man, dressed as Giuseppe always is, in a long black scholar's robe, is scowling at me from the other side of the gate.

"I wish to see Giuseppe Castiglione," I say.

"Brother Giuseppe has retired for the night, to pray and sleep," says the man.

"I must see him," I say. "It is very urgent."

The man shakes his head, looking at my crumpled maid's robe and bare feet, no doubt wondering what possible business I could have with Giuseppe. "You can see him in the morning," he says.

"Please," I say. "Please. I can't wait till then. I will freeze to death."

"Then go home to your master," he says and turns to go.

"Please!" I cry after him but he ignores me and walks away, his lantern bobbing in the darkness until it disappears into the grey stone.

I have to get warm. Now that I know where Giuseppe is, I can return in the morning and waylay him before he reaches the Forbidden City. But I will not last till dawn without more clothes or some shelter. I look about me.

On the corner of a street is a cobbler's. A lit brazier gives off a dull red light from the embers, which are burning low. The cobbler will not work much longer, for the light is almost gone and he will not want to keep a costly lantern flame burning. The small lantern he does have casts a weak glow over his busy hands, finishing the last shoe of the day. Behind him sits a woman, probably his wife, cutting up scraps of leather, making little decorations out of those scraps that are too small to be useful in making shoes but might serve to make the petal of a flower. Both of them have their heads bowed low, straining to see in the poor light.

I'm drawn to the brazier's heat. I shuffle forwards, as close as I can get without drawing attention to myself. I cannot feel the full warmth of the fire, but even a faint whisper of it is worth edging a little closer for.

"Stop hanging about, girl," says the cobbler, frowning down at his work. "What do you want?"

"Please," I say. "I'm very cold. I just need to stand by the fire for a little while."

"And then what will you do?"

"I don't know," I say. "I need to find some shelter for the night but I have nowhere to go."

I stand in silence for a few minutes, hugging my body, trying to preserve what little heat I have. I edge a little closer to the fire, hoping the cobbler will not chase me off. I wonder how long it will be before he finishes work for the night and douses the fire, leaving me alone in the dark and cold. I try to think of where else I might shelter but I don't know any of these streets and I daren't go too far from the church in case I lose my way and miss Giuseppe in the morning.

"Here," the cobbler says, without looking at me.

Something hits my leg and I look down in the glowing red darkness to see two old worn slippers. They are scuffed and worn away at the toes, and far too big for me, but I seize them and slip them on. The difference is immediate. My teeth almost stop chattering in surprise at the release from the frosted earth against my bare soles. I approach the cobbler until I am stood right in front of him, my white hands gripping the edge of his workbench. "I will repay you for your kindness," I tell him, trying not to cry. "And I will thank you every day in my prayers."

He grunts, looking down at his work as though uninterested.

I shuffle away, back towards the little fire when his wife speaks to me. "Girl!"

I look back.

"Take this," she says, holding out something shapeless. "And save your prayers for yourself, you look as though you need them."

I reach out a hand for the shadowy item. It is a jacket, thick but full of holes and with a greasy feel to it, perhaps used as a rag for polishing the finer shoes. It feels better than any of the furs and silks Huan ever ordered for me. I wrap myself tightly in it, then wipe away the tears that have fallen. "Thank you," I say to the woman. "You have saved my life."

She shrugs, embarrassed at my tears. "If you're still on the streets tomorrow come here and I'll give you bread," she says, her voice gruff. "I don't want to find you dead on the street, you'll scare away my best customers. Now be off with you. We've finished work for the day and I must put out the fire. There may be somewhere to shelter near the church."

I nod and back away. "Thank you," I say. "I will never forget your kindness."

The church is surrounded by a wall. At least it will provide some protection from the wind and keep me out of sight of any passers-by with less than good intentions. I make my way along the side of it until it turns a corner and curl myself into a small ball, pulling my thin robe down as low as I can to cover my feet, then wrap the jacket tightly about me. I rest my head against the wall and hope to make it through the night. I am not sure I can sleep.

"You took some finding."

The figure standing over me is only a mass of shadows and his voice has lost the humour and confidence that it used to have.

I wriggle away from him and stand up, wary of being too close to him. "How did you find me?"

"I came looking for you."

"How did you know where I would go?"

"How many friends do you have in Beijing?" Nurmat asks. "Giuseppe would have been your only hope of help."

"How did you know your way round these streets?"

He laughs. It's not a happy sound. "I wander through the streets of Beijing every night, Hidligh," he tells me. "I walk and I drink. And I hope for enough strength not to return to the Forbidden City. To leave this place and these lies and Iparhan. But every dawn I find myself presenting my tally at the Meridian Gate and re-entering my nightmare."

We're both silent for a moment.

"What do you want, Nurmat?"

His voice is very low. "I think she is going to kill him, Hidligh."

I don't ask who. I know. "She said she wanted to raise a rebellion…" I say. I know I'm stupid for even clinging on to this old lie, but I believed it for so long it comes out, even now.

"That was before she even saw you," says Nurmat. "She wanted revenge. I believed, like you did, that a rebellion would give her that. But what greater revenge could she have than to press a dagger into the Emperor's flesh and watch him die before her very eyes? She cannot wait any longer. She cannot play a part. You've seen her. She wants to see him die and nothing else matters. I was a fool not to see it long ago, but I wanted to believe her. Just as you did."

"She will die for it," I say.

Nurmat begins to say something and then stops. There's a sound like a sob before he speaks again. "She does not care about dying."

"She cares about you," I say. "And you still love her. Aren't you still loyal to her? Aren't you going to help her?"

"She's gone, Hidligh," says Nurmat. "She is gone. The woman I knew and loved from when we were little more than children – she is gone. There is a ghost in her place. A hungry ghost who seeks her revenge, by whatever means."

I shiver.

"Stop her," says Nurmat. "Help me stop her."

"Why would you care if the Emperor dies?" I ask.

"Because it would break your heart," says Nurmat. He is standing very close to me now and I take a step backwards, still wary of his loyalties.

"Why do you care if my heart is broken?" I ask.

His arms come around me in the darkness. I try to struggle away, afraid that he will seize me, drag me back to Iparhan to carry out some new part of her plan, but he holds me gently, my face pressed against his shoulder, his head bowed to rest against my hair. I stand still and listen to his sobbing breath before he lets me go and steps away. When he speaks he almost sounds like the old Nurmat I used to know, the one who loved Iparhan and still believed she would one day love him enough to seek his embrace rather than her revenge.

"My own heart has been broken enough times," he says. "I thought I loved you once. You were Iparhan, but in a gentle form. You were the Iparhan I could have been happy with. I longed for you because I longed for her. But you have found your own love and now you are your own woman. And Iparhan is gone."

"And what will become of you?" I ask.

"I will die loving her," he says. "And that will be enough."

We stand in silence for a moment.

"They have already eaten," he says. "He was with her in the bedchamber and then he left her to sleep in the other room. She will try to kill him while he sleeps. We have to stop her now or it will be too late. Are you with me?"

I reach out in the darkness and slip my hand into his. He holds it tightly for a moment and then we walk through the dark streets. He walks quickly, certain of his way and I shuffle behind him in my slippers, my hand gripped in his.

The Eastern Gate looms above us. Nurmat lifts a fist and hammers at the door. It creaks open a chink and a guard's suspicious face peers out. At the sight of Nurmat he nods and motions him forward. As we step into the light of the lanterns Nurmat suddenly grasps me roughly by the shoulder and jerks me forward. It hurts and I let out a yelp. Nurmat ignores me and holds out a small flat rectangle of wood, the size of a man's palm, the precious tally allowing him to re-enter the Forbidden City. "This one tried to run away after her mistress caught her stealing," he says. "I knew where to find her and she'll be given a beating when I get her back to the palace."

The more senior guard approves the tally and one of the other men opens the gate. Nurmat all but drags me through, raising his other hand to the guards in thanks. For a moment I'm desperately afraid that he has lied to me, that he is still on Iparhan's side, but as soon as we are out of sight he lets me go and grasps my hand again.

Hand in hand we run through the courtyards. We keep to the shadows, to the bases of the walls, the edges of the great temples and halls, keeping away from the well-lit areas where the guards congregate. The distances have never seemed so great. I am out of breath in moments. I tug at Nurmat's hand and we pause for a moment while I kick off the worn slippers. They are too hard to run in and I am afraid of the noise they make. Barefoot, I run on with Nurmat pulling at me, trying to make me run faster.

The Inner Court is quiet. Lanterns lead from one palace to another, little paths marked out with softly glowing orbs of yellow and red light. We hurry past the gates of my own palace, too brightly lit with lanterns signalling the Emperor's presence. Instead we make our way to the covering darkness of Ula Nara's still-empty palace and use her gardens to get closer to my servants' quarters.

There is silence everywhere. We avoid the sleeping quarters, where the servants have now retired for the night and make our way through the living quarters and then into my own reception hall. The room is in darkness and through the windows we can see into my courtyard. There, lanterns are lit but the guards and Emperor's servants seem mostly to be asleep. The Emperor has made his way to his bedchamber, his concubine is in her own room. There are no more tasks until the morning and every servant knows better than to waste the chance to sleep.

We make our way quietly through the rooms until we come to my bedchamber. I stop outside the door. "There will be a eunuch on guard," I say.

Nurmat shakes his head. "I was on guard," he says. "But she had me sleep outside the door, not inside. I knew she was planning something and did not want me to see that she did not go to sleep. She will be awake," he adds. "Be careful. I will go first."

He eases the door open. The room is dimly lit, with only one lantern. It is not enough light to see the whole room. He edges into the room and I follow him, a pace behind. I can just see that the bed seems empty and I look back over my shoulder, fearing that we are too late. She may have already gone to the Emperor's room.

In the moment that I hesitate I hear a gasp. There is a heavy sound and then Nurmat groans. I don't think. I enter the room and feel the door swing shut behind me, a gust of air on my cheek as the lantern is blown out, leaving me in darkness. I stand motionless. From somewhere in the room I can hear Nurmat's ragged breathing. I want to call out for help, to light a lantern and look down at him to see if he can be saved, but I feel a presence close to me and then the sharp tip of a dagger against my throat.

"Give me the perfume. I need more of it."

I shake my head, feeling the dagger slip on my bared throat as I do so, scratching the skin.

The dagger presses tighter. If I shake my head again it will draw blood. "Give me the perfume."

"Ask Nurmat for it," I say.

"He stopped giving it to me," Iparhan says and I hear a tiny catch in her throat.

I take a deep breath. "I cannot let you kill the Emperor," I say. "Kill me, if you must. I will not give you the perfume. I cannot let you go to him."

"Fool," she spits at me. I feel the dagger shake in her hand and brace myself for its thrust. "You think because you are to be promoted that he loves you?"

"I love *him*," I say. I try to back away but she follows me in the dark, her dagger kept tight to my throat. I find myself against the edge of my bed and stop. *I am going to die*, I think, and find myself speaking again, as though clinging onto my life through words. "When I am in his arms I am happy and when I am not I long for him. When he sees me his eyes are bright and he reaches for me with such desire that I find myself running to him, however unseemly it may be."

She snorts. "You must be the only Emperor's concubine in history who is happy to sit in her golden rooms, being pampered until you die of boredom."

"You forget where I came from," I say.

"Ah yes," she says. "The street rat turned lady. Is it the warm bed and the food that brought you crawling back here?"

"No," I say. "It is the care of my closest servants. It is the friends I have made here, those who rise above scheming. It is being free to pray with an open heart rather than a starving stomach. It is playing with my animals and being held by a man whom I love and who cares for me."

"And the jewels, and the clothes – they mean nothing, I suppose?" she taunts me.

"Not really," I say and as I say it I know it is true. "They are beautiful but they are not what has made me happy here."

"How virtuous."

"Iparhan," I say. "Take Nurmat and go away from here. Think how it would be to lie in his arms – the man you love – instead simpering at the Emperor, whom you hate, in the hopes of being taken to his rooms so that you might kill him. Think what it would be not to pretend to love."

"Too late for that," she says and her voice is choked.

"Nurmat would take you to his heart," I tell her. "He is only angry because he sees you with the Emperor when he wants you in his own arms."

"Too late," she says. Behind her Nurmat's rasping breath continues in the darkness.

I put a finger on the dagger, trying to lift it away from my neck. She holds it steady. I let my eyes close for a moment, trying to find some strength to carry on. "Iparhan, stop your crazy notions of revenge. Xinjiang is part of the empire now. You are not going to change that alone. It would take generations of fighting to reclaim it from the empire."

The dagger pushes tighter and I feel it prick my skin. "*Xinjiang?* You call our homeland *Xinjiang?*"

I have made an error but now I am growing angry. "You should have spent more time convincing me of your plans if you wanted a comrade in arms. You took a girl who needed food and shelter, who was starving for kindness and love and that is what you got. You never asked yourself whether I agreed with your ideals. Or your plans."

She makes an impatient sound and pulls the dagger away from me. My fingers go to my neck at once and I feel a little wetness on my fingertips. I put my fingers to my mouth and taste blood. She has nicked my throat, just where the little rough patch was. Now she stands above me in the darkness. I slide away from the bed and make my way toward Nurmat. I move slowly, afraid a sudden movement will find me with a dagger embedded in my side.

"If I fail they will execute you for treason. You had better pray I succeed," she says, watching me, a dark shadow in a dark room. "If I get away and nobody knows who killed him you will still live here as a concubine of the dead Emperor. You will have a full belly and a warm bed till the end of your days. Isn't that what you wanted? Isn't that the reason you agreed to my plan?"

"I agreed because I had nothing else in my life," I say. "No choice. And now I do."

"He will die for what he has done to my family and my country," she says, her voice shaking.

I've reached Nurmat's side. I kneel by him but it's too dark to see him properly. "Nurmat," I whisper. "Speak to me." I run my fingers over him, wary of what I may find. I try to lift him a little although I'm wary of moving him too much. His breath is too hard and rasping to answer me, but he lifts a hand and places it on mine. Above us looms Iparhan's shadow. I am suddenly angry. I lay him down and stand to face her. Our features hidden by the darkness, I can feel the heat of her body, we are so close. "You loved him!"

"He loved *you*," she answers, lowering her head.

"He did not, Iparhan."

"He let you back into the Forbidden City."

"And you killed him for his last shred of decency?"

She turns away. I stand watching her, shaking. Now I am truly afraid of her. If Iparhan has killed Nurmat then she can kill anyone. The Emperor, me, herself. There was no one she loved more than Nurmat and she has not hesitated to take his life. Nothing I can say now will dissuade her.

She strides towards the doorway, stepping over Nurmat's body without pause. She is heading towards the courtyard, where a door on the walkway leads to the Emperor's bedroom.

At my feet Nurmat gasps and I want to comfort him but I cannot. I run, barefoot, after Iparhan.

In the courtyard all is silence and darkness. The lanterns are growing dim. Their faint lights play on the carvings and make every shadow a person. My feet are cold on the walkway and I shiver. The guards and eunuchs who accompanied the Emperor are now all asleep, my courtyard littered with bodies as though a battle has already been fought and lost here tonight.

There's a small sound near the door leading to the Emperor's bedchamber and suddenly I am running along the walkway and throwing myself at Iparhan. She turns at once to grapple with me.

She's strong. I knew it, of course, but I've never had to pit myself against her. Now we clutch at one another, her hands unforgiving as she reaches round my back and presses hard on my spine. She is wearing the perfume, but its scent has faded beneath a mixture of sweat and fear, rage and the cold damp night air. I clench my teeth in pain but she does not slacken her grip and at last I do the only thing I can – I jerk forwards and bite her cheek hard, my teeth coming down on the raised line of her scar. I feel flesh give way and taste blood. She makes a groaning sound and pulls away. I open my jaw and let her fall backwards with the effort she has made to escape me. I've only a moment before she is on me again but this time I'm quicker, expecting her. I run into the courtyard, out of the gates into the little lane outside my palace and as I do so stumble against a pillar. She follows me, her hand coming out to rest on the pillar as she grabs for me but the pillar is already rocking from my weight and suddenly from it a figure falls – a giant golden guardian lion – and crushes her from the waist down beneath its bulk.

Even in her agony she manages to remain silent, only a gasp tells me she should have screamed. I wriggle away from her flailing arms and stand over her. She is trapped – her pelvis and legs crushed beneath the golden weight. Her fingernails scrape on the cobbles as she tries to pull herself away from it but the weight is far too much for her. I come closer and she twists and tries to grab at my robe but I step away.

"Bitch," she curses under her breath. "Traitor."

I stand and watch her. Her efforts are causing her greater pain but she does not stop writhing.

"Keep still," I tell her. "I will help you if you keep still and promise not to attack me again."

She becomes a little more still and I approach her. I kneel by her side but as soon as I am close to her she grabs for me and brings my face close to hers, her arm around my neck. Her hot breath is on my cheek and her hand, wet with the blood from my bite, pulls at my hair. I struggle and she spits in my face. "You will die," she hisses. "You and your precious Emperor and all your pampered court."

"Half your body is crushed," I tell her, still struggling to escape from her. "You will die if I leave you here. You will not be able to kill anyone."

She lets go of me suddenly, her arms weakening with the pain filling her body. "You're wrong," she pants, wiping blood away from her eyes. "The poison will kill all of you – you, the other whores and the Emperor."

"Poison?"

She tries to sit up and then gasps with pain as something else in her legs gives way. "You won't find it. But all of the court will die."

I hear steps nearby and turn quickly. A shadowed figure stands between the gateposts a few paces away. I've been expecting someone to arrive; there's been too much noise to go unnoticed.

"Reveal yourself," I say, my voice shaking. If it's a guard I am dead.

The shadows change and Huan steps forwards. I stare at him for a long moment and he looks back at me, then down at Iparhan. He takes in the clothes she is wearing, which are mine, and her hair, dressed in sparkling stones. He looks back at me. I open my mouth to speak but he raises a hand to stop me.

"I was right," he says slowly. "She took your place."

I nod. "How did you know?"

He shakes his head. "I am not sure," he says, looking between the two of us. "I am not sure," he repeats as though in a daze. "I knew but did not know. Until now."

I let my body slide down so that I am squatting before him. My head lowers and I stay in silence for a while.

At last I look up at him. "Do what you must do, Huan," I say. "If you must raise the alarm, do so."

He's gone. I've grown used to the eunuchs' skill in walking quietly so as not to disturb their masters, but even so his footsteps are like air. I'm alone again in the darkness with Iparhan. Time passes in silence and my thighs ache, I'm unaccustomed to squatting now, though it used to be my natural resting pose. "He'll be back soon," I mutter. "With guards."

Iparhan tries to move again and then becomes still, looking over my shoulder. I twist to look up. Huan has returned. He must have been running, for his breath rises and falls quickly in his chest but still he made no noise approaching us. He keeps his mouth open to breathe more quietly.

"Are they coming?" I ask.

Huan looks behind him. "Who?"

I shrug. "The guards. Other servants. The Emperor. Whomever you called for."

"I called for no one," he says. "I brought this."

He passes me something that seems to glow softly in the darkness, something pure white and soft to the touch. I hold it. It seems to be a white silk scarf but I am stupid with tiredness. "I don't know what this is," I tell him.

"It is for an honourable death," he says, his voice still soft despite his quick breath.

I turn it over in my hands. "Suicide?"

He bows his head.

I twist it in my hands, look down and feel its strength. "Is that what I should do, then? Is that what is expected?"

He snatches it back from my hands. "For *her*," he hisses. Not for you."

I rock back on my heels to look up at him and almost topple over. I am too tired to balance. "She doesn't want to die," I say. "She wants to kill."

He lifts his chin to indicate Iparhan and I turn to look at her. Her hands are reaching out towards the scarf.

I throw the scarf through the air and it twists and turns before floating into her outstretched hands. She wraps it about her neck and tries to pull it but even I can see at once that she will not succeed. She tries harder but at last lets go, leaving it crumpled round her neck.

Huan steps forward. "It is a task I can perform," he says.

I grab at the base of his robe. "You don't know anything about this," I say to him. "How do you know you should still be loyal to me?"

He looks down at me and at Iparhan. His hand comes to rest gently on my tousled hair for a brief moment, before he steps forward again.

I tug at him harder, stopping him. "Can't she be taken away?" I ask in a whisper. "We could get her out of the Forbidden City. She could go away," I add, although I know that Iparhan would do no such thing.

Huan shakes his head. "She will die by dawn," he says. "She can die quickly or slowly." He steps forward again but I hold up my hand.

"It is mine to do," I say.

He is silent for a moment and then nods. "I will find the well," he says.

I frown at him. "Well?"

"She said she had poisoned the court," he says. "She must mean a well. There are many in the Forbidden City but only a few large enough to provide enough water to be sure of harming so many."

I'd forgotten her threats. I look at her face and see from the bitterness on it that Huan is right. "Go," I say and he's gone before I can take another breath.

I make my way over to her and when I'm close I wait for her to attack me again, watching her hands carefully, but she doesn't move, only looks at me.

"Are you happy?" she rasps. "Happy in your golden cage while our homeland is crushed by your lover?"

"It's over," I tell her. "Your plans for rebellion and unrest – your plans to kill the Emperor. All over."

"The people will rise again," she says.

I shake my head. "The Emperor will crush them if they rise against him."

"Then they will rise again. And again and again. Until there is no Emperor, nor empire, and they will be free."

I nod, take the ends of the silk scarf in my hands and look down at her. My hands shake.

Her face softens and she strokes the silk at her neck, her eyes closing. "I loved Nurmat," she says, her voice soft and gentle as I've never heard it before. "Tell him I always loved him."

It takes a long time for her to die. I hoped only a few moments would suffice and I begin to release my grip on her too early. She twists violently as soon as the pressure eases, trying to take the breath that will save her and I'm forced to grasp the scarf again more tightly although my hands ache and the white silk cuts into my knuckles until I can hardly feel them.

At last her body grows heavy and slowly falls against me instead of struggling away. I'm wary, thinking she is playing dead to fool me, knowing how strong she is. I let go of the white silk finger by finger but she doesn't move and when I unwind its coils I bring my ear close to her mouth and there is no warm breath on my cheek.

I sit in the darkness and hold her for a while. I try to cry for her but I'm too tired for tears. My whole body is weak with the fear of the past two years draining out of me. At last I get to my feet and place my hands under her arms, bracing myself against her limpness. I need one last burst of strength to protect myself and then I will be free.

I begin the journey back to my room, staggering under the weight. It's not far but she's heavier than I expected and by the time I reach the bedroom I'm dragging her body rather than carrying it, her shoes making a noise as they bump into hard objects and her clothes swishing against doorways. A few guards and servants mutter in their sleep or roll over as we pass them but no one wakes.

My bedchamber is dark. Only one small lantern is lit and everywhere are shadows. I stumble through the doorway and rip off the old jacket and the maid's robe, then use it to wipe my face, removing my painted scar. I feel about for my silken sleeping robe and pull it on, then kneel by Iparhan's body. In the dim flickering light I wipe away her makeup, revealing her scar, pull away all of her gemstones and ribbons, leaving her hair unbound. I replait it, my fingers clumsy, the little red maid's ribbon badly tied. Throughout this I can hear deep rasping breaths close at hand and I keep up a whispered comfort. "One moment, Nurmat," I beg. "One moment and I will come to you. I must finish this. I must." I tug at her clothing. Her limp corpse resists me and more than once I hear the fabrics tear. At last she is naked and I use the stained cotton robe to cover her again. Dressed, she lies in the middle of my chamber floor, a crumpled broken shell, her pale skin flickering with dark shadows.

Now I make my way to Nurmat's side, lifting the lantern onto the floor so that I can see him better. He is half draped on the bed and when I touch the coverlets they are wet with blood. I kneel by his side. "Nurmat," I whisper. "Nurmat. Speak to me."

His eyes open but when he tries to speak blood gurgles from his open mouth. I wipe it away with my silk sleeve and then lay a finger against his mouth so that he will not speak but he tries again. I can make out only one word. "Iparhan."

I hold him closer with one arm. With the other hand I reach for my vial of perfume and hold it open, close to him, so that the faint scent that always clings to me is magnified a thousandfold. He breathes, hard and fast, and the smell of delicate spring blossom and rich summer fruits enters his nostrils. He stills in my arms, breathing slower and more deeply.

Then I close his eyes. "I am Iparhan," I whisper to him. "And we are married now. I am your wife and we will leave this place today. We will journey back to Kashgar and there we will live, you and I. I will bear your children and you will love me always."

His eyes flutter, trying to open. He tries to focus on me. "Hidligh."

I place a hand across his eyes, blocking his sight and whisper again, while his breathing grows ragged. "I, Iparhan, will love you for ever, Nurmat. Forever."

His breath is gone and his body grows so heavy I can no longer hold him to me, even with both arms. I let him go and he slides to the floor, leaving his blood soaking into my pale silk coverlets, staining them from palest pink to deepest scarlet.

I stand, every part of my body aching. Slowly, as though in a trance, I conceal the vial of perfume and rip the bed curtains, use the water bowl to clean my feet before binding my own hands, then drape myself across my bed.

Only then do I scream for help and hear Huan come running, his footsteps suddenly grown loud and heavy, as he echoes my cries and forces the heavy-eyed servants out of their slumbers.

Dawn comes and as soon as the gates of the Forbidden City open Huan sends for a man who will release me at last of the weight hanging over me. He may not see my face, of course, so I sit on one side of a painted screen and he stands on the other. I hear him kowtow, his forehead touching the ground nine times while I gather up the strength to speak.

"The casket is currently in the care of my chief attendant, Huan," I explain. "It must be treated with great respect. I require the best carriers and there must be mourners sent to accompany the casket."

"Yes, my lady. May I ask – who is the deceased?"

Within the casket lie two bodies, Iparhan's and Nurmat's, intertwined at last. Huan has concocted a romantic story for the court, hailing Nurmat as a hero for having given his life to protect me from an unknown assassin and cherishing Iparhan as a lovestruck maid who took her own life rather than live without her eunuch husband-to-be. Huan and Jiang carried her body to the casket, her crushed body hidden beneath the faded blue of her cotton robe. The Emperor sent additional guards to my palace to ensure my future safety and was assured that my other servants had learnt to cook Nurmat's dishes. At my request he granted me many taels of silver to send my loyal servants westwards to rest in our homeland.

I stay silent, thinking of this and of Huan's search in the darkness of that night for the poisoned well. Without his knowledge of the Forbidden City many of the courtiers and women here would have died in drawn-out agony.

"Your relative," the man surmises after a long silence has elapsed. "All due care shall be taken."

"It is a long journey," I remind him. "Do not let me hear that once gone from Beijing your care of the casket fell by the wayside." I know I need to say this, to threaten him, even though the silver he will be paid is more than enough to make him care for the casket as though it were his own mother's. He will never have been paid so well, even though he has over one hundred people to accompany him – to carry the casket, to mourn, to guide the way through the trade routes and finally to lay the casket to rest.

"I shall be by its side until your relative is laid to rest," he promises.

"It must be laid in Kashgar," I clarify. "There must be a tomb of great beauty for the people of that land will wish to honour it."

He probably thinks I am attributing too much importance to my unknown relative but I have the silver and he wants the job. "The tomb will be a place of pilgrimage for ever," he says in tones of dutiful piety.

I insist on specifying the inscriptions, the colours of the tiles adorning the tomb, the route they must take which retraces our steps from Kashgar to here. I wish I could have them buried in the Taklamakan Desert by the side of Iparhan's father, but there would be too many explanations and, besides, the dunes will have shifted by now and no-one could find that old poplar tree. I would be lost trying to find it myself.

I leave my rooms, now filled with servants and guards, and make my way to the pond, where I kneel among the grasses and murmur prayers for the dead. The air is cold, very soon the winter months will be here. Tears fall then, but silently, and I stay still for such a long time that the greedy heron joins me and gobbles fish without casting me so much as a glance. When I rise he stalks away, indignant over my interruption of his repast. The ripples of Iparhan's daggers slipping into the water make him turn back to see if the glinting metal is in fact the scales of a fish, but by the time he has returned they are gone from sight and I am already walking away, leaving him to continue his investigation of the edible inhabitants in peace. Huan is already waiting for me. The ceremony to promote me to a higher rank will take place soon and everything must be ready. Jiang has just returned from his errand: he sought out the cobbler and his wife and gave them more silver than they have ever held in their lives. They gasped their gratitude to him but it is I who will give thanks for their kindness every day of my life.

The stiff golden-yellow silk cocoons me. I look down at the imperial dragons raging around my high collar and the swirling ocean waves decorating the robe's hem, feel my triple pearl earrings sway forward as I do so. The movement hurts a little, for the piercings are still fresh. The horseshoe-shaped sleeves trimmed in fur all but cover my hands, so that only the tips of my fingers emerge, showing my golden nail shields, studded with tiny pink rubies. They hide the scrapes across my knuckles and my own broken nails, the last remnants of my attempts to climb the red walls. I had thought the elaborate Manchu hairstyles of the other concubines would be hard to balance but golden combs and green jade pins hold lotus flowers firmly in place, the very last of the season, rising above my head like a tiny garden. Lady Wan sent her hairdresser to help Huan and their final choice is beautiful but simple, all the attention focused on the pale and vibrant pinks of the lotuses. Amongst the flowers sits a tiny green jade tortoise, my only request, cunningly wrought by a court jeweller. I reach up to touch its curved back and think of Mei. Huan tells me he picked the flowers for my hair himself. That is, he stood on the bank of the lake and screamed ever more irate instructions at two lesser eunuchs getting their sleeves wet stretching out from a boat, berating their incompetence and general inability to spot a suitable lotus flower when they saw one.

I stretch out a hand to him. "You have performed a marvel," I tell him and he bows, his face suffused with pleasure. When he straightens I see the shine of tears in his tired eyes.

"I am proud of you, my lady," he says. "Your honour is my honour."

I clasp his hand more tightly. "It is indeed, Huan," I say and make my way towards the waiting chair.

From his throne the Emperor smiles down at me as he turns a magnificent green jade *ruyi* in his hands, topped with gold lotus flowers. I know the jade was brought here from Xinjiang, that one of my countrymen, stooping in a riverbed, touched its smooth shape with his bare feet and knew it for a treasure before it was lifted above the water and made its way travelling the trade routes just as I did two years ago. I smile, step forward, balancing gracefully on the hand-height platforms of my golden shoes, then kneel and begin my kowtow to the Emperor and his mother. My voice is steady as I wish them ten thousand years and rise to my feet in one easy movement as the Chief Eunuch calls out my new name.

"Lady He is promoted to the order of *Fei*, Consort of the fourth rank. Her name will henceforth be Rong Fei - Consort of Harmonious Beauty!"

The scribes and officials hurry to update the records and put into motion all the new privileges that will now be mine – more servants, larger rooms, richer clothes. My new name will be Lady Rong, a name encompassing harmony, beauty, the lotus flowers in my hair and on the *ruyi* about to be presented to me. And perhaps, with only the slightest change of tone, the meaning of martial valour.

From his place at the back of the room Giuseppe nods to me. The Emperor has commissioned a new painting. A hunting scene: the Emperor at full gallop on a horse, an arrow loosed from his bow at a falling stag. By his side on a dappled horse, rides a woman who passes him another arrow while her plaits fly in the wind. It is a private portrait, for the Emperor's own pleasure and mine.

To my right, the ladies of the court watch me. Lady Wang's lips are pressed tightly together but she does not permit herself a scowl. It is dangerous to insult a higher-ranking concubine, especially a favourite. I smile at Lady Wan, who clasps her hands in happiness for me. Ladies Qing and Ying nod to me, their friendly smiles broadening as I return them. Imperial Noble Consort Ling, now the highest-ranked of us all, meets my gaze with steady eyes before each of us bows our heads to the other. Our two name chips are still those most often chosen on the silver tray in the Emperor's rooms. I know that her children will be chosen as his future heirs. She knows that I have a place in the Emperor's heart. Each of us is happy to walk the path laid out before us.

In the imperial records of this dynasty I am reborn for the third time. A new name, a new status, a new being. All that came before this moment is swept away into rumours and exaggeration, stories to be told behind closed doors or whispered one to another with much embroidery along the way.

I take the *ruyi* from the Emperor and smile up at him. He leans in a little to breathe in my perfume as he lightly caresses my cheek. His eyes soften as they did the first time he smelt my scent. He cups my face more firmly and kisses me, his lips warm on mine. It's a lingering kiss more suited to a bedchamber than here in front of the whole court and I feel myself grow flushed but when his lips leave mine I am still pressed against him, relaxing into his warmth. He chuckles into my neck.

"I have a surprise for you," he murmurs. "Someone from your homeland."

I thought I was free. I pull away from him and turn very slowly, my fists clenching, wondering who can be left from those days. I wonder if I have the strength to fight for my life again.

Kneeling on the floor, the old man makes his obeisance to us. His eyes were failing him even then and now they are milky-white. As he looks up towards where the Emperor and I stand he will see only two columns of yellow and gold, shining in the dim light of the throne room.

"A storyteller," says the Emperor. "I thought you would like to hear stories from Kashgar."

I look up at him. He is hopeful in his latest gift. "Do stories help with homesickness?" he asks.

My smile is wide and unforced. I place a delicate golden-tipped hand on his sleeve and feel a wave of tenderness overwhelm me. "My home is here, Your Majesty. By your side. I have no more homesickness. I am happy."

He nods, content in his benevolence. "Begin, storyteller," he commands, and settles himself back on the throne while the rest of us gather round and arrange ourselves comfortably for the performance, the eunuchs hurrying to provide thick cushions on which we may recline.

The storyteller is old and blind but he still knows his craft. He straightens himself and spreads his hands wide to bring all of us into his circle. His voice is strong and confident, honed over many trading days in the market of Kashgar. From my place close to the Emperor, cushioned by soft silks and wrapped in glittering colours, I watch the storyteller and wait to hear the words I heard so long ago.

"All legends are true, even the ones that never happened," he begins.

My scarlet-painted lips move soundlessly with his.

For in them we find ourselves.

Notes

Legends of the Fragrant Concubine

IN CHINA, APPROXIMATELY IN THE year 1760, the Emperor Qianlong conquered Turkestan, also known as Altishahr, an area to the west of China. He renamed the area Xinjiang, the New Dominion, and took a local woman into the Forbidden City as his concubine. From this union came the legends of the Fragrant Concubine, although the stories differ wildly depending on the storyteller.

In China they tell of a beautiful Muslim concubine sent from Altishahr to the Emperor's court in Beijing. Her body emitted an irresistible natural fragrance and the Emperor was besotted with her. But the woman, known as Xiang Fei – the Fragrant Concubine – was homesick. The Emperor tried many things to make her feel at home. He built her a mosque and a bazaar, but nothing would stem her tears. At last, at her request, he ordered the silver-leaved, golden-fruited oleaster tree to be brought from her homeland, and with this gift the lovely concubine was homesick no more and they were happy together.

But in Altishahr the local Uyghur people say that the beautiful Muslim concubine came from a family of rebels. She was named Iparhan – Fragrant Girl – and the Emperor seized her from her husband and family, bringing her to court by force. But Iparhan refused to allow the Emperor near her, keeping daggers hidden in her sleeves to protect her honour. At last the Empress Dowager, fearful for her son's peace of mind, offered Iparhan the honourable option of suicide while the Emperor was away hunting. Returning, he found Iparhan strangled by a white silk scarf, whether by her own hand or that of the palace eunuchs is unknown. The Emperor held her in his arms and cried bitter tears. Her body was sent in state back to her homeland, where she was buried in a tomb that is still a place of pilgrimage today.

Official court records from the time show that there was indeed a Muslim concubine brought to court at the time of the conquest. She was the sister of a local noble who had aided the Emperor in his conquest of the region. She was named Rong Fei – Consort Rong – and it seems she was a favourite of the Emperor, who arranged for a Muslim cook named Nurmat to serve in her household so that her dietary requirements would be met. The Emperor built an observatory tower in the palace that looked out onto the newly created Muslim quarter within Beijing. He indulged the concubine with Hami melons brought from her homeland and sweetmeats on her birthdays. He had many portraits painted of her, including one showing her in full battle armour, an unusual image for a concubine. She was twice promoted within five years of her arrival at court, ending her life there as a highly-ranked consort. She began her life at court in her own traditional dress but on being promoted ordered court clothing to be made for her. On her death many years later she was buried with all due honours in the imperial tombs near Beijing. There is a private portrait, intended for the Emperor's eyes only, of the Emperor hunting with a woman riding alongside him, a very unusual image. He is shooting an arrow at a stag and she, mid-gallop, is passing him another arrow for his bow. She is dressed as a high-ranking concubine and her hair hangs in two plaits, a style not used by Manchu women but by the women from Xinjiang. It is surmised that this could well be a portrait of Rong Fei, out riding and hunting with the Emperor. I found this portrait only *after* I had written about their riding together in the hunting grounds, an activity that I thought I was taking quite a lot of poetic licence inventing, so it was a wonderful find for me!

Key characters

I HAVE TRIED TO BE AUTHENTIC to the period and setting, incorporating as much of the history as possible, however I have also allowed myself some freedoms to enable better storytelling – and in the spirit of all legends being true whether they happened or not.

The period covered in the novel is only two years, while the key historical events described actually took place over about five years (1760-1765), from the concubine arriving at court to Empress Ula Nara cutting off her hair and including the grand tour. The Emperor Qianlong was very fond of hunting, which was an annual event as well as travelling, going on a number of grand tours of his empire. There were two in the period covered, which I have conflated into one. The portraits of the Fragrant Concubine described in the novel all exist.

Lady Wan lived to over 90. She was promoted to honour her long service to the Emperor, whom she outlived.

Imperial Noble Consort Ling was the mother of the future Jiaqing Emperor, heir to the Qianlong Emperor. Because of this she was posthumously raised to the rank of Empress.

Consort Qing raised the Jiaqing Emperor (Prince Yongyan in this novel). He was fond of her and when she died he had her posthumously promoted to the rank of Imperial Noble Consort.

Consort Ying raised the Jiaqing Emperor's younger brother

(Imperial Noble Consort Ling's second son) who was also very fond of his adoptive mother, presenting her with gifts on her birthdays.

Lady Wang managed to be promoted again following her disgrace and later bore the Emperor a daughter who became his favourite child.

The Jesuit painter and architect Giuseppe Castiglione lived in the Forbidden City from his youth until his death, serving three Emperors, the last of which was the Qianlong Emperor.

The Dowager Empress began life as a fairly low-ranking concubine to a prince, until the choice of her son as Emperor made her the most senior woman in the Forbidden City. The Qianlong Emperor was very devoted to her and when she grew too old to travel stopped all of his tours of China. She died aged eighty-four. She is the main subject of a future novel I plan to write: *The Forbidden Palace*.

Empress Ula Nara did cut off her hair and was banished from court. She died a year later and was buried without the honours due to an Empress. There is still a debate on why she acted as she did. Rumours at the time suggested jealousy over another woman. The Emperor Qianlong refused to have another Empress appointed during his lifetime.

For readers

THE FRAGRANT CONCUBINE IS ONE of four existing and forthcoming books set in the Forbidden City. Characters such as the Emperor Qianlong and his mother, Giuseppe Castiglione, Empress Ula Nara, etc., all feature in each book. You can get a free eBook of *The Consorts*, a novella featuring Hidligh's friends Qing and Ying, via Amazon.

You can also sign up for my Reader's Group on my website, where you can download a free copy of *The Cup*, a novella that begins a series set in Morocco in the 10th century. My Readers receive a monthly newsletter with free and promotional reads and are always the first to hear when I bring out a new book.

www.melissaaddey.com

Your Free Book

The city of Kairouan in Tunisia, 1020. Hela has powers too strong
for a child – both to feel the pain of those around her and to heal
them. But when she is given a mysterious cup by a slave woman,
its powers overtake her life, forcing her into a vow she cannot hope
to keep. So begins a quartet of historical novels set in Morocco
as the Almoravid Dynasty sweeps across Northern Africa and
Spain, creating a Muslim Empire that endured for generations.

**Download your free copy at
www.melissaaddey.com**

Biography

I MAINLY WRITE HISTORICAL FICTION, AND am currently writing two series set in very different eras: China in the 1700s and Morocco/Spain in the 1000s. My first novel, *The Fragrant Concubine*, was picked for Editor's Choice by the Historical Novel Society and longlisted for the Mslexia Novel Competition.

In 2016 I was made the Leverhulme Trust Writer in Residence at the British Library, which included writing two books, *Merchandise for Authors* and *The Storytelling Entrepreneur*. You can read more about my non-fiction books on my website.

I am currently studying for a PhD in Creative Writing at the University of Surrey.

I love using my writing to interact with people and run regular workshops at the British Library as well as coaching other writers on a one-to-one basis.

I live in London with my husband and two children.

For more information, visit my website www.melissaaddey.com

Current and forthcoming books include:

Historical Fiction
China
The Consorts
The Fragrant Concubine
The Garden of Perfect Brightness
The Cold Palace

Morocco
The Cup
A String of Silver Beads
None Such as She
Do Not Awaken Love

Picture Books for Children
Kameko and the Monkey-King

Non-Fiction
The Storytelling Entrepreneur
Merchandise for Authors
The Happy Commuter
100 Things to Do while Breastfeeding

Thanks

Many thanks are due. First of all to my mother, who not only taught me to read and write but is also the best storyteller I know. To the members of www.YouWriteOn.com for their feedback and encouragement for chapter one. To Professor James Millward of Georgetown University for his fantastic article *'A Uyghur Muslim in Qianlong's Court: the meanings of the Fragrant Concubine,'* and his enormous kindness in reading my manuscript and giving me a real education in everything from noodles and accents to tea and mountains. All errors are of course mine. To the British Library and the School of Oriental and African Studies library – your resources are amazing. Thank you to my Bookclub Ladies as well as Bernie and Camilla for cheerleading, Helen for detailed feedback right at the start and Ryan for constant love, encouragement and precious writing time. To Seth for arriving late and to Isabelle for taking regular naps enabling me to keep writing. Thank you to my agent Lisa for being excited, my editor Sam for seeing what had been left out and the Streetlight Graphics team for making the book both real and beautiful. All of you made it a better story.

Made in the USA
Monee, IL
11 March 2020